MW01043189

**Detective Ryan Doherty had never seen a murder so twisted, so bizarre, until rapper Terrico James came down on a cross. Dead.**

"I read that Terrico James was raised as a God-fearing Christian, Detective," he began, as if he were telling the group a bedtime story. "But somewhere along the line his faith was misdirected. He deluded himself into thinking *he* was the Son of God. It was a tragedy, what happened last night. But did you ever consider he may have done it to himself?"

"Crucify *himself?*" asked Di Santo. "That would have been pretty tricky to get the last nail in, don'tcha think?"

"I don't mean purely by himself, but perhaps he had another lost and twisted soul help him up on that cross. That is our theory, anyway. Maybe he had finally repented for his unholy hubris and recruited a friend to help him commit suicide."

"Interesting theory, but our evidence shows he was already dead when he was nailed to the cross. Stabbed in the heart."

When rapper Terrico James claimed to be "mightier than Jesus," nobody took him seriously…until someone did. Terrico's dead body ends up nailed to a cross and Chicago Detective Ryan Doherty is on the case. Was it a fringe religious sect making a statement? Or Terrico's protégé, Mandy Ross, a petulant pop star who sheds hearts like glitter in her path? With the help of his partner, Matt Di Santo, and the spirit of his dead partner, Jon, Ryan fights his way through cultural divides to find the murderer.

Catharine Lulling is ready to venture outside of her estate for her first real date with Ryan. But even her special abilities can't save her when she reveals a secret she's been hiding from him—one that could destroy their relationship for good.

KUDOS for *Taking the Rap*

Moss takes us on a seamless journey from her two preceding books, *Town Red* and *Way to Go*, into a plot that contains both twists and surprises. She interweaves the Ryan and Catharine romance with the search for the killer that keeps us turning pages. A must read. ~ *Charles Alvarez, author,* Dressed to Kill

Jennifer Moss has done it again with *Taking the Rap*. In the third installment of the *Ryan Doherty Mysteries*, we find our hero Ryan searching for the killer of a rapper who was killed then hung on a cross. In the background, Ryan's lover Catharine has to testify at the trial of the man who tried to rape her in book 1. Her testimony leads to the revelation of a secret that devastates Ryan and splits the two of them apart. As always, Moss's characters are highly realistic and well developed. Her plot is strong and filled with surprises that keep you turning page after page. ~ *Taylor Jones, Reviewer*

*Taking the Rap* by Jennifer Moss is the third book in the *Ryan Doherty Mysteries* and, like the other two, this one's a great read. Just when I think that Moss will run out of interesting stories to tell about Ryan, she proves me wrong. This book has some unusual twists in that the murder is a hate crime and the usual suspects are unusual, to say the least. Everybody seems to have a motive in this one. As with the other two books in the series, *Taking the Rap* is filled with interesting, well-developed characters. The plot is fast-paced and intense and will keep you on the edge of your seat from beginning to end. Way to go, Moss! ~ *Regan Murphy, Reviewer*

# TAKING THE RAP

## JENNIFER MOSS

## *A Black Opal Books Publication*

Black Opal Books

BECAUSE SOME STORIES JUST HAVE TO BE TOLD

GENRE: MYSTERY/DETECTIVE

This is a work of fiction. Names, places, characters and incidents are either the product of the author's imagination or are used fictitiously, and any resemblance to any actual persons, living or dead, businesses, organizations, events or locales is entirely coincidental. All trademarks, service marks, registered trademarks, and registered service marks are the property of their respective owners and are used herein for identification purposes only. The publisher does not have any control over or assume any responsibility for author or third-party websites or their contents.

TAKING THE RAP
Copyright © 2014 by Jennifer Moss
Cover Design by Chuck Reaume
All cover art copyright © 2014
All Rights Reserved
Print ISBN: 978-1-626942-29-5

First Publication: NOVEMBER 2014

Published by Black Opal Books **http://www.blackopalbooks.com**

*Dedicated to*
*Peggy Moss*
*(1933-2014)*
*My biggest fan, my champion, my mama.*

# PROLOGUE

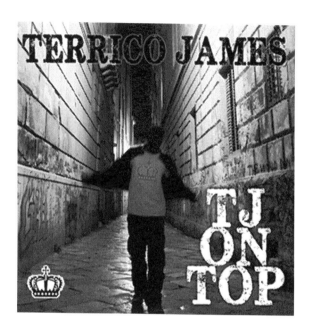

I'm mightier than Jesus!" the rapper announced, holding the newly won trophy above his head. "'Cause Jesus didn't have my gifts and my gifts make the world go around, know-what-I'm-sayin'?"

Apparently none of the two thousand awards show guests knew what he was saying, since the auditorium was

silent but for a few coughs. Several people in the back rows
booed. He raised the platinum trophy a bit higher and concluded, "So I thank Jesus but, most of all, I thank *me!*"

His publicist, Kim Barnett, popped a Xanax into her
mouth and dry-swallowed the bitter pill with a shiver. She
panicked at the silence until the orchestra conductor looked
to the stage manager who encouraged him to start playing
with an enthusiastic nod.

"This is the second award this evening for Terrico
James," the announcer voiced over the music. "Just last
month, James won three Grammys for his fifth album, *TJ on
Top.*"

During the commercial break, Kim made her way to the
wings of stage left and spotted Terrico bumping shoulders
and shaking hands with the other award winners and pre-
senters.

One of the younger members of his entourage was given
the task of standing beside him to hold the trophies. She
waved until she caught the rapper's attention.

Terrico sauntered over to her, arms flung wide for a hug.
"He-e-e-y, Kim. My girl," he said with a wide smile. "Two
wins tonight, baby! I'm on fire!"

"Yeah, TJ, that's good news," Kim said, remaining rigid
throughout his bear hug.

Terrico's gaze went roving around backstage as he pulled
away. "You seen my man Quince? I think he's due up to
present soon." He beckoned the trophy guy to follow him.
"Stay right by my side, brother! For the photographers!"

The young man complied.

"TJ, *what the hell?*" Kim tried to whisper above the din.
"I told you to stop the Jesus talk! You're gonna get yourself
in some deep shit and I can't keep picking your ass up off of
the floor!"

"Settle down, baby, it's a'ight." Terrico James was oblivious to the public relations shit storm he had just created.
Actually, perpetuated. "Look, I'll see you at the after-

parties, 'kay? You just stay here and talk to the media after I give them their Terrico photo op they been waiting for."

He flashed a brilliant white grin before he disappeared into the circle of his entourage. The trophy guy rushed to open the pressroom door and the group moved into the room of awaiting reporters.

Kim inhaled deeply and lifted her chin, preparing like a gladiator for what would come next. At least the Xanax had started to kick in.

# CHAPTER 1

Question religion, question it all.
Question existence,
until them questions are solved.
~ *Jay-Z*

Waiting out the final eight minutes until end of shift, Detective Ryan Doherty tossed a green tennis ball across the desk pod to his partner, Matt Di Santo. A new four-days-on, two-days-off schedule had been implemented for all detectives in the Chicago P.D., which was why they were working this particular Saturday in late June.

"Harry Caray," Di Santo announced, continuing their impromptu game. With each toss, they had to name a prominent Chicagoan from their own ethnicity.

"Caray isn't an Italian name," Ryan challenged.

"His real name was Carabini or Carabina, something like that. He's a *paisan*, believe me."

Ryan accepted that, but he'd look it up later. "Mayor Daley," he said tossing the ball across the desk pod. "Both of them."

"Peter Cetera. Chicago. The band." The tennis ball flew through the air back to Ryan.

"I know who Peter Cetera is. Vince Vaughn."

"Love that Vince!" his partner said, and tossed the ball back. "Al Capone."

Ryan chuckled as he held the ball. "I was waiting for that mistake, my friend. Capone was born and raised in New York."

"Well he contributed to the city, and Chicago is whole-heartedly identified with him."

"*Contributed* to the city? He was a criminal."

"He contributed to the economy. He provided the booze of which many of *your* people bought and consumed."

Ryan grimaced. "The economy?"

"Yeah, yeah, and he's still contributing to it," Di Santo answered. "You know how many foreign tourists come here expecting to see the 'bang-bang' old-fashioned gangsters? They still visit the Clark Street address where the St. Valentine's Day Massacre went down, even though it's now an empty lot. Capone is *big* business for the city of Chicago, trust-you-me."

He glanced at the clock. Three minutes to go. "Well, if we're going all *Law & Order*, then I call the entire Chicago police force Irish." He tossed the ball back, extra hard this time, but his partner caught it nonetheless.

"'Cept for DiLeonardi and Jaconetti—they're legends. And *my* guys." Di Santo said, tapping the ball against his chest. Ryan's cell rang and he picked it up with one hand while catching the ball with the other.

"Homicide: Doherty," he said by rote, forgetting for a moment that he had answered his cell and not the department's landline.

"Hey, Ry!" He recognized the voice as Duke, one of Catharine's twin sons. Since Ryan had started dating Cat six months and twenty-eight days ago, he'd had a fairly good relationship with the boys—Duke better than Hank, who half-respected him and half-resented him.

"What's up? Is your mom okay?" Ryan asked.

"Yeah, yeah. Mom's fine. It's about work." Duke was

shouting above the crowd on the other side of the line. "You know we're doing security work at Payton Arena, right?"

Ryan pulled his legs off of the desk and sat up in his chair. "*Security*? Your mom didn't say you were doing security. She just said you guys had a summer job there. How'd you get on security?"

Duke sighed as a preface to his explanation. "They recruited half the university football team. Me, Hank, and some of the other guys. But we've got a problem here. You know Terrico James?"

"Terrico James the rapper? I don't really know his music, but yeah, I've heard of him."

"Well, he's missing. They can't find him anywhere," Duke said, trying to keep his voice down and shouting at the same time. "Payton's in your district, isn't it? Lincoln Park? I thought you guys could come over and just help look into it. His people aren't saying anything, but I can tell they're getting really nervous."

Ryan glanced over at Di Santo who bucked his chin in inquisition. "It's Duke," Ryan answered. "He wants us to go over to Payton Arena and check on a missing person."

Di Santo scrunched up his face. "Now? We're almost off!"

Duke must have overheard their conversation because he raised his voice in appeal. "Please, Ry. I was just hoping you could come over and like, look into it on the down-low. Not an official police thing. Hold on—" The other end became muffled, but Ryan could distinctly hear him arguing with his brother. The nineteen-year-old twins were almost joined at the hip, even in college, when most brothers would have gone their separate ways. He figured they had to stay tight, being raised by a single mother since they were toddlers, their father only sporadically in and out of their lives.

"Duke?" Ryan called into the phone. "What's going on?"

He glanced over at Di Santo, who was pointing to the wall clock. Little hand on seven, big hand on twelve. The

*Flinstones* quitting bird whistled in his head as Di Santo started straightening up his desk.

Duke came back on the line. "Sorry, that was Hank. I've been assigned to Terrico's team and Hank is with Mandy Ross. Could you just stop by here on your way home? If they find him by that time, you and Matt can just stay for the concert if you want."

"Yeah, I'm not into rap music, nor am I a pre-teen girl. But I'll swing by to make sure everything is okay."

"Thanks, I'll put you guys on the VIP list! See you." Duke disconnected.

"So, someone is missing?" Di Santo asked, stuffing his laptop into a brown leather case.

"Possibly. Hank and Duke are working security at the concert tonight, and they want us to check it out, discreetly."

Di Santo nodded. "Terrico James? They've been playing his songs all morning on WGCI, probably because of the concert. Not really my style of rap, but he's okay."

"Your style of rap?" Ryan chuckled, half-shocked that his partner listened to WGCI and actually had a rap preference. Something he had never known about Di Santo in the two years, eight months and twenty-three days they had been partnered. "Okay, well Duke is assigned to James's team, and Hank's covering Mandy Ross."

Di Santo stopped packing up his gear. "No shit! Mandy Ross? I love her!"

"Wait, she's like sixteen—"

"She's *eighteen* now, thank-you-very-much, and so what? I like her music. It's catchy. I've got all her albums." He shook his ass like Mandy in the video that rocketed her to stardom. "*Shake it, shake it shake it, baby. That is how we make it, baby.*" He held out his arms and bowed to no applause.

"Stick with police work, okay?" Ryan said. "So I take it you're coming along, now?"

"Yeah, I'll stop in with you," Di Santo said waving the

back of his hand, as if he hadn't just admitted he was a raging fanboy. Ryan unplugged his own laptop and stuffed it into a padded backpack, grabbed the keys to the department-issued Impala and headed out, his partner jogging behind him.

The Chicagoland temperatures remained mild from the late spring. Ryan was grateful for the postponed heat and humidity when he walked into a crowd like the one in front of Payton Arena.

His phone displayed the time as 7:22 p.m., thirty-eight minutes before the show was scheduled to start. The red-gold sun bathed the scene in front of the main entrance: concertgoers lining up to get in, news vans with reporters readying their cameramen, and energy drink hawkers with their booth babes working the crowd.

There were also several groups of protestors. One of the picket circles was more vocal than the others with a loudmouth on a megaphone denouncing Terrico James and his latest decree that he transcended their Lord and Savior.

Ryan nudged his partner and nodded toward the group. "Let's go let them know we're here." As they approached the picketers, Ryan scanned the text of their picket signs: *Terrico=Terrorist*, *God Hates False Prophets*, and *JC >TJ*. He pulled his jacket aside so the demonstrators could clearly see the gold shield mounted on his belt.

"Do we have an organizer here?" he asked to the group, in general.

A smaller man stepped forward, holding a Bible atop a clipboard in one arm. He appeared to be about thirty, dirty blond, wearing a starched blue shirt buttoned up to his neckline and freshly pressed black cotton pants. His black loafers reflected the light as if he had just buffed them.

"Hello, officers. We are demonstrating within the confines of the law here," the man said with a slight, but noticeable Southern dialect.

"And you are?"

"Pleased to meet you, sir. I am Warren L. Smith, director of the ODL." He handed both detectives a brochure and held out his hand for a shake.

Ryan took the man's hand, which was damp with perspiration. "ODL?"

"We are the One Divine Life, an organization dedicated to helping others live their lives in the path of Christ. We're based out of Atlanta."

"Well we are the One Chicago Police," Ryan said, half-mocking the man. "We're introducing ourselves to all the groups out here. If there's any trouble, we won't hesitate to take anyone in."

"We're being peaceful here, Officer." He gestured toward his fellow picketers. "We don't plan on provoking any violence. You see we are a religious group, in the name of Christ."

"Yeah, like there's never been any violence in the name of religion," challenged Di Santo, with an exaggerated roll of his eyes.

"I assure you fine gentlemen that we are just here to spread our message and will be staying outside the perimeter of the arena."

A reporter had sidled up to them, pretending not to be listening. Ryan hated how the media leeched on celebrities, although it was almost a symbiotic relationship. Without the press, there would be no fame of celebrity, and without celebrities, there would be nothing to write about. His hatred of the media didn't extend to his baby sister, Finn, who had worked for the *L.A. Times* until they'd laid off a majority of the staff. This particular reporter, with his scruffy face, nose ring, heavy-lidded eyes and bony frame, was not made for television. Probably a blogger. The conversation stopped and Ryan glared at the dude until he got the hint and moved on.

"Okay, Mr. Warren L. Smith. Thank you for your cooperation." Ryan handed the man his CPD business card and they left the group to walk in their circle.

He and Di Santo stopped a couple of other picketing organizations that were less substantial, only three to four members each. Ryan gave them the same warning along with his card. In return, they offered him their literature, which he stuffed into his back pocket.

In order to make their way to the arena doors, they had to round a news van, behind which stood an attractive, young Asian reporter standing opposite a cameraman. She stopped and touched the earpiece in her right ear. "We are just now getting word that Terrico James may *not* be performing at the concert tonight. Mandy Ross will still go on, as planned."

"The news is spreading," Ryan said, leaning in to Di Santo.

"I guess we'll find out what's really going on when we see Hank and Duke. Are we going backstage?" Di Santo took off his suit jacket and swung it over a shoulder, hooking the collar with a thumb. He was woefully overdressed in the crowd of teenagers and rap fans. Even Ryan, who was sporting jeans and a CPD-issued polo shirt, might as well have been wearing a sash with *NOT A FAN* across his chest.

"Promise me you won't hit on her, will you?"

"Who, me?" Di Santo said, feigning innocence. He hit on every new woman he met, five-three and under.

"She's eighteen, dude...just remember that."

They approached the north side of the venue and Ryan tapped on the glass door. When they caught a security guard's attention, they both held their shields up to the glass. The guard nodded, accepting their credentials, and opened the door, admitting them into the lobby of the arena. He pointed them to a set of double doors, which they found unlocked, and they proceeded into the auditorium and down the main aisle.

At the edge of the stage they encountered a genuine 300-

pound, six-foot-six muscle-bound behemoth of a guy wearing a navy security tee.

"We're looking for Hank and Duke Lulling?" Ryan said, holding his shield up to the guy's eye-level. The giant nodded and led them around backstage to a long green hallway. There were several white doors off of the hall, each labeled with a gold glittery star and a name. The dude pointed to the second door and Ryan knocked.

"Probably can't hear you. Just go in," the security guard said before heading back in the direction of the stage.

Ryan pushed the dressing room door open and saw that the suite was filled with people mingling, drinking, dancing and chattering away. He stepped in with Di Santo behind him, scanning the room until he eventually spotted Duke on the far side, standing next to a red velvet couch. On the couch sat several people, including Hank, who was sitting so close to a petite blonde girl she was practically on his lap. Ryan recognized the girl immediately, as her face was constantly plastered on magazine covers and television: Mandy Ross. The megastar appeared tinier in person, about five-foot-two with long blonde wavy hair, framing a trim, dancer's body. Although her face was already stage-painted, Mandy lounged in a pink velour hoodie and cutoff shorts. One of her bare feet played footsie with Hank's ankle.

When Ryan caught Duke's eye, the boy held up a hand in greeting and made his way toward the detectives.

"Hey, guys, thanks so much for stopping by," Duke said. "Glad you got in okay."

"Tough job," Ryan said, eyeing the party.

"Yeah, well our jobs tonight were to be liaison assistants to the talent. Like I told you over the phone, I was assigned to Terrico's team but he never showed. I'm getting a bad feeling about it. His people won't tell me anything and they won't let me into the dressing room. So I was hanging out here with Hank, waiting for you."

As fraternal twins, Hank and Duke Lulling looked no more alike than standard siblings. Hank had blond hair and light-skin with brooding brown eyes, while Duke had light brown hair, olive skin and his mother's eyes of sky blue. The boys did share an identical frame, athletic and large. Ryan marveled at how these enormous young men had come out of Catharine's petite body. As far as character, Hank was the more extroverted of the two while Duke's temperament hovered at serene.

Ryan glanced over at Hank and Mandy, holding hands on the couch. She whispered into Hank's ear and the boy grinned.

"And what's going on over there?" he nodded toward the couple. "That part of his 'liaison' duty?"

Duke smiled, and dropped his gaze—an expression inherited from his mother. "Well, Mandy kind of took to him from the start. And as you can see, he doesn't mind."

"Fast work."

"C'mon, I'll introduce you," Duke said, gesturing for the detectives to follow. When they arrived at the red velvet couch, Hank's jaw tightened. He was clearly pissed.

"I told him not to call you," Hank said. "As far as I can tell, nobody's dead."

The pop star chuckled a bit uncomfortably and nuzzled in closer to him.

Duke interjected with an introduction. "Mandy, this is Ryan. He's a cop." Di Santo nudged Duke's elbow. "Oh, sorry. And this is his partner, Matt."

"Oh, you guys are such a cute couple! My assistant's gay," she said, pointing to a man standing nearby. The man cringed.

"No, n-n-no," Di Santo stuttered. "We're not a couple. We're partners. *Cop* partners. Keeping the city safe and putting away bad guys and all that." He puffed out his chest like a superhero.

Mandy announced to the room, "Hey, everybody, we've got cops here! Put all the drugs away." Ryan scanned the hands of the party guests, but found no contraband visible. Just a joke. Good, because he didn't want to play narc to-

night. He just wanted to put Duke at ease and get back to
Catharine.

"Miss Ross, this is such an honor," Di Santo gushed.
"I'm a *big* fan." Mandy giggled and offered up a limp hand
as if she expected him to kiss it. Di Santo looked like he
was considering it. Ryan couldn't wait to tell the guys back
at the 18th about this whole scene.

"What's your name again, baby?" she said, slithering up
to Di Santo.

He cleared his throat and loosened his tie a bit. "I'm
Matt. Detective Matt Di Santo."

"De-tective Di-Santo," she repeated, playing with the al-
literation of his name. "You staying for the show, De-tective
Di-Santo?"

"Absolutely! If we can."

"Of course, you can. You're in, aren't you? Come backstage again afterwards, okay? Join the party." She straightened Di Santo's collar then flashed him a grin that made
him stand up a bit straighter. Di Santo stood about five-foot-
six, but his overblown personality made up for his small
stature.

Before Ryan could stop him, his partner had whipped out
his cell phone and asked the singer for a picture.

"Only if I can hold your gun," Mandy said. Di Santo
froze. "Just *kidding*, babe! Of course you can." She made a
gun out of her thumb and forefinger, pretending to blow on
the "barrel" for the photos. Di Santo was in heaven and
Ryan knew the pictures would be online within the next six-
ty seconds.

After the third click of Di Santo's cell phone camera,
Ryan grabbed his partner by the shirt and pulled him back
toward the door, turning his back to the room so the boys
couldn't hear. "What did I say? She's eighteen, for Chris-
sake."

"Yeah, but she's an *old* eighteen," Di Santo said looking
back at her. Mandy winked at him in return.

Ryan shook his head. "Jesus. At least avoid her for Hank's sake. I don't need any more of his teenaged wrath."

"Okay, okay. I just want to see the show."

Ryan let the shirt go and gave his partner a slight slap on chest. "I'm going to go call Cat. See if she can do her thing with this Terrico James situation. Stay here and watch over the kids." He stepped out into the hall and walked down to a corner space so he could shield himself from the clamor of the backstage crew.

Catharine answered without a greeting. "Hey, are you coming for dinner? I already started preparing some salmon."

"I'm at Payton Arena," Ryan answered. "Duke asked me to stop by. One of the artists is MIA. I thought maybe you could use your..." He lowered his voice after glancing around for potential eavesdroppers. "...*finding* powers and help? See if you can picture him anywhere?" He gave her the address and a brief description of the rapper. He heard her scribbling notes on the other end.

Once Catharine had proven to him that her "abilities" were genuine, Ryan got her approved with the department as a consultant. Besko was as skeptical as Ryan had been at first about using a psychic empath to help with cases. Their skepticism was normal for cops who were trained to trust the evidence. Since their first case together, she had "impressions" on cases, and helped find missing suspects and a child held captive. He really didn't understand the full extent of her abilities, but his close rate had risen to almost 90% on the cases on which Catharine has assisted. That was all the evidence he needed.

"I'll work on it now," she replied. "I do hope they find him. And not just because I was hoping to see you tonight."

"I love you," he said, cupping his cell. "Hey, did Jane stop by, yet?"

He heard her take a deep breath on the other side of the line. "She's due any minute."

# CHAPTER 2

Jane's schedule had been jammed for the past month, but she knew it was no excuse for postponing this meeting until the last minute. But before she met the woman she had to get some food in her stomach. Fridays were always a bitch. She called and left a message for Catharine before she stopped at Panera, grabbed a salad and reviewed the case file.

In two days Catharine Lulling was to give her video testimony in the trial of Todd Elliot. He had attacked her in her home during the Town Red case at the end of last year and the trial was just now coming up on the docket. It was Jane's job as Assistant State's Attorney to make sure Elliot was convicted for breaking and entering, aggravated battery, and attempted rape. Seemed to be a slam-dunk, but Jane hadn't met the victim yet.

"Destination on right," announced the GPS on Jane's Lexus. She had set the voice to a British male thinking it would be James Bond sexy, but it ended up sounding like a tight-assed butler. She made a mental note to change it as she pulled up to an imposing black iron gate.

"Holy crap," she said under her breath, as she scanned the gate and the mansion behind it. Her brain froze for several seconds, taking in the image of the estate and lush surrounding property. "It's fucking Downton Abbey."

Before she had a chance to use the intercom, or even roll down the window, the gate swept open. Catharine had been watching for her.

Ryan had recently explained to Jane that the woman didn't leave her house. Agoraphobia. Which was the reason the judge had agreed to accept her testimony on video. When Ryan first disclosed the affliction, it had totally thrown Jane for a loop. She couldn't imagine that the great Detective Doherty would settle for a relationship so limited. He was so normal. And hot. And he knew it. Ryan was one of the top detectives in the department and he could have any woman he wanted.

Gazing up at the massive white mansion, she knew it would be awkward, although she had that feminine curiosity—tinged with a hint of envy—to meet the proverbial other woman. Jane had been attracted to Ryan since the day they'd met, in court, several years ago. She thought she had been getting the same signals from him, but when she'd outright propositioned him a couple of months ago, he refused, citing his new relationship with Catharine. Then he had shown up at her door drunk and propositioned her back. But she discovered it was just a rebound due to a lovers' quarrel he'd had earlier in the evening. After all that chaos and awkwardness, Jane and Ryan agreed that the best tack moving forward was to remain friends.

She parked her Lexus at the front of the circular drive, checked her image in the rear-view mirror, flung her briefcase strap over her shoulder, and steeled herself. Just in case it didn't go well, Jane had already planned to meet her girlfriends at McGinty's later in the evening.

She locked her car with a chirp and ascended the white marble steps of the estate. But before she reached the massive double doors, the one on the left was already opening, and in the threshold stood the woman she was there to meet.

Catharine Lulling was gorgeous—a Disney princess with her petite frame, big blue eyes, and long brunette curls that ended an inch or two below her waist.

In contrast Jane felt like an Amazon at five-ten. It brought her right back to junior high school where she was the tallest and homeliest girl in the class. Even with her nose job and Ivy League education, she still felt defeated. She couldn't possibly compete with this woman.

"Welcome. You must be Jane," Catharine said, holding out a hand.

Jane shook it, nodding. "Hi, Catharine. Pleased to finally meet you." She took a deep breath to calm her nerves and forced a smile in return.

"You can call me Cat. I feel like we're already good friends." Catharine moved in to embrace her. Jane leaned in with an obligatory pat on the back. In another surprising move, Catharine took her hand, ushered her into the house, and closed the door behind her. "Did you find the house okay?" she asked.

"Yes, fine." *How could anyone fucking miss it?* But just as she was thinking about the grand exterior, Jane was silenced by the unusual sight directly in front of her. In the middle of the home was an oversized garden—with flowers, a stream and even several trees, which grew up past the second story. Four open corridors surrounded the garden in a square.

"I love your…your…courtyard, it's really nice."

"Thank you. The atrium is my pride and joy. Come, I'll show you. It's the perfect place to sit and talk." Catharine led her down two steps to a path leading through the most verdant home Jane had ever seen.

"Did you build this house yourself? It's so…unusual."

"I designed it, yes. All the rooms surround the atrium, in four wings. We came in the south entrance. East is my study, then the dining room. North is the kitchen and the doors out to the back gardens. To the west is my dance studio and the boys' entertainment room. Pool and gym are on the lower level and the bedrooms are upstairs. Very simple, actually."

Simple for the Queen of England. "You have a dance studio?" Jane asked. "So you dance…"

"Well, I used to. Ballet. I still like to practice for myself, now, for fun. I also use the room for just meditating or listening to music," Catharine explained. "Let's get you settled. I'll show you where you can put your things down."

Catharine led her down a stone path through the atrium while Jane took several deep breaths and shook off the encroaching envy that had no place at this meeting. She had to be professional. She was a state prosecutor, for god's sake.

When they arrived at the center of the atrium, Catharine took Jane's briefcase and placed it on a round table in the middle of it all. A tray with a pitcher of iced tea sat waiting for the women, and the hostess proceeded to pour two glasses. Jane followed a beam of light upward toward the ceiling where a grand skylight let in the setting rays of the sun.

Catharine glanced up and smiled. "I have one in my bedroom, too. We like to watch the stars at night."

The pronoun hit Jane harder than expected. She took a sip of the tea and avoided eye contact by taking out the files for the Elliot case. Back to business.

"So the judge has agreed to do the video testimony here, in your home. Will there be a quiet place to record the video where we won't be interrupted?"

"My study would be the best," Catharine responded. "Since my boys live on campus—they're at Northwestern—the only other person here will be my personal assistant, Sara. I will advise her not to disturb us." Catharine reached over and touched Jane's arm. "Thank you so much for arranging for it to be done here. I really do appreciate it."

"No problem," Jane said, pulling back. She shuffled several papers to make it seem like she wasn't flinching from the woman's touch. "If you could just walk me through what happened, start from the very beginning. Try not to leave any details out."

"All right. It started in the back, in my gardens. Come."

Catharine stood up and led Jane to a large double door, out and into her backyard. As if the atrium weren't enough, the back gardens were ten times as opulent.

"You don't mind if I record this? It's easier than taking notes."

"No, no problem," Catharine responded.

Jane started a voice recorder app on her cell phone and nodded for Catharine to begin.

"I had just made coffee and let my dogs out, as I do every morning," Catharine said, her gaze distant. "But they didn't come when I called them back in. I was worried. I had a bad feeling. Not a psychic thing, really. Just a skin crawl."

Oh, yes, Jane remembered, the *psychic* thing. She'd heard that Catharine did some psychic consulting with the police on several cases, and was honestly stunned that Ryan's sergeant had bought into it.

"As you can see," Catharine continued, "the property is gated, so there really was no way the dogs could've gotten out."

As if hearing the story, two dogs came running up to her—one large black power breed and one little funny looking poof with its tongue hanging out.

"This is Bully, my Rottweiler," Catharine said, introducing them. "And this little guy is his little brother Buddy. A Shih Tzu."

Jane nodded to the dogs while Catharine crouched down to give them motherly love. She pulled two treats from her pockets for them and gestured them into the house before continuing her story.

"I thought I had heard them barking in the far side of the yard, so I walked out to call them again. And he—Todd—grabbed me right here." Catharine stopped on a stone path that led to a greenhouse about fifty yards away. She raised a fist and said, "He grabbed me by my hair and then pulled me back into the house…" She stopped the narration, pantomiming the action of Elliot dragging her back into the house as she led Jane back through the double doors.

"Did he say anything?" Jane asked, stepping inside again. "That's very important. Try to recall what he said to you. That goes toward intent."

Catharine rubbed her mouth and thought for a moment. "He accused me of killing Scott and Carly."

"You will have to explain who Scott and Carly are to the jury."

"Oh, yes. Scott and Carly owned the advertising agency, Town Red, where I worked years ago. Todd was a co-worker. When they sold the company, I had earned...do I have to say the number?"

"I'm afraid so."

"From the stock that I was given when I worked there, I earned thirty million dollars from the sale of the company. Apparently Todd didn't. Something was wrong with his stock agreement and he didn't get anything. He was angry at the inequity. He kept saying things like 'It's nice you have all *this* and I have nothing.'"

"And he kept accusing you of killing the Reddings?"

"Yes, with my mind. That's what he said: I killed them with my mind. He was ranting."

"That's good. Make him out to be crazy. That will be good for us."

Catharine didn't look pleased as she moved deliberately through the atrium, Jane following. "I fell down onto the path, right here." She pointed to a spot next to an indoor oak tree.

"You fell onto the path? Or Todd pushed you?"

Catharine thought for a moment. "I don't recall. He may have pushed me."

"Then say that: he pushed you."

"But I don't—I'm not sure."

"He pushed you."

"Probably."

"Then say it in your testimony. And keep saying his name. 'When Todd pushed me.' Continue."

"When—when Todd *pushed me*—" Catharine glanced at her for approval, and Jane nodded. "I fell and hit my head on a rock. That rock." She pointed to one of the decorative stones that lined the atrium pathway.

"Any damage? Permanent or otherwise?"

"No, just a bump. Not even blood."

"Then what happened?" Jane prompted. Catharine's head dropped and she rubbed her forehead, her eyes squeezed shut on a painful memory. "Catharine, I know this is diffi-cult, but the more you tell it, the easier it gets."

"He got on top of me." Catharine paused, staring down at the path as if she were watching the scene unfold. "He got on top of me and started to lift my skirt. He said I was 'hot' and—" She stopped.

"And you were afraid he was going to rape you."

"Yes. I was afraid he was going to rape me. Then the dogs broke through the back door and attacked him. While they were biting him, I grabbed his Taser and shocked him."

"You didn't mention he had a weapon. That's important. You have to bring that up sooner in your testimony. He *threatened* you with the Taser. Call it a 'weapon' as often as you can. Say you were threatened. Use that word: threat-ened. Language and word choice are important."

"Okay."

"And that was it?"

"Well, yes. I ran to the door and Ryan was there."

"Ryan knew about the attack?"

"No, he had come to ask me questions about the Redding case. He *also* thought I had killed Scott and Carly! I mean, at the time he did."

"You don't have to say that. Just say Ryan—Detective Doherty, actually—had some follow-up questions about the Reddings. You definitely don't want to validate Todd's rant-ings and you don't want to paint yourself as a homicide sus-pect."

"Okay." Catharine answered. She walked back to the center of the atrium and sat at the table. Her mood had picked up considerably, now that they were beyond the attempted rape scenario.

They both took a moment to enjoy the ginger tea. Jane flipped through the file to see if she had covered everything. There was one question she hadn't asked: "Were you involved with Ryan at the time of the attack?"

"No. Not yet."

"Good. That will help his credibility."

"Todd won't be here, will he? I don't want him in my house again."

"No, no. The defendant doesn't have to attend, and I requested it."

Catharine let out a sigh of relief. Jane had a brief revelation of why Ryan was attracted to her, other than her obvious physical beauty. The woman seemed frail, vulnerable. And Ryan was the consummate protector. He loved to rescue.

"Who will be there?" Catharine asked.

"It will be the judge, me, Elliot's attorney, a court reporter for the record, and I'll probably bring along a paralegal for help."

Catharine nodded, accepting the guest list.

Jane's phone vibrated from her briefcase. She dug it out to read a text from Ryan.

– *How's it going?*

She smiled as she shook her head. "It's Ryan, checking on us." A rush of assorted feelings accompanied the text: glee that he was thinking about her, a competitive satisfaction that he had texted her and not Catharine, and a tad of discomfort that she was standing in front of this man's significant other.

If Catharine had minded, she didn't let on. "Tell him we're fine and not to worry," she said, with a slight nod of the head.

Jane thumbed the message back to him and then tucked the phone away in her briefcase, along with the files.

"I have to go," she said, eager to leave the strange mansion and the woman along with it. "I'll see you on Monday morning. If you have any questions or concerns about the testimony, please call or email me."

"Oh, well I know you ate dinner already, but I was going to ask you to stay for dessert," Catharine said, a bit discombobulated.

"Dessert? Oh, thank you, but I can't. I'm meeting some friends tonight. Maybe another time," Jane said, knowing she would do her best to avoid *another time.* Too complicated. As Jane followed Catharine through the atrium, toward the front of the house, she took in the surroundings and couldn't, for the life of her, picture Ryan in it. For sure, she could see the appeal: Catharine was beautiful, vulnerable, and had a shitload of money. But the house, with its ridiculous indoor forest, was light-years away from their everyday realm of policing, prosecuting, criminals, and death. Did Ryan really prefer this fantasy world to the real one?

When they reached the front door, Catharine opened it and hugged her again before she knew what was happening. This time, Jane just stood in place, tolerating the embrace until it was over.

"You care about him very much," Catharine said, her blue eyes locking onto hers.

Whether it was her "psychic abilities" or just a woman's intuition, at that moment Jane knew that Catharine knew. But Jane remained stoic, a practice learned from years of performing in court.

"And he cares about you, Catharine. You're all he talks about." It killed her to say it, but it was the truth.

Catharine smiled and bowed her head slightly as a goodbye. The princess had dismissed the lady in waiting.

# CHAPTER 3

Ryan spent the next few minutes getting the lay of the land, exploring the various hallways, nooks and crannies of Payton Arena's backstage. He stepped aside while large black equipment boxes were rolled past him down the hall. A man with a headset kept referring to a clipboard in his hand and sighing pure stress.

When he found the door marked "Terrico James" he listened closely to see if he could overhear anything through the door. He couldn't. Before he could knock, the door opened and several people walked out, stopping short in front of him.

"Can I help you?" A short black man around Di Santo's height addressed him. He wore an expensive leather jacket and an even more expensive gold watch.

"Detective Doherty, Chicago PD," he said, introducing himself. He scanned the group as he flashed his gold shield. "I hear Terrico James may be missing?"

"I'm Clancy Ray, TJ's manager," the man responded and held out a hand to shake. Ryan took it. "We really don't want that to get out, yet, until we know what's goin' on. Know what I'm saying? Wouldn't be good for publicity." Ryan nodded in agreement. Mr. Ray rubbed his hand across the top of his head. "He's never missed a show. Ever."

Ryan handed him a card. "Is he usually here by now? I

mean, Mandy is opening, right? When does he usually arrive for his set?"

"You know, it's all good. We good. Was it that kid spreading this rumor? I told him not to say anything, now the cops are here. Shee-it." Ray cracked his neck and looked behind him, as if pleading for someone to bail him out of the conversation.

"When was the last time anyone saw or spoke with Mr. James?"

"Um, last night. At the hotel. But this is *not* an investigation. Not yet!"

"What's going on?" A tall, stately woman interrupted them, stepping out of the dressing room.

"Hey Kim!" Ray said, visibly exhaling. "Could you please handle this? This is Detective Doherty of the Chicago Police. Detective, this is Kim Barnett, Terrico's publicist." And with that, the man practically ran away down the hall.

"*Police*? We didn't call the police," Barnett said. She was an attractive woman, about five-foot-seven, with wide brown eyes. She looked at Ryan as if he bore a contagion.

"Actually, we're not here on an official capacity," Ryan said. "I've got friends on staff and we heard Mr. James hadn't arrived, yet. Just offering to help." Ryan took another card out of his wallet and handed it to her. Barnett accepted the card and took the time to read it.

"*Homicide*?" she gasped. She handed it back as if it, too, was repugnant. "Look, nothing's happened here. TJ is not missing, he's just late. This is Chicago, for God's sake. His hometown. *He'll show*!" she announced, as if verbalizing it would make it so.

"Okay, no problem. But if you need our help, we'll be around for a while."

Barnett ended the conversation as she turned and went back into Terrico's dressing room, slamming the door behind her.

"Nice meeting you, too," he quipped to the door and headed back in the direction of Mandy's dressing room.

He knocked again before entering. With no response, he opened the door and was relieved at the scene. Most of the people from earlier had cleared out and Mandy had already changed for the performance, with more glitter on her face than clothing on her body. She paced in circles while she shook out her arms, humming one of her number-one hits. Hank, Duke, and Di Santo were still there, huddled together and leaning against the bar. Only two other people remained. Duke introduced them as Mandy's manager, Brooke Hale, and her personal assistant, Vincent.

"The rest of Mandy's friends already went in to watch the show," he explained, then turned to the manager. "Ms. Hale, are there any extra seats for my—for the detectives, here?"

Ryan got that the boys still couldn't label who he was to them. He wasn't their father, and there was really no good title for the-man-who's-sleeping-with-my-mother. At thirty-eight, the word "boyfriend" seemed a bit juvenile.

"Sorry, all accounted for. But they can watch from backstage with you. That's usually where the liaisons perch, in case we need them."

Di Santo accepted that with a grin while a text message pinged on Ryan's phone. He stepped away from the entourage to retrieve it.

*– Are you sure Terrico's missing? I keep getting that he's there. At Payton Arena.*

Ryan took a beat to absorb that thought. Maybe Terrico had just arrived in the nick of time. Well, technically, he had all of Mandy's set to get ready for his show.

He texted her back:

*– I'll check it out, thanks for the help! <3 U, see U soon.*

"Anything?" Di Santo asked.

"Cat thinks Terrico's already here. And she's usually right, so case closed." Then to the boys, "I can stay for ten, fifteen minutes, but I've promised to have dinner with your mom."

He did want to stay for a while, just to confirm that James was all right. He wouldn't mind getting a photo with him, either, for his Facebook page.

A man with a headset popped into the doorway. "Three-minute warning, Ms. Ross," he announced, pointing a finger at her.

Mandy pecked Hank on the cheek and ignored everyone else as she strutted out of the dressing room. Hank trailed her, gesturing for his brother, Ryan and Di Santo to follow. When they arrived in the right wing of the Payton Arena stage, Mandy proceeded onto the set and up a dark stairway from which she would begin her show.

With the curtain still closed, the band started playing Mandy's current hit single, "Shake It," with the bass pounding out through the arena. Di Santo's head started bobbing to the beat as the audience roared in anticipation of the pop star's imminent entrance. Even though Ryan didn't care for this vapid form of pop music, he did feel a charge from the whole scene, picking up on everyone else's energy.

Di Santo and the boys started whooping when the curtain lifted and the staircase lit up to reveal Mandy in her full sparkling glory. Multi-colored lights swam across the set and faux fog rolled in from both wings. An eight-by-eight grid of video screens served as Mandy's backdrop as she threw up her arms and began singing into her headset.

"*Shake it, shake it, shake it, baby. That is how we make it, baby. Shake it, shake it, shake it toni-i-i-ight!*"

The sixty-four video screens flashed behind her with three, two, and one-second clips of her face, her hair blowing in the wind, and the Santa Monica surf in a perfectly choreographed music video timed to the live performance. Out in the audience cell phone screens sparkled like stars in the galaxy—an homage to the lighters of past decades. While Mandy descended the grand staircase, the steps lit up as each silver sequined boot made contact.

Several male dancers swooshed past them and onto the stage, performing moves around Mandy that felt a little too mature for her pre-teen fan base. But Mandy was in her element, executing the perfect bump-and-grind along with her backup dancers. She belted out the repetitive chorus when the crowd roared unexpectedly, drowning out her performance. A thunder of feet pounded the arena floor and their screams escalated. Whistles bounced off the walls.

Something was descending down from the rafters directly behind Mandy's head. She clearly wasn't expecting it, because when it caught her eye, she stopped mid-shake. She glanced back out at the crowd and resumed the song, apprehensively at first, and motioned for her dancers to move downstage to avoid getting hit by the thing. When the apparatus was in full view, the music stumbled to a halt. Mandy pivoted around to see Terrico James, arms spread open, on a huge cross.

Mandy's microphone picked up the first part of her irate rant: "TJ, what the hell are you doing? You're fucking up my show for a *publicity* stunt? You—" and then her mike went dead. The audience's cheers died slightly while they continued to applaud. Ryan didn't know what was happening but assumed Terrico James was going to let go of the cross and break into one of his self-aggrandizing rap numbers.

He was wrong.

The contraption stopped when the rapper's feet were approximately six inches from the stage floor. Even with her microphone muted, Mandy's scream echoed throughout the arena. Hank ran onto the stage and took the girl into his arms. He glanced up at the rapper on the cross, then ushered her offstage, yelling, "Close the curtain! *Close the curtain*!" When Hank and Mandy reached the huddled group in the wings, Hank made a solemn announcement.

"I take it back—somebody's dead."

# CHAPTER 4

Terrico's people were clamoring for answers and pushing to see the body, but Ryan had instructed the security team to keep everyone off the stage while he called in the homicide of America's most infamous rapper, Terrico James. It took only seven minutes and twenty seconds for the extra police units to arrive, some from the 18th and some from the downtown unit on call to assist. Although Ryan and Di Santo weren't technically on duty, they took charge of the crime scene until the acting sergeant could work out an official assignment. Ryan ordered the uniformed officers to help usher out the audience, cordon off the stage, and prepare for the Medical Examiner and Evidence Tech Team to arrive.

Due to the twenty thousand cell phones in attendance, the news traveled instantly that the rap star was not ill but most definitely dead and additional news vans soon appeared in the parking lot. Di Santo volunteered to corral the press and help keep the reporters at bay while Ryan managed the crime scene.

Payton Arena management was miffed at the spectacle and had ordered security to get the concertgoers out as calmly as possible. Ryan sequestered Hank, Duke, and Mandy in the dressing room and told them to remain there until further notice.

His first order of business was get back to the body. As he walked onto the stage, he spotted Zach Sloane from the Cook County Coroner's office approaching through the center aisle with an older gentleman behind him, both transfixed on the suspended cross. The curtain had since been lifted, again, and Ryan ordered the stage manager to turn on every light in the arena, making it better lit than a night game at Wrigley Field.

"Zach," Ryan said, snapping his fingers to get the M.E.'s attention. "Glad you're here."

"Oh, hey, Doherty. This is some crazy shit," Zach said, shaking his head. "Oh, do you know my boss, Dr. Barone?" He turned to the man behind him. "Dr. Barone, this is Detective Ryan Doherty. Best homicide cop on the north side."

Dr. Barone ascended five steps to the stage and shook Ryan's hand. "Detective," the doctor greeted him. Barone's face was mapped with deep lines of discontent. "The superintendent called and wanted me here to oversee the examination of the body." Ryan glanced at Zach to gauge his reaction. In the five-odd years that that Dr. Zach Sloane had been working their stiffs, he had never been supervised. He was one of those people who were socially awkward but highly intelligent and Ryan respected him for it. He not only memorized Grey's Anatomy—the text, not the television show—but he had also stashed almost every forensic body trauma detail in that brain of his.

"Dr. Barone is accompanying me due to the fact that this is a high-profile case. It's not uncommon for him to come out into the field sporadically," Zach said, answering Ryan's unspoken question.

"Okay, well, this is it," Ryan began, turning to the cross. "He came down from up there." Ryan pointed to the rafters above the stage. He couldn't see anything past the first level catwalk, with the lights shining directly down upon them. "Believe it or not, as far as I can see, the victim has been...*crucified*. Like really crucified. According to the stage manager, Terrico usually dropped down on the device in a body harness that hooked onto the cross from the back. But as you can see—" He looked up at the body and the doctors' eyes followed. "He had no harness on. The body was secured to the device by nails. In the hands and feet."

As a Catholic, this didn't sit well with Ryan. It was definitely a statement, and with all of Terrico James's recent religious proclamations, he wondered if it was some kind of publicity stunt gone bad. Barone began to photograph the body with a full-bodied digital SLR camera while Zach set down his bag and removed several pairs of latex gloves. He handed one pair to Ryan and one to his boss. All three men put on the gloves before they proceeded with the examination.

"Can we get him down from the cross apparatus so we can begin to collect the evidence and study the body?" Zach asked.

Ryan gestured over a couple of patrol officers from the auditorium and asked the stage manager to slowly lower the contraption until the five of them—the two uniforms, Ryan, Zach, and Barone—could bear the weight of the cross. The men slowly laid it down onto the stage floor, with James facing up. Ryan shook out his arms, crouched down next to the supine corpse and studied it from head to toe.

"There's not enough blood," he announced. "Look at the hand wounds."

Zach was already hovering over Terrico's left side, lifting the rapper's shirt with a metal instrument.

"Yeah, that was the first thing I noticed," the ME said. "No blood on the stage, either. Looks like Mr. James was crucified post-mortem. See these stab wounds?" He moved aside to show Ryan Terrico's exposed torso. "Dried blood trailing away from his wounds toward the sides and back. He was horizontal when he bled out. Multiple stab wounds, but this particular puncture near his heart is the probable COD." Zach lifted the corpse's chin. "This is interesting. See his neck? The veins are distended and enlarged. That's an indicator of cardiac tamponade. The knife wound caused the heart sac to fill up, which pressured the heart to the point of failure."

Ryan nodded, taking it all in while counting the stab wounds. There were four. "Any idea about time of death?"

"Well, rigor's pretty much set in. We won't know for sure, but I'd venture to say at least eighteen to twenty-four hours. We'll know for sure when I take the liver temp."

"So this isn't the primary crime scene." Ryan's cop brain was already trying to determine whether Catharine's boys were going to be suspects.

"From the lack of blood, no. But if I were you, I'd make your next stop those rafters." Zach pointed above to a cat-walk of black iron, suspended twenty-some feet above them.

Ryan blew out a breath and looked up again, straining to see the origin of the wires holding the cross. He wasn't a fan of heights. Maybe he could coerce Di Santo to climb the narrow spiral staircase.

"I'll leave that to the tech team for now," Ryan grumbled as he started formulating the crime in his head: if Terrico hadn't been killed on site, then the perpetrator would have had to bring the body in, somehow, already deceased, and string him up in the rafters without anyone in the arena no-ticing. His hypothesis was interrupted when Di Santo walked onto the stage, stopped three feet from the body and crossed himself with his hand.

"Jesus Christ—no pun intended," Di Santo said. "Oh hey, Zach. What d'ya got so far?"

"TOD could be as long as twenty-four hours ago," Ryan replied. "There are four knife wounds on the torso and chest, one of which went right to the heart." They both glanced at the body, almost in reverence. "Zach says the nail wounds were most definitely post-mortem," Ryan contin-ued. "No blood."

"Shit, he was really nailed—"

"To the cross. Affirmative."

"Da-a-a-a-mn," Di Santo said and crossed himself a second time.

"Would you stop with that? This guy wasn't a saint, he was a rapper. And from what I've read, a borderline sociopath."

"Detective Doherty!" called a voice from the wings of stage left. He recognized the southern drawl and looked up to see all two hundred and twenty-some pounds of Detective Wyatt Fisk emerge out of the wings. The man was fully suited up with a navy and red striped tie pinned to a white shirt with old-school tie clasp. On the clasp was a small Celtic cross, causing Ryan to wonder if Fisk was an Irishman, too. His gold shield swung back and forth from a chain around the man's neck. What a tool. Although it was common to see that on television, real cops avoided that practice. Too easy for a perp to grab.

"Fisk," Ryan greeted the man with a firm handshake. "That was quick, you on duty tonight?"

"I was going to say the same exact thing. You two seem to swarm to dead celebrities like flies on shit!" Fisk said in his trademark drawl. He was an old-school cop who had transferred in from Atlanta when his wife got some kind of executive promotion. She worked at a top finance company in the Loop, and rumor had it Fisk compensated for his marital inferiority complex by being a huge dick on the job. Fisk laughed at his own joke and then leaned in to Ryan and Di Santo as if divulging a secret. "This here is a side gig for me. Moonlighting. Sometimes I step in and head up the security team here at Payton on my off hours. You?"

"We were visiting my—two friends who were actually working on security tonight. Lulling twins. Do you know them?"

"Oh the new guys! Football players. Yeah. Good kids."

"Sons of the woman I'm dating. One had been assigned to Terrico's team and was worried when he went missing. Asked us to come poke around. Guess his instincts were correct. Did you see anything unusual?"

Fisk rubbed his hand across his mouth, shaking his head. "Unusual, no. Everything was going smoothly until this guy came down on the cross. That was a spectacle!" Fisk bellowed with inappropriate laughter. "Well, fellas, this isn't my case, so I cannot conjecture," Fisk said, as he circled the large cross with Terrico's body still attached. "So, we've got two boys who are practically related to you that are all up in this incident. And now you want this to be your case? Good luck on that one."

The extra flesh on the man's chin wobbled as he shook his head. Ryan figured he and Di Santo must've caught the case or else Fisk wouldn't be harassing him like this.

Ryan decided to call Fisk's bluff. "Well! We're done here, then."

"D?" Di Santo said, questioning the statement. Ryan threw his partner a look and he caught it with a nod. "Oh, yeah, we've been on shift since nine this morning, so I don't need this." He emitted an exaggerated yawn that fooled nobody.

"Hold on, hold on," Fisk said waving a hand in the air. "I already called this in and I was told it is the preference of our fine Superintendent of Police that you two are the primaries on this case." *And there it was.* "But since this here homicide was discovered with me on site, the sergeant on duty agreed that I should help out with the investigation. I will give you my full statement. And seeing that I am both a Chicago police officer and an employee of Payton, I should be making any and all announcements to the press."

The man straightened his tie as if already preparing to step in front of a camera.

"The press is yours, Detective," Ryan said. He hated the media anyway. "We'll start by interviewing Terrico's people while the docs work on the body. They'll give you the details we want to disclose. When the tech team gets here, we need them to go up onto the catwalk where the cross was suspended, photograph, and gather trace."

Fisk's gaze followed the cables that were still dangling

from above, although disengaged now from the cross. With his chin in the air, he almost lost his balance and had to catch himself with a quick step back. "Yeah, we'll wait for the tech team for that," he said, gathering his composure. "I've already taken statements from Terrico's people, but I'm not sure I can trust them. They all seem pretty shady to me." Ryan wondered if "shady" meant "black" to the Bible-belt Southerner. "They all told the same version of what happened, but of course since no one had *separated* them, they could have all coordinated their stories."

"Listen, it was complete chaos when Terrico James came down on that cross," Ryan justified. "We had to deal with the scene and getting the audience out of the arena."

Fisk held up a palm. "Hey, hey. I'm not being accusatory. Just stating a fact. I'm suggesting every one of them go into your suspect pool since they were close to the vic. Next, while we wait for the tech team to arrive, I would like to go talk to that little Miss Mandy Ross and your boys, if you don't mind. You and your mini-me partner can tag along, if you wish."

Ryan was usually good about holding back with ass-holes, but this comment threw him over the edge. He held his finger up to the detective's face.

"One, they're *not* my boys. Two, *we* will interview them and *you* will observe. And three, you *don't* disrespect my partner. Ever. *Got it?*"

Every person on the stage jumped when a blast of music pumped out of the eight-foot amps. A colossal image of Terrico's face appeared on the video grid, rapping out the middle of his current chart-topper, "I'm da Man."

"My hood is black and his is white.
How long we gonna fight this fight.
Over or under the Mason-Dixon line,
There are dicks of all kinds who wanna kill my rhyme.
But I'm Da Man."

The music stopped abruptly, along with the video. Everyone stood silent, all eyes peeled on the video display as if Terrico had just come back from the beyond. A voice called out from the back of the auditorium, "*Sor-ryyyy!*"

Fisk pulled back, chuckled, and turned to head off stage. Ryan shuddered from the incident then followed the detective, intentionally hanging back twenty feet, Di Santo at his side.

"Aw, you like me, you really, really like me," Di Santo said, elbowing Ryan in the ribs.

Ryan ignored the comment while they made their way offstage and back to the dressing rooms, his partner practically bouncing down the hall beside him.

Di Santo was always giddy at the beginning of an investigation. "The supe asked for us by name, did you hear that? I guess we're still golden with him. Musta been the Town Red case and the fact that we closed the Jessica Way homicide in four days. We're getting quite the rep!"

Ryan wasn't as thrilled as his partner. For one, he was supposed to be off duty and enjoying a nice dinner with Catharine in Evanston right now. Secondly, he wasn't enthused about having to work with Fisk. They had worked a couple of other cases on the same team, and Ryan had noticed more than once that Fisk didn't work too hard to conceal his bigoted beliefs. He lacked in detecting ability, too. How the 18th ended up being the recipient of his transfer, he couldn't comprehend.

"If it's between Fisk or us, there's no contest," Ryan told his partner. "So don't let it go to your head. This is going to be the biggest one of all. I'm not sure I even know where to start."

"Hey, you and me, we're a great team. I have no doubt we'll close this one, too. And with Catharine's woo-woo stuff, well, that's our ace in the hole. So, you got any feelings about this? Your cop intuition seems to be getting stronger and stronger with each case. I'm starting to believe that Cat's 'powers' are rubbing off on you." Ryan audibly scoffed at the idea. "Listen, it happens! And if it rubs off on you, it'll rub off on me."

Di Santo was spiking energy, as if it were Christmas morning in June. Ryan shook his head in amusement. His former partner, Jonathan Lange, had always been laid back, always in control. It had been a two years and almost ten months since Jon had been killed in a highway accident. Ryan remembered how he'd bucked being reassigned to another partner so soon: two weeks, five days, to be exact. He told his sergeant he didn't want anything to do with the newly promoted beat cop, but Besko had drafted the two of them into the Police Officer Mentorship Program— probably as therapy for his loss—and he had no choice. And so there sat Detective Matthew X. Di Santo, adjusting his nameplate on Jon's desk, jonesing for his first case like a Chihuahua on coke. But the "other D," as they called him in the squad, had grown on Ryan and was a decent investigator.

Ryan shook off the memory as they arrived at Mandy's dressing room. Fisk was already introducing himself, shaking hands with the same five people who had been there just prior to the show: Hank, Duke, Mandy, Mandy's assistant Vincent, and her manager, Brooke. When Duke spotted Ryan and Di Santo, he stood up and came over, still visibly shaken.

"You guys okay?" Ryan asked, patting him on the back.

The six-foot-two boy ran his hand through his hair. "Yeah, this is just so crazy. I'm so glad you were here, Ry. I just talked with Ma and let her know we're okay." Duke looked from him to Detective Fisk, waiting for the next move.

"We need to ask y'all some questions," Fisk began.

Ryan took it from there. "Let's go sit down," he said, gesturing to the seating area at the other side of the suite.

Mandy stood up from her makeup chair, wiping away remains of the stage paint, her eyes red and swollen. She took Hank's hand as they headed back to the red sofa. She had already changed back into her sweats.

Ryan let everyone find a seat while he took out his notebook. He always carried his notebook. Some cops had transitioned to taking notes on their cell phones or tablets, but he would never be able to type that fast on a touchpad.

"I know this is a difficult time for you," he began, directly addressing Mandy. "Just a few questions, Ms. Ross, and then we'll let you get out of here." She nodded and leaned in closer to Hank. He couldn't help but think that the boy was setting himself up for a big fall. "How well did you know Terrico James?"

Mandy couldn't stifle a sob before she began speaking. She took a wadded-up tissue and dabbed the corner of her eye. "I didn't know him very well...I mean, except for the tour."

"You didn't know him very well?" Di Santo questioned her. "He discovered you! He produced your first album!"

Ryan was impressed, if not embarrassed, at his partner's knowledge of her career.

"Well, yeah. I mean we worked together. It's true, he produced my first album but kind of let me fly on my own with the second. Hadn't seen him much lately until the tour. It was the promoter's idea to tour together. Double the fan base, y'know? My fans are not his fans—"

Ryan held up a hand to stop her babbling, which was quite common with trauma victims. Either they babbled or were shocked into silence. He was relieved that at least she was talking. "Do you know of anyone who would want to hurt him?" he asked, proceeding to the next by-the-book interrogation question. He could hear Fisk's labored breathing, directly behind him. Almost felt it.

Mandy answered, "No, no. No one would want to hurt TJ. Everyone loved him. He had a huge fan base. Well, except all those religious nuts. They hated him."

Ryan flashed on the picketers and kicked himself for ordering everyone out of the parking lot. They were probably gone by now. He patted his back pocket and thankfully the brochures he had collected from the groups were still there.

He turned to Di Santo. "Check with the press and see if any organization has claimed responsibility. If it is one of those groups, they'll want to announce it."

Di Santo nodded and ran out of the room on his mission.

"Tell us what happened before the show. Before we got here," Ryan continued, turning back to Mandy.

Hank sat up straighter and answered Ryan's question. "When Mandy arrived, Terrico's people were already here—"

Ryan held out a hand. "Hank, I need to hear it from her, first. Sorry." Hank's jaw tightened. "Ms. Ross, please tell me from the beginning. When was the last time you actually spoke or saw Mr. James in person?"

"God, I don't know." She pulled her cell phone from the pocket in her hoodie and swiped the screen with her finger. "Last night. No, not last night. I—I'm confused. A couple days ago. We were talking about the concert. It was important to him. He's from Chicago, you know. That's why it was so weird when he didn't show up."

"He has family in town?"

"Mm-hmm. His mom and brothers, they all live here."

Ryan documented the information for notification purposes. He and Di Santo would want to speak with the family next. Get some insight into the man. "Did he visit his family? Do you know?" The girl shrugged. "Where was Terrico staying?"

"At the Westley. We're all staying there. We have a floor. *Brooke!*" she screamed for her manager, who was standing less than five feet away.

Brooke jumped up from her chair. "What do you need?"

"I'm sad and I'm tired and I don't want any of this anymore," she said, waving her hands in Ryan's direction, as if she could just make him disappear.

He didn't know whether to laugh or be livid.

"With all due respect, Ms. Ross, we have to get through

this tonight," Ryan said to the singer, as well as the rest of the room.

Mandy ignored his presence.

"Miss Ross has been through hell tonight, Detective," answered her manager. "And she has just lost one of her very, very close friends. Can we finish this up in the morning?"

Ryan glanced back at Fisk, who was scowling at the prospect, and made a split-second decision. "Okay, but we'll want Ms. Ross to come into the station and give a full statement in the morning, when she's rested. I'll follow up getting the details from Hank and Duke. I know where they live."

His attempt to lighten the mood in the room didn't work.

"Oh, we can talk, now?" Hank remarked.

It was never easy with Hank. He had been a pain in the ass ever since Ryan had started dating Catharine. The boy was overprotective of his mother and gave Ryan a hard time every step of the way.

Duke took over, always the diplomat. "It's our first time working a big concert like this and our first time backstage," he said. "I tried to introduce myself to Terrico's manager, but they wanted nothing to do with me. Terrico was missing and they were all upset about that. They said no one had seen him all day."

"And you didn't see anything suspicious, say, like someone carrying a body up to the rafters?"

The twins glanced at each other and shrugged, simultaneously. "Dude, we were in here most of the time," Hank said. "They wouldn't let Duke into Terrico's dressing room, so we hung out with Mandy. I mean, you saw: there were like twenty, thirty people in here. That's our alibi. All those people."

Ryan took a deep breath. "I'm not saying you're suspects."

"Everyone's a suspect, dee-tective," Fisk challenged him from behind.

"Okay, that's it for now," Ryan said, ignoring the man. He stuffed his notebook back into his pocket.

Mandy jumped up from the couch and started pacing in front of her wardrobe rack. "And what the hell am I supposed to do *now*?" the pop star cried. "I can't go back to the hotel. The press is going to be swarming it. *Vin-cent?*"

Both the manager and her assistant jumped to attention.

"I need somewhere else to stay tonight. I can't handle the press yet. Maybe in the morning when all this is cleared up and my head is straight. But now I just can't deal. Can you figure out a place I can go? Like *now?*"

"You could stay with us," Hank suggested, and glanced at his brother. Duke nodded. "We've got a pretty big house," he continued. Mandy was listening. "Huge house, actually, two guest rooms. No one would find you there, and it's only like twenty minutes north of here."

Ryan had to give Hank credit. It was actually a decent idea. With the girl at Catharine's house, Ryan could keep tabs on her and make sure she got to the 18th district station in the morning for questioning.

He addressed Fisk, but made sure Mandy's manager heard, too. "Sounds good to me. It's a gated house, with good security."

"It sounds like a good plan, Mandy," Brooke chimed in. "The press will be expecting you back at the hotel. Vince and I could even divert them there with the limo."

Mandy thought about it for a beat and then agreed with a shrug and a nod.

"I'll call your mom," Ryan told the boys. He walked out into the hall to place the call.

"Here? In *my* house?" Catharine sounded as if she was panicking. "I suppose it's fine, at least I had the cleaning service in today. But what do I need to do? Should I roll out the red carpet?"

"She's just a teenager, Cat. You don't have to go all out. She just needs a bed for the night. The reporters will be expecting her back at the hotel."

"Is she all right? How are the boys?"

"She seems okay. The boys are fine, too. Oh, and I should mention: Mandy and Hank seem like they've gotten pretty close in the past couple of hours. I think something's going on with them."

"*No*! Seriously? *My* Hank? With Mandy Ross?"

"Yeah, your Hank. I didn't want you to be surprised when they showed up hand-in-hand. But I also have to warn you—" He lowered his voice and walked a couple of steps farther from the dressing room door. "—this girl is a piece of work. She's used to being waited on hand and foot. Don't let her bully you."

Catharine laughed. "Nobody bullies me in my own house."

# CHAPTER 5

It was close to midnight when the dogs broadcast the visitors seconds before Catharine heard the rumble of Hank's SUV in the driveway. She had just finished making some oatmeal cranberry cookies for the imminent celebrity houseguest. She rushed to set the plate of cookies on the table in the center of the atrium, corralled the dogs in her study and made it to the front vestibule just as the three were entering.

"Are you all okay?" she asked, scanning their faces.

Before they could answer, she planted a grateful kiss on each of her twins' cheeks.

"Yeah," Hank said. "It was just a crazy scene, but we're good. Oh, Ma? This is Amanda Ross."

He pointed to the small blonde girl who was hovering behind the boys, biting on a fingernail.

Catharine offered her hand. "Hello, Amanda, nice to meet you."

Mandy offered a limp hand as if expecting Catharine to kiss it. "Hi, I love your hair," she said. "Is it Indian?"

"Indian?" Catharine answered, not quite understanding the question. She reached for her own her long, brunette curls.

"Yeah, your extensions. Are they from India? Those

people have the best hair quality, I swear. Really shiny and soft."

"No, that's my mom's *real* hair," Hank answered, ushering Mandy down two steps into the home.

The boys laughed as Catharine led them along the path through the atrium, still bewildered by the statement. She was proud of her natural waist-long mane, which hadn't been cut for several years. Did it look like fake hair? She unconsciously brushed her hair back with one hand, as if to prove it was hers.

"Whoa, this is crazy!" Mandy said, strolling through the large gardens in the center of the house. "My place is about twice the size of yours, but this layout is sick!"

"Sick?" Catharine said, turning to Hank to interpret once again.

"Cool," he said, chuckling under his breath.

Catharine nodded, not knowing how to respond to the backhanded compliment. "I have prepared the blue guest room for Amanda. Have you all eaten? I made some cookies, but I could make sandwiches if you'd like."

"I'm not hungry," Duke answered. "I'm wiped out. I think I'm just going to head up to bed." He kissed his mother and made his way to the staircase.

"*I'm* hungry," Hank said. He turned to Mandy for her answer.

"I just barfed," the girl announced. "I got carsick on the ride. Or maybe it was seeing TJ up on that—anyway, I could do with a soda. You have Diet Sprite?"

Catharine was getting thoroughly flustered by the girl, but her mothering instinct quickly took over. "No, I don't. I'm sorry, but let me get you some ginger iced tea. Ginger will help settle your stomach."

Mandy agreed with a nod. Catharine left her son and the pop star and made her way back to the kitchen. As soon as the door swung closed, she texted Ryan.

– Kids made it home and you're right, Mandy is a little rough around the edges.

– *Told you :) So they're ok?*
– Yes, fine. You coming back tonite?
– *I'll try. Keep the bed warm for me.*
– Will do. Don't forget to eat something.

Catharine was disappointed that she wouldn't see Ryan tonight, but she understood the requirements of his job. A budding relationship was hard enough to navigate, but then there was the added constraint of her affliction. They could only be together at her home. Her fault, entirely, and she was working to remedy it.

As she prepared the sandwich in the kitchen, she thought about how she wanted so desperately to be a normal couple. For the most part, their relationship was ideal. They rarely fought. They cherished their time together. But lately, she'd had this haunting feeling that a big storm was around the corner. She quickly dismissed it with a shake of her head, chalking it up to insecurity.

As she put the sandwich on a plate and neared the door to the atrium, she could overhear snippets of Mandy and Hank's conversation from the atrium. "Wow, your mom is pretty hot for an older lady," Mandy was saying. "No wonder that cop hangs around."

*Older lady.* Offended for a moment, she realized it was only a matter of perspective. She pushed the swinging door open with her hips and re-entered the atrium, head held high.

"No, no, don't do that. Don't pick the flowers," Hank said to the girl. "They're not for picking."

Catharine arrived to see Hank standing between Mandy and Catharine's prized daisies, one of which had already been plucked and placed behind her ear. She ignored the girl's faux pas and lowered the plate down onto the table, gesturing for both of them to take a seat.

Hank avoided his mother's gaze and attacked his sandwich, while Catharine sat and studied Mandy, who was busy thumbing her phone.

She was tiny, about Catharine's height, but about ten to

fifteen pounds lighter, almost too thin. Circles under her eyes betrayed her exhaustion.

"Mandy, where are your parents when you're on tour? Do they come with you?"

Mandy took several seconds to finish a text and then looked up at her. "My mom stays back in L.A. to take care of my brothers. They're also in the business—acting on commercials and TV. She needs to take them to their acting classes and auditions."

"My dad's an actor," Hank said, grabbing a handful of cookies. He handed one to Mandy. "He lives in L.A., too."

She took a miniscule bite out of the cookie and put it down. She was done. "I thought you said he was a body-guard?"

"Yeah, well, between acting jobs he does security and personal training and stuff."

The girl ignored him and turned her attention back to her phone. "They're planning to develop a TV show for me," Mandy finally said, looking up. "A reality show about me on the road." She laughed. "All wild and shit!"

Catharine glanced at Hank, who shrugged non-responsibility for Mandy's language.

Mandy's cell rang, crooning one of her own hit songs, which broke the awkward silence. "What," she said, answering. Mandy paused while listening for several seconds. "Seriously? We're not going to Columbus? Fuck. How long do I have to stay in Chicago?" she whined.

A shadow fell over Hank's face. Catharine had tried to accept this girl without prejudice since her son was obviously smitten with her. There weren't many people she outright disliked, but it was difficult to connect on a human level with Mandy Ross. The girl's broken personality was most likely a manifestation of an unfortunate child being thrust into an adult career.

The pop star continued into her cell phone, "Okay, well the cops sent me to my friend's house. Up in...where are we?" she asked, turning to Hank.

"Evanston."

"Evanston," she said into the phone. "Yeah, just let me know. Thanks, bye." She took a sip of iced tea and then filled in Hank and Catharine, as if they were waiting with bated breath. "That was Brooke, my manager. They're probably going to have to cancel the tour with Terrico and then start another one just for me, alone. Business stuff."

Catharine scrutinized Hank's reaction, wondering if he had picked up on the extent of Mandy's narcissism.

"Brooke said we have to go into the police station tomorrow to give a formal statement to your *boyfriend cop*," the girl continued. "But he'll go easy on me, right? They all do," she said with a wink.

Riled, Catharine was about to chastise the girl—someone had to teach her manners—until she realized Mandy was baiting her. Catharine took a deep breath and remained calm as she stood up from her chair and announced, "Okay, well! I'm going to turn in. Hank, you show Amanda the guest room." She then addressed the girl. "I hope you have a restful night here. There are toiletries and a new toothbrush in the guest bathroom. I've laid out a clean nightgown on the bed if you need one."

"I won't need one," Mandy said and threw another wink in Hank's direction.

Catharine walked behind the girl's chair and mouthed the words, "*Guest room!*" to her son.

He nodded and waved goodnight, promising nothing.

# CHAPTER 6

Ryan was conferring with Sam Matello, the ornery head of the Evidence Tech Team, when a wiry blond man tapped him on the shoulder. He huffed at the interruption and the man jumped back like a frightened foal.

"Oh, hi! Detective, is it?"

Ryan nodded and rubbed his neck, fatigued. The older he got the harder it was to pull off two shifts in a row.

"I'm Charles, one of the event managers here at Payton Arena?"

The younger generation had an irritating way of ending each sentence like a question. It made him sound as if he was unsure of everything—even his own name and job title. There was even a new term for it: up-talking.

"Yes, Charles. How can I help you?"

"Well, we found something that I think you might want to check out. A couple of our staff members kept smelling something funny in the wings of the stage? Smells like bad meat or a dead animal or something? And so I opened the storage closet and there was this big equipment case. It *really* stinks, like sick and sweet at the same time? Anyway, it has Terrico's logo on it and in light of what just happened, I told them not to touch it until you guys checked it out."

"Good call. So, no one has touched it or opened it?"

"No, I locked the closet so no one would go in, and believe me, no one really wants to! I'm not opening that box. God! Do you think there could be another dead—"

"Just lead us to it," Ryan instructed. Charles nodded and beckoned Ryan and Di Santo to follow him as if they wouldn't. "You did the right thing. Can I have your last name for the record?"

"Epperson, that's Charles Epperson. E-P-P-E-R-S-O-N."

Ryan appreciated the spelling, as he had to classify every staff member as a person of interest. In fact, everyone in the goddamned arena was a person of interest, but they had to start somewhere.

"Hey, Ryan!" a woman called out from behind them.

Ryan turned around to find Jane Steffen catching up to them, trying to run in heels.

"Plain Jane," Di Santo said. "Always showing up at crime scenes. If I didn't know any better, I'd think she was the perp."

Since she was out of earshot, he greeted her with a short wave and fake smile, not bothering to hide his disapproval of her presence.

When she caught up to them, Ryan made the introductions. "This is Jane Steffen, Assistant State's Attorney," he said to the manager. "Jane, this is Charles Epperson, one of the managers here at the arena." They shook hands while Jane caught her breath. "Charles was just about to show us a closet in which he thinks there's another body." Both Jane and Charles recoiled while he enjoyed their reactions. "Okay, so we don't know for sure if there's a DB in there, but we're investigating. Here, put these on." He handed Jane a pair of rubber gloves.

She remained stoic while pulling them on. "I can't stay long. I've got court in the morning."

"Do I smell…*alcohol* on your breath?" He leaned into Jane with a grin, but she pulled back.

"Yes. I was at McGinty's when I got the call from Stan. I told him I'd check it out since I was in the neighborhood."

"Mmm-hmmm," he teased her. "Hey, how'd it go at Catharine's place?"

"You mean *Queen's Landing*?" Jane said. Ryan acknowledged the joke with a smirk. "She did fine, no worries. I'll tell you about it later. Let's go check this out."

Epperson led them through the auditorium, up the stage stairs and through the wing on the right.

"That's the closet there," he said, pointing to a door in the corner of the black space. Epperson pulled out a key ring full of keys and fumbled through them.

As they approached the door, Di Santo leaned in and took a big whiff. "Definitely de-comp," he said. Ryan didn't even have to lean in, he could smell it, too. He gestured to Epperson to hurry up and open it.

Epperson's eyes widened. "Man, I don't even want to look," he said. He unlocked the closet door and leaped back again, as if the boogeyman had jumped out at him.

Jane stood a couple of feet back while Ryan and Di Santo rolled a three-by-four-foot black equipment case out of the closet with gloved hands. As described, it bore a white-stenciled logo on each side of the box: the initials TJ with a crown over them.

Ryan rocked it back and forth, feeling the weight of the box. "Doesn't feel like there's a body in there. Too light."

He decided to open it quickly, like tearing off a bandage, and flipped all three silver latches that held the sides to the top. The sides collapsed outward and the smell was ten times stronger than it had been a second ago.

"Foo!" Di Santo exhaled and covered his nose with his sleeve. Ryan did the same. Jane groaned.

"What's in it? What did you find?" Epperson yelled from thirty feet away.

"Nothing," Ryan answered. He didn't even see blood or hair at this point, but it was still dark backstage, despite the arena lights. "Just the smell." Then to his partner: "This is probably how they got the body in here without anyone seeing. Equipment cases go in and out all day." Ryan pulled out his cell and called Matello to get some tech team members over ASAP to process it.

When he hung up, Epperson had approached the group again, gawking at the black box, holding his sleeve under his nose. Ryan and Di Santo pulled up the sides up and latched it again while Jane turned away from the box, wanting nothing to do with it.

"Charles, how did the cross get lowered? Was there a switch? A lever that you used for the performances?"

"There's a switch, but the stage manager uses the remote during the show. Many of the artists use it for their entrance."

"On a cross?" Di Santo asked.

"Oh, no. Terrico was the only one who came in on a cross. P!nk came in on a trapeze, Gaga on this really cool spaceship. Same mechanism, though."

"And where is the remote now?"

"Hold on, I'll get it." Before Ryan could object, Epperson had leapt off the stage and returned with a remote control. "Here it is."

Ryan took it by its sides so he wouldn't obfuscate any fingerprints on it and dropped it into an evidence bag. He sealed it with tape and signed it.

"You're going to have to give us your prints for elimination," he told Epperson. "See Sam Matello. He'll get someone to take them."

"No problemo! I've got nothing to do with this. By the way, do you have any idea how to get rid of that smell once we get that thing out of here?" Epperson asked, his hand back underneath his nose.

Ryan handed him a card for a company called the Crime Scene Cleanup Croo. He often got that question and always carried their cards.

Jane stepped in. "Does the arena have video of the loading dock or backstage?"

"No, we only record the performances," Epperson answered with an over contrite frown.

By then, several members of the Tech Team rounded the curtain. Ryan presented the equipment box while they pulled on evidence gloves.

"Step back, gentlemen!" Matello boomed. "And, lady," he amended, bowing to Jane. "What are ya doin' poking through closets anyway, detectives?"

"Um...detecting!" answered Di Santo.

"Don't give me your crap, Di Santo, I have enough to do here. Shit."

Matello was rough around the edges, but top-notch at his job. And with the square footage of the arena, they needed him at his finest. All night. So Ryan elbowed Di Santo, who agreed to behave with a nod. They ushered Jane and Epperson away from the box while Matello waved over two of his team.

The equipment box was their first viable lead of the evening causing Di Santo's energy level to shoot to eleven. "I want to go up to the rafters and check out the thingy that lowered Terrico to the stage," he announced then turned to Epperson. "Can you show me how to get up there?"

Epperson agreed, but only if Di Santo was accompanied by an experienced member of the backstage crew. He picked a blue-eyed brunette staffer around twenty-five years old who looked more like someone who should be on stage rather than behind it. She wore a black Payton Arena logo tee shirt and tight faded jeans ripped at the knees. She told Di Santo to follow closely behind her as they climbed the black metal spiral staircase, and he was extremely happy to do so.

Ryan watched them ascend into the rafters until he heard their footsteps far above him on the catwalk. He didn't even want to look.

"So, what are you thinking?" Jane asked. He'd almost forgotten she was there. "You think they brought him in in the box?"

"Zach said James has been dead eighteen to twenty-four hours, due to the rigor in the body. If I had to guess right now, I'd say he was killed somewhere off-site, brought into the arena in that box, and then nailed up on the cross. Why, I don't know yet. We find the motive and we'll find the perp."

"Who would do such a thing?"

"People are crazy," Ryan said. "Who knows? Someone who was trying to send a message. We've got all the uniforms and detectives from the night shift interviewing the staff. I'll have to go over it in the morning. Hey, so tell me about the meeting with Catharine. Do you think she'll be okay?"

Jane frowned. "She seems to be fine. We went over the testimony and I coached her. She's pretty smart, she'll do well."

"When is the taping again?"

"Monday."

Ryan had planned to be with Catharine during the taping, or at least in the house to support her. Reliving the attack from her coworker could bring up a lot of traumatic feelings. He was worried that she'd regress when it came to her agoraphobia, but she'd already gone through several months of therapy and was doing well. She even managed to walk the dogs around the block with minimal anxiety.

"Anyway, I need to go," Jane said, interrupting his thoughts. "I'm juggling five cases at the moment, so I probably won't be assigned to this one, but I'm eager to know how it turns out. And if you need anything—"

Ryan held up a hand as goodbye as his attention was drawn back to his partner who was already descending the iron staircase from the rafters. Di Santo nodded to the girl and watched her walk over to the other side of the stage.

"Get anything?" asked Ryan.

"Yeah, her number."

Ryan shook his head. "Seriously, you never stop."

"A guy's gotta do…ya know? Anyway, there's a good chance the perp left prints up there," Di Santo added. "It's really dusty and at least a hundred feet up. You gotta hold on to those rails for dear life. Believe me, even the arena girl got dizzy and I had to hold her in my arms."

Ryan snickered. "Yeah, sure, dizzy. Isn't she staff? She goes up there all the time."

"It was my charm that made her dizzy." Di Santo said, straightening his tie.

Ryan rolled his eyes and hit his partner on the back of the head. "Dizzy Di Santo. I like that."

# CHAPTER 7

Ryan drove directly to Cat's house after the team wrapped up at Payton Arena, arriving at 7:34 in the morning. He wanted to catch Mandy Ross before she had a chance to take off. And he wanted to see Cat. He called out her name and heard the dogs answer from upstairs. By now, they knew Ryan's walk, his keys, and his voice. They didn't even bother to meet him at the door or defend their territory, as he was now part of it.

Ryan headed up the large wooden staircase to the second floor. All was quiet. He figured no one was up yet, and made his way around the periphery of the two-story atrium to the north side of the house. He quietly opened Cat's bedroom door and observed her bed rumpled. The shower was running in the en-suite bathroom to the left. It only took him 4.3 seconds to shed his CPD polo shirt, jeans, shoes, and socks and get to the bathroom door. Steam hit his face as he entered. "You got room for one more in there?"

He knew there was room for five, as her white marble-lined shower was about the size of his entire bathroom.

"Oh! Ryan. You scared me." Catharine's voice came from the other side of the glass door.

He pulled it open and stepped in, savoring the hot pounding water on his tired flesh. He also savored the vision before him.

"Ms. Lulling…"

"Detective."

He loved the sound of his title in her voice, and she knew it. He pulled her slippery body in close to his. "There's only one thing more beautiful than you naked, and that's you naked and wet."

Catharine smiled and blessed him with a kiss. "How'd it go? Did you get all the interviews done?"

"Tedious, and yes."

"Anything helpful?"

He gathered her wet hair and swept it back, behind her shoulder blades so he could have an unobstructed view of her perfectly formed body. "No one saw Terrico James being nailed to the cross, if that's what you're asking."

"That would have been too easy, eh?" she joked.

The smell of her body wash, her shampoo, and her slippery body urged him to forget about the investigation. He planted an enthusiastic kiss on her lips and backed her up against the marble wall, made warm by the hot spray. He focused all the remaining energy in his body on making love to her.

Afterward, they stepped out of the stall and Ryan helped Catharine dry her long locks. They dressed, making small talk. He took her hand as they walked down the hall, but she stopped short at the guest room. The door stood slightly ajar. Cat pushed it open, peered in, and let out a disapproving *humph*.

"The bed is made," she said, lips tight.

"She could've made the bed this morning."

"Does she strike you as the type of girl who would make her own bed?"

"No, you're right. She's in Hank's room."

"That *girl*!" Catharine chided, shaking her head. "And in his mother's house!"

"Cat, they're adults. We just went at it in the shower. What's the difference?"

"The difference is that he's my son. I'm not a prude, I'm

just being protective," she said, closing the guest room door as quietly as she opened it. "I just know this isn't going to end well."

He leaned in and whispered in her ear. "Let him have his fun in the meantime, Mama Bear." She smiled, reluctantly, while he jostled her left shoulder. "Come on, it's not every day a boy gets to hook up with a big celebrity. Think of all the cred he'll get on campus."

Catharine pulled away from him and proceeded down the stairs, mumbling, "Hook up. I despise that term—*and* its implication. And I have no interest in Hank's 'cred' on campus. That's all male-mentality nonsense."

From a long history with women, Ryan knew that he wasn't going to win any argument that had to do with the male mentality, so he let it go and followed her downstairs and through the atrium.

When they entered the kitchen, his stomach grumbled from the smell of rich coffee and breakfast. He hadn't eaten since yesterday's lunch. Duke sat on a stool at the island while his girlfriend, Vanessa, was in the process of placing two more pancakes onto his plate. They both greeted Ryan and Cat with a wave.

"Oh, hello, you two. Breakfast is served," Vanessa sang out.

Duke and Vanessa met the first week of college and had been steady throughout the school year. The girl was a classic beauty, in a studious sort of way. She may have had an inch on Catharine but seemed just as tiny next to her athletic boyfriend.

"Good morning!" Catharine said, visibly impressed. She put her arm around the girl and then leaned over to kiss her son. "Wow, what a spread. You must have gotten here early, Vanessa!"

The girl handed Cat and Ryan full steaming mugs of dark French roast. "Yeah, well Duke texted me about your 'special guest.' I told him I'd come over and make everyone breakfast if I could just meet her. I *love* Mandy Ross!" she said, whispering the last sentence. She punctuated the sentiment with two tiny jumps.

Catharine raised her brows at her son.

"What?" Duke squawked, sporting a guilty grin. "I didn't want you to be overwhelmed."

"Duke, you're showing off. You know Vanessa was the only one you could tell. However, this is a lovely gesture. Thank you." Catharine opened the refrigerator door and asked, "Have you seen the love birds, yet?"

Vanessa caught her comment and giggled. "No! Not yet. They haven't made an appearance. Hank and Mandy Ross, I can't believe it! Cat, can you believe it? Your own son?"

Catharine closed the refrigerator without responding.

Vanessa looked to Ryan for a response. He shook his head at her, discouraging the subject. "So! Terrico James. It's all over the Internet this morning. Are you in charge of the case, Ryan?"

"Yeah, but we have to work with one of the other detectives who happened to be there, off-duty. A real dick, no one likes him." Catharine looked up in reaction to his language. Sometimes he forgot to keep the cop vernacular in the squad room, as she put it. "Well, he is, Cat. There's no other word for it."

She let it go as she took a breakfast plate for her and one for Ryan and placed both at the table next to Duke.

"Will Hank and Mandy want breakfast, you think?" Vanessa gushed. "I hope they want breakfast. Look, I've made eggs and pancakes and bacon."

"*Bacon*!" Ryan and Duke cried out in synch. They slapped hands.

Cat answered while she let the dogs out into the backyard. "I'm sure they will. Hank will never turn down a meal. I'm not sure about Mandy. She wouldn't eat last night but she's awfully thin. Try to get her to eat something."

"Mandy Ross—I still can't believe it," Vanessa repeated as she flipped the flapjacks. "Do you know how long she's staying?"

Catharine shrugged her shoulders. "I hope not too long. Her energy doesn't work in my environment." Ryan and Duke exchanged smirks.

"I hope he uses protection," Ryan said to Duke in between bites. "Who knows where that girl has been?"

"*Ryan!*" Cat cried out.

Her son laughed. "Don't worry, Ry, we're not fourteen. We know about STDs."

Ryan slapped him on the shoulder. "I know, but I just had to get that out there."

"Do you use protection with *my mother?*" Duke challenged him.

"*Duke!*" Cat cried again.

Vanessa giggled.

Ryan knew Duke was jibing him, but he didn't expect the question and choked on his scrambled eggs. "Um…I…the thing is…"

"I think we can stop talking about my sex life at the breakfast table," Catharine interjected.

The men chuckled again as the kitchen door swung open and Hank walked in. He ran his hand through his bed hair and tightened the drawstring on his blue cotton pajama bottoms.

"Hey, Ma," Hank said and kissed the top of his mother's head. "Broh. 'Nessa."

Apparently Ryan didn't warrant a greeting.

"He-e-e-y, Ma!" Mandy echoed, following Hank through the swinging door. She was wearing one of his Evanston High School football jerseys, the hem of which fell below her knees. Vanessa fumbled with the spatula, almost dropping a pancake on the floor. She let out a squeak and got it back into the pan.

Hank scanned the kitchen scene. "What's all this?" he said.

"Vanessa made breakfast," Catharine responded as she set two additional plates on the island.

Hank threw a smirk at his brother, immediately comprehending what was going on, and nodded consent to share their brush with fame.

Duke put down his fork and wiped his hands on a cloth napkin. "Mandy, this is my girlfriend, Vanessa."

Vanessa cleared her throat and held out a hand.

"Hey," Mandy said without making eye contact. "Oh, that reminds me, I need to call Brooke." She stepped out into the atrium, leaving Vanessa visibly disappointed that the celebrity encounter was so brief.

Hank sat down next to his brother at the kitchen island and stabbed a fork into the stack of pancakes. "After breakfast we need to go to the hotel so Mandy can change," he said. "She was supposed to check out today, but we've decided to go back and stay there until she leaves."

"*We?*" Catharine questioned. "You will be staying with her?"

"Ma, don't start."

Ryan changed the subject. "I need to speak with Mandy at the station before you guys head off. About the case. She has to give her statement, remember?"

"Can we eat first?" Hank responded. "I promise, you can talk to her before we leave."

"Oh, you're in charge of her schedule now?" Ryan challenged him. "When did this happen?"

Cat put her hand on Ryan's shoulder, a clear signal to calm down.

Hank went back to his food. "You guys, she has been through a lot in the past twelve hours. Just chill." From the next room, they could hear Mandy cackling on her cell.

"Yeah, I can tell she's completely traumatized," Ryan said.

They finished their plates without speaking until Mandy came back into the kitchen.

"Brooke said we could go in through the hotel's kitchen and up the service elevator. The staff has been prepped and they won't bug us." She took a stool next to Hank and fixed her gaze on his plate.

"Mandy, would you like breakfast?" Catharine asked her.

"I'll take a slice of wheat toast. Plain. And a half-orange, half-apple juice with a squeeze of lime, please."

Ryan wrapped an arm around Catharine before she could detonate.

"We don't have apple juice," Cat answered.

"I could run and get some," Vanessa chimed in. "That would be no problem!"

Catharine held up a hand. "Is plain orange juice okay, Mandy?"

"No. Not okay," said the singer. "Bottled water then. Bubbly, if you have it."

Cat went to the fridge, took out a bottle of Aquafina, and plopped it in front of the girl. Mandy stared at the water bottle it as if she expected someone to open it for her, and Hank obliged.

"Thanks, baby," she cooed.

Ryan wiped his mouth with a napkin, leaned back on his stool, and addressed the pop star. "So when would you like to come give your statement?"

Mandy's head turned slowly to Ryan as if she had not granted him the right to speak to her. She dramatically inhaled and exhaled. "I've decided I am not going to any police station. The press would crucify me. Ha-ha! Crucify." She looked around at the room while everyone else froze. "What, too soon?"

"The police station has a back door too," Ryan said to the girl. "And you *will* be there."

The 18th district detective squad was in a frenzy when Ryan entered. Amy-Jo Slater, the Department's press liaison, paced back and forth in front of his desk, screaming into her cell phone.

"No, we don't have official cause of death yet. Yes, we

are pursuing several leads. No, he was not killed by crucifixion. Yes, he was actually nailed to the cross. As soon as
the coroner's report comes in, there will be a press conference in front of the Payton Arena. I promise I'll let you
know."

Ryan circled around her to his desk and nodded to Di
Santo, who was already in place across from him.

"Mandy and Hank were right behind me," he said. "They
should be in any minute. No coroner's report yet?"

Di Santo opened his email and scrolled a bit. "Nothing."

Ryan's cell phone tinged with a text from his sister. Finn
Doherty ran a celebrity crime blog, which was gaining some
fair readership. The downside was that she always wanted
an exclusive from him.

– *Terrico James—any deets?*

He was about to text her back "No" when the landline
rang. He answered it on speakerphone, "Homicide:
Doherty." The caller ID stated it was from the intake desk,
but no one responded. "Hello? Vic?" He had just passed the
desk sergeant, Vic Firenzo, on the way up, so he knew the
guy was there. Finally, a voice responded.

"Hey, yeah, Ryan, there are two people here to see you."
The desk sergeant changed to a loud whisper. "And one of
them is *Mandy Ross,* I swear-to-God!"

Ryan grabbed for the receiver, but not before there was
an audible reaction in the squad room. Shit. He didn't want
to make a scene. "Okay, send them up."

As he hung up the phone, Di Santo jumped up out of his
chair, buttoned his suit jacket, and ran a hand through his
hair. The other cops in the room laughed and whistled at
him.

Ryan put his hand up as a warning. "Calm down, you
guys. She's just a kid."

"She don't look like no kid!" responded a cop from the
corner of the room.

Ryan kept an eye on the double doors until he saw Mandy and Hank through the windows and got up to escort them

before there was too much of a commotion. The pop star was now dressed in a hot pink ripped top over black leggings and sequined heart-shaped sunglasses on top of her head. She appeared so young to him. That's what happened when you got to be forty-minus-change, he thought. The celebrities started to look younger and younger.

"Hey, Ry," Hank greeted him when they got to the door. "Where are we going to do this? And can we get it done quick before the reporters find out she's here?" The boy eyed a detective who already had his phone up, about to snap a photo.

"No pictures!" Ryan shouted to the room.

He motioned Hank and Mandy to the back of the squad toward the interview rooms. He and Di Santo followed, instinctively shielding Mandy from the rest of the squad.

The four of them settled into IR-3, the interview room farthest from the squad. Ryan motioned for them to take a seat at the metal table, while he and Di Santo sat on the opposite side, facing them.

Ryan felt an uncomfortable level of attention from the girl as she seemed to scrutinize his build. She licked her glossy lips while her gaze settled on his shield clipped to his belt. At least he hoped she was looking at the shield.

Di Santo handed him a crisp new brown folder labeled JAMES, TERRICO in black and white. As Ryan opened it to review what they had so far, Hank rocked back on his chair, arms folded across his chest in a gesture that clearly gave off a "Fuck you, let's hurry this shit up" vibe.

Ryan took a little more time than necessary to review the file. It was a tactic to put the suspect on edge. Get them to talk first. And it worked.

"So what else do you need to know that I didn't tell you last night and you couldn't have asked me over breakfast?" Mandy said, implying an intimacy between them that was nonexistent.

Ryan took a deep breath before responding. "Why don't you walk us through your entire day yesterday? From the moment you woke up to the moment on stage when you realized Terrico James was dead."

Mandy rolled her eyes as if he were her father asking her where she'd been all night.

"I woke up. Vincent came in with my breakfast tray and went over my schedule for the day while I ate." Mandy leaned forward in her chair with wide eyes. "One egg, a carrot, and a Diet Coke." She flashed her flawless white teeth and added, "Put that in your notes."

"What time was that?" Ryan asked, refusing to react.

"Two o'clock. Around two."

"You woke up at two in the afternoon?"

"I was out late on Friday. At Cuvée—that's a *club*," Mandy explained as if he were a geriatric tourist.

"Yes, we know Cuvée. Was Terrico James there that night? At the club?"

"Terrico? *Ha*! No, he wasn't with us. We don't really hang in the same circles."

"I was wondering about that," Di Santo said from Ryan's left. "How did you two get on a ticket together? Don't you have different types of fans?"

"We're with the same label, and our promoters thought it would double the chance of filling the arena. *Because* we have different types of fans. Pretty genius, if you ask me. And it's worked so far. Twelve cities sold out."

Ryan wasn't as impressed as she wanted him to be. "So back to Saturday. After the egg, carrot, and Diet Coke, then what?"

Mandy thought for several seconds. "Oh, yeah. I went shopping at Macy's. But some girl spotted me and started screaming, so I had to get out of there. I went back to my room at the Westley, changed, and then headed to the arena. That's where I met *this* guy!"

Mandy took Hank's arm and pulled him closer. Hank didn't mind. Ryan couldn't help thinking that when this girl was done with him, she was going to toss Hank aside like a used makeup sponge.

"And in any time during the day did you see or have contact with Terrico James?"

"No," Mandy responded, as she pulled her pink cell phone out of her pink purse. She pressed some buttons and held the phone up to her ear. "Are we done now?" Before Ryan could answer, the girl stood up and began a conversation on her phone. "Hi. Any word about getting out of Chicago? Fuck, Brooke, I am just so tired of this whole scene! Tell Brad to call me A-S-A-P so I know what's going on."

"Do you have anything to add?" Ryan asked, turning his attention back to Hank. The boy shook his head.

Mandy was still whining into her phone. "It's one thing to do a show together. But TJ's fans are not going to just want to see me, you know? I'm going to lose half my audience." She paused several times between "whatevers" before ending the call with a "fuck." The singer turned to the three men in the room. "What if the person who killed Terrico is after *me*? What are you going to do to protect me?"

"We don't have the resources—" Di Santo began.

Hank turned to her. "I'll protect you, don't worry. I won't leave your side."

The girl sat down, pouted, and leaned up against him. "Aw, you're just the sweetest thing. Will you be my bodyguard, honey? Just until I leave?"

Hank put his arm around her in response.

Aside from being sickened by the girl's manipulation, Ryan didn't like the idea of Hank being put in that position. "You aren't trained to be a bodyguard, Hank. This is not a good idea. I won't allow it."

"You won't *allow* it?" Hank said, leaning forward in challenge. "Our dad's a bodyguard!"

"It's not genetic, Hank, there are specific skills you need, and extensive training. Look, the Westley's not in our district, but I'll talk to the sarge and see if District 1 could send over a unit to watch over her."

"Can we go now?" Mandy said, standing up to end the conversation.

Ryan couldn't concoct anything else to keep them there, so he agreed. "I think we have all we need. Please fill out this information form before you leave, though, so we have your contact information."

Mandy gave him a wry smile. "Yeah, well, you wish. I'll give you Brooke's number. She knows how to get a hold of me."

Ryan had had enough of this brat. He slapped the form onto the table in front of her. "*Your* information, Ms. Ross. This is a homicide investigation, I'm not asking for an autograph."

Mandy's fake blond extensions bounced as she fell back down into her chair and dutifully filled out the form. When completed, she handed it to Ryan, took Hank's hand, and left the station without a word.

# CHAPTER 8

After Mandy left the station, Ryan reviewed the brochures he had collected from the religious groups at the concert. "Warren L. Smith," he said, reading through the brochure for their organization, One Divine Life. He recalled that particular group and their antagonistic picket signs.

"Let's see if we can catch those guys before they fly back to Atlanta." He dialed the phone number on the brochure and waited for an answer.

"One Divine Life, are you havin' a blessed day?" the female voice greeted him with a saccharine-infused drawl.

He paused for a second wondering if he really had to answer the question or if it was rhetorical.

"This is Detective Doherty with the Chicago Police. We're trying to get a hold of Mr. Warren Smith. Can you tell me if he's still in Chicago?"

There was a suspicious silence on the other end of the line and he thought he heard her whispering.

"Mr. Smith is out of the office today, Detective. Is there something I can help you with?"

"We need the location of Mr. Smith." There was another silence. "Hello?" He glanced over at Di Santo with a frown, who echoed it back to him.

The woman finally came back on the line. "Yes, well I'm

going to have to get back to you with that information, Detective. Where can I reach you?"

He gave her his number and spelled his name out for the
message. She politely bid him farewell with a friendly sug-
gestion he live his life in the Way of the Lord.

"She's probably calling their lawyer," Ryan said.

Several minutes later, the phone rang and he noticed the
incoming area code was the same as the ODL office. The
caller ID only displayed a location: Atlanta, GA.

"Atlanta. This has got to be Smith."

"De-tective Doherty," the voice bellowed on the other
end, pronouncing the H. He hated when people pronounced
the H. "This is Harlan Copeland the third. I represent Warren L. Smith and the church of the One Divine Life. How
can I help you today?"

He mouthed the word "lawyer" across the desk pod and
Di Santo scrunched up his face. Ryan then explained to the
Harlan Copeland the third that they had met Mr. Smith at
the concert and had some follow-up questions for him.
"We're thinking that Warren or another member of the
group may have remembered something since last night. It
was so hectic at the arena. Often witnesses have more information the day after. Just any kind of small detail would
really help us narrow down the timeline." He knew attorneys and hoped he could get the group to talk to him without one present.

"I see, I see," said Harlan Copeland the Third. "Well, if
you are giving your word that they are not direct suspects..." Ryan would do nothing of the kind. "Then I guess
it's okay if they speak with you. I'm sure they'll want to
cooperate in any way that they can."

Copeland's last comment almost seemed to be a directive
for his client. Ryan's intuition kicked in with the thought
that Warren L. Smith could have been silently conferenced
in on the line.

Copeland continued. "They are taking a couple days to
commune with some sister-churches in Chicago. They are

staying at the Westley on Wabash." The attorney paused for a response, but Ryan was busy taking notes. "They *will* report back to me, Detective, after your conversation. So please mind your professional manners?"

"Absolutely. We appreciate your help in this matter, Mr. Copeland," he said nodding to Di Santo. He then asked for Smith's cell phone number and the attorney obliged. After he hung up, Ryan recapped the conversation to his partner.

"The Westley huh? Same hotel as Terrico," Di Santo said. Ryan had also taken note of that particular detail. "Interesting that a church organization would spend that kind of dough. Aren't they all 501(c)(3) and all that?"

"Yeah, the Jesus business must be booming."

Ryan dialed Smith's number and the man didn't seem exactly surprised to hear from him, strengthening his suspicion that Smith had been on the previous call. They agreed to meet at noon at Uno's, a pizzeria famous for catering to the tourist crowd, located less than a half mile from the Westley Hotel.

"It's always the pizza for tourists," he mused to his partner. Ryan didn't mind, though. By noon he'd be hungry again, and looked forward to downing a couple of slices of thick crust. "The ME's report came in from Zach!" he said, reading his new incoming email. "Official cause of death: cardiac tamponade due to invasive trauma. Terrico James most likely died within minutes of being stabbed."

Di Santo frowned. "Tamponade? Isn't that a French olive-relish-thingy?"

"That's *tapenade*," Ryan corrected him. "Imagine death from olive tapenade?"

They laughed along with some of the other detectives who had been listening in.

Ryan went to back his email to retrieve the autopsy report. "The murder weapon has been characterized as a nonserrated blade, approximately six inches in length, one to one and a half inches wide," he read aloud. "Cardiac tamponade. Too bad it wasn't olive tapenade. Now I'm getting hungry."

He glanced at the clock. One hour, twenty-one minutes until 'za time.

"Good afternoon, Detectives. Do you have Jesus in your heart?" was the way Warren L. Smith greeted Ryan and Di Santo as they walked into the North side pizza parlor. Uno's was a favorite with the tourists, always landing on the top of the "must-eat Chicago pizzas."

Smith was one amongst a party of twelve, seated at the helm of four checker-clothed tables set together in the center of the restaurant. The two chairs directly adjacent to Smith were empty, courteously saved for him and Di Santo.

"Yeah, I grew up with the guy," Ryan answered as he took the chair next to Smith. "We went to Catholic school together." A wave of chuckles broke the ice. Smith introduced the other eleven members of the ODL, nine of whom were male, all buttoned up a little too tightly for the hot June sun.

Ryan had started the voice recorder before entering the restaurant, and checked it with a tap of two fingers. Not many civilians were aware that every interview, every interrogation was recorded—whether casual or structured.

After the table reviewed the menus and ordered, Di Santo opened with some small talk—a tactic they often used to put people at ease at the opening of an interview.

"You guys do any sightseeing while you're in town? Art Institute? Navy Pier?"

Smith scanned his flock and then took a drink from his water glass before answering. "Y'all have a great city here, Detective. This is my first time visiting. After our early morning services our group took a walk over to Millennium Park. So lovely. We were particularly amused with the big bean-like mirrored structure. What is it called? Gateway something?"

"The Cloud Gate," answered Di Santo. It was one of Di Santo's favorite tourist attractions, probably because the distorted reflection made him look taller than he really was.

"Yes, the Cloud Gate," Smith echoed, while an affirmative reaction rumbled through his companions at the table. "Really a lovely city so far, I must say. And not too hot or humid."

"Yet," Ryan interjected.

"Have you ever been to Atlanta?" Smith asked.

The group tittered. Must have been a joke, but he answered nonetheless.

"I have not. Hot?"

"They say it's so humid in the summer you have to cover the fishbowls to keep the fish from swimming out!"

Ryan smiled, gratuitously. "What time did you arrive at Payton Arena last night?" He was done with the chit-chat.

Smith raised his eyebrows. "Oh, so we're there now, already. Okay." He addressed his people as he answered, his voice dipping into a preaching cadence. "We arrived at six p.m. and left at 8:45 when the police cleared everyone out of the parking lot."

The others nodded in unity—a move that just slightly creeped Ryan out. Was this a legit organization or a cult? Or something in between? He shook it off to continue the questioning. "Did you notice anything or anyone suspicious entering the arena?"

Smith looked around the table for help with this question. "Well, I was busy organizing and handing out flyers so I wasn't really keeping an eye on the arena itself. Please define 'suspicious' and I'll do my best to answer you."

"Any crosses go by with—oh—a large rapper nailed to it?" Di Santo quipped. He meant it as a joke, but it didn't go over very well with this particular crowd.

Smith cleared his throat and folded a napkin into his lap. "I read that Terrico James was raised as a God-fearing

Christian, Detective," he began, as if he were telling the group a bedtime story. "But somewhere along the line his faith was misdirected. He deluded himself into thinking *he* was the Son of God. It was a tragedy, what happened last night. But did you ever consider he may have done it to himself?"

"Crucify *himself*?" asked Di Santo. "That would have been pretty tricky to get the last nail in, don'tcha think?"

"I don't mean purely by himself, but perhaps he had another lost and twisted soul help him up on that cross. That is our theory, anyway. Maybe he had finally repented for his unholy hubris and recruited a friend to help him commit suicide."

"Interesting theory, but our evidence shows he was already dead when he was nailed to the cross. Stabbed in the heart."

At that unfortunate moment, the waiter arrived with three large deep-dish pizzas. The two detectives didn't hesitate to reach for the cheesy slices and quickly stuffed their mouths with the fine Chicago cuisine. The others moved a little more slowly in taking their pieces of the gooey red pie. One of the women declined and placed a glass of ice water to her forehead.

"No man should die at the hand of another," she proclaimed quietly. The others nodded, some trying to sever the strings of cheese tethered to their mouths from the chunks of pizza in their hands.

Ryan considered the quote for several seconds. "An idealistic sentiment," he said. "But what about 'An eye for an eye'?"

"Old Testament," replied Smith. "We'd prefer to live by the teachings of our Savior. As in Matthew 6:14."

The table was suddenly abuzz with agreement and amens.

Ryan shook his head. "Sorry, it's been a while?"

"'For if you forgive men when they sin against you, your heavenly Father will also forgive you.'" quoted Di Santo.

Smith appeared impressed. As was Ryan.

"Do you think Terrico James sinned against you?" Ryan asked, picking up on the quotation.

"Detective, Terrico James was a sick man in a sick occupation. We just wanted to get our message across to the people who needed it the most: his fans. Like I said, we were within the confines of the law."

A phrase that he no doubt had learned to recite by heart.

Di Santo cleared his throat and asked the question. He was good at asking *the question* and Ryan let him, in most cases. "So, we need to ask you, Warren, for the files: where you were on Friday night, six p.m. to midnight?"

Warren L. Smith wiped his mouth with a red cloth napkin before he answered. "Well, Detectives, our plane arrived around five-thirty p.m., so after we got our luggage and picked up our rental van, we didn't get to the hotel until about seven. You can check with the hotel and confirm our check-in time. We got a block of rooms on the fourth floor. After settling in and calling my mother to tell her I arrived safely, I took a shower. Then Mr. Diehl—" He paused to nod at the man on his left. "Mr. Diehl, Mr. Kellan, and some other associates of ours went down to the hotel restaurant because we were famished by the time we settled in. You can check our account, as we charged the meal to my room."

Ryan noted the details in his small spiral notebook, making a note to himself to check the hotel records. "And about what time did you pay your bill and return to your room?" he asked.

"Not sure of the approximate timing, Detective, but around eleven."

Ryan and Di Santo were satisfied with the religious leader's answers. At least, temporarily. They spent the rest of the lunch discussing the best Chicago tourist spots and hidden treasures for the group to visit. And Ryan charmed the woman with the ice water to at least *try* the pizza that was sitting in front of her. She did, even finishing off one more slice after that one.

On their way back to the station, the two detectives discussed their different experiences growing up in the Catholic faith. Irish Catholic, Roman Catholic—it all came from the same place. The same teachings and all the same guilt.

"I had no idea you had your Bible down like that," Ryan said to his partner, recalling his off-the-cuff quote.

"A product of all those years of Sunday school, I suppose."

"You still go every Sunday?"

"To church? Sure. My mom considers it quality family time and it's really the only time we can all be together. Tradition." It was funny how they had worked together for two years and nine months, and yet they had never really discussed religion. "I gather you don't?" Di Santo prompted.

"Nah. My sisters used to be more faithful than I ever was. They used to badger me to go with them every Sunday when they all still lived in town. But the more they bugged me, the more I resisted. Doesn't really mean much to me now. Especially after everything I've seen on the job. Hard to believe there is some master creator up there wreaking this kind of havoc upon the world. It's easier for me to believe in the chaos theory—that nothing happens for a reason. It just happens. In a way, that's more comforting to me than believing there's some kind of divine entity up there deciding that this is the day he's going to kill babies. Or mothers. Or rappers. Or allow men to commit suicide while they murder three thousand innocent people. Or allow a psychopathic dictator to kill six million. I don't like that God. That's not a God I want to worship. That's not the world I want to live in."

Di Santo nodded, taking it all in, politely. Ryan wasn't trying to convince anyone of anything. In fact, he rarely spoke of religion. But his partner had asked.

"'We went to Catholic School together. That was a good one, D!'"

Ryan chuckled at his own wit. "You know, those guys seem to be legit on the surface, but I got a bad gut feeling from them. Not just because they're hyper-religious, but it was almost—"

"Cult-like?" Di Santo answered. "Yeah, my gut was acting up, too. Although it may have been the sauce. Kinda spicier than usual."

Ryan decided to keep Warren L. Smith and his ODL on the back burner.

Upon entering the station, Ryan recognized a man sitting in the row of chairs across from the intake desk.

"Mr. Ray." Ryan offered his hand to Terrico James's manager. "How is everyone doing?"

The man clasped Ryan's shoulder as they shook. "Not good, not good. I wanted to come by and see what was going on with TJ's, you know, case? I hope you don't mind I came in. I got the address from your card."

"Of course," Ryan said. "Let's go upstairs and I'll tell you what we've got so far," Ryan said.

He and Di Santo exchanged a look as if they had caught the next big fish. The drill: pretend to fill him in on the details while surreptitiously conducting an interview. They brought Ray up to the detective squad and Ryan pulled over a spare chair to the side of his desk. No interview room this time. Just keeping it casual, as if they were lending a sympathetic ear.

"As far as we can tell, he was stabbed, which was the actual cause of death," Ryan explained. "We still do not know how he ended up in the arena. We've got detectives interviewing possible witnesses and Payton personnel. The autopsy is almost complete and I believe that the coroner's office might be fine with releasing the body as early as tomorrow. I'll give you their number to coordinate." He looked up the number on his phone and wrote it down for the manager.

"I appreciate your help, Detective. This is a terrible loss for his family and his friends. And his fans." The man looked down at the desk and stared at Ryan's coffee mug. Following Ray's eyes, he cringed. The mug was a gift given to the whole department as a gag at the end of last year. Bold white letters against black stated:

*CHICAGO HOMICIDE DIVISION*
*Our day starts when yours ends.*

Ryan turned the mug around and continued the conversation. "When was the last time you actually saw Terrico James?"

"Man, I've gone over this in my head again and again. I saw TJ on Friday night, after rehearsal. We all went out for dinner. The Italian Kitchen, I think it was called. Then we came back to the suite at the Westley. We were having drinks, watching TV, and talking about the concert details. Then TJ gets a call on his cell phone. He wouldn't tell anyone who it was. He said he had to step out for a second, meet someone in the lobby, and that he'd be right back. He even told Roman and Dex to stay put. They're his bodyguards. Well, he didn't come right back. He never came back."

"What time was that?"

"Around 11:00, 11:15."

"And when he didn't come back, you tried to call him?"

"Yeah, man, of course we tried to call him. After about an hour we were all like what the fuck? Oh, excuse me."

"That's okay. But you didn't call the police?"

"No. Kim, you know, TJ's publicist? She wouldn't let us call the police. She said give him time and he'll turn up. And you know, he's a guy. Sometimes he runs into a female fan, and—you know what I'm sayin'—stays out for the night. Although, he usually brings chicks back to his room. But we're thinking, okay, so maybe he got some female. Yeah, so then we all went to our rooms and turned in for the night. No partying without Terrico, man."

"And in the morning?"

"I usually give him till noon to let the chick clear out, so I didn't try calling or texting until then. He didn't answer, so I knocked on his hotel room door. Nothing. By Saturday afternoon we were worried. We didn't know if we should go to the venue or not, without him. But we figured maybe he was out and it was getting late. We had to figure out what to do with the show, you know what I'm sayin'? We told the promoters TJ was sick and probably couldn't go on. But deep down we were hoping he would just show up. And then that's where we met you. At the arena."

"Do you know of anyone who would want to hurt him? Did he get any credible threats? Hate mail?"

"Man, have you been following Twitter? He pissed off a

lot of people at that awards show. That kind of shit can escalate quickly. Kim kept trying to get him to publicly apologize, but his ego was too big. I don't think I've ever heard him apologize for anything in his entire life."

"Any concrete death threats?"

"You should talk to his security company about that. Celestial Security. Hold on, I got a card." Ray pulled a black billfold out of his pocket, opened it and handed Ryan a business card. *Celestial Security – Celebrities, Dignitaries, Executives.*

"They handle everything from his mail to his bodyguards. Dex and Roman are from Celestial, and I believe they already gave their statements to your associate, I think. A Detective Fisk?"

Ryan shuffled through the forms in the file and found the bodyguards' statements, taken by Wyatt Fisk. Pretty short and sweet, only a half-page each. He skimmed both, which were consistent with Clancy Ray's accounting of events.

"So you, personally, haven't witnessed anyone threatening Mr. James?"

Ray thought for a moment. "Well, there is this one funky-ass religious group. Pretty scary. They come to every one of our shows, but we just try to ignore them. The DLL or somethin' like that."

"ODL?" Ryan showed Clancy the pamphlet he was given when they questioned the group. "One Divine Life?"

"Yeah, yeah. That's them. Crazy mofo crack—I tell you, they tend to show up everywhere we go. I've started to recognize the faces. I wouldn't be surprised if they had something to do with this whole thing."

"Have they ever been violent or threatened to be violent?"

"Naw, man. Just picketed our shows. I don't know, maybe I'm wrong. I don't want to go accusing people of shit, I'm just…it's been a bad coupl'a days, you know?"

"I do. And again, I'm very sorry for your loss. If you could please fill out the rest of this form while you're here, it would be helpful to the investigation. We need to have details on anything or anyone you could think of."

Ray took a pen from his shirt pocket and wrote some notes on the form. "Pret-ty scary dudes, let me tell you," he added while writing. "But they never threatened us or anything. Just kept showing up, like zombies. Always there. Creeped me out, I'll tell you that."

"Can you tell us about Terrico's family? Mandy Ross told us he grew up in Chicago. She said he could still have family here?"

Ray put the pen down. "Yeah, definitely. We're all from here. East Side."

Ryan gestured for Ray to note that on the form, and the man picked up the pen again. "Was Terrico on good terms with his family?"

"Well, yes and no. You know they all church-going people and sometimes they weren't happy when he, you know, said all that stuff in public. His mama didn't like it, for sure, and she would call and blast him into next week. But she didn't *hurt* TJ if that's what you're thinking. No, man, she's like 80 years old." Ray looked to the back of the squad room and out the window. "Starting to get hot in this city, isn't it? I forgot about this Chicago humidity, bein' in L.A. for so long." He patted the hair on the top of his head.

Ryan knew from experience that when someone changed the subject, there was a good reason. "Is Terrico's mother the only family he has here?"

"No, no. TJ's got two brothers, both still living in the city, I think. One has a family, the other lives with the mama. In and outta rehab, a druggie type."

"Do you have an address? Where the mother lives? Or a name?"

"Yeah, she still down in the East Side," Clancy replied, looking down at his lap. "Same house they grew up in, I think. I don't remember the address—it's been a shitload-a years since I've been back there. But the house is on Avenue M, just south of 98th."

Ryan locked eyes with Di Santo, probably thinking the same thing: with all of Terrico's earnings, why would his mother still be living in that neighborhood? The East Side was a misnomer of a neighborhood, as it was actually located on the southern-most tip of Chicago proper. Unlike its sister neighborhoods across the city, there was no way this place was ever going to be gentrified. It was a beaten down stepchild of a 'hood—an area you wouldn't want your mother living in by choice, especially if you had the means to move her.

Clancy picked up on the silent judgment. "TJ was a little tight with his cash, know-what-I'm-sayin'? He didn't want to end up like *some* rappers, all broke and shit after a couple of hits. He put his money away in the bank vault and it stayed there. Didn't let friends *or* family do the mooch thang." He sniffed and looked around the room.

Di Santo piped up, "Hey, D, maybe it's worth going down and talking with them. Pay our respects and see what they have to say."

"Mae Robinson," Clancy interjected. "That's his mama's name, Mae. Oh, and you best call him Terrence to her. That's his real name: Terrence James Robinson. She won't talk to you if you call him Terrico. He also went by TJ among friends and family."

Ryan noted the names in his book.

"Tell Ms. Mae I'll be calling on her soon," Ray said as he slid the report form back to Ryan. "Thanks for talking with me, I appreciate it."

They stood up with the man, thanked him in return, and ushered him out of the squad room.

"Huh, interesting twist about the money," Di Santo said when Ray was out of earshot.

"Yeah, let's check out the family. This isn't going to be easy, today of all days, but we have to do it. The sooner we get there, the more likely they'll all be there."

"Great. On to the East Side. Should we get some backup from the 4th?"

"Yep," Ryan confirmed, checking his weapon. "And we'll need the vests."

# CHAPTER 9

Ryan called Research for Mae Robinson's address and then asked to be transferred to the 4th District. He requested a patrol from the East Side meet them at the house and made it clear that they didn't want any strife over territory. The sergeant on duty was an old friend of Besko's and complied without a hassle.

When they pulled up to the Robinson's home the first thing they noticed was the urban shrine that was set against the front chain-link fence: various types of flowers, stuffed animals, photos of Terrico, and notes left for him in the afterlife. A blue and white police sedan idled about fifty feet south of the house. Ryan approached the unit and told the officers to just hang out and stay watchful. They'd check back again when they were finished questioning the family.

Ryan and Di Santo approached the house, an older structure constructed of cheaper materials with concrete steps and a long porch covered with green turf-like carpet. A white iron security door barred the threshold, with enough latticework that it was impossible to see through. Ryan could clearly hear voices behind the iron door.

"Can I help you?" said a disembodied male voice.

"Hi, I'm Detective Ryan Doherty, and this is Matt Di Santo with the Homicide Division, Chicago P.D." He and Di Santo held up their badges to the security door and waited for a response. There was none. "We're here about Terrico—I'm sorry, *Terrence*," he continued. "We'd like to speak with Mrs. Robinson, if she's available?"

A latch was thrown and the iron door swung toward them. The voice belonged to a tall, fit black man about thirty years of age. "Hi, I'm Christopher. I'm Terrence's brother." He offered his hand to Ryan, then Di Santo. "My mother is in the living room with family. As you can imagine, it's been a very rough day for her. Please be gentle."

"We're sensitive to that fact and will proceed accordingly."

"Okay, thank you. Follow me."

It was a scene that they had witnessed many times before: people mourning, weeping, eating, talking, and hugging. Two small girls sat on the rug, oblivious to the grieving around them, building some kind of multi-colored structure out of Legos. The house was modest but extremely clean, with beige carpeting, overstuffed furniture, and plastic plants sprinkled about the interior. On the far wall above the couch hung a replica of Da Vinci's *The Last Supper*, shrunk to about two feet wide.

"Mama, this is the—"

"You must be PO-lice," the woman interrupted.

She was already in black—a lace covered one-piece dress that ended past her knees. Six inches below the hemline two black orthopedic shoes grounded her as she struggled to get up from the recliner.

"Don't get up," Di Santo said, taking her hand. "We're so sorry for your loss, ma'am." Matt was always good at the comfort part.

"You gonna find out who killed my boy?" she challenged them, her chin up for emphasis.

Mae's eyes were small, compared to the rest of her features. Yellow from age, and red from tears.

"We're working on it Ms. Robinson," Ryan said, taking a seat on an ottoman beside her. "That's why we're here. We were hoping we could ask you and your family a couple questions."

She patted Ryan's arm. "You can call me Ms. Mae. Everyone calls me Ms. Mae."

Ryan was almost attacked by a horsefly that was buzzing around his head. He swatted it away from his ear.

"Don't you go batting my TJ!" Mae admonished him.

"Ma'am?"

"TJ! My boy!" Ms. Mae spat.

Ryan looked to Christopher to translate.

Chris shook his head and explained, "She thinks the fly is my brother."

"This fly *is* your brother!" Mae waved a finger up at Chris. "He come to tell me he's okay. You see, Mr. Po-lice Detective, the very minute I heard my Terrence had crossed over, this fly came in the house and never left my side."

Ryan nodded. Whether the woman was just in the denial stage of mourning or was fighting dementia, the best approach was to just go with it.

"I'll tell you, with that big ol' black head and stubborn attitude, I'm almost believing it," Chris said. "The thing seriously won't go away."

Ms. Mae agreed with a "Mmm-hmmmm!"

"Very well, then. Ms. Mae," Ryan said, flashing his famous smile. He knew he could soften any woman with his Black-Irish smile, especially the elderly. Old ladies loved him. "Do you know anyone who would want to hurt your son, Terrence? You know—the old Terrence—who was human?"

Ms. Mae shook her head and addressed the fly, which had landed on the arm of her recliner. "I tol' him to stop all that religious talk, just stick to your music and make people happy, I said. Now look where it took him! He's going to be with the *real* Jesus now, mm-hmm, the *real* Jesus, who I hope will kick his ass for me! You hear that, TJ? You go saying that blasphemous crazy stuff, the real Jesus gon' *kick yo' ass*!" The fly took off and went to the window. "Okay, you ignore me now, but you'll see!" she said, waving a hand over her shoulder.

Ryan nodded in sympathy, half expecting the fly to cry out "*Helllllp-meeeeeee*!" like the movie.

A pretty young woman bent over to Mae Robinson, placing a hand on her shoulder. "Ms. Mae, you want something to drink?" she asked then nodded to Ryan and Di Santo.

Mae Robinson declined by pursing her lips and putting up her palm. The younger woman turned to the detectives.

"Hello, I'm Tracey Robinson, Chris's wife," she said. "TJ's sister-in-law. You may not get much from Mae today, but Chris and I would be happy to help you, if we can."

"That would be great. Is there somewhere we could talk privately?" Ryan said, lifting himself from his seat.

"Let's go out on the porch," Tracey answered. She turned to the kids playing on the rug. "Simone! Watch Tyree for me while I talk to these men. Don't let her wander!"

A little girl in pink denim pants looked up, nodded, and put some blocks in front of a smaller, freckled girl, in diapers. Chris opened the front iron door and let his wife and the detectives through before closing it behind them. The couple took a seat on a porch swing, while Ryan and Di Santo each pulled up a plastic lawn chair, facing them.

"We just finished talking to Clancy Ray down at the station," Ryan began.

Tracey sneered. "That snake, what did *he* have to say?"

Christopher took her hand, in a gesture meant to calm.

"He said that Terrico was pretty stingy with his money," Ryan answered, trying to provoke a conversation.

"He should talk! All them came outta this neighborhood and what do they do? Play it big over in L.A. in their mansions and their Bentleys—forgetting their roots—forgetting where they came from!"

"Trace…" Christopher said.

"I'm sorry, but he never sent your mama a dime above what she had needed to survive. That's just not right. Not right for the millions—or billions—or whatever he made."

"It's been an issue in the family," Christopher explained. "I mean, we're okay. I have a good job, and Tracey works. We can take care of our family *and* my mama, but it's just the principle of it."

"And what about now? Where does Terrico's money go?" Ryan asked. "Who would be his beneficiary? Does he have any children?"

Tracey looked at Christopher, who shook his head. "No, no kids. I can't even think about the will, at this point. Everything's just happened, you know?"

"His money will probably go to one of his hoes," Tracey said, poking her finger in Chris's chest.

Christopher continued. "We haven't spoken with an estate attorney yet. I assume TJ had a will, but we're not expecting any grand gestures. Not from his history of giving. Or *not giving.*"

"Do you think his money went toward drugs?" asked Ryan.

"Why do you say that?" Tracey spewed. "Because we're *black*? We're all junkies?"

"No, no, Ms. Robinson. I'm sorry, you misunderstood," Ryan said. "I said it more because he's in the entertainment business. Not because of his race."

The woman smirked without comment.

"TJ had no interest in drugs," Chris answered. "Not that I know of. Reggie's the one that has a problem—my other brother. Been in and out of jail and rehab a couple times. I really don't think that was Terrence's thing, but honestly I wouldn't know. My brother turned into a different person after he became popular and his music blew up. I don't *think* he would get into that shit, but I have no idea what his life was like. Last time I saw him was a about a year or so ago when we visited L.A."

Ryan noted the details. "Did Terrence ever visit your mom when he was in town? Did he visit this time?"

Christopher humphed. "Nah. Like, he sent us all tickets to the show, but none of us really wanted to go. Why would we want to go to a Mandy Ross concert with screaming teenagers? It was a weird mix with the two of them. Good thing we didn't go, too, seein' what happened. I wouldn't have wanted to see him like that." Chris started to hold out his arms in an attempt to copy the crucifixion pose, but stopped when his wife flashed him a grimace.

"Your other brother you mentioned, Reggie, is he around?" Di Santo asked Christopher.

"Reg? He was here earlier. I think he went up to the city to try to get a hold of the old gang. They work with TJ now. He gave them all jobs in his '*entourage.*'" He accompanied the last word with air quotes.

"Anything else you can think of that could help?"

"Nope. That's all," said Christopher. "I told Mama to stop watching the news. She don't need to see that image of TJ on the cross like that."

"We hid the remote from her," added Tracey.

"That's a good plan," Ryan said and handed the man his card. "If you think of anything else that may help us, no matter how small, please call or e-mail me."

The detectives thanked the couple and left down the front steps. Ryan approached the patrol car, still idling a few hundred feet away. He was embarrassed in retrospect for ordering the unit since the family was extremely cooperative and the neighborhood relatively calm. Eyeing the fans' display of mourning, he mentioned it might be a good idea to keep patrol on the house until this whole thing died down—at least a week. The patrols agreed to run it by their sarge.

"So, any thoughts on the scene?" Di Santo asked as he started up the Impala.

"I want to get TJ's cell records, to see who called him down to the lobby of the hotel. We should also go see if the Westley's security team has video on the lobby for Friday night."

It was 4:43 pm when they returned to the station, and although they weren't officially working a shift, Ryan promised himself he would leave at five. Thirty-three hours with no sleep took a toll on his thirty-eight year old body.

He ordered the phone records from Research and contemplated the Robinson family and their resentment toward Terrico James. Was it enough for murder? He had to find out about beneficiaries. He called back Research and added that they needed to find out about the will and insurance policies. He made it clear this it was P-1: top priority.

"I want to talk to the second brother," Ryan muttered aloud as he stuffed his laptop into the case.

"I'll track him down, D, and we can interview him in the morning. Take the night off. See your woman."

Ryan turned his attention out the window to the blue water of Lake Michigan. The summer sun wouldn't set for another couple of hours and he wondered if he could make it to Cat's in time to have dinner with her in the back gardens.

# CHAPTER 10

On the way to Evanston, Ryan stopped at a little Italian market and picked up a nice bottle of red table wine and a loaf of fresh bread to have with dinner. When he let himself into Cat's estate, he smelled dinner grilling from the back patio. He was exhausted, but not too exhausted to pass up a Lulling meal.

A cousin of Catharine's had visited the prior week, bringing along a box of homegrown corn from their farm in Iowa. Although July was the best month for the crop, the early fresh ears were still mouthwatering. Especially when grilled with pinwheel steaks, rolled with spinach and garlic.

Ryan and Catharine ate on the back patio, with the soft sounds of the double waterfall in the background. The combination of aromas of the cooked meat and the green of the gardens were enough to bring about those sweet summer endorphins.

"I better start working out again," Ryan said, leaning back on his chair and patting his stomach. "I'm spoiled with all these home-cooked meals."

"You look fine to me, Detective. I'll let you know if you get a little paunchy." Cat took a moment to stare off into her gardens. "Were you able to interview Hank and Mandy today?"

"Yeah, he brought her into the station, as promised. And

thanks for taking her on short notice. I think she needed a home. And some adult supervision."

"You're welcome, but the supervision was very short-lived. I don't think she's used to being supervised."

"Nope. Mandy Ross is a spoiled brat. Used to getting whatever she wants, and has come to expect it."

"Including my son?" Cat asked, raising an eyebrow.

"He'll figure it out, Cat," he assured her. "There comes a time when the mama bear has to let go of the cubs."

She dropped her head and looked up at him with those eyes. Today they were deep blue, reflecting the perfectly clear summer sky.

"He wants to go back to L.A. with her," she said.

Ryan frowned. "What? Are you serious?"

"Completely. The boys already had a trip planned to Los Angeles to go see their father. Hank asked to move it up so he can go back with *her*."

"When?"

"Tuesday."

Ryan sat up straighter in his chair. "*This coming* Tuesday?" Catharine nodded. "Well, I don't like the fact that she's taking off so soon." He tried to come up with a legal reason to keep Hank and Mandy in Chicago, but couldn't think of one off the top of his head. "How long does he plan on staying in L.A.?"

"Only a week."

"Is Duke going too?"

"No, he wants to stay and work at Payton. Make some money. Hank already quit. I don't know if it was the murder or if he just wants to stay with that girl. It bothers me. I don't like her," Catharine said, and took a hard bite of a carrot.

Ryan chuckled. "I agree, there's not much to like about her. I do think Hank's heading for a fall, but he has to figure that out himself. You have to let him go."

After dinner, Catharine took Ryan's hand and pulled him into to her library to rest and let the meal settle. He lay down on the sofa while she kicked off her shoes and nestled in beside him. Pyxis, Catharine's midnight-grey cat, jumped up and started preparing a resting spot on his stomach. He'd gotten used to the cats making themselves at home on him. In a way, it was kind of endearing. Made him feel part of the family.

Catharine seemed distracted as he brushed several strands of wavy hair from her face.

"You still worried about Hank?" he asked.

"You never like to see your children hurt, and it's worse when you're powerless over the situation."

"I'll have a talk with him if you think that'll help."

She smiled up at him. "You're a good role model. I'm glad you're around."

"I'm glad I'm around, too."

She suddenly sat up, causing Pyxis to jump wildly from his lap. "Oh, I have to show you what I found when I was going through my old files!"

She padded over to her desk, barefoot, shuffled through some papers and came back with a magazine in her hand. She handed it to Ryan and knelt down next to the couch.

Three people graced the cover of this particular issue of *Fast Company* magazine, all staring straight at the camera: a couple, who he recognized as Catharine's former employers, Scott and Carly Redding, since deceased. It was their double homicide that had brought him and Catharine together.

Behind them stood a severe-looking woman with her arms folded, her ebony hair pulled back in a tight bun. She wore a black business suit over a starched white shirt and a pearl choker around her neck.

It wasn't until he got to the woman's ice-blue eyes that he thought he recognized her. "That's not—"

Catharine crossed her arms and tried to mimic the severe expression in the photo, but her twinkling eyes, loose hair, and free spirit all thwarted the imitation.

"No way!" Ryan said, looking at her and then back at the

cover. "I would *never* have recognized you. If I walked into a magazine stand and saw this on the rack? Never!"

Catharine giggled. "It was ten years ago. Seems like a lifetime."

"Scott and Carly look so young," Ryan said about the couple as if he had befriended them in life rather than how he had actually met them, as lifeless bodies at the scenes of their own deaths.

"And I look so old!"

"Older than you do now. God, Cat." He shook his head in disbelief. "Can I have this?"

"No! I don't want anyone seeing it. You are not taking it to the station, no!"

"But Matt would get a kick out of it—"

"No!"

"Okay, okay." He looked back down at the magazine and his mind returned to the double murder case that had brought them together just over a half a year ago. His thoughts turned to Todd Elliot, Catharine's former co-worker, who had attacked her viciously during that same time.

"How do you feel about your testimony tomorrow? Do you want me to be here?"

"You know, I actually ran my own life before you came along, Detective," Catharine said. "I am a fully functioning adult!"

He raised his eyebrows, challenging her statement.

"Well, okay, *semi*-functioning. But I'm working on that. I'll be fine."

"You *are* fine, Ms. Lulling," he said.

His mood lifted as he looked her over, with Catharine-the-executive playing out a lovely scene in his imagination. He placed the magazine on the floor as he leaned over to kiss her.

"Speaking of which…" Catharine said, pulling out of their kiss. "You know I've been working with Sandy, my therapist, on my problem. And she says I should start going on outings. A little farther than around the block."

"Really? That's great!"

"Yes. She says I should go with someone I trust, someone who makes me feel safe," she said, putting her hand on his.

"You know I'll go anywhere with you," he said. "Where do you want to go?" He picked up her hand and kissed it.

She smiled. "Sandy says I should start small and go somewhere that doesn't have a lot of people around because that's really what bothers me…when there are a lot of people around." He nodded, letting her talk it out without interruption. "It's like…well as you know, I'm really sensitive to people's energy, and that's good for what I do: working with pain and clearing negative energy. But it's *not* good for me when I go out. Especially in crowds. I get bombarded with their energy. Lots of energy. And I get incredibly overwhelmed. But Sandy and I are working on turning it off. The sensitivity. Turning it off like turning off a radio. No incoming signals."

"So we should have our date in a place that doesn't have a lot of people?" He ruminated on that and sorted through all the places he eventually wanted to take Catharine. When she was well again.

"Right. And not too far away. Yet."

"No police stations," he teased.

She smirked. About a month ago, Catharine had been required to come into the 18th to give a statement to an FBI agent. It hadn't gone well.

"Hey, I think I know of a good outing. I pass it every time I come here and I think of you." That got her attention. "The Rose Garden? It's over on Lake Street. I looked it up one time and it said it has over two hundred types of roses and they all seem to be in bloom now. Is that somewhere you would maybe like to go?"

"I remember the Rose Garden! My dad used to take me there when I was little. I loved it. Probably what started my passion for flowers, now that I think back. Are there a lot of people there, though? During the day?"

"We can go early. How about in a couple of days. Early one morning, when this Terrico thing dies down a little."

"I'd love that, Ryan."

"I'm excited!" he said, patting the sofa for her to get back on. "It's a date."

"Our first date!"

As she snuggled in, he marveled at the fact that in the seven months they had been dating, he and Catharine had never gone out on a real date.

"So…I have a question," he said.

"Hmmm?"

"Do you still have that business suit?"

Catharine giggled as he moved in on top of her.

# CHAPTER 11

Thirty-five hours and nine minutes of no sleep caused Ryan to hit Catharine's bed early Sunday evening. He was dead to the world until she nudged him awake Monday morning at eight.

"You sure you don't want me with you at the taping?" he asked while they were still in bed.

"I'll be fine, Detective. Jane had me practice. It would make me more nervous with you in the room. Too many people."

He kissed her nose, wished her good luck, and got out of bed.

Showered and shaved, he grabbed a breakfast burrito and got into the station by 9:03, only to find Detective Wyatt Fisk wedged into his own desk chair, gabbing with Di Santo.

"Fisk," he greeted the man. "You on duty today?"

"Doherty! Just the man I wanted to see. I'm checking in on the Terrico James case, wanted to know what you have so far, and offer my fine services."

Ryan stood over the man and motioned him out of his chair. After heaving and puffing, Fisk pulled himself out of the desk chair and Ryan sat, shuffling some papers to find the James file. Turned out Di Santo had it and handed it over the desk pod to him.

He opened the brown folder and reported, in a monotone, what they had so far. "We found an equipment box at Payton Arena, in a back closet. Had definite odor of decomp. Tech team confirmed hairs and fibers inside were from Terrico James. Probably how the murderer transported his body into the arena to get him on the cross.

"We conducted an interview with Mandy Ross and Hank Lulling. They had no knowledge of James's body entering Payton Arena. She hadn't seen or socialized with James since they hit town. At the approximate TOD, she was at a club called Cuvée. Alibi checked out.

"Di Santo interviewed the anti-Terrico groups, the most vocal one being One Divine Life, led by a Warren L. Smith. We spoke with them again yesterday and they seemed to be a peaceful bunch. No knowledge—didn't take credit for—the murder or the 'crucifixion.' Need to check out alibi that they were at the hotel restaurant.

"Clancy Ray, Terrico's manager, came into the station yesterday but didn't have much to add. He said to talk to the family, since there was some infighting over money. We then visited Mae Robinson, Terrico James's mother. Also in attendance was Chris Robinson, brother, and Tracey Robinson, sister-in-law to the deceased. Family indicated no drug use. Contention over money was that James didn't share his. They seem to be doing okay, though. Brother is employed and supporting the family. There is a second brother, Reginald Robinson, who was not available for interview. Alleged drug user.

"So now we're heading to the Westley Hotel to check stories and see if they have any video footage of Terrico leaving the hotel Friday night, when he disappeared," Ryan concluded. "He was killed sometime between eight and midnight."

Fisk shook his head. "A lot of work for a piece of crap rapper, I'll tell you that much."

Ryan scowled at Fisk's casual dismissal of the victim's life. Terrico James might have been a tad delusional and narcissistic, but he wasn't a criminal and certainly hadn't done anything worthy of being strung up like a piece of meat in a butcher shop.

"I'd place my bet on one of his entourage guys. I didn't like them a-tall, a-tall," Fisk continued. "As for the religious groups, well, they're okay. I spoke with that Smith fellow several times and he seems like an upstanding citizen. I can run his sheet, if you want."

"We already had research do it. Some minor harassment charges, consistent with organizations like his. But if you want to dig deeper, that would be okay. See what his reputation is in Atlanta, since that's your old stomping ground."

Fisk flashed them a big grin, his teeth shiny with spittle. "I'm on it, Detective. Anything else you need from me?"

Ryan squinted at Fisk. The man never volunteered for anything. "Naw, not right now, thanks. We'll keep you posted and you do the same."

"Ten-four." Fisk waved a goodbye and waddled out of the squad room and down the stairs. His office was located on the first floor, next to the intake desk. Probably because he didn't want the extra effort of climbing to the second floor, where most detectives were homed.

Ryan closed the James file and headed back out with Di Santo to the Westley Hotel. The hotel kept all video for one week, so they were in luck. The time-consuming part would be wading through the footage. The manager of security agreed to copy all video from Friday through Saturday to DVDs for them while they talked to some of the hotel employees. They started at the front desk, where they learned that two of the reservation agents had actually worked Friday night, their shift ending at 1:00 a.m.

One was a young-looking blonde, who wore the company uniform well: a light blue blouse under a navy blue blazer and skirt, with the gold W logo on the left shoulder of the jacket. Her ponytail was tied back with a pink scrunchie.

"Terrico James! Yes. Usually celebrities will check in with pseudonyms. Like Mandy Ross? She checked in under

Fifi Scarbinksi. Can you believe that? Fifi Scarbinksi! But Terrico James was Terrico James, so everyone knew he was here."

"Did you see his group come in on Friday night?" Ryan asked her. They had a procedure: Di Santo always let Ryan lead with the women.

"Yes, I remember because they were loud. And then some people from the lobby asked to take pictures with him. He was nice that way. He stopped and took pictures with his fans."

"And around 11:30, 11:45—did you see Terrico come back down to the lobby?"

The girl thought for a minute. "No, I don't think I saw him after that. After they came in."

"I saw him," said the second employee, a thirty-something white man who was prematurely graying at the temples. "He came down and started fighting with another guy, right over there by the door."

"What did the other guy look like?"

"He was black. A little shorter than Terrico. Was kind of jittery, like his arms were waving all around and stuff."

"Could you hear what they were saying?"

"No, but at one point the guy shoved Terrico and I thought 'Oh no, maybe it's a crazy fan' so I went over and asked Mr. James if he needed any help. If he wanted me to call security. He was like 'No, thanks, we're just having a conversation here.' He was really nice about it, but I could tell he really wanted me to skedaddle."

"Did Terrico James leave with this man?"

"I think so, yes. I got preoccupied with a guest who had late check-in and a lot of luggage, so I really didn't pay attention after that."

"So you had a close up view of the guy he was with?" Di Santo asked.

"Yeah, like I said, he was shorter than me, shorter than Terrico, about five-foot-seven or eight. Kind of skinny."

"Any distinguishing marks? Tattoos? Remember what he was wearing? His hair short or long?"

"His hair was short, I remember that. I don't know about what he was wearing...a dark tee shirt, I think? And jeans? I wouldn't have seen any tattoos."

"Thanks, that helps."

The man was genuinely pleased with the praise. The detectives took the full names of the front-deskers and went back to the security office of the hotel. Ryan asked specifically to see the video of the lobby from Friday night from 10:45 p.m. to midnight. After a couple of minutes, he saw Terrico James on the screen. James entered the lobby and approached another guy, but unfortunately the other guy's back was to the camera. The unidentified subject wore a dark gray tee shirt with angel wings on the back. After several minutes, they saw the scene that the front-desker recalled: the shorter guy shoved Terrico and the desk agent intervened. Terrico quickly waved the agent away, just as the man had stated. He took out his wallet, counted out ten bills, and handed them over to the unidentified man.

After about three more minutes of what looked like a heated discussion, the man turned around and the two men walked out of the front door of the Westley Hotel, Terrico following the suspect. They had the security manager freeze the video just after the man turned around. Although the video was black and white and fairly low-res, they could spot one more identifying characteristic on the man in question: he had a goatee.

They took copies of the videos and thanked the security team. As they headed toward the front door, Mandy and Hank walked right by them.

"Hey!" Ryan called out to them.

Hank turned around first. He slid his Ray Bans down his nose, already playing Mr. Hollywood. "Oh, hi, Ryan. I didn't see you guys. What are you doing here?"

"Investigating," Di Santo answered, shaking the boy's hand.

Mandy hung back, hands on hips, appearing annoyed at the interruption.

"What are you guys up to?" Ryan asked him, nodding toward Mandy.

"We were just shopping. Well, Mandy was shopping. I was tagging along."

"New sunglasses?" Ryan asked, almost teasing.

"Yeah, how'd you know?"

"'Cause you're wearing them indoors."

Both detectives chuckled at the jibe.

Mandy let out an over-exaggerated sigh from the elevator bay. "Hello! I'm going up to the room," she called, obviously perturbed.

Hank slid the sunglasses back up on his face. "Yeah, well, gotta go, guys. See you later." He held up a palm as a goodbye and rejoined the pop star.

"Hey, Mand-eee!" Di Santo called out to her. She jumped back, mortified, and pressed the elevator button repeatedly, as if a thousand screaming fans were going mob her. There were no fans, and no one had noticed.

"She's a piece of work," Ryan said, when the two disappeared into an elevator car.

"You know, the girl started her career at the age of five," Di Santo said. "And she was touring by sixteen. Has got to take a toll on a kid."

Ryan thought about that kind of life for a child. To him, it was no different than putting your kid to work in construction. It was labor. It was a job. A kid should be allowed to have a childhood before being put to work, and it should be their decision to do so. "I just don't get it. What kind of parent allows that?"

"One who wants her to keep bringing home the bacon! You know, you're sounding more and more like a father." he said, and slapped Ryan on the back.

Ryan ignored the comment, his attention being pulled back to the mystery man last seen with James. He called for a department sketch artist to meet them at the hotel and work on the description of the man with the staff. By the afternoon, they had an image in hand of a thin black man, angular face, with one eye a tad droopier than the left. Di Santo took a picture of the sketch with his phone and emailed it to Amy-Jo Slater to disburse to the media.

"Tell her to tag him as an 'Unknown suspect last seen with Terrico James before he was killed,'" Ryan instructed. "Get the pictures on the ten o'clock news. Tonight. See if we can smoke this guy out."

He scanned the ceiling to spot the cameras that had provided the footage they had just reviewed. It was amazing to him that no one bothered to look up. *Not one person bothers to look for cameras unless they are thinking of committing a crime or investigating one*, he thought. *Everyone is on camera 24/7 and either they don't realize it or don't care anymore. And when they're not under public surveillance, they pull out their phones and document themselves.* Following that train of thought, he called Research. He instructed them to find out the service provider of Terrico's cell phone. They called back with the information in four minutes.

"What're you thinking, D?" Di Santo asked after he terminated the call.

"I'm thinking that we never found Terrico's cell phone on or near the body, did we? So someone else might have it. If GPS is enabled, we may be able to see where he was murdered—before he got to the arena. If we're lucky, though, the murderer may still have the phone."

"Kind of a stretch, but it couldn't hurt," Di Santo said.

Ryan called AT&T and explained the situation. "Is it possible to locate the phone now? And how long would it take for a list of calls going back one month?"

"I would be happy to help you with your questions," the customer service rep answered in a scripted monotone.

Ryan couldn't place the accent, but had a feeling the call center was located somewhere on the other side of the world. He waited while keys clicked away on the other line, probably searching some knowledge base for what to do with a phone record request. He wondered if he should have had Research handle this task. He had to ask twice for a supervisor, and then to be transferred to a manager in the U.S. Still, he couldn't get very far.

"We can provide you with phone records if you fax us a copy of your warrant, along with your supervisor's requisition and—"

"*Fax*? Who faxes anymore? You know what, just tell me if it's possible to find the phone now."

He clearly should have let Research make the connection with the telecommunications conglomerate. They could always get him the records.

"I'm sure that it's a possibility to find the phone now, if the battery has any power left. However, again, we would need a requisition from your supervisor, along with a local warrant and—"

Ryan cut the guy off by hanging up. He called Research and within twenty-two minutes they called back to tell him that AT&T would be emailing the phone records and would begin a triangulation of the cell phone.

"I owe you a beer," he said to the research coordinator.

"You keep saying that, Doherty, but we never find a six-pack on our doorstep!"

# CHAPTER 12

Jane arrived at Catharine's door a half an hour before the video testimony was to begin. They were still expecting Todd Elliot's defense attorney, a paralegal, and a court reporter.

Sara had set out some croissants, orange juice, and a pot of coffee in preparation for the guests.

"As I said, my library is the best room to do the testimony," Catharine explained to Jane. "It's quiet and should look good on camera. With the books behind me, I will look sophisticated, intelligent!"

She smiled at the attorney, but received no response. Catharine swallowed her pride and led Jane to the east wing of the house, into her study.

"This is good," Jane said, setting her laptop bag on the sofa. Two club chairs faced each other on either end of the sofa, accommodating the group of five that they were expecting. Jane addressed her again, "I hope you practiced in the last two days. How are you feeling?"

"A little shaky, but so grateful you arranged to do this here, in my home. That helps tremendously."

Jane nodded and removed some papers from her bag. "Any questions or concerns before the others arrive?"

"No, no. Just tell the truth, right?" She let out an involuntary giggle, her nerves getting the best of her.

The attorney wasn't amused as she took out a file folder, a yellow legal pad and her laptop computer. "Where can I plug in?" she said, surveying the room.

Catharine helped Jane set up and wrote her Wi-Fi password on the legal pad.

Several minutes later, the doorbell rang. Catharine and Jane greeted Judge Arnold Geithner at the front vestibule of the estate. He was an older man, late sixties, with a briefcase in one hand and his black judge's robe draped over the opposite arm.

"I'm so grateful you have agreed to come here for my testimony," Catharine said to the judge, but his attention was drawn to the atrium, behind her. She was accustomed to this particular reaction from visitors who entered her home for the first time.

"That's—that's just incredible!" the judge said, as Cat took his robe. "I've never seen anything like it."

Catharine smiled. "I'm happy to give you a short tour before we begin our meeting." She handed Jane the robe at the same time the judge handed Jane his briefcase.

The assistant state's attorney raised an eyebrow at Catherine, who silently mouthed "please" to her. Jane exhaled and carried the items to the library while Catharine escorted the judge through her lush atrium and around its perimeter.

After they returned to the library, the rest of the group had arrived. Jane introduced Catharine to the defense attorney, Victor Brant, a severe man with an angular face, wearing a very expensive suit. Catharine smiled and made eye contact as they shook hands, but the man didn't soften. All business.

As they settled in and set up, Catharine sobered quickly as she watched the judge don his robe, as if the deposition were to determine her fate instead of the fate of the man who had attacked her.

Sara entered, making sure everyone was comfortable, pointing out the coffee and croissants. The paralegal grabbed her share while the attorneys declined. The court reporter held up a water bottle she brought with her to indicate she was fine.

Catharine settled into her wingback chair and brushed back a rogue curl from of her face. The paralegal had set up the video camera in front of library's tall windows, allowing the summer day's sun to illuminate the scene. Catharine sat opposite the camera, with the two attorneys perpendicular to her on the sofa, side by side. Jane sat closest.

The paralegal adjusted some settings on the camera and framed her subject on the screen. "You're so pretty," she said to Catharine. "I would die for those eyes!"

Catharine flushed a bit, embarrassed at the compliment. Jane coughed.

"Okay, we're recording," the paralegal announced.

Jane put both feet on the floor, cleared her throat, and set her computer on her lap. Catharine waited for her to begin, softly cleared her throat, and snuck a peek at the camera lens. A big black eye glared back at her with unspoken hostility.

The judge spoke first: "This is an official video testimony for case number Q-2343-2014, *the State of Illinois versus Todd Elliot*. Present in the room is Jane Steffen, Assistant State's Attorney for the County of Cook; Victor Brant, attorney for the defense; Ashley Singleton, paralegal; Vaneta Wise, court reporter; and myself, Judge Arnold E. Geithner; with the witness for the prosecution, Catharine M. Lulling. Ms. Lulling, do you understand that you are testifying under oath and that giving your testimony here, on camera, is no different than appearing in front of a jury in a court of law?"

"Yes, I do," Catharine stated.

"Do you swear to tell the truth, the whole truth, and nothing but the truth, so help you God?"

Catharine nodded to the judge. "I do."

"Please state your full name for the record."

"Catharine Mireille Lulling," She wasn't sure whether she should look at the judge, Jane, or the camera. Feeling awkward at the camera's presence, she decided on Jane.

"Ms. Steffen, your witness."

Jane took a deep breath and turned to face Catharine. "Ms. Lulling, could you begin by walking us through what happened the morning of November ninth?"

"Sure," Catharine replied, nodding. "I was in my back gardens, looking for my dogs. It seemed like they had gone missing—they didn't come when I called them. I stepped out into my back garden and Todd—Mr. Elliot—attacked me from behind. I didn't know it at the time, but he had used a Taser gun on my dogs. They were stunned, but not hurt. Todd grabbed me by my hair and dragged me into my home *by force*. He threw me to the ground and held me there, against my will."

She paused, and Jane nodded her approval. Catharine was pleased that she had remembered how to describe the attack.

"Where, exactly, in your home did Mr. Elliot drag you by force?"

"Into the atrium—that is the indoor garden in the center of my house."

"Were you injured in this attack?"

"Yes. Todd—Mr. Elliot—pushed my head into a rock several times when he was on top of me. And he kept pulling my hair. Hard."

"You say he was on top of you. What happened, exactly? Please take us through it sequentially."

"Yes, okay." Catharine glanced in the direction of the camera and cleared her throat. She took a minute to take a drink from a glass of water she had set beside her.

"He—Todd Elliot—dragged me into the house, threw me to the ground, and was yelling at me. He said that I killed Scott and Carly Redding, our bosses who had just been murdered. Well, they were my ex-bosses at the time. I hadn't worked for them for almost five years. That's how I knew Todd."

Jane pursed her lips and Catharine got the hint that she wanted her to go back to the attack.

"So then Todd slammed my head down against the rock again. He was planning on—" She stopped.

"Was planning on what?"

"He was going to rape me," she said softly, holding Jane's gaze.

Victor Brant spoke up. "Objection, speculation on intent."

"Sustained," said the judge.

"Rephrasing," Jane said, nodding to the judge. "Ms. Lulling, what gave you the *impression* that Mr. Elliot was going to rape you?"

Catharine swallowed and willed her memory to go back to that morning. "It was his attitude, his tone. It changed. Todd had a lascivious gleam in his eyes. I can't explain it, but he started to talk about my body, about how I looked." Catharine's memory flashed back to Todd holding her down, his drool landing on her face. She blinked several times. "That, and the fact that he was sitting on me, pinning me down on the ground."

"What exactly did Mr. Elliot say to you? About your body?" Jane prompted.

"He said I looked different, that I was 'hot'—yes, that's what he said, that I was 'hot,' and he started to pull up my skirt." Catharine looked at the rug, playing the scene out in her head as if she were an observer. "He also threatened me. Todd said I was going to get what was coming to me, things like that."

"Then what happened?" Jane's voice was softer now, more sympathetic. Woman-to-woman, that was how she was playing it.

Catharine looked back up at her. "Then my dogs broke through the back door and they attacked him."

"What exactly did your dogs do?"

"They bit Todd. They were fighting with him. I saw that his Taser gun had fallen out of his jacket, so I took it and shocked him." Catharine made a jabbing gesture with her fist, recreating the motion.

"And then what happened?"

"I ran outside the front door and the police were already there. And Ryan was there."

"Can you explain exactly who was outside your house, Ms. Lulling?"

"Yes, Detective Ryan Doherty of the Chicago Police. He was investigating Scott and Carly's murder at the time. We met and he...we...became friends. The Evanston police came soon after."

"And then?"

"Then they arrested Todd and that was all."

Jane made some notes on a legal pad, leaned back on the couch and said, "No further questions. Thank you, Ms. Lulling."

Catharine exhaled. Half done. But that was the easy part. She feared the defense attorney wouldn't be so accommodating.

"Let's take a short break before we continue with the cross-examination," Judge Geithner announced.

The court reporter stopped typing and the paralegal paused the video camera. Jane checked her phone. Catharine stood up and walked behind the couch, hoping to catch some kind of impression from her. Usually she could get a reading on the people in the room, even without touching them, but there was a barrier with the attorney, an obstacle she couldn't break through, mentally.

Catharine shifted her attention to Elliot's attorney, Victor Brant, who had made his way to the other side of the library, reviewing his notes before his turn at the questioning. Catharine didn't like the fact that he had quickly separated himself from the group. She took several deep breaths, finished off her glass of water, and returned to her seat in the wingback chair.

Victor Brant switched places with Jane on the sofa, taking the seat closest to Catharine. He signaled the paralegal behind the camera, who turned it back on and flashed a thumbs-up to the room.

"Victor Brant representing Todd Elliot," he began.

Catharine didn't need her sixth sense to know this wasn't going to be a friendly interview.

"Thank you for testifying today, Ms. Lulling, I know this is probably difficult for you."

Catharine nodded.

"Audible answers only," said the court reporter. The first words she had spoken since they started.

"Oh, sorry. You're welcome, Mr. Brant." Catharine folded her hands in her lap waiting for the next question.

"Ms. Lulling, you stated that prior to the attack, you and Mr. Elliot had worked together."

"That is correct. We worked together at Town Red Media."

"Can you explain exactly how you met and what each of your positions were with the company?"

"Sure. I was the Vice President of Operations, and Todd was hired as Vice President of Business Development. That was sales."

"So, you were at the company prior to his arrival?"

"Yes, I was there for a total of five years. He was hired about a year before I left."

"A year before you left. Did you blame Mr. Elliot for being fired?"

"I wasn't fired. I left on my own accord."

"Okay, but why, just after his arrival, did you decide to leave the company?"

"It wasn't *right* after his arrival. It was about a year later, like I said. I wanted more time with my children. I have two boys. In my position at Town Red they expected me to work long hours, nights, and weekends. I didn't want to do that anymore."

"I have here an interview you gave to Chicago Police detectives last year. In it, you said that Todd was, quote—instrumental in pushing you out—unquote. What does that mean?"

Catharine recalled that interview. It was the day she and

Ryan had first met. She hadn't realized that their conversation had been documented and was available to Elliot's attorney. However, it did make sense, thinking back, since it was a murder investigation.

She took a deep breath and organized her thoughts about her time at Town Red.

"Todd was ambitious. He wanted to be the second-in-command, and he quickly edged himself into that position. He was competitive from the beginning."

"Competitive with *you?*" asked the defense attorney.

"Yes, but I was planning to leave the firm on my own."

"I see. So you regarded Mr. Elliot as a competitor? An adversary?"

"No, not really," she answered. "Well, I think that's how *he* considered *me.*" She wondered where he was going with this line of questioning.

Brant leaned forward as if coming in for the kill. "Ms. Lulling, did you and Todd Elliot have an intimate relationship?"

Catharine's breath hitched in panic, not knowing how to answer. Not knowing how Jane would want her to answer. Jane looked up from her notes, awaiting Catharine's response.

"Ms. Lulling, did you hear the question?" Brant asked.

"Yes," Catharine said softly. Her heart ached.

"Yes you heard the question, or yes you had an intimate relationship?"

"It was one night," she mumbled.

"I didn't hear you," said the court reporter.

"One night," Catharine repeated. "*Only* one night. It didn't mean anything. I mean, we weren't a couple. We had a bottle of wine, and things just—happened. He asked to take me home. I said no. I got a cab. It was just that one night and I immediately regretted it—*Jane?*" Catharine pleaded with the ASA but Jane broke eye contact, shaking her head.

Brant's smug expression revealed his joy in throwing

her. "So that is a 'yes,' you had sexual relations with the defendant?"

Catharine closed her eyes for a beat then opened them again. She managed to say it again. "Yes."

Brant leaned back a little in his seat. "So you and the defendant had an intimate relationship. How could that happen, since you two were so-called 'adversaries'?"

Catharine rolled her lips into her mouth. She swallowed again, before she answered, her voice now slow and methodical.

"We were working late. We were alone. We drank. It was a mistake. Like I said, it only happened once. Never again."

"So considering this new evidence: that you had sexual relations with the defendant—" She cringed slightly when he said *sexual relations*. "—how do we know that he was *really* about to rape you? Maybe he was just picking up where you two left off!"

"Objection, badgering," Jane said, without looking up from her screen.

"Withdrawn," Brant interjected before the judge could rule.

Catharine couldn't believe the attorneys were being so cavalier about this. It was her life, her privacy—now on public record.

She thought of Ryan. Her boys. They'd know.

"Ms. Lulling," Brant continued, with false sympathy in his voice. "I'm sorry, but we have to ask. Did you want Todd to come into your home?"

"No."

"Did you *invite* him into your home? Maybe you wanted to continue the intimate relationship that you had started several years earlier?"

"No!"

"And maybe when your boyfriend showed up you *panicked*?"

"*No*! That's not how it was! Ryan wasn't—"

"You had to give him a story. A story why you and Todd were going at it in the atrium."

Catharine was so filled with rage, she started shaking. "He *attacked* me! In my home! How can you say that?"

"What is your relationship with Detective Ryan Doherty?" Brant was so smooth, it scared her.

"Excuse me?"

"You heard me. Are you intimately involved with Detective Ryan Doherty of the Chicago Police Department?"

"Objection," Jane interrupted. "Relevance."

Brant turned to the judge. "This goes to show that she may have altered her story for the detective's benefit," he explained.

"I'll allow it," the judge ruled.

Jane nodded at Catharine to answer the question.

"Detective Doherty and I are seeing each other. *Now*."

Brant smirked like a cheetah with its prey. "You are seeing each other *romantically*?"

"Yes."

"Ms. Lulling, did Todd Elliot attack you or is that the story you told the detective because you didn't want to tell him the truth? That you and Todd were having an affair?"

"We weren't 'having an affair.' He *attacked* me. That was the truth. That *is* the truth."

"Okay, so you say." The attorney took a moment to review his notes. "Ms. Lulling, what was the exact extent of your injuries? When your head hit that rock, did you bleed?"

"No, I just had a bump."

"You said that Mr. Elliot pulled your hair. You have beautiful hair, by the way." She didn't respond to the flattery. "Did he pull any of it out?"

Catharine thought for a moment. "No, not that I remember."

"No, what?"

"No, he didn't pull out any of my hair."

"And what were the extent of Todd's injuries? Do you remember?"

"My dogs bit him on the neck and on the shoulder. He got stitches, I believe."

"Do you recall that Todd got a total of one hundred and twenty stitches from the dogs tearing at his flesh?"

Jane shook her head, but didn't object.

Catharine responded, "I didn't know that, but okay."

"So *you* had a bump on the head, and *Mr. Elliot* was shocked with a deadly weapon *and* had his neck torn apart by vicious dogs. Who, exactly, is the victim here, Ms. Lulling?"

"Objection," interrupted Jane.

Brant held his hand up. "Withdrawn. No more questions. Thank you, Ms. Lulling."

The judge addressed Jane. "Ms. Steffen, any redirect?"

Catharine exhaled with gratitude. She would take the opportunity on Jane's redirect to explain—

"No redirect, your honor," Jane said.

"This concludes the testimony of Catharine M. Lulling in the case of *the State of Illinois versus Todd Elliot*, case number Q-2343-2014." The judge closed his folder and the paralegal turned off the camera. The court reporter pulled a USB drive out of her machine and handed it to the judge.

Catharine felt like she had just been bludgeoned. "But wait. This is where we leave it? Can't I even defend myself?" she asked the group.

"You're not on trial here," the judge stated. "That's all the testimony we need."

"Jane?" Catharine said, glaring at the prosecutor.

"*Catharine,*" the attorney responded, obviously peeved.

Without so much as a glance, Jane stuffed a legal pad into her laptop case and shut down her laptop. This time, the attorney's thoughts were broadcasting loud and clear, or else Catharine was projecting: Jane had been blindsided by the fact that Catharine didn't tell her about the night with Todd

Elliot. Still, the attorney's sudden chill seemed a bit out of line.

Catharine lifted her cell phone and dialed Sara. "Please come see our guests out," she instructed her assistant, then left the library without saying goodbye.

# CHAPTER 13

Back at the 18th, the detectives took turns answering the continuous stream of phone calls about the face in the police sketch. As it turned out, Amy-Jo had successfully convinced three out of the four local news stations to run a "Special Report" showing the police sketch, along with a plea for any information about the mystery man. They were running anything and everything to do with the Terrico James murder. The media hadn't been in this much of a frenzy since Michael Jackson.

Ryan picked up the line for the sixth time that afternoon, already exhausted by going through the same routine with every person who thought they knew a neighbor or friend-of-a-friend who perfectly matched the police artist sketch. This call was different, however.

"Dee-tective! Why you put my boy's face on the news? Huh?"

"Excuse me? Who's calling, please?"

"This is Miz Mae. Mae Robinson. I seen my son's face on the news."

"Oh, Mrs. Robinson. Are you watching TV? I thought Christopher told you not to. Did you see the story on Ter-ric—Terrence, ma'am?"

"Not Terrence, you fool! It was Reggie I seen. On the television just now. They say that the *po*-lice is looking for my boy, Reggie. Now what you come bothering my family for again? What'd he do?"

"I'm sorry, I don't understand. Where did you see Reggie?"

He heard a scramble on the other end of the phone line. Then a man got on.

"Detective? Hi, I'm sorry about that. This is Chris. The sketch you put out on the news—that's my brother Reggie. You have to take it down. He's terrified. He won't even come out of his room. He thinks the police are going to come for a shootout. You're not sending SWAT for him or anything, are you?"

Ryan covered the mouthpiece and relayed the news to Di Santo. "The sketch is Terrico's brother, Reggie. The one we didn't meet. We have to head over there." Then back into the phone, "Chris. Man, I'm sorry. We'll be right over. Do you know if Reggie is armed?"

"Reggie? Naw, he doesn't have any weapons." There was a pause on the line. "At least I don't think so."

"We're on our way. Try to keep Reggie at the house, do you hear me? It's really important that he doesn't leave. No SWAT, no patrols, just us. Just keep him calm and occupied. It should take us twenty, twenty-five minutes at the most."

"Okay, sure, yeah. I'll try to keep him calm. But like I said, he's freaked out. He doesn't do well with stress."

"We'll be there very soon. Just hold on tight." Ryan hung up the phone and led Di Santo out of the squad, half-jogging to the car.

"You think Terrico's own brother whacked him?" Di Santo asked, pulling on his suit jacket while trying to catch up.

"Considering their family dynamics and that he seems to have been fighting with Terrico at the hotel, he's a solid suspect. Let's just hope he's still there when we arrive. Call Amy-Jo and tell her to pull the sketch from the news, if she can, but *don't* tell the media that we've identified the suspect. I'll drive this time."

When they had to get somewhere fast, Ryan insisted on driving. Di Santo would never break a speed limit, even with the cherry light on the hood. Ryan could push 30 over and still stay safe—at least that was what he kept telling himself. As they pulled out of the 18th parking lot, Di Santo dialed Amy-Jo and told her to pull the sketch. They argued a bit before Di Santo hung up in a huff.

"Nothing is ever easy with that woman! She pisses me off. For someone who is supposed to interface with the public, she sure is snippy."

Ryan chuckled. "I think you like her."

"Never."

"Never would you ask her out? Or never would she give you the time of day?"

"Ha. Ha. The latter. I mean the former. I'd never ask her out."

Ryan gave his partner a sideways glance, still grinning. It reminded him of elementary school when he kept pulling Kelly's red braids. He admitted in retrospect that he had liked her, even back in second grade when girls had cooties. Kelly was less cootified than the rest of the girls. She was tough and played as hard as the boys. He liked that, and they eventually got together in high school. After attending separate colleges, they lived together for a few years before she got tired of his indecision and indifference. She made the decision for him when she left his ass for a job on the East Coast.

Twenty minutes later Ryan and Di Santo arrived at the Robinson's house. A crowd had gathered outside, neighbors and looky-loos, who had probably seen Reggie's picture on the news.

The detectives pushed their way past the onlookers. This time the door was closed, and all the window shades were pulled.

"Excuse me, folks, Chicago PD," Ryan said, raising his shield over the crowd.

"Did Reggie do it, Officer? Did he kill TJ?" asked a man in a yellow-stained undershirt.

Ryan went up onto the first step, turned around, and addressed the crowd. "Nothing has been determined yet. We are just questioning Reggie Robinson. We have no evidence that he is involved in his brother's murder. Now please go home. There is nothing to see here."

A grumble emanated from the crowd as they started to disperse, including several kids who mounted their bicycles and rode away. One followed on a skateboard.

When he was satisfied they could now do their job in peace, Ryan turned to his partner. "Now, there's a chance Reggie is armed. But we go in slow and friendly, okay?"

Di Santo nodded quickly, his adrenaline level showing in the expanding pupils of his eyes. He unsnapped the strap on his .38.

Ryan stopped. "What did I just say?"

"What? You said he might be armed!"

"I also said let's go in friendly. You can keep the holster open, but the gun stays in it. For now."

"Okay, D."

"Don't make this a situation."

"*Okay*, D."

They climbed the front steps of the Robinson house and Ryan knocked. He heard the door open but, once again, could not see beyond the white security door.

"Oh hey, Officers," a disembodied voice greeted them. It was Christopher's. He unlatched the security door and let them in.

"Hi, Chris," Ryan said, shaking the man's hand. "Is Reggie still here?"

Chris nodded. "Yeah, he's still here. Up in his bedroom, hiding out." Christopher led them into the living room "Why don't you stay here and I'll see if he'll come down and talk to you. Nice and calm-like."

Di Santo looked up at Ryan for an answer.

Ryan didn't like the plan, but he also didn't want to ratchet up the tension. He agreed with a short nod.

Chris went up the main stairs and Ryan spotted Tracey in the kitchen, holding the toddler in one arm and cradling the telephone against her shoulder. It was one of the old-fashioned wall phones, olive green, with a curly cord connecting the unit with the handset. The older child sat at the kitchen table coloring. When Tracey turned around and saw them, she gave a short wave, and they both waved back.

Ryan scanned the living room, completely deserted compared to the previous day. The blue recliner that had been occupied by Mae Robinson sat empty, like a queen's throne that had been recently vacated.

"Mama's gone to church to visit with Minister Eli," Christopher said, coming back down the stairs. "Reggie's up there. I can hear him breathing. But he won't answer me and he won't open his door. Do you want to go up and try?"

Ryan calculated the risk, attempting to analyze the situation they were about to step into. "Chris, I don't want to alarm you. But just to be safe, you should get Tracey and the kids out of the house while we go up there. You said Reggie was using. Is he on anything now?"

Chris dropped his head. "Pot. A little meth. On and off."

"A little *meth*?" Di Santo asked.

"He on the way up or coming down?" Coming down from crystal meth could include a heightened sense of anxiety, paranoia, and even psychosis.

Chris rubbed a hand across his mouth. "I don't know, man. He just ran in the house like a crazy man and locked himself in the room. He might've had some in there. I don't know."

"Okay. Get your family out of here, but don't scare them. Take them for a walk or something." Ryan glanced up the staircase. "Which room is Reggie's?"

"First door on the right at the top of the landing."

While Chris got Tracey and the kids out of the house, Di Santo rocked back and forth on the balls of his feet.

"Think we should call for a backup unit?" he said.

Ryan shook off the idea. "It's one guy. I think we can do this. But *now* you can draw."

Di Santo pulled out his .38 while Ryan drew his Glock and they ascended the carpeted stairs as quietly as they could in an old house with creaky floors. When they got to the top, Ryan pointed to the first door on the right. It was well worn, and they noticed a silver padlock hung from a hook on the doorjamb, unlocked. Ryan glanced at his partner and frowned, wondering why it was on the outside. Did the family lock Reggie *in*? Maybe during detox.

They flanked the door, weapons drawn but at their sides.

Ryan knocked.

"Hey Reggie," he said in an upbeat tone. "I'm Ryan and I'm here with my pal Matt. We're from the Chicago Police—we just want to have a chat with you. We're not going to hurt you. Think you can come out and talk to us?"

"You ain't gonna shoot me!" Reggie shouted from the other side of the door.

"No, we're not going to shoot you."

Ryan heard something slide and then thump. Reggie had thrown his window open.

"He's running!"

Ryan turned the knob and the door opened. The smell of burning meth attacked his nose and he saw the remnants of the man's leg disappear out the window. Di Santo turned and ran back down the stairs while Ryan went to the open window. Somehow Reggie had made the two-story jump, probably with the help of an old striped patio awning. He saw the man limping across the back yard, and for a second almost jumped after him. But he couldn't risk a broken leg, so he left the way he came in and ran down the stairs, taking them two at a time.

He hoped that Di Santo could catch up with him and decided to run down the street to head Reggie off around the corner. He spotted the man cutting through a strip of grass in between two neighbors' homes with a pistol firmly gripped in his hand.

"He's armed!" Ryan called out, warning Di Santo.

His partner picked up his pace, trying to flank Reggie from the side, but the suspect jumped a chain link fence into another neighbor's yard.

The meth in Reggie's system was granting him extra speed. Di Santo came back around and ran behind Ryan on the sidewalk, parallel to Reggie's trajectory, as he kept weaving through hedges from yard to yard.

At the last house on the block, three kids were playing on a swing set.

"Reggie, stop! Now!" Ryan called, already out of breath.

Reggie spotted the children, stopped, changed direction and ran across the street. Ryan darted off after him, still about a quarter of a block behind, and Di Santo accelerated, passing him.

Sirens whooped in the distance, causing Reggie to stop short. He turned around to face the detectives and put the muzzle of the gun to his own chin.

"Whatcha think about this, huh? Is this what you want?" he shouted at them.

Ryan stopped short, panting to catch his breath, about twenty feet from the man. "Reggie, no. We don't want that. We just want to talk." Di Santo caught up a couple of seconds later.

"You gonna kill me anyway, aren't you?" Reggie shouted. "You think I killed my brother. My own brother! I'mma get the death penalty, man! I might as well just do it now."

Ryan caught his breath, holstered his gun, and lifted up his hands, as if he were the one surrendering. "Look, Reg, no gun. I'm not going to hurt you. But if you don't put down that gun, my partner over there may have to. Just put the gun down and we can talk. No death penalty. Just a talk."

The kid on the skateboard rushed past in the street. He circled around, kicked up his board and stood to watch.

"Leave, now!" Ryan ordered. "This is a police situation."

The kid dropped his board and skated over to the opposite side of the street. He turned back to watch from a distance.

The sirens grew louder and Reggie started jiggling in place, whimpering.

"Reggie, you're going to put the gun down. Look, there are kids around here. Like your nieces. You wouldn't want to accidentally hurt a kid, would you?"

"I'm just gonna hurt myself. See?" Reggie jammed the revolver farther up into his chin.

Ryan winced, expecting the shot, when a blue and white patrol car turned the corner. He pulled his shield as a signal for them to stay back. They either didn't get it or were complete dicks, because they rolled up right beside Reggie and whooped the siren. He jumped and turned to look at the car. In the one second Reggie's attention was diverted, Ryan and Di Santo both pounced. Ryan took his gun and maneuvered him face down onto the hood of the squad car. Di Santo put the cuffs on, opened the patrol's rear door, and shoved Reggie into the back seat before the two patrol cops could even get out.

Ryan leaned into the driver's open window. "Get this guy to the 18th. Homicide suspect."

"Yeah, we know, Terrico James. A one 'Christopher Robinson' called it in. Thought you might need help."

"We appreciate it." Ryan banged the top of the car as a thank you.

The officer in the driver's seat shook his head. "You guys need to call us when you're down in our area."

Ryan wanted to respond, "Why, because we're *white*?" But he held his tongue, agreed, and thanked them for the assistance. Sometimes it was best to be diplomatic for the sake of the department.

The uniformed officer saluted and then pulled out. Di Santo rolled his eyes. "I'm glad they came, D, but they said that like we couldn't handle the East Side. Fuck them!"

"Let it go. Just a territory thing." Ryan shook out the last of his adrenaline.

"Yeah, yeah. So, you okay there? You look a little peaked."

"I'm fine. But I think it's *definitely* time to get back to the gym. It's all those Lulling meals," he said, rubbing the little roll that popped out over his waistband. "I'm turning into the sarge."

# CHAPTER 14

The patrol officers from the 4th had beaten them to the station, waiting in reception with Reggie Robinson in tow and vending machine snacks in hand. Reggie scratched his head against the wall, his hands still cuffed behind him. Ryan requested the officers wait ten more minutes so he and Di Santo could settle in.

Up in the squad room, they updated Sergeant Besko on the chase and Reggie's arrest. "We may have a small window of opportunity, Sarge," Ryan explained. "He's already coming down from a meth high and he's going to start hurting soon. We may not get anything out of him."

"Why don't we let him come down off the high first, and then talk to him?" Di Santo suggested.

The sergeant agreed and called down to the officer in charge of holding, giving orders to escort Robinson to a detox cell.

Back at their desks, Ryan started going through his voice-mail messages while his gaze roamed to the framed 4x6 photo of him and Jon grinning, arms around each other. It had been right after the CPD v. CFD charity game at Wrigley Field—Popos v. Fifis as they called it in the squad. That year they'd kicked the Fifis' asses, six to zero. He and Jon had been like brothers.

"My brother-from-a-honky-mother," Jon had called him,

knowing the word always cracked him up. Straight out of old Richard Pryor stand-up from the '70s. Ryan chuckled as the memory of Jon's camaraderie flowed though him like a glass of warm milk.

He deleted a message from the Officer's Union. They kept trying to recruit him for a management position now that it was close to nomination time. Next, his mom, saying she was leaving a message on his work line because he didn't return her message on his cell and he just wanted to make sure it was working and that he wasn't lying dead in a ditch somewhere. Flawed Irish-mother guilt trip. If he had been lying dead in a ditch somewhere, how would he have gotten her message at the station?

He pressed a key for the next message. "Amy-Jo confirmed the media pulled the sketch," he relayed to Di Santo. Next. Next. "Several messages from people who actually identified Reggie," he said, a little surprised. He deleted those messages and kept listening. "Clancy Ray. Asking why we didn't ask him before broadcasting the sketch—he could have told us it was Reggie. Good point, actually, we should have."

At the last message, Ryan sat up a little straighter and took notes on his spiral pad. Di Santo took notice and bucked his chin in inquisition.

"AT&T," Ryan responded, flipping pages in his spiral notebook to find a blank page. "They have a two-block radius for the phone. It's downtown, near the Westley. I hope to God the battery's not dead yet. Let's go." Ryan ripped the page from his notebook, opened a desk drawer, and pulled out two pairs of blue rubber evidence gloves and a plastic bag. "*You* drive this time!" he said, and threw Di Santo the keys to their beater of a car.

They were on the list for a new sedan, as the Chicago PD had just gotten in a new fleet of unmarked Fords. He couldn't wait. The dented brown Impala had seen finer days. Plus, it all but screamed "unmarked police car." They weren't fooling anyone.

Ryan parked the car in the valet turnaround of the West-ley Hotel and placed a CPD placard in the window. They started their search in the lobby, where Terrico was last seen, near the door. Ryan dialed James's cell number from his phone. A toddler wailed right next to the reservation desk. Both detectives flashed the parent a look to shut the kid up. The mother must have felt the glare, as she picked up her child, stuffed a pacifier in his mouth, and walked to the other side of the lobby.

"I don't hear any ringing," Ryan said. "You?"

"No, D. Nothing."

He feared that Terrico's cell might have lost power al-ready. They moved outside to the circular drive and Ryan hit redial. He thought he heard some tinny music, but he wasn't sure. He hung up and hit redial.

"Wait. You hear that?" he asked.

"Maybe…" Di Santo answered, cocking his head.

"That way," Ryan said.

He pointed toward Burger King, just north of the hotel. Ryan dialed again and distinctly heard a ring tone this time—a rap song pounding out from the alley between the Westley and the Burger King, where they had parked. Di Santo searched the left side of the alley and Ryan took to the right. They kicked over some empty fast food bags and cardboard boxes, flattened to parallelograms. Ryan came upon one with a crimson brown stain on the corner. He crouched down to study it. Definitely dried blood.

"Hey, D, look at this," Ryan said to his partner, pointing to the box. "That's blood. I think we may have found the primary crime scene."

He redialed Terrico's number and after a three-second delay, the rap song echoed from the dumpster.

Di Santo winced. "Okay, so who's goin' in?"

"I've got seniority, you're the newbie," Ryan said, hand-ing over the rubber gloves.

"Newbie? Two and a half years and I'm still a newbie?" Di Santo said, throwing his arms up into the air. Ryan deadpanned. "Shit." Di Santo surrendered and put the gloves on. "We have to call for the Evidence Team, anyway. Can't we—"

"Get the phone!" Ryan commanded.

He interlocked his fingers to give his partner a boost into the dumpster. Di Santo stepped up, jumped into the dumpster, and let out a moan.

Ryan redialed, causing Terrico's voice to sound out again from the pile of garbage. Di Santo foraged around and eventually found it. He raised the phone above his head like an Indy 500 trophy then dropped it into a brown paper evidence bag that Ryan held out for him.

They debated whether they should go through Terrico's calls, texts, and photos. A cell phone always held a shitload of useful information. Ryan was just itching to turn it on, but they agreed to follow protocol and let the Evidence Techs go over it first.

Ryan called dispatch for the tech team and formulated a plan to go over every inch of the alley.

"Aw, man. We have to go over it *now?*" Di Santo complained. "I smell like dumpster!"

"Then you'll fit right in!" a voice called out from the alley.

A man was sandwiched between two flattened cardboard boxes. They approached him, slowly, hands on their weapons. When Ryan got within arm's reach, he grabbed a corner of the top box and flipped it off the man who sat curled up against the brick wall of the hotel. He did smell like dumpster. And urine.

"What's your name?" Ryan asked the man.

He was white, mid-forties, disheveled as the homeless are. He had dirty blond hair with lowlights of sweat and grime. He squinted up at them, eyes adjusting to the light.

"Name's Ben," he croaked, eyeing them up and down.

His gaze settled behind the detectives, as if there was a third person lingering there, with enough conviction to make Ryan look. Glancing back at him, Ryan noticed more blood on the blanket that Ben had pulled up to his chin, despite the fact that it was pushing eighty-five degrees out.

"Hey, Ben, can I see your blanket?" he said, crouching down next to him.

"No, you can't see my blanket! It's mine. And I'm cold."

Ryan glanced up at Di Santo, who pulled out his wallet and handed Ryan two twenties.

"I need that blanket, Ben, so I'm gonna pay you for it. How about forty bucks?"

"Shit, here y'are." The man threw the blanket at Di Santo while he grabbed the two twenties from Ryan.

"Don't say I never bought you anything," Di Santo quipped to his partner.

"So where did you get this blanket, Ben?" Ryan asked, lifting himself up again. "Did you get into a fight?"

"Naw, man. I didn't get into a fight. I don't have the energy. You see, I've got the plague. AIDS. I'm wasting away."

"Shit," Di Santo said. He dropped the blanket onto the pavement.

"You've got gloves, D. You're good," Ryan reassured him. "Go get a paper sack and bag it for processing." Di Santo ran across the street to a small convenience store while Ryan turned back to the homeless man. "Is that your blood on the blanket?"

"No, not my blood. I don't think I even have that much left. It was from the other night. There was a fight here in the alley. All sorts of hullabaloo goings on."

"Hullabaloo? What happened?"

"You know what? You can go away, now. I—I don't want to talk about this." The man curled up and reached for the box, attempting to pull it back over himself.

Ryan crouched down to his level and spoke to him, quietly. "I'm sorry, Ben, but this is really important. If you saw something, we need to hear it."

Ben's eyes unfocussed, recalling the memory. "Okay. I gotcha. There were two guys in the alley. They were

fighting at first, but then they calmed down and started talking nice. One of the guys started to cry. Really freaked me
out, and I thought I should give them some space. Plus, I
didn't want to get involved or anything. So I went down to
the end of the alley and ducked into the water heater closet.
The lock on the door is broken and sometimes I nap in there
if I get cold. I gave them about ten, fifteen minutes and then
peeked out. That's when I saw the abduction."

"An *abduction*? Exactly what did you see?"

"A van. A bunch of white guys were putting a black guy
in the back of a van and drove away."

"Was the black guy alive or dead?" Di Santo asked.

"I don't know. I couldn't see that much. He wasn't kicking or screaming, that's for sure. When they left, I came
back to my spot. Turned out they got blood all over my
stuff. I had to get another box, but I wanted to keep my
blanket. I just dried it overnight and it was fine."

Ryan asked Ben to step of the box he'd been lounging
on. Underneath, the blacktop was coated with a dried pool
of blood. Primary crime scene. He ushered Ben to the other
side of the alley and instructed him not to go back to his
spot, as they needed to collect evidence. "Did you see what
the van looked like?" Ryan asked him.

"Plain white van. No writing on it."

"Year, make, or model? What about the guys? Tall?
Short? Big ears? License plate number?"

"Man, too many questions. Leave me alone. I don't
know anything. You push me and my story goes away and
I'm not testifying or anything. Not worth my measly time
on earth."

Ryan wrestled with the fact that this man had no
healthcare and was dying on the streets. A star witness to an
abduction—possibly a murder—and no one had noticed
him. He was one of the invisible people the city called
homeless.

He crouched down to the man. "Ben, is there any place
you can go? Someone who could give you a bed for the

night, or a shelter? You won't be able to stay here, in the alley."

"Yeah, there's a shelter down the street. They'll feed me and put me up for the night. Can I come back in the morning?"

"Of course, as soon as you don't see the yellow tape, any more, okay?"

The man agreed, flashed a melancholy look at his bloody blanket, and walked away, passing Di Santo on the way back. Ryan pointed out the blood pool to Di Santo, who sidestepped it to pick up the blanket and place it in the paper bag.

One of the managers from the Westley Hotel exited a side door and approached them.

"Woah," Ryan warned her. "Please stay back. We have a crime scene here."

She recoiled. He asked about Ben.

"The staff calls him 'Gentle Ben' and takes care of him as much as they can," the manager explained. "We have an understanding. As long as he stays in the alley and not in front of the hotel, we'll feed him and make sure he's okay."

"What about getting him to a doctor?"

"He won't budge. But occasionally we bring one here. There's a local doc that works over in the Carlson Building—Reichert—who checks him out and makes sure he's comfortable. That's about all we can do."

Ryan nodded, not satisfied but not dissatisfied, either. At least the man was cared for. He explained to the manager that they believed the alley was the primary crime scene for the James murder and they'd need to cordon it off for a while.

"Our evidence team is on the way," he told her. "Is there a doorman working the front door? Someone who may have witnessed the scene on the night of the twenty-third?"

The woman stepped away from Di Santo, not hiding the fact that she was repelled by his odor. "We do have a door-man, however, we allow him to remain inside the door during summer and winter—because of the weather. The valet ends at ten p.m. We then put up a sign to direct guests to self-park." She rubbed her nose, attempting to disguise the fact that she was holding her breath.

Di Santo hit Ryan on the shoulder, taking the hint. "Hey, D. I'm going home to get the stink off. Meet you back at the eighteen."

Ryan nodded and then addressed the woman who had since exhaled. "I'll need the name of the doorman who was working that night."

The manager retreated into her office and returned with a name, which he noted it in his phone.

He made the call while the manager retreated back into the hotel. The doorman reiterated that he only remembered Terrico leaving the hotel with the "other guy," as he put it. He remained at the concierge desk and could only say that Terrico did not return before the end of his shift, at midnight. So there were no wits other than a dying homeless man who refused to testify.

Great.

When the evidence techs arrived, Ryan briefed them on the scene and then hitched a ride with a patrol car back to the 18th. He took a side stairwell down to the lower level where the detox cells were located in a converted wing of the police station's basement. Two cells lined either side of a cement-floored hallway. At the end, a small medical office was set up with a part-time nurse practitioner and a round-the-clock medical technician. They attended to the prisoners who were coming down from a high or sobering up from an alcoholic binge.

Ryan checked in with the med tech on duty and asked after Reggie Robinson.

"Looks like he had a bad couple of hours," the tech reported. "But we have him on painkillers now. He seems to be doing better."

"From meth to Vicodin, eh?" Ryan quipped. The tech wasn't amused. "Think he can answer some questions?"

"Yes, I think he'd be up to it." The tech led him to a door and entered a code to unlock it.

They passed through to a narrow hallway lined with more locked doors on either side, making it appear like a mental institution. Ryan couldn't recall the last time he had been down in this unit.

"He's over there, in cell four," the tech said.

Ryan peeked through the bars of a twelve-inch square opening on the door. Reggie was standing up in the middle of the room, staring straight back at him. It was eerie.

Ryan cleared his throat. "Hey, Reggie? How are you feeling?" he asked, peering through the small opening while he waited for a guard to unlock the door.

"Who'zzat?" Reggie replied, looking around the room.

When the door opened, Ryan stood at the threshold. "Hi Reggie. I'm Detective Ryan Doherty. Do you remember? Me and my partner, Matt, chased you down the street, right?" Reggie scratched his head then yawned. "I have a few questions to ask you about your brother. Is it okay if I come in?"

Reggie backed away from him, closing one eye as if trying to remember an old classmate from twenty years ago. After a beat, he raised his hands in agreement. "All right, whatever."

Ryan instructed a guard to stay close. The guard nodded back, affirmation without expression.

"I'm Reggie, Reggie Robinson," Reggie said, holding out a hand. He obviously had no memory of the events earlier in the day. "So when can I get out of here?" His head jerked uncontrollably every couple of seconds from withdrawal.

Ryan checked the upper corner of the room for a video camera and, sure enough, one was mounted near the ceiling. A red light indicated it was operating. Probably recording, too, which meant he'd have to play it by the book.

"Well, Reg, you are going to have to stay in here for a while, until you feel a little better," Ryan said.

"Yeah, man, okay." Reggie's eyes kept flickering to the open door. Ryan felt secure that between him and the guard, they could keep him from fleeing. "So whaddya want?"

"The quicker we get through this, the quicker you can get out of here and get some help," Ryan said.

"Mmm-hmmm," Reggie said with his mother's tone.

"Take a seat, Reggie. Relax." Ryan pointed to the edge of the cot. Reggie took a seat while Ryan pulled up a metal chair for himself. "You know, this is informal, but I have to do this." He pulled a card out of his wallet and read him the Miranda warning. Not that he didn't have it memorized. It was a deliberate bit of play-acting: pull out the card, make it seem like no big deal. Treat the Miranda like an inconsequential necessity and chances are, the suspect would waive. He finished with, "Do you understand these rights as I have read them to you?"

"I don't need an attorney, man." Reggie dismissed the idea with the back of his hand. *And score.* The man rolled his lips into his mouth, licking them on the inside. "I didn't do anything. 'Cept try to shoot my own face off. That's not a crime."

Ryan shifted. "Well, actually it is, Reggie. You brandished a firearm. But that's not why you're here. I need to talk to you about your brother, Terrence. Do you remember talking to him at the Westley Hotel before he died?" Reggie looked down at the floor and frowned. "Do you remember going to the hotel?"

Reggie started nodding, slowly. After a couple of seconds, he lifted his head. "Yeah, yeah, I went to ask him for a little green, you know, brotha-to-brotha. I'm between jobs, know-what-I'm-saying? I tried Chris first, but he won't give me any more money. He says the money tree's been chopped down."

Ryan transcribed the man's responses in his notebook and wondered if he should wait for Di Santo to arrive before going too much farther. But knowing his partner, he could have been taking a two-hour shower.

"When you went to ask Terrico for some—*green*—you met him in the lobby, right?"

"Yeah, right. And the name is Terrence. Terrence or TJ! None of this Terrico shit with me. That wasn't his name."

"Sorry, Terrence. You and Terrence had words, and then you two walked out of the hotel and into the alley."

"Umm...naw, man, I don't think we went into any alley."

"I think you did. Think again. You went out of the front door, turned left, and then there was an alley."

"Alley? What alley?" Reggie's eyes rolled up into his head. "Um, oh, right. The alley. We talked a bit in the alley, yeah. Then I walked down the street and had a smoke at the fountain on the corner."

"Wait, hold up," Ryan said, his bullshit meter spiking. "We have witnesses that said you and Terrico were fighting. So let's go back to the alley. Walk me through that. What did you and Terrence discuss that got him upset?"

Reggie shook his head and stared at a spot on the floor. "TJ—man, he told me to get cleaned up. I told him I couldn't. I am who I am. You know, like Popeye, man! He wasn't yelling at me mad, he was yelling at me like a brotha. Concerned-like. He told me if I got clean and sober and stayed that way, he'd give me a hundred thousand dollars." He lifted his head and pointed directly at Ryan. "That's six zeroes—no, five zeroes. A one and five zeroes. Green, man. A lot of green."

Ryan took a moment. For someone who was supposedly so cheap with his money, that was a pretty generous offer for Terrico James.

"You sure he said he'd give you a *hundred thousand dollars*?" he said, leaning in a little closer to the suspect.

"Yeah, man, can you believe it? A hundr'd K. Well, I started crying. I bawled like a baby. Then I asked if he could give me some of it up front, you know, like an advance."

Ryan smirked. He knew where that advance would have gone.

"TJ say 'No way, Reg, a deal is a deal and you gotta go

through the program. I send you to this place in Malibu, you come out clean and stay that way for six months, you a rich man.'"

"And then what happened?"

"Then I agreed. Hell, wouldn't you? It's a hundred thousand dollars! I figured it would be a good, you know, *incentive* for me to do so. Then we shook on it, and we hugged, man." Reggie wiped one eye with his thumb. "He just hugged me right there, and I started bawling again. He said he would take me back to L.A. with him after the show." Reggie's eyes started to moisten and he pinched them with two fingers. "I just didn't know he had it in him. He was a Jesus that night, for sure. To me he was. I could feel the healing start happening right then and there."

"Then what happened, Reggie?"

"Then nothing. Like I said, we hugged good night and I went down to the corner where they have that fountain. I sat and had a smoke before I got in my car and went home. I parked at a meter about a block and a half down from the hotel."

"Did you see a white van when you were at the fountain? Or in the alley? A van that may have taken Terrence?"

"A van? No, I didn't see no van."

"So when you left the alley, where did Terrence go?"

"I don't know. Back to the hotel, I suppose."

"But you didn't see him go back to the hotel."

"What is this?" Reggie angled his head in inquisition. "What are you sayin'?"

"One question, Reggie. When you left Terrence, was he alive?"

"Hell *yeah*, he was alive!" he said, jumping up from the cot. "What, you think *I* killed him? I knew that's why you were after me! Chase me on down my street! Am I gonna be put away for this?"

Ryan rose to calm the man. "Hey, hey, Reg. This is just a conversation."

"How can you think I killed TJ? He's my brother! He

was gonna *help* me!" Reggie was tapping his chest furiously with two fingers. "I needed that dough, man. I wouldn't a killed him. Seriously, after I found out TJ was gone, I went to Clancy and asked him about the deal, you know, if it was still on. He said he didn't know anything about it and to get tha fuck out of his sight. Mothaf..." He shook his head without finishing the word.

After a moment, he blew out a breath, turned his back on Ryan, and stared out the barred window at the far side of the cell. It looked out into the precinct parking lot. Ryan felt sorry for the man. He certainly didn't have the attitude of a killer, even for a meth addict.

"You can go now, dee-tective," Reggie said, without turning back to him.

He was definitely Ms. Mae's son, with similar mannerisms. He had her soulful eyes, too. Eyes that made Ryan want to believe him.

Ryan left the detox unit and took the elevator up to the second floor detective squad. He rarely took the elevator, impatient at its lack of efficiency. It took over three minutes to ascend two floors. But this time, he wanted the extra time to rehash his talk with Reggie. The man did seem pretty lucid and Ryan almost believed his version of the events. Reggie had correctly described the direction and location of the fountain, a half a block south of the hotel. And if he was telling the truth about Terrico's offer, he would have had no motive, whatsoever, to kill his brother. In fact, it was the opposite. He seemed eager and ready to go along with the rehab plan.

Di Santo was sitting at his desk when Ryan got to his.

"Spiffed up and smelling groovy!" his partner announced. Zegna Sicilian Mandarin cologne hung heavy in the air, Di Santo's signature scent.

"I just got back from checking on Reggie," Ryan said. "I did an informal interview."

"Without me? Thanks, partner." Di Santo threw the tennis ball to him, a little too hard.

Ryan caught it anyway and sat down at his desk, his palm stinging from the catch. "He didn't say much. Claimed they had a conversation in the alley, but then left him there. Alive. Said that Terrico offered him a hundred grand to sober up, so he had no motive to kill him. Terrico was his bank."

Di Santo took a beat for the story to sink in. "Guess we could check that with Clancy Ray. Maybe he knew of this deal. Oh, by the way, Fisk just stopped by. I told him we had nothing new. He's such a bug! Do we really have to keep him posted on the investigation?"

Ryan glanced at the sarge's office. "Nah, fuck Fisk. He's just getting in the way. You did the right thing." He started straightening his desk in preparation for leaving for the day and then abandoned it, realizing it would never be as tidy as Di Santo's.

"I may be a little late tomorrow," he said, trying not to arouse his partner's suspicion. It didn't work. The little bugger was nosy.

"What? What you got going on tomorrow morning? Another interview without me?"

"No, and I said I was sorry about that." Or maybe he hadn't. "Anyway, I'm taking Cat out. We're trying a little outing. A date."

"Hey, that's terrific!" Di Santo said, just a little too loud.

"We'll see," Ryan said, flashing on the day Cat came into the station.

He hoped tomorrow morning's excursion would be more successful. At least there would be flowers. She liked flowers.

# CHAPTER 15

Ryan's cell alarm went off at 7:15 a.m. Tuesday morning. He'd set it extra early for his date with Catharine, eager to embark on their first real date. He rose from her all-white bed to turn off the annoying fog-horn and made a mental note to change it. Cat had already vacated her spot next to him, so he got up out of bed and checked the bathroom. But it, too, was empty. He took a quick rinse then wrapped one of the thick white towels around his waist and stepped back out into the bedroom.

Catharine emerged from her dressing room and stood on

the opposite side of the bed. He took a moment to absorb the vision of the woman and thanked God she was his.

She wore a crisp summer dress, white lace on top with two thin straps. The skirt was tiered in lavender sections, each a slightly darker shade, ending just below her knees. Her long hair was swept up and pinned loosely on her head, with some pieces falling softly around her face.

"Do you like it?" she asked him. "I bought it especially for our date."

She twirled around in a dancer's pirouette, stopping gracefully with a grin in his direction. He was speechless. As beautiful as she always was, she had never really dressed up for him.

"Cat," he said, closing the distance between them. "You are...do we have time for a quickie?"

"No!" she said, pushing him back with both palms. "Hands off! I want to see the roses. And don't you dare take that towel off!" He smirked and reached for the wrap at his waist, causing her to scream and giggle like a schoolgirl. "No! Ryan! I'm not looking!" She ran up the two stairs to the bedroom door and turned to him. "Get dressed, Detective. I'll make coffee."

After their morning ritual of greeting the animals and downing a mug each of caffeine, they walked out the front door, hand-in-hand and Ryan led her to the passenger side of his prized '66 Night-Mist-Blue Mustang convertible. He had been working on the pony for several years when Catharine had had it fully restored for him as a Christmas gift. It was an amazing present and today was the first day that she was actually going to ride in it.

"What a great chariot!" Catharine said, complimenting both his car and her gift of restoration simultaneously. Ryan opened the passenger door and held it for her. "And what a gentleman!"

He smiled and bowed at the compliment, while she got in. He tucked her skirt into the car, shut the door and took his place in the driver's seat. He glanced at her for permission to drive. She smiled and nodded as she buckled her belt.

It was only a nine-minute trip to the Rose Garden and, being 8:23 am, they found a spot right in front, on Lake Street. Ryan scanned the grounds to see if there were people who might upset Catharine's equilibrium. Only two people were walking the Rose Garden paths, and traffic was sparse. Perfect.

"Are you okay?" he asked her.

"Yes!" she said and was already opening the door, grinning at the rainbow of fully bloomed roses in front of her. "Oh, look at that! Let's start on this side!"

She pulled him along by his shirtsleeve toward a path on the right side of the garden.

When he caught up to her, Ryan was pleasantly relieved at the sight of Catharine taking in the sights and smells of the populated rose patches. He kept a hand on her back, while his eyes darted around the gardens, across the street, and to each corner, as if he were a Secret Service agent seeking out potential assassins. Catharine stopped to examine each variety of rose and read the signs in their entirety. Several times, she reached down and caressed the underside of the petals, cupping the flower as if it were a child's chin.

"Don't touch the flowers, ma'am," said a woman who appeared in front of them on the path. Her green uniform identified her position at the City of Evanston Parks and Recreation Department by a patch on the sleeve.

"Oh! I'm so sorry!" Catharine said, automatically stepping back. "I pet the roses in my garden and totally forgot it's not appropriate elsewhere."

The city worker nodded and strolled away, her attention already wandering to the one other visitor in the park.

"She's worried about her daughter," Catharine said, looking after the woman. Her eyes started to glaze over. "The baby is sick and she wants to go home and take care of her."

"Hey, turn off the radio, remember?" Ryan said, tapping her temple.

Catharine bowed her head with a smile and nodded in compliance. They strolled down the colorful pathway and Ryan mused, silently, how he had never—literally—stopped to smell the roses, only passed this place in his car. Catharine delighted to take in every single variety and stopped to read every information plaque along the way, noting which of them also grew in her gardens. Occasionally she would throw a glance back at the car.

"You okay?" Ryan asked.

She nodded as they continued their stroll. "*Belle de Crécy*," she read from one of the plaques. "A member of the Gallica family. Thought to have been raised by French dramatist Alexandre Hardy at the home of Madame de Pompadour at Crécy, France. Huh!"

"Pompadour like the hair?" asked Ryan.

"Yes, I think the Madame invented the hairdo," Catharine said and put her hand high above her head. They strolled down several more paths in the back of the garden, one of which ended at the old three-tiered fountain—a historical relic, rehomed from Evanston's Fountain Square.

Ryan handed Catharine a penny from his pocket and she closed her eyes and tossed it in.

"What did you wish for?" he asked.

"It wasn't a wish. It was a thank you. I have everything I could ever want."

She hugged him around the waist and he kissed her forehead.

This woman was so entirely different than any he had ever dated—different than any woman he had ever met, actually. Effervescent, uplifting, and secure. He took another penny from his pocket and tossed it in, behind her back, saying his own private thank you. He lifted her chin for a kiss, but she wouldn't make eye contact.

'*She's hiding something from you*,' he heard in his late partner's voice. It had been a while since Jon had "spoken" to him. Ryan was at the point where he wasn't shocked to hear his deceased partner, anymore, as he knew it usually came when something important was about to happen. Whether it was a communication from beyond or a hallucination or just a memory, he had learned to just go with it.

Catharine, of course, believed it was Jon's spirit communicating with him from beyond. But Ryan leaned toward the more practical explanation—that it most likely developed from the residual pain of losing his partner and best friend.

Jon's accusation hung heavy in the air.

Ryan turned her around to face him.

"Cat?" he said, the unspoken question being, *Is there something you want to tell me?*

"Let's keep going." She took his hand and pulled him along the path as if she had heard the unspoken part and was intentionally avoiding it.

'*See? Something is up,*' Jon said in Ryan's head. '*Something feels off.*'

They were making their way down the east side of the garden when church bells rang out from St. Mary's Cathedral, across the street. A group of people had gathered in front of the gothic doors of the large Catholic Church.

Catharine stiffened, fixated on the crowd. Her breathing quickened, her brows furrowed.

"Cat? Are you okay?" he checked again. Her right hand started to tremble and he immediately took it, but she jerked it away as if she was in pain. "Cat—"

"Stop asking me that!" she replied and backed away from him, almost in a trance.

Ryan tried to reach for her, but she was too quick. She stumbled off the path and into a patch of pink roses, confused and disoriented. Her eyes darted around the garden, seeking escape.

"I'm so sorry, Ryan," she said, tears welling up in her eyes. "I hurt you."

He had no idea what she was referring to. "Cat, you

aren't hurting me, but you aren't supposed to be in there. Come out." He held out his hand to help her back onto the path, but she wouldn't take it.

"Ma'am! Ma'am!" the city worker shouted at her from across the garden.

When Cat saw the woman approach, she turned to run and slammed directly into a maple tree. The force threw her backward into a sea of pink blooms. Ryan stepped in and pulled Catharine up, out of the roses, and into his arms in one move.

"You absolutely *cannot* walk in the rose beds!" the woman shouted at the two of them, waving her finger like a schoolteacher.

"Yes, we know, we know," Ryan assured her as he set Catharine on her feet. "We're leaving now."

He wrapped an arm around Catharine's waist and walked her slowly back to the car. She remained silent as he pulled some leaves and stems from her dress, opened the passenger door, and set her down. When he leaned down to help swing her legs in, he noticed they were cut and bleeding from the thorns. He found an unused fast food napkin in the back seat and dabbed the wounds, then placed her hand on top for pressure.

"You'll be okay." He was trying to soothe her and determine her mental state at the same time. "Everything's okay. We're going home now."

She stared out of the car window, almost catatonic. He let her be silent while he drove just a little too fast to get her back to the estate.

Several minutes into the drive, Catharine came out of her stupor. She pulled her dress up past her knees and assessed the damage to her legs. "Ow," she said, acknowledging the pain after the fact.

"I didn't know they had services this morning. I'm so sorry," he said, feeling the guilt of a thousand Catholics.

"It's not your fault, I loved it. The roses were beautiful." She wet her thumb and tried to wipe away some of the blood, but it just smeared a thick red line across her shin. She lowered her dress, abandoning the attempt to clean up.

"We can keep trying. You're doing great," he told her. "All in all, it was a success. We got out. We had a date! The roses were beautiful, weren't they?"

"Yes, they were," she said, placing her hand on his cheek. "Thank you." Ryan took her hand and kissed it. Catharine pulled it back, folded her hands in her lap, and stared back out the window. "Did Terrico James have children?"

He didn't quite understand the change in subject, but decided to go with it. Let her forget about the roses. "No, I don't believe so. He never married. No kids."

"Huh."

"Why, what are you getting? Are you getting something?" he said, referring to her sporadic metaphysical abilities. Sometimes she could summon them; sometimes they just popped in like a genie.

"Just a child," Catharine answered. "A girl. Maybe I'm still picking up the sick child of the park manager. That's possible." She paused to look back out the window while they crossed Chicago Avenue. "My boys, they're going to leave me someday."

Ryan took his eyes off the road for a second to absorb her melancholy. "Cat, I know it's hard that Hank is going off with Mandy, but he's only going to be gone a week. At some point you have to let go. Yes, the twins will leave home. That's natural. But they're never going to leave you. And I'm here for you. I'm not going anywhere," he reassured her.

Catharine whispered something in response, something that he couldn't quite hear but sounded vaguely like, "*You will.*"

# CHAPTER 16

After dropping off Cat, Ryan drove into the 18th to continue investigation on the James case. Di Santo was already at his desk poring through a printout when Ryan came into the squad.

"The LUDs from Terrico's phone," his partner explained. "I just got them from Tech. Oh, hey, how was your date?"

"Talk about it later."

"That good, huh? Poor Cat." He *tsked* a few times and went back to the printout. "Sarge was asking for you."

"I told him I'd be in a little late. It's only 10:03," he said, looking at this watch. He glanced at the squad's wall clock to make sure they were in sync. Almost to the second.

After putting his laptop down on the desk, he rounded the desk pod to Di Santo's side to read the phone detail report. Tech had come through for them. It listed all incoming and outgoing calls and texts for the last month. Standing next to his partner, Ryan scanned the lines of data with his fingertip.

"Okay, here's Reggie's call, at the very end," Ryan said.

He turned one page back and ran his finger from the bottom to the top, trying to see patterns in the numbers. He flipped through the report backward.

Di Santo pointed to one of the numbers. "This one shows up a lot on the text list. But it's listed as private."

Ryan punched the speakerphone button on Di Santo's desk phone and dialed the number. It started with a 310 area code, which he knew to be the L.A./Beverly Hills area.

One ring, two rings, three rings.

*"Hey-yay! This is Mannnnndy. If I'm not answering then I'm busy or you're a loser. Ha-ha! Okay, leave a message."*

He punched the speakerphone button again to disconnect and looked back at his partner.

"So Terrico was texting Mandy," Di Santo announced the obvious. "But why? About the tour?"

Ryan raised his eyebrows. "Let me see those call records again." He paged through last couple of pages of the LUDs again. Picking up a red pen, he put a check mark next to each line with Mandy's number on it.

"Look, he texted her every night. Like around ten, ten-thirty. Every night, up and until that Friday. Every night. 10:30." Ryan's gut clenched, mainly for Hank. "You know what those are?"

"Yep!" Di Santo smacked the desk with his palm. "Booty calls!"

Ryan pulled out his cell and called Catharine. "Cat!" he shouted a little too loud when she answered. "Where are Hank and Mandy?"

"I told you, on their way to L.A. He packed last night."

"*Shit!* I forgot they were leaving today. What time is their flight?"

"Let me check. He's already left to pick her up. I can call him if you want. Why, what's wrong? Ryan?"

Ryan put his hand over the phone, even though that rarely muted it. "Cat says Mandy is leaving for L.A. today and she's taking Hank with her. We've got to stop them." Then back into the phone. "No, Cat. Don't call them. Do you know if they were going on a private jet or taking a commercial flight?"

"American, I think. Hold on, I have the flight number," Ryan heard Catharine's footsteps and then her typing on her keyboard. "Here it is: American flight 311. Departs at 11:40. Ryan? Should I be worried? Is Hank in trouble?"

"No, it's Mandy. We found some evidence that proves she lied to us. Looks like she could have been sleeping with Terrico James. We need to follow up with some more questions."

"That little—"

"*Cat!*" He stopped her before she finished her derisive comment. Catharine never swore. Although it would be funny to hear her do it.

"You see what she does to me, Ryan?"

"We'll take care of it. Just do not call them. We don't want her to run." He hung up and held out his hand. "Keys, please."

"To O'Hare?" Di Santo asked, tossing the Impala keys over the desk.

"To O'Hare."

On his way out, Ryan's cell rang. He looked at the caller ID and let out a string of his own expletives. He threw the phone to Di Santo.

"Please take care of her," he begged his partner as they got into the Impala. "If I don't answer, she'll just keep calling every hour on the hour."

"Finn Doherty!" Di Santo said, answering the call. "How is the redheaded love of my life today?"

Ryan could clearly hear his sister's over-amped voice on the other end. "Oh—em—gee, *Matt*? He won't even answer my call?" she said. "Put my douche-ass brother on the line!"

"No can do, sweet cakes. We're on a case. In fact, we're headed out now to apprehend a suspect!" Di Santo grinned at Ryan for approval.

"*Suspect*? Who's the suspect? Is it Mandy? I'll bet it's Mandy! Can I print that it's Mandy?"

"No, n-n-n-no!" Di Santo's glee turned to panic.

"Shit, Finn, don't print anything!" Ryan called from the driver's seat.

"See I knew he was there! *Put Ryan on the line!*" she screamed.

Di Santo hung up. "Your little sister's a hottie, but boy, is she a bug," he said, placing the cellphone in the console between them. "Is she still writing that crime blog?"

"Yeah, Finfamous.com." Ryan laughed. "It's really taking off, which is making her more of a bug. She just hit one million visitors last month."

Di Santo whistled. "Miss Tabloid Journalist makin' some bucks! She still single?"

"What do you think?" Ryan answered, heading onto the highway heading east toward the airport. The phone rang again. "Just text her and say I'll give her an exclusive if she just waits until we have solid evidence."

*Sisters.*

"I need to get two people off of American flight 311," Ryan explained to the TSA agent. He and Di Santo shoved their gold badges and department IDs under his nose. "It leaves in ten," he added, hoping for sympathy.

The Filipino man, encroaching on middle age, frowned at them as he grabbed the radio on his chest. "Uyuh—I have two Chicago police officers that need to get to a gate. Uyuh. American. Uyuh." He paused for several seconds, listening to something in his ear bud, then read their credentials into the radio. The passengers they had cut in front of started to make noises of irritation. Finally the TSA agent lifted his latex-gloved hand and waved them through.

"*Thank you!*" Ryan said, almost jumping the barrier before the agent pulled it back.

They weaved through security and jogged down the long, long terminal. O'Hare was one of those airports that went on for miles. And miles.

Finally arriving at gate B-45, they repeated the routine

with the woman who was checking in the residual line of boarding passengers. Ryan pulled her away from the passengers and explained that he needed to get passengers Ross and Lulling off the plane for questioning.

"*Mandy* Ross?" she questioned.

Ryan nodded. "Discreetly, please."

The woman stopped the loading of the passengers and disappeared down the breezeway to the plane. After several minutes she returned, followed by a fuming Hank and Mandy.

"Fuck this shit. You'll be hearing from my lawyer!" Mandy said, pointing her index finger at the ticket taker's face. Hank spotted Ryan and Di Santo first, standing near to the check-in counter. When he pointed them out to Mandy, she hissed obscenities under her breath.

"Ry," Hank said, coming up to the detectives. "Seriously, what is up?"

"We need to take Mandy to the station for more questioning," he answered.

"*Now*?"

Di Santo grabbed Mandy's arm, and Hank tried to force himself between them.

"Hank, you're going to want to step back," Ryan said.

"Dude, don't be so rough with her. Is she under arrest?" Hank moved into Ryan's personal space, attempting to intimidate with his size.

"No, she's not under arrest. We just have to talk with her."

"But our flight's about to leave." Hank took Mandy's hand and tried to pull her away from Di Santo's grip.

"Hank, stop resisting. Let go," Ryan ordered. "You want us to take you both by force? You know that will be all over the Internet in five minutes."

Hank scanned the waiting area. People were already gawking at them. At Mandy, mostly.

He squinted at Ryan and exhaled in defeat. "Okay, but I'm going, too."

"No, you're not," Ryan said, leading them out of the terminal. "You're going home."

"Screw you. You can't tell me what to do. You're not my father."

Ryan stopped short and turned back to face him. He stepped in closer and put a finger in the boy's face. "No, I'm not your father, but I am a cop. And *that* gives me every fucking right to tell you what to do." He pulled his handcuffs out from the back of his belt. "You want to come down to the station? If so, hold out your hands."

"Seriously? You brought *cuffs*?" Hank said, in disbelief. Ryan didn't back down. "Okay, okay. Let's go," the boy said, waving to the front of the long terminal walkway. "So, where's our luggage gonna end up?"

"They said they'll pull it," Di Santo answered. "They can deliver it wherever you want."

Hank shook his head, but knew better than to buck them now.

"You're reimbursing me for these tickets!" Mandy whined.

"Shut up," Ryan snapped.

# CHAPTER 17

Catharine soothed herself by working the gardens. She had the atrium in the wintertime, but now that it was warm, she could spend her time outdoors in the lush backyard. Her naturalist, Lisa, was somewhere down the garden path, planting some new peonies. Lisa came three to four times a week in the spring and summer to help her take care of it all. She was more than an employee, they had become friends. In fact Lisa and Sara were more like sisters to her. Maybe they even had been, in a different life.

Other than the birds chirping and the occasional clip of the pruning shears, it was quiet. Peaceful. Until Catharine's cell phone rang. The screen indicated it was Jane and Catharine almost didn't answer. She wanted to put the trial out of her mind, pretend it didn't exist. But she had to, knowing she had to get through it to have it be over.

"Catharine," Jane began. "I was calling to tell you that your video testimony is most likely going to be played at the trial tomorrow morning. Depends on the opening statements, if we get through them today. I am on a five-minute break, so I can't talk for long."

"Tomorrow? That's so soon! But I haven't—" She began to panic. It was her intention to tell Ryan about her past indiscretion with Todd, but everything happened so quickly. The Terrico case was on his mind, then their date at the

Rose Garden was ruined. She couldn't find the right time. "Can't they hold off for one more day?"

"Sorry, Catharine. The victim speaks first. It will be more effective this way."

Jane didn't seem very sympathetic. In fact, Catharine sensed a wave of aggression traveling through phone line— an acidic feeling she couldn't shake. She knew not to continue the conversation. Jane wasn't her friend.

"Thank you," Catharine finally said and disconnected.

She had waited too long to tell Ryan, but every time she had remembered that night with Todd, she had been too ashamed to share it with him.

She fell to her knees on the dusty garden path, feeling the weight of her guilt and the impending fallout from her testimony. Her knees still stung from the confrontation with the roses. She hadn't realized the thorns had cut so deeply.

Lisa dropped her trowel and ran to her. "Cat, are you okay?" she asked.

"Stop asking me that! Why does everyone keep asking me that?" Catharine couldn't help the flood of tears that emerged. Her shoulders trembled with sobs that she tried desperately to hide.

"Cat, I am so sorry, I didn't mean to upset you!" Lisa crouched down and put her arms around Catharine. "Oh-my-god. What's the matter? Do you want to talk about it?"

She helped Catharine up and walked her over to the patio table and helped her into a chair. Catharine buried her head in her hands, still weeping, and Lisa remained silent, offering quiet sympathy with a hand on her shoulder.

"It's the trial," Catharine eventually said, wiping her tears with her sleeve. "You know, the man who attacked me last year? The trial is this week and I gave my testimony yesterday."

"You gave your testimony? Where? Did you go out of the estate?"

"No, they took it here, at the house. On video."

"They can do that?" Catharine nodded. "Well, that's

good," Lisa continued. "So what happened? Didn't it go well?"

Catharine shook her head and looked down, smoothing her skirt. Several tears rolled down her cheeks and took a dive into her lap.

"Did you talk about it with Ryan?"

"I can't."

"Why not?"

"Because the man who attacked me—Todd Elliot—his attorney brought up the fact that we had—slept together."

"Oh-my-god, *what*? When?"

Lisa was always up for drama. She thrived on it. Normally Cat didn't feed it. However today she needed their female support.

"It was six years ago. One night. I'd had some wine—we shared some wine. It was a mistake. But Todd's lawyer—he made it seem like we were still—he said, 'Maybe you invited him into your home. Maybe you picked up where you left off.' Now that's going to be shown to *everyone*. At the trial tomorrow. And I haven't told Ryan, yet."

"You haven't told him? Why?"

Catharine shook her head. "I don't know, I don't know. I just haven't found the right time. And now—now he's all wrapped up in this big case and I didn't want to sidetrack him with this."

"Oh, Cat. I understand," Lisa said, patting her arm. "Let me get Sara to bring out some tea." She took out her phone and sent a quick message. "Okay, she's on her way. So, tell me the story. How did it all happen?"

Cat wiped her remaining tears on the napkin and gathered her thoughts. "It was one night when we were both working at Town Red Media. Todd and I both stayed late to work on a pitch for a big client—some energy drink company that Scott and Carly really wanted to land. We were going over the campaigns that the art department had put together. We were the only ones in the office, out came some wine."

"Yep, I know how that is," Lisa said.

"What made it worse was that afterward, Todd had completely misinterpreted it. I knew it was a mistake from the minute I got home that night. I took a long shower, trying to get the smell of his cologne off of me." Catharine shuddered at the memory. "The next day, I was eating lunch with some of the staff and he came up and put his arms around my shoulders from behind. I was mortified."

"Oh-my-god! Was he, like, in *love* with you?"

"No, nothing like that. I think he was trying to make a statement. That I was his. It was possessive," Catharine said. "I immediately jumped up and told him to come to my office. He misinterpreted that, too. As soon as the door closed, I was fighting him off. I told him I had no intention of *ever* seeing him again outside of work and that we needed to forget about the previous night."

"What did he say?"

"He got angry. Mean. Said I was the one who seduced him, called me every name in the book from a…FB to a…FC."

"What an ass!"

"Everything went downhill from there. He hardly spoke to me after that, but that was fine by me. I had been planning to leave the firm anyway."

"And this was the guy who *attacked* you? Did you have to say all that on the video?"

"No. His attorney just used the incident to discredit my charge that Todd was going to rape me. *But he was*! He had me pinned down and he was lifting my skirt when—" Catharine buried her face in her hands again, trying to erase it all from her mind.

When she heard the screen door open, she lifted her head. Sara came out of the back door with a tray of ginger iced tea and three glasses. Lisa signaled her to sit down and join them.

"What's going on?" Sara asked.

Cat accepted the tea, took a drink, and fixed her gaze at a

beautiful Japanese maple in the garden. Its red leaves danced in the breeze.

Lisa asked, "Can I tell Sara? About Todd Elliot?"

Catharine nodded, keeping her eyes on the leaves. Lisa repeated the story of Catharine's admission in her video testimony as Cat calmed herself. *Just breathe*, as her therapist had instructed her. *Breathe and be present.*

"Wow. Well, I knew it had been rough on you, because you left the library so quickly," Sara said. "You didn't even walk them to the door. What did Ryan say about it?"

"Well, that's the issue," Lisa said, under her breath. "Cat, are you going to tell Ryan before they play it in court?"

Cat shook her head. She couldn't even face him right now. And in the last couple of days she'd had this vision of him leaving her. Physically and emotionally. He was going to leave her if she told him. From the corner of her eye she saw Lisa and Sara exchange a look.

"Cat, I think you should tell him," Sara said, her dulcet voice comforting.

It had a low, rich tone that Catharine had noticed the minute she interviewed her. It was excellent on the telephone, authoritative, unlike her own voice, which was breathy and melodic. That was one of the reasons she had hired Sara as her assistant, beyond her credentials.

"Then again, if Ryan blows up before the trial, it may ruin their chances of convicting him," Lisa said. "Who knows? He could go crazy and beat the guy up or something. Didn't you say he tends to get jealous? Maybe it's best if she just lets it play out, and then they can deal with it later. Maybe it won't even be a big deal."

Catharine broke her tree study and turned her attention to the two women discussing her life. Her love.

"I disagree," Sara countered. "It's going to affect the trial—you know the defense will use it. You have to tell Ryan. He can't get too angry. I mean, it has nothing to do with your relationship *now*."

Catharine nodded and wiped the remaining moisture from her eyes.

Lisa shook her head. "Sara, it was six years ago. The more she makes of the issue, the worse Ryan will take it. If she treats it like it's not a big deal, then it isn't. Listen, Cat, you've been under a lot of stress this week with the date this morning and the testimony. You should take it easy for a while. It'll all be over in twenty-four hours."

"Guess we agree to disagree, then," Sara said. "It's your decision to make, Catharine."

Perhaps the best decision, Catharine thought, was not to make one.

# CHAPTER 18

Mandy Ross

Shake It

The ride back from the airport was tense, to say the least. Ryan drove while Di Santo sat shotgun, trying to start a conversation with Mandy in the hopes of getting her to spill information without an attorney present. Mandy ignored Di Santo and pulled out her phone. She called her manager, Brooke, arranging for their luggage to be sent back to Chicago and delivered to the Westley Hotel.

When she completed her call, Mandy addressed them in

general. "Are you going to tell me what this is even about? I didn't kill Terrico, if that's what you're thinking. I was at the nightclub. Didn't you check that out? That's your job, isn't it?"

"Shut. Up." Ryan said, pinching the bridge of his nose, as a headache was threatening his temper.

"Are we going to the station?" Hank asked.

"We're dropping Matt and Mandy at the station. Then I'm taking you home."

Hank sulked silently in the back seat.

"So *Mandy!*" Di Santo turned around to face the girl. "The reason we picked you up is that we found Terrico's cell phone." The pop star didn't respond. "In fact, we got a printout of all his phone calls going back for months."

"So?" She said, sounding like a petulant five-year-old.

"So, it was very interesting information."

Ryan glanced briefly into the rear-view mirror, but couldn't get a fix on her face. He worried about Hank, how he would react to their little affair. But as he had told Cat, the boy wasn't a boy anymore. Heartbreak came with growing up.

"Yeah, what was so interesting about it?" she asked in a monotone.

"Well, think about it. We reviewed the time, date, and number of every phone call and every text that Terrico James made. Incoming, Outgoing. Lotsa outgoing."

Mandy remained silent. Hank looked interested, though, as he turned his attention from outside the window to what Di Santo was saying.

"Seems like there were quite a lot of texts to *you*, Mandy. Especially at night." Mandy huffed and looked out her passenger window, away from Hank. "What was *most* interesting," Di Santo continued, "is that we wondered how far back these calls and texts went, and they went way back—like two to three years. *Every night.* To Mandy Ross."

Ryan looked in the mirror again to gauge her reaction. And Hank's.

"So? We were planning the tour, so what," Mandy said.

"Planning the tour?" asked Di Santo. "At 10:30 every night? *For two years?*"

Hank looked at over at her and she snapped her head back in his direction. "What, Hank? You don't *own* me. I didn't even *know* you a week ago."

"Mandy, were you—"

"Fucking him? So what? I didn't kill him."

"Evvvvv-ery night," sang Di Santo. "And I can see you're so torn up about it. About Terrico's death, I mean. I don't think we've even seen you shed one tear."

Ryan felt bad for Hank, and a little guilty about how he had treated him at the airport, but he had to pull the cop card. The boy could have taken him in a minute, having three inches and thirty pounds on him.

"He was an idiot," Mandy spewed. "I just used him. I knew he had the hots for me from the beginning, so my mom told me to work it. And because I worked it, I got on his label, got him to produce my album, and got him to agree to tour together. Yeah, *I* had the idea to put us together and it was genius. The major cities sold out in three minutes. *Three minutes.*" She held up three fingers as if they would be impressed.

Ryan risked another look and saw that Hank was looking at the girl, shaking his head. She tried to take his hand but he pulled it away from her.

"Classy, Mandy, real classy," said Di Santo. "When we get to the station, you're going to tell us the truth this time, so don't plan on going anywhere soon. You know, we could charge you for obstructing justice. Impeding an investigation. Lying to the police."

Mandy threw them the bird along with a "BFD," and remained silent until they pulled in front of the 18th.

Ryan dropped off Mandy and Di Santo and told his partner to hold her in an interview room until he got back. He was going to drive Hank back to Cat's and then return. He'd already clocked the drive from the 18th to the Evanston estate at twenty-seven minutes, barring traffic.

Hank remained in the backseat, silent, for the length of the drive home. Ryan didn't push it. When they got to the Lulling house, Hank ran up to his room and slammed the door. Hearing their entrance, Catharine walked up to the vestibule to greet Ryan.

"What happened there?" she said.

"He found out his girlfriend was a skank. I guess it's best, in the long run. And we both knew it was inevitable." Catharine nodded and let out a sigh. "I'll tell you, that girl showed her true colors back there in the car—and they weren't pretty."

Catharine took Ryan's hand and tried to lead him to the atrium. "Can we talk?" she said.

"I can't, not now. I gotta get back to the station to question her."

"Oh, okay. But we do need to talk. My testimony is going to be played at the trial tomorrow—"

"Yeah, Jane just texted me. She said it will be tomorrow morning at nine a.m. sharp." He kissed her hand as a goodbye and turned to leave. "Don't worry, babe. I'll be there for the whole thing."

As soon as Ryan entered the 18th, Di Santo jumped up from his chair. "Mandy wised up and refused to talk without an attorney present," Di Santo said. "I put her in holding."

Ryan chuckled. "You put *Mandy Ross* in holding?"

"Don't worry, she's alone. Although it would have been fun to put her in with the hookers. Too bad we don't have any hookers today."

"How long do you think she'll stay in there before she gets someone to complain to the sarge?" Ryan looked over at Besko's office. The blinds were drawn.

"I've been thinking about this girl, D," Di Santo said, plopping back down into his chair. "The chick weighs ninety pounds soaking wet. If that. Do you really think she could've taken out Terrico James? He was pretty tall. And hoisting him up on that cross? Impossible."

"I don't really think she killed him, no, but she's been intimate with him for over two years, which she refused to disclose. So she knows more than she's saying."

"Gotcha."

While waiting for Mandy's attorney to show up and get her out of holding, Ryan checked in with the sarge and completed some paperwork. Finally, the pop star threw open the double doors to the squad room with attorney in tow. At least, he guessed it was her attorney, because the guy was in a full three-piece suit carrying a briefcase, but he looked to be about four days shy of twelve-years-old. He had maybe a half an inch on Di Santo and sported a thick head of strawberry-blond hair with matching freckles across his nose.

"I'm Miss Ross's attorney," the man-boy announced. "Where can we go to speak?"

Mandy's smug expression gave the impression that she had trumped them, but the game wasn't over yet. Ryan picked up the case folder while Di Santo adjusted his tie. They then led Mandy and her attorney back to Interview Room 3.

Before Ryan could close the door, Sergeant Besko appeared and introduced himself to the new visitors.

"Miss Ross, thank you for coming in," the sarge said. Di Santo scrunched his face at Ryan, questioning Besko's sudden hospitality. "I apologize for the inconvenience, and for detaining you. However, this is standard procedure. I hope you understand. We appreciate you stopping by to answer some quick questions about the deceased. It won't take much of your time."

Besko had a grandiose smile plastered on his face while he shook Mandy's hand vigorously. She cringed, pulled her hand from him, and wiped it on her jeans.

The sarge turned to Ryan and Di Santo. "Detectives, a minute outside?"

They followed their superior officer out into the hallway and Di Santo closed the door behind them.

"You guys stopped this girl from getting on a plane? And then put her in goddamned *holding?*" Besko didn't wait for an answer. "I get a call this morning from the mayor. The *mayor,* goddammit. Who gets a call from Arnold. Yeah, that Arnold. Apparently a friend of hers."

"What *kind* of friend?" quipped Di Santo. Ryan back-handed him on the arm.

"Look at her," Besko said, pointing to the two-way. "That Barbie doll didn't whack Terrico James. Why is she here?"

"Sarge, she lied to us. In the first interrogation she said she didn't know Terrico well. Now, she admits that they've been sleeping together since she was sixteen," Ryan said.

Besko's eyebrows went up to his hairline and then back down again. "But that was Terrico's crime, not hers. Statutory."

"She may have some inside information on him. On his friends. Who might want him dead."

"Tread lightly, boys. I don't want the Terminator comin' in here and kicking my ass. She's out of here in fifteen minutes!"

"Yes, Sarge," they said in unison.

The two detectives re-entered the interview room and the lawyer spoke up. "I was under the impression you had Terrico's brother in custody for his murder?"

"We have his brother in custody for a different matter," responded Ryan.

"Oh, so you still have no leads?"

"We're not at liberty to discuss the status of the case, Mr…"

"Denney. Craig Denney, with an E-Y. I'm with Pepper, Chase, and Brant."

Ryan noted it was the same law firm representing Todd

Elliot. They were one of the largest firms in the world, based out of DC, with a clientele ranging from heavy politicians to top celebs.

"Mr. Denney. We just have a few questions for your client," Di Santo said, leading them into the interview. "Miss Ross, you admitted to Detective Doherty and myself that you had an ongoing personal relationship with Terrico James."

"Yeah, so?" she answered. The attorney put a hand on her shoulder. "What?"

"Let me answer before you do," he coached her.

"Whatever."

"How long have you been—intimate—with Mr. James?"

Mandy leaned over to her counsel and whispered in his ear. He took a moment and then whispered an instruction back. She took in a breath and held it for a beat.

"A little over two years."

Di Santo frowned. "Two. Years. And how old are you, now?"

"Almost nineteen. I'll be nineteen in August."

"So you have been sleeping with Terrico James since you were—*sixteen*?"

Ryan remained silent, allowing Di Santo to play prosecuting attorney. It amused him.

"Gee, I guess so," Mandy snickered.

"And Terrence—Terrico James. How old was Mr. James at the time you two started sleeping together?"

"I dunno, twenty-two, twenty-three?"

Ryan looked down at the file in front of him. He saw that Terrico James was thirty at the time of his death. "Twenty-eight," he corrected her. "He was twenty eight and you were sixteen."

Mandy squinted at both of them. "Ooh, then why don't you *arrest* him?"

Her attorney dropped his gaze and thumbed notes into his phone. Ryan couldn't believe she was so heartless to be joking about Terrico's death—and her loss of innocence.

"What happens now, to the tour?" Di Santo said, ignoring her sarcasm.

"No final decisions have been made," answered the attorney. "But it's probable that the current tour will be canceled without the headliner. Miss Ross will most likely suffer a substantial financial loss from this whole situation. Terrico James was her patron—a major investor in her career. She will not benefit at all from the death of Terrico James."

Ryan wondered how long he had practiced that speech on the ride over. It was probably there on his phone, like a cheat sheet.

Ryan cleared his throat. "Seeing that you were so—familiar—with Mr. James, can you think of anyone in his immediate circle, or even a fan, maybe, who wanted to hurt him?"

Mandy got serious and stared down at the table. Her eyes darted around as if she was trying to recall something. "He did say he got hate mail, but he really didn't take it very seriously. You know, there were those cray-crays that would picket in front of his house. Out by the gate. Those Bible thumpers. They'd wave those signs at us every time we went past them."

"Do you remember their names?"

"No, I didn't stop to introduce myself," she sneered. "I tried to ignore them. But TJ wasn't scared of them. He kind of liked it, actually, because he said it brought him publicity. You know, being all controversial and shit. He just did it for the publicity. That's why I thought he was, you know, jacking my show. I thought he was doing it for the publicity."

"Other than the religious stuff, did he pull any other stunts for publicity?" Di Santo asked. "Something that may have offended anyone?"

"Well, in one of his shows, he was going to have his backup dancers in white hoods. Like that KKK, you know? Then he was going pretend to shoot them. But I think his crew talked him out of that whole scenario. That woulda been too much."

Di Santo typed on his tablet for a minute while Ryan closed his eyes tightly and shook his head to get that image out of his mind.

"Anything else you can think of?" he prompted.

"No. Talk to Kim. Kim Barnett, she might have more stories for you."

They heard a speaker crackle and their sarge's voice say, "Double-D, time's up!"

"That's all we need now, Mandy," Ryan said, then to the attorney. "Thank you for your time."

*"That's* what you got me off the plane for?"

The attorney put his hand on her arm and whispered into her ear. Mandy closed her mouth.

Denney spoke for her. "Thank you, detectives, for keeping it brief. Miss Ross is going to return to Los Angeles, and if you need anything else, you can contact me." The Howdy-Doody lawyer handed a card to each of them.

After Mandy and her attorney left the station, Ryan and Di Santo spent the remainder of the day poring through the reports from forensics and the research department.

Ryan read the report out loud to his partner, "The only discernable prints on the remote control for the cross belonged to Charles Epperson, who had handed it over to them. The back of the remote seemed to have been wiped down. They looked for epithelial cells, but there were none. The blood from the alley and the blanket from the alley ended up matching that of Terrence Robinson a.k.a. Terrico James. The Evidence Team also found a meth pipe in the dumpster, which tested positive for Reggie's and Terrico's prints, but that doesn't exactly prove they were both in the alley at that time. Nothing else pertaining to the victim or his brother. I want to talk with Terrico's security team," he said, slamming the report back down on his desk. "They're based here in Chicago. I can stop by tonight on the way home."

Di Santo nodded, then hit the speakerphone and speed-dialed someone. "Amy-Jo Slater," the woman on the other end announced.

"Hey, Amy-Jo!" Di Santo said, with a big grin on his face and in his voice. "I got a little something-something for you."

"I said I wouldn't go out with you, Di Santo."

"Not that something-something, another something-something. You know anyone at the tabloids?"

"A couple people, why?"

Ryan interjected. "What are you doing?"

"Maybe if the whole Terrico-Mandy thing gets out, she'll be a little more cooperative. Pressure her into giving us more information." Then into the phone, "Hey, AJ, meet me at the Black Bear in a half an hour. We can split the story fee."

"You're despicable. You just won't give up."

"Can't blame a guy—"

"Okay, but make it seven. And you're buying. And don't call me AJ." She disconnected.

Amused, Ryan shook his head as he prepared to go home for the day. "Good luck on your date tonight," Ryan said. "And make sure Finn gets the scoop, too, or I'll never hear the end of it."

# CHAPTER 19

Rather than love, than money,
than fame, give me truth.
~ *Henry David Thoreau*

Ryan had already called ahead to Celestial Security, and its managing partner agreed to stay after-hours to speak with him. The firm was located in one of the newer skyscrapers on Wabash Avenue and smelled of fresh carpet and high-end cologne. In the lobby, dark mahogany wood paneling was accentuated with blue neon pin lights.

Jordan Cartwright came out when he heard Ryan enter and greeted him with hearty handshake. Cartwright was a medium-skinned black man with piercing blue eyes, always a striking combination. Although the man wasn't suited up, his casual slacks and designer shirt exhibited a style of dress far above Ryan's budget. When he caught a glimpse of the man's watch, he almost proposed. "The emerald Oyster Perpetual Day-Date," he noted out loud.

"Oh, you like Rolexes?" Cartwright responded.

Ryan laughed. "Who doesn't?" Truth was, he had a thing for watches. All watches. But he dreamed of owning a piece like the Oyster someday.

Cartwright ushered him into a conference room overlooking the bustle of the Loop, and the top of the El tracks encircling it. It took almost an hour to go through Terrico's file, and Ryan was impressed at the level of investigation they conducted on anyone who had sent a suspicious e-mail, physical mail or gift to the celebrity. The firm had fully co-operated, giving him details on various religious groups and fanatics that they had investigated. Only one had plagued Terrico James regularly.

"The ODL," Cartwright said, presenting him with a dossier. "They seemed to pop up at every Terrico appearance. Concerts, airports, even at restaurants when he's with a lady or his friends. That's because TJ tended to tweet, instagram or check-in at every public establishment he visited. He loved it, but we constantly advised him not to be so 'social.' We told him that if he wanted to check in at a restaurant, do it when he was leaving so he wouldn't attract the stalkers. He never listened."

"What did you turn up on the ODL? Anything?" Ryan wanted to see if the security firm had a different take on the group.

"Tried speaking with the leader a couple of times. Even in person. Although he tried to be respectful, I found an undertone of hostility toward us. Toward blacks, in general. But they've never crossed the line. They know the law— they even have some big lawyer on retainer."

"Somebody Copeland the third?"

"Yeah, that's him. Southern fellow to the core. The ODL has caused some controversy, sure, but it seemed that's exactly what Terrico wanted. He liked controversy. Kept him in the headlines."

"Aside from the ODL was there anyone else on your radar? An over-obsessed fan or anyone from James's circle?" Ryan asked.

"I did a little investigating on two fans that we had an eye on." Cartwright handed Ryan two one-sheets, similar to what they had at the Department. "But they both were clearly not in Chicago at the time of the murder. First thing we checked. We've got local eyes on them, and they were both in their home states."

Ryan nodded as he reviewed the sheets. One woman from Maine and a man who changed his own name to Terrico, from L.A.

"Any of them own a white van?"

Cartwright searched through the records. "Sorry, no."

"Anyone else you can think of?" Ryan asked.

"We did have our eye on his brother, Reggie. He surfaced every now and then to ask TJ for money. Always broke, always a junkie. Reggie had some low-level connections to drug dealers and minor gangs, but very low-level. I don't think it was enough for them to lift a finger for him. His other brother, Chris, keeps him in line."

Ryan lifted his head. "Oh, you know Chris?"

"Yes, that's how we got Terrico's business. Chris works here part-time while he's finishing up his bachelor's at UI Circle. Great guy."

Ryan thanked the man for his time and apologized for such a late visit. By the time he left the security firm it was almost nine p.m. He decided to go sleep in his own bed in his apartment in Rogers Park, since it was closer to the courthouse for the morning's trial. He decided to call Di Santo on the drive home. When his partner picked up, he heard a loud television in the background and glasses clinking. Must still be at the Black Bear.

"Anything with the publicist?" Ryan asked.

"Yeah, Kim Barnett confirmed what Mandy said about the Klan fiasco. They even had the costumes on order. White hoods, can you believe it? She said she finally convinced Terrico not to do it—told him she would quit if the number got on stage. You don't think the real Klan got wind of it and decided to put an end to him?"

Ryan tried to visualize that musical number and shuddered, slightly. "How long ago was James thinking of doing this?"

"About a year ago, she said."

Ryan scrubbed his face with one hand. Too far back. "Anything else?"

"She mentioned the ODL. They wanted to do a joint press conference or a debate or something with Terrico. She told them no. That was last month, at the beginning of May."

"I feel like we're going in circles," Ryan said. "You coming to the courthouse tomorrow for Elliot's trial?"

"Yeah, I'll be there. I want to see them put that scumbag away!" Di Santo had had it in for Todd Elliot from the beginning of the Town Red case.

"Okay. Then after court we can question Reggie again. If he's the last person to see his brother alive, maybe he's remembered something more he can give us. And we need to ask him about that pipe."

"Okay, see you, D. Nine a.m. sharp."

Back at his apartment he tried calling and texting Catharine, but she was silent. Probably recovering from the Rose Garden outing. He kicked himself for taking her out of the estate, especially during the trial. She didn't need any more stress than she was already handling. He put it all away and fell down into his bed at 10:31 p.m.

A fly buzzed at his bedroom window, trapped between two panes as the bottom was lifted to let in the summer air. He chuckled, thinking about Ms. Mae clutching onto Terrence's memory to the point where she had anthropomorphized her housefly into her deceased son. The humor of the memory quickly faded. It wasn't that funny after all. He knew the pain of loss well. A pain so permanent that it always stayed with you in some form or another. How was Ms. Mae and the fly any different than he, himself, talking to the ghost of his partner who died two years ago? It wasn't.

"So why can't you just tell me who did it?" he called out to Jon. "Just tell me who killed Terrico James? You're up there, all knowing. Why can't you just feed me the info?"

He waited for an answer, but the room was silent with the exception of the intermittent buzz of the frustrated fly.

As he drifted off into that half-dream-half-lucid dream state, the image of the stage cross flashed across his psyche. But instead of Terrico, it was Jon hanging from it. Head hanging, blood dribbling from the thorns in the crown around his head.

With eyes closed and head still hanging, Jon spoke. "I'm not your savior. I don't know any more than you do. But you'll figure it out. You always do."

The image was disrupted by the rumble of the El, drowning out Jon, drowning out the fly, transporting Ryan into a deep, black sleep.

In the morning, Ryan put on one of the two suit jackets that he owned, a plain white button-down shirt, and his one navy-blue tie. He wanted to be prepared. Jane had told him there was a chance that he could be called to testify after they played Catharine's video.

Just as he reached courtroom number 46, he received a text from Di Santo, asking where he was. It was only 8:47 a.m. He wasn't late. He opened the double doors, spotted Di Santo seated in a middle bench on the right side of the courtroom, and took the spot next to him.

The bailiff began the court proceedings, ordering them to rise and be seated at the entrance of the judge. When Todd Elliot was escorted into the courtroom, Ryan studied the man from head to toe. He appeared to be just as much the executive that he used to be, complete with designer suit, expensive tie, and horn-rimmed glasses. The gray hair that had started to sprout on his temples in jail was now colored again and newly coiffed in a short, conservative cut.

The judge took a little over ten minutes to instruct the jury, delineate the charges, and explain how the day was going to proceed. He mentioned Catharine's video testimony and explained nothing about the witness except for the fact that she was not able to be present in the courtroom. He advised them to accept the testimony as if she were there, sitting on the witness stand. The jury members nodded and took preliminary notes.

Ryan leaned back on the gallery bench when he saw Catharine's image appear on the large flat-screen television placed just in front of the witness stand. Di Santo elbowed him with a smile, and he nodded back. She was just as beautiful on screen as she was in person. The courtroom hushed as they watched Catharine clear her throat and fidget in the chair waiting for the questioning to begin.

The first part of Catharine's testimony went well as Jane conducted her portion of the questioning. Catharine came across confident and sympathetic and answered the questions succinctly.

Ryan searched for Jane up at the prosecutorial table. She was poring through volumes of legal books, spread around her on the table, paying no attention to the video. Made sense—she had sat through it only a couple of days ago and had probably reviewed it several times prior to the trial.

Ryan's attention was drawn back to Cat's testimony when she said the word "rape." He threw a murderous look at the defense table. Brant leaned over to Elliot and whispered in his ear. Elliot nodded and they both turned back to the video.

Di Santo elbowed Ryan again when his name was mentioned in Catharine's testimony: "Detective Ryan Doherty of the Chicago Police." Ryan glanced around the courtroom to see if anyone there would know him, but he didn't recognize anyone other than the legal teams, and most of the spectators were thoroughly engrossed in the video.

The screen went blank after Jane's direct examination, and the court took a ten-minute recess. Todd Elliot and his attorney stood up and Elliot stretched.

Smiling, Victor Brant leaned over and said something to Elliot that made the both of them laugh.

"What the hell're they so happy about?" Di Santo said.

"I don't know, but I don't like it," Ryan responded and looked back over at the State's table. Jane was still seated, still flipping through the pages of the legal books. He decided to check in with her.

"Hey, Jane," he said, approaching her.

"Oh! Hi, Ryan." She took off her glasses as she looked up from her legal books. "I didn't see you here. Looking good. I don't ever think I've seen you in a suit."

Jane's assistant flashed him a smile he didn't expect.

"So it seems like it's going pretty well, don't you think?" he asked.

"I wouldn't speculate until the day's over. We've got to get through the cross-exam."

"Are you going to need me on the stand today?"

"Ummm…" Jane flipped through her notes. "Probably not. We're going to bring up the Evanston officers who were first on the scene, the two that arrested Elliot, and that will probably go the rest of the day. Probably tomorrow, though. I'll let you know for sure by the end of the day."

"Okay, good luck," Ryan said and turned to take his seat. As he passed the defense team, his eye caught Brant's and the attorney shot him a wide smile. He ignored it, walked back to the gallery, and sat back down next to his partner.

"What'd she say?" asked Di Santo.

"They won't need me today, but I want to see the rest of Cat's testimony."

"Yeah, of course!"

"All rise," announced the bailiff.

The judge took his seat and gave the official statement to the record and the jury that the trial was proceeding. Jane clicked a remote for the television and the video started up again. Catharine answered questions about working at Town Red Media, about why she left, and about Todd Elliot's ambition. She talked about Todd being competitive.

"Ms. Lulling, did you and Todd Elliot have an intimate relationship?" Brant's voice bellowed from the video.

Ryan snorted and threw Di Santo a smirk. But when Catharine didn't answer, his amusement turned to apprehension. He looked back at the video—at the image of her face on the screen. Her lack of an answer closed in on him like an anaconda.

"Ms. Lulling, did you hear the question?" Brant said from the screen.

"Yes."

"Yes you heard the question, or yes you had an intimate relationship?"

Ryan swore he'd heard Catharine murmur, "It was one night."

He denied it to himself until she said it again, more distinctly.

"One night. *Only* one night." Ryan's heart seized. "It didn't mean anything. I mean, we weren't a couple. We had a bottle of wine, and things just—happened. He asked to take me home. I said no. I got a cab. It was just that one night and I immediately regretted it—*Jane*?"

There was mumbling in the courtroom. Out of the corner of his eye, Ryan saw Di Santo stare him down. But he sat frozen, staring at Catharine's panic on the video.

"So that is a 'yes,' you had sexual relations with the defendant?" Victor Brant questioned, in a more jovial tone. Ryan glanced over at the attorney in the courtroom. Brant placed his hands behind his head and leaned back in his chair. This was not good.

"Yes," Catharine said on the video.

The dull ache in Ryan's stomach turned into a sharp pain. He looked down at his shoes and tuned out the entire courtroom and the video, trying to process what Catharine had just admitted. He tuned back in again when he heard her say, "…we drank. It was a mistake."

At that point Todd Elliot turned back, caught his eye, and mocked his surprise with a grin. Ryan was about to pounce when he felt Di Santo's hand on his shoulder, holding him back.

"D—" Di Santo warned.

Ryan jerked away, shaking off his partner. "Don't fucking touch me. And *don't* say a word." He stood up and left the courtroom.

# CHAPTER 20

At ten minutes after ten o'clock, Catharine got the call from Ryan that she had been expecting. She knew this wasn't going to be a good day for either of them. She walked to the center of the atrium and sat down in a chair before answering.

"Hello?"

"Cat, I'm coming over," he said. It was his official voice. His cop voice. Cold.

"Okay—"

He had already hung up. Catharine dropped her head and wept silently. After several minutes, she dabbed her eyes with a tissue and waited among her flowers and trees until she heard him at the door.

Ryan stormed down the atrium path, knowing exactly where to find her.

"*Why*? Why didn't you tell me?" he began.

She stood up for the confrontation. "I'm so sorry Ryan, I—I didn't think it would be brought up."

"You didn't *think*? What about *after* you gave your testimony? On Monday? What about all day yesterday? You *knew* I would see it in court this morning. You couldn't have told me? *Prepared* me?"

Catharine tried to embrace him, but he shook her off.

"I tried to tell you!" she whimpered. "I tried, but there wasn't a good time. Please, calm down."

"No! I don't accept that. Anytime would have been a good time. I tried calling you yesterday. You didn't respond. And how many times did we see each other in the last two days? You could have said 'Oh, by the way, Ryan, in my testimony that will be *broadcast to the public*, I admitted to the world that I f—'" He stopped the sentence by rubbing his mouth. "And *Elliot*? I mean, *God*, Cat!"

"It was six years ago, Ryan. I was a different person then. It was a completely different time. It was—a mistake." He shook his head and paced in front of her. "Sit down," she pleaded.

"No."

Feeling weak, she decided to take a seat, hoping it would calm him as well. "Ryan, I care deeply about you. You know I love you. I don't want this to get between us."

He kept shaking his head slowly, side to side. He wouldn't even make eye contact. "I just don't get it. Why didn't you just *tell* me?" he said, lowering his voice slightly. "We've been going out seven months. Seven months! All that time we talked about Town Red. Todd Elliot. The case. Not once did you mention you two had—"

"I was ashamed, Ryan. It's not me. Not me *now*, at least. I was newly divorced, lonely. And so I didn't tell you because I thought you'd think less of me. Remember when you came over that time for dinner? You propositioned me—after we had known each other for only two weeks. I told you it was important to me to be in love before—"

"Oh, I remember. You told me you wouldn't have sex until it was a 'spiritual union!' What a hypocrite. Where were your intimacy rules *then*? Was that *a spiritual union*, Cat, *was* it?" He glared at her, waiting for an answer.

"Why do you think I have those rules now?" She started to weep again. "I never wanted to feel that disgust ever again. That disgust with myself!" She didn't even bother to wipe the tears, anymore. There were too many. And she had deserved his wrath.

"Cat, I—I—just don't know what to do with this."

"Ryan, I'm not perfect. I'm a human being. Sometimes I think that you treat me like a fantasy. A china doll. Something you can take out every now and then for fun and then put away when you're done. When you have to go back home or go back to work. A perfect doll in a perfect dollhouse that's there for your amusement."

"I have *never* treated you like that!" he said, pointing directly at her.

"I'm *human*, Ryan, I make mistakes. I don't want to be that doll. I'm sorry that I can't be out there with you. In your 'real world.' I'm *sorry*. But I'm still human. I'm not *perfect*."

"Don't make this about you, Cat, and your affliction. You're not crippled. Nothing is stopping you from walking out that door." Ryan had a new look on his face, one she hadn't seen before. Instead of love and adoration, there was anger, judgment. "This is about the fact that I sat in that courtroom and Elliot laughed in my face because he knew he had *fucked* the woman I love. The woman I thought I could spend the rest of my life with. The woman who I thought had no secrets from me. But you did. He was laughing at me because *I didn't know*. Because you didn't have the decency to tell me."

She couldn't speak. There was nothing to say. He was right.

Ryan started to back up toward the front door, hands up in surrender. "You know what? I'm done," he said. "I just...need time. I gotta go." He turned and walked out of the atrium. Seconds later, the front door slammed.

And he was gone.

Ryan couldn't go back to the station in his state of mind, so he took a detour to the lakefront. He found a secluded spot on the beach, picked up some small stones and threw them as far as he could into the surf, one by one by one.

He thought about their confrontation, and the last fight they had before this one. It was about some kid who was coming onto her, and she wouldn't admit it to him. Another time she had withheld information. Lies of omission. How could he ever trust her again?

'*Dude, this can't be it. It can't be over,*' Jon said in his head.

"I don't know," Ryan answered aloud. "Not sure we can get past this. Not sure *I* can get past this."

'*You love her.*'

"I loved Kelly, too. And she left me."

'*Boo-hoo, grow up. People leave, relationships end. Are you going to let that ruin your whole life? So what—you're pushing Catharine away before she hurts you?*'

"She's already hurt me."

'*So at the first sign of trouble, you're out.*'

A jogger on the lakefront path slowed, eyes on Ryan. Probably wondering whom he was conversing with. Ryan put a finger to his ear pretending he had a Bluetooth headset in, and said, "Uh, yeah, nice talking with you. Bye."

The jogger took off, unimpressed.

Ryan climbed to the top of a large boulder at the edge of the lake and looked out over the horizon. "I just need time," he said, under his breath. The *swoosh* of the surf soothed his anger. He hurled several more stones into the oncoming waves and then sat down on a flat rock.

'*Was Catharine right? Are you idealizing her?*' Jon asked.

Ryan thought about the question while he hurled another rock. *Splat.* Maybe he had idolized her, put her on a pedestal. The great goddess had fallen.

His thoughts went back to the testimony and he couldn't help visualize Catharine and Elliot together. Was it his office or hers? Town Red's conference room? Did Elliot kiss her? Undress her? Ryan dropped his head into his hands and grabbed his hair so tightly his scalp started to ache. He lifted his head and gazed out at the surf for another four minutes and made the decision to shelve the pain. He was good at compartmentalizing life. Personal on one side, the job on the other.

He maneuvered his way off the boulder, jumped down onto the grass, and jogged back to his car.

"I'm done with this for a while," he explained to his built-in guardian angel. Or maybe it was to himself. At the car, he unknotted his tie, shed the dress shirt, and exchanged them for the spare CPD polo he kept in the trunk. He revved up the pony and floored his pain, back to the 18th.

There was no doubt the news had travelled fast in the department. When Ryan entered the squad room the usual unruly chatter quieted to a low buzz and he sensed the other detectives stealing sideways glances at him. Even Di Santo grew silent when Ryan took his chair on the opposite side of the desk set. Di Santo was never silent.

Ryan turned to his computer and after a couple of minutes of checking his email, the normal din of the squad room resurfaced. Di Santo filled him in on the remainder of Catharine's testimony: about the comparison of injuries that she and Elliot had sustained, and that she and Ryan were a couple. He closed his eyes and rubbed them, dreading his turn on the stand. He assumed he'd only have to talk about the attack and arrest, and now he had to put his personal life on public record. In addition to the shame of Catharine's indiscretion.

"I dunno, D. Bein' realistic, I'm not sure they're gonna nail him now," Di Santo said.

"But you think the jury believed her, right? About the attack?"

"Yeah, I think she came off sympathetic. She was really pretty, too. On the video."

Ryan blew out a breath and focused on his laptop keyboard, only because he had no clue where to go and what to do from here.

"Jane said to tell you you're up tomorrow first thing. She wants you to call her so she can prep you for your testimony."

Ryan stared at the phone for about ten seconds before he reached over and picked up the handset. As Jane's line was ringing, Di Santo said, "It was a long time ago, D."

Ryan closed his eyes to get the image out of his head.

"Jane Steffen," she answered.

"Hey, Jane. I hear I'm testifying tomorrow?"

"Yes. Matt said you didn't stay for the whole video. Sorry about that." He didn't know what she was sorry about, that he didn't stay or that Catharine was skewered by the defense. "You free for dinner tonight? We can go over your testimony."

"I'm not really in the mood—"

Jane paused for a moment. "So she hadn't told you?"

"I don't really want to talk about it, Jane."

"No prob. Let's meet at Buca di Beppo. After your shift. Buca's cheesecake can cure all ailments. Even of the heart." He chuckled, devoid of amusement. "Come on," she coaxed. "See you there at seven?"

"Okay, seven." He hung up.

"So there were a million prints up on that catwalk," Di Santo said, studying his partner's face. "Nothin' we can really use. *But* there were also prints on the equipment case. Two different individuals. We're running them through AFIS now."

"Yeah, okay." Ryan forced his mind back to the Terrico James case. His cell rang and he looked at the screen. Catharine. He pressed ignore.

"You talk to Cat?" Di Santo asked, guessing at the caller.

"Can I please have *one person* not up in my business to-day?" Ryan snapped.

Di Santo leaned back in his chair, hands up, in apology.

An officer with a county-jail uniform entered the squad room and announced, "Detectives R. Doherty and M. Di Santo?"

Ryan and Di Santo raised their hands.

"I got a delivery for you."

Reggie Robinson stepped out from behind the officer.

# CHAPTER 21

They escorted Reggie into the back and the guard followed. Di Santo told the guard to wait in the hall while Reggie got situated at the metal table in IR-2. The detectives took the two chairs across from him.

"What's up, Reggie? How're you doing? You eating?" Ryan asked. He didn't know why, but he felt some strange sort of compassion for this guy. That didn't happen very often with suspects.

"Yah man, got three squares up in there," he answered like a true veteran of the county-jail system.

"Good. We'll try to make it easy on you. Is there anyone working on your bail?"

"Well, Chris come in to see me yesterday," Reggie answered. "But I told him I ain't going nowhere."

"Why not?"

Reggie shifted in his chair, angled his head from side to side and said, "'Cause I have decided to tell the truth. Ya see, I did it. I killed TJ."

Ryan inhaled and leaned forward. "Reggie, do you understand what you're saying?"

"'Course I do. I said I did it. I—stabbed him. In that alley, like you said." He pantomimed a stabbing motion into the air. "And yeah, well, that was it."

The detectives glanced at each other. "But that wasn't it,

Reggie," Di Santo said. "Terrence's body wasn't discovered until a day later. What happened in those twenty-four hours? How did you get him up on that cross?"

The door to the interview room opened, interrupting the conversation.

"Gentlemen!" Detective Wyatt Fisk bellowed. "I'd like to be in on this interview, if I may."

Ryan clenched his jaw, aggravated that their momentum had been stopped cold. He waved the detective in. Fisk took a metal chair, turned it around and sat on it backward, with his stout thighs open.

"Okay, so Reggie," Di Santo continued. "We asked you what happened to Terrence from the time you killed him Friday night to the time he came down on that cross during the concert."

Fisk cleared his throat as if he was going to add to the question, but remained silent. Reggie glanced at all three detectives and then rolled his eyes upward, as if trying to remember.

"Um, I said I *stabbed* him. I didn't say I strung him up and shit. I didn't do all that business. No, sir."

Ryan's head was spinning. "Then who got the body to the arena and put him up on that cross?"

"I don't know, maybe those weird white dudes. They're always hangin' around us. You know those religious guys? Maybe they did all that. Wasn't me."

Fisk cleared his throat again, which started to irritate Ryan. He glared from Reggie to Fisk and back to Reggie again. The suspect's head twitched as his gaze bounced around the room.

"Can you excuse us for a second? We're going to step out," Ryan announced, jerking his head to his partner. "You too, Fisk."

When the three detectives had gathered in the hall, Ryan made sure the interview room door was closed.

"I'm not sure what to make of this. Let's bounce it off of the sarge."

"The guy said he did it," Fisk said. "What's not to make? Brother against brother is the oldest story in history. You know, Cain and Abel and all that? You just closed this red-ball case."

Ryan ignored Fisk and walked down the hall and into Besko's office.

"Yeah? What d'ya want? You identify the perp yet?" the sarge asked.

"Well, Sarge, that's just it," Ryan said, rubbing his chin. "Reggie Robinson just confessed."

"Excellent! We're done then! Oh hey, Fisk. Did you help our detectives here? If so, then good work."

Ryan bristled. Fisk had nothing to do with it, and the pieces weren't fitting. "Well—hold on, Sarge," he said. "It doesn't add up to me. Reggie said he killed his brother in that alley, but had nothing to do with the crucifixion. Said someone else did that."

"What doesn't add up? Sounds legit to me. You said we had his and Terrico James's prints on his meth pipe, so that puts both of them in the alley, right?"

"No, it just proves they both touched the pipe. You know that there is no timetable on prints."

"Well, it's enough for an arrest warrant—especially with a confession, D. You're running the prints on the equipment box, right?" Ryan nodded. "Maybe we'll get an ID on the second half of the crime, desecration of a corpse. Maybe Reggie did it, maybe not."

Fisk piped up, "I say he did the whole thing. He could'a been so pumped up on meth that he did that crazy crucifix thing too."

"Let's wait for the prints on the box," the sarge replied.

Fisk cleared his throat again, almost in protest. The sarge pulled open his desk drawer and offered him a Halls throat lozenge. He accepted. "I'll call for a warrant for Reggie's car to see if there's any evidence of a body being transported in the trunk. In the meantime, you guys go back in there and get him to give you a full statement. You just went from walking around with your heads up your asses to closing the Goddamned case! *Take it*!"

Wyatt Fisk was now making sucking noises on the lozenge, which bugged Ryan more than his throat clearing.

"We can take it from here, Fisk," he said, dismissing the man and giving the sarge a clear indicator that he wanted the detective out.

Luckily, Besko always backed him up and ordered Fisk to go get a warrant to impound the car.

For the next ninety-three minutes, the detectives questioned Reggie and had him explain—in detail—the circumstances from the time he met his brother at the hotel, to the confrontation and stabbing. Ryan pressed forward on the crucifixion, but Reggie stayed adamant that he had nothing to do with it. His story contained a few inconsistencies, changing slightly at each telling. At the end, they made him write it all down on paper and sign the statement. Sarge had ordered them to take the confession and Ryan had no choice but to do so, despite gut feelings.

After the guard escorted Reggie out of the squad room, Ryan called the state attorney's office to hand the case over to them. He spoke with George Demopoulos, one of the senior ASAs who was given the James case because of its celebrity status.

"Stan will love the confession, Ryan, you guys did a great job."

"Well, we're still waiting on more evidence. I hope it works out for you," Ryan said, still apprehensive about the unexpected case closure.

After he hung up, his focus remained on the large black phone unit for several minutes, studying the display, the numbers, the red hold button. He picked at his mouse pad and thought about the confession. Thought about the Elliot case. Thought about Mandy Ross and her Howdy-Doody attorney. Thought about his relationship. Had he and Catharine just broken up? Did he want to break up? Nothing made sense lately.

The universe had somehow completely reversed upon it-self.

He needed to get out. "I'm going to talk to the sarge, get off a little early," he informed Di Santo.

His partner approved with a wave.

Ryan poked his head in Besko's office and knocked on the open door. "Hey Sarge?"

The sergeant, wrapped up with something on his computer screen, greeted him silently with a wave to come in. When Ryan got closer, he saw his boss was engrossed in a game of solitaire. He decided not to mention that the red ten could go on the jack of clubs.

"So I was thinking…" Ryan began, leaning up against a filing cabinet. "We just closed the James case. And I've got to be in court tomorrow. I was wondering if I could take the rest of the day?"

Besko squinted at him, settled back in his chair, and crossed his arms in front of his wrestler's chest. No reply.

Ryan continued. "And then after I give my testimony, I'm glad to put in some overtime. Any hours you got, I'll take them. Help some of the other guys out with their cas-es—"

"Sit down, D," Besko interrupted.

Ryan knew that when the sarge asked a detective to sit down, someone was about to get a lecture. He decided to just suffer through it, because he desperately wanted the extra work time. He needed it so he didn't miss his personal time. So he could avoid being alone.

"D, I know you, don't I? How long have we known each other? Like twenty years?"

"Almost eighteen years. I was twenty-one."

"Twenty-one. You were a cocky little shit. Your sister, Erin? She was a sweet kid. Didn't deserve what happened to her, that's for sure."

Besko was a beat cop at the time that Erin had been date-raped on prom night. He was one of the first-responders to the 9-1-1 call.

Ryan was finishing up his junior year at U of I and decided to take the following semester off to help the family cope. He'd needed to step in as the man of the house since his dad's death a year earlier.

Distraught over the incident, Ryan had followed Besko around, pestering him until he agreed to let him help with his sister's case.

Later, the sarge put in a good word for him at the academy. "I always knew you'd make a good cop," the sarge continued. "Glad we put that scumbag football player away. How's Erin doin' now, anyways?"

"She's great. Lives in Phoenix now. Two kids."

"Good, good. So, extra hours, eh?" Besko rubbed his chin. "The last time you asked for extra hours was when that Irish girl broke your heart." Besko studied him with a frown. Ryan was about to argue that Kelly hadn't actually *broken* his heart, but thought better of it when the sarge continued. "Let me tell you something about women, may I?"

Ryan blinked his eyes to suppress a scream.

"All women come with baggage. Sometimes that baggage is good, like when the lady got a gazillion dollars, for example. And sometimes the baggage is not so good, like maybe she got some previous indiscretions. But you know what love is?"

Ryan closed one eye and jiggled a leg, awaiting the answer.

"Love is forgetting about the baggage and making your own. Your own memories, I mean, not baggage. Start fresh. You got it?"

"Yeah, Sarge, I got it." Ryan saluted. "Can I still have those extra hours?"

"For now. But be nice to your lady. Make up. Buy her some flowers."

"Okay, Sarge."

He would never do that. Catharine raised flowers and the boys instructed him once, and only once, to never buy her cut flowers. Cut flowers were dead flowers. Catharine likened them to "dead kittens."

"Now get out of my office," the sarge said.

And he did.

# CHAPTER 22

When Ryan eased the Mustang into the restaurant parking lot he spotted Jane leaning against the building, thumbing her cell. He pulled into an empty space to the left of her Lexus, got out, and put up the convertible top.

Jane slipped her phone into a purse pocket as she walked up to him. "You okay?" she asked, opening her arms for a hug.

"You know, I was thinking on the way over. Why didn't *you* tell me? It's bad enough I don't hear it from *her*, but you're my *friend*, Jane."

She took a step back. Her arms dropped to her sides. "Ryan, first of all, I had no idea she didn't tell you. How do I know what you've discussed with each other? And second, even if I *was* aware you didn't know, that's between the two of you. I don't go around gossiping about people's ex-lovers." Ryan cringed at the word. "It was none of my god-damned business."

He leaned back against the brick wall of the restaurant and raked his fingers through his hair. "God, it's so fucked up."

"It was a long time ago, Ryan—"

"Why does everyone keep saying that? It doesn't matter how long ago it was. The thought makes me nauseous.

Physically *sick.* That sleaze touching her—and he laughed at me in court. You didn't see it, Jane, but he turned and—like he *knew* they were springing it on me." Ryan pointed at a phantom defense table as if he were back in the court-room.

Jane pulled his arm down and kept hold of it, speaking deliberately. "We'll fix it. You'll go up on that stand tomorrow morning and act like you *did* know, and it doesn't faze you one bit. Don't let that creep get to you. That's exactly what they want."

Ryan softened at her touch. He closed his eyes and put his head back against the wall.

"Come on, let's go in," she said, tugging at his sleeve.

"No." He dropped his head, staring down at the black tar pavement of the parking lot like a petulant child.

Jane stepped up to him and angled her head. "Ryan—"

Without thinking, he wrapped his arms around her and pulled her in for a tight hug. The move pulled her off-balance, and she fell into him, her torso pressed up against his. Their "friendship" had always been tenuous, one on the brink of acknowledged attraction, and she had only agreed to be his friend if he respected that line. He wasn't sure if he wanted to at this point.

"Ryan, what the *hell*?" Jane cried out. She pushed off of him and righted herself.

"Sorry. It's just—"

"It's just *nothing*! Every time you have a fight with Catharine, you come on to me. That's bullshit. I thought we were friends." Ryan looked up at her under his bangs, trying to be adorable. It wasn't working. "Is that the kind of boyfriend you are? As soon as the going gets rough, you go out and get yourself another piece of ass?"

He chuckled at her accusation. "Jane, you're overreacting. And you're not a piece of ass. I mean—you *know* what I mean. I'm fucked up right now."

She shook her head and tucked her hair behind her ears. "Ew, I can't believe you. You're just as much a sleaze as Elliot."

That sobered him a bit. "Don't say that. Come on. Let's go eat," he said, pulling himself up off the wall. He jerked his head toward the front of the restaurant.

She was still seething. "Screw you. I don't even know why I become involved. You always find a way to piss me off. Stop playing with people's feelings."

"Jane. C'mon." He bowed to her. "Forgive me my indiscretion, my lady. Thou art hot. The end. Now let's go eat cheesecake and go over my testimony. Please, come on. I haven't been in a restaurant in months." He could tell she was softening a bit. "Cheeeeeeeese-cake..." He reached out to her.

"Keep your hands to yourself, or I'll call my BFF Catharine and tell her what her boyfriend does when she's locked up in her Barbie Dreamhouse." Jane turned and started walking briskly toward the entrance of the restaurant, Ryan jogging to keep up behind her.

"I thought you didn't tattle," he said.

"On *you*, I'll tattle," she said, and flashed him a sardonic smile. "I hate the woman but she likes me, and don't think I won't use that."

Before she could open the door, he reached for it and let her in, continuing his mock chivalry. He didn't think she liked Cat, but "hate" was a pretty harsh word.

After they were seated on opposite sides of a wooden booth, Jane pulled a thumb drive from her purse and placed it in on the table front of him.

"This is the video of Catharine's testimony," she explained. "You need to watch the rest of it before you go on the stand tomorrow. It will give you clues to the defense strategy, and insight into what Victor Brant may ask you."

"Okay." Ryan put the drive into his pocket and brooded at the thought of watching it again. He picked up the restaurant menu and propped it up on the table, creating a laminated wall between them.

"I've never cheated on her, for your information," he mumbled from behind the menu.

"Oooh, call the *Sun-Times*. How long have you been going out, six months?"

"Seven."

"Then good for you."

They both stopped talking to pick out their dinner choices. She reached over and pulled down the menu between them.

"What about the previous girlfriend? Didn't you have a long-time thing before Catharine?"

"I never cheated on her either," he said, closing his menu. "Although we were on-again-off-again. And when we were off— mean mutually, agreeably off—we saw other people. I want spaghetti and meatballs."

"Stop fucking up, then," she said, still reviewing her menu. "When I met her, I got it."

"Got what?"

"I got why you're all into her. She's a little skewed— with the agoraphobia and psychic stuff and all—but she has brought out the best in you."

"And you bring out the worst."

"Yeah, okay, Ryan, it's my fault," she said, then slapped her menu closed. After they ordered, Jane brought the conversation back to the trial. "So the first thing they'll probably ask you is if you were sleeping with Catharine at the time of the attack."

"Why?"

"Just for reference."

"I wasn't."

"Okay, then say so."

"We were just friends at the time."

"Friends, right," she said, pursing her lips. "Well, I might just ask you about your relationship in direct exam to get it out of the way. Dispel any hint of impropriety in it."

"Impropriety?"

"They can make it look any way they want, Ryan. A cop and a suspect? A suspect turned victim—"

"Well, there was no *impropriety*, so I'm not worried about that." He took a drag of his root beer as if it were real beer. He wished it was.

"I'm not the one you have to convince. They'll also try to make it look like Catharine *invited* Todd into her home, like it was a friendly situation that got out of hand. Make it look like Todd was the victim and Catharine lied because she didn't want you to know."

"Son of a—" Both of his hands went into fists and she covered one with her hand.

"You *can't* freak out. They're going to push your buttons. Brant will do his best to trip you up. Get you angry. Make you and Catharine and her dogs look like the bad guys. I want you to remain calm, cool, and completely cooperative on that stand. You understand me?"

"Sure," he said. His hand relaxed, and he laced his fingers in hers. "Thanks. Not many prosecutors would be doing this for their witnesses. Your friendship means a lot to me. I won't fuck it up."

A girl who was not their waitress came and deposited the plates of food in front of them.

"Careful, hot plate," the girl said to Ryan, flashing him a wide smile. He ignored the waitress and pulled his hand from Jane's. "How 'bout I find another cop for you to date?" Ryan said, in between bites.

"Yeah, no thank you," Jane said, forking her salad in the humongous bowl.

He never understood why people ordered salads in a restaurant. They were way overpriced and didn't fill you up at all.

"I don't need you to play matchmaker, Ryan. I do okay on my own, believe it or not."

"Are you seeing someone?" he said, a meatball halfway to his mouth.

"I'm seeing several someones, actually. No one serious."

"Who?"

"No one you know."

"Oooh, online dating."

"No!"

"Yeah." He laughed. "You wouldn't dare date anyone in the SA's office. You're too worried about your rep. So that leaves either bars or online."

"Neither. Friends of friends."

"See? Friends of friends, that's what I'm saying. I can set you up."

"You mean *hook* me up. I'm not dating a cop."

"Once you go blue—"

"Shut up, Ryan, and eat your meatballs."

He chuckled. After a few moments of silence as they enjoyed their meal, he said, "Hey wait a second. You said that their theory is that Cat and the scumbag were seeing each other and so she invited him into her house, right? But I have evidence that clearly disproves that."

He waved his fork at her. Jane dodged the drops of marinara sauce flying off of it.

"What evidence?" she said.

"During the Town Red investigation I had Catharine's LUDs pulled for six months prior to the murders. I wanted to see if she had any contact with the Reddings or anyone over at Town Red. She didn't."

"So you're saying there were no calls between Catharine and Todd for six months up and until the attack?" Jane asked. Her face lit up at the new evidence.

"Yep."

"You checked work, cell, home—"

"Cross-referenced all numbers," he said, nodding.

"Then they couldn't have been seeing each other!" Jane said, a wide smile forming on her face. "Can you send that report to me before tomorrow? I'll get it into evidence."

"Yeah, I think I still have it on my laptop. If not, it's on the server in the Town Red folder. I'll email it to you."

She held her hand up for a high-five and he obliged. "I think we'll do okay, Ryan. Just get a good night's sleep and no alcohol tonight."

He agreed. After they finished their dinner and shared a gargantuan chunk of cheesecake, Jane said her goodbye without a hug and peeled out of the parking lot.

Ryan pulled out his phone and texted her:

*– Don't drive so fast. And stop texting while driving.*

He heard a double-honk a couple of blocks away. Clearly an "FU" from afar.

Back at his apartment, Ryan pulled out his laptop from the case and placed it on the coffee table. Before he settled in, he logged into the PD's server, opened his file from the Town Red case, and found the Local Usage Detail report he had run on Catharine's phone lines.

After emailing the report to Jane, he went to the fridge and took out a Goose Island. Recalling her directive, he placed it back in the fridge and grabbed a San Pellegrino instead.

He unscrewed the top, took several gulps of the cool carbonated water, and pulled the thumb drive from his pocket, trying to decide whether he should even watch the video. Maybe he could wing the testimony without it. No, he had to know everything he was up against. He needed Todd Elliot to go down. He inserted the drive into the laptop. He opened the folder and double-clicked on the video file.

When the video player launched, a still image of Catharine's face appeared with a large play button superimposed on it. He studied her expression—composed, with a hint of fear—while he replayed their relationship in his mind. He thought he had found his other half. As soon as they had met, they connected on such a level he felt like they had known each other for years. Decades. The betrayal cut deep.

He quickly clicked the mouse and the video started. Catharine cleared her throat and fidgeted. Unlike the first time, as he watched her prepare for her testimony, he didn't reflect on her beauty. This time he knew what was coming, and it killed him. He let it run, tolerating the first half again just to see her speak, hear her voice, see if she appeared different to him. He wanted her to be pure, virginal, to be his alone. Even knowing Cat had been married, bore two sons, and divorced—somehow he had imagined that she hadn't been with anyone but him. When they came together, it felt like they really did have an "extraordinary union," as Catharine put it. That image had since been shattered, like a glass house pummeled by thousands of stones.

"Victor Brant representing Todd Elliot." His attention went back to the video. He pressed fast-forward.

"...wanted more time with my children. I have two boys..."

Forward.

"Ms. Lulling, did you and Todd Elliot have an intimate relationship?"

This was it. The question sounded different this time around—it had lost its absurdity now that Ryan knew the answer.

"Ms. Lulling, did you hear the question?"

"Yes."

"Yes you heard the question, or yes you had an intimate relationship?"

"It was one night," she mumbled. A pause.

"I didn't hear you," said a female voice off-screen. Probably the court reporter.

"One night," Catharine spoke up. "*Only* one night. It didn't mean anything. I mean, we weren't a couple. We had a bottle of wine, and things just—happened. He asked to take me home. I said no. I got a cab. It was just that one night and I immediately regretted it—*Jane?*"

He tried to remain neutral while he watched the testimony for the second time, but it still pained him. Her voice, pleading, panicked. The image of the two of them together. Elliot's triumphant grin in the courtroom. Ryan took a deep breath and forced himself to turn his attention back to the video. Catharine's expression had changed from soft to hard in a matter of seconds. She glanced to the right of the camera, her chin up.

He recognized the falsity of her composure. It was the hint of fear in her eyes—the same fear he had seen in the Rose Garden.

"So that is a 'yes,' you had sexual relations with the defendant?"

Catharine closed her eyes and opened them before answering. The irises so light blue, they looked almost white. "Yes," she replied.

This was where Ryan had tuned out the first time, so he upped the volume and leaned closer to the computer.

Victor Brant asked, "So you and the defendant had an intimate relationship. How could that happen, since you two were so-called 'adversaries'?"

Catharine wet her lips before responding. Lips that he could taste, even now, her kisses so engrained in his psyche. "We were working late. We were alone. We drank. It was a mistake. Like I said, it only happened once. Never again."

Ryan fidgeted in his chair.

"So considering this new evidence: that you had sexual relations with the defendant..." Brant said on the video. He saw Catharine cringe, maybe not perceptibly to others, but he could see it. "How do we know that he was *really* about to rape you? Maybe he was just picking up where you two left off!"

"Objection!" Ryan said aloud, in synch with Jane's on the video.

"Withdrawn." Brant took a beat. "Ms. Lulling, I'm sorry, but we have to ask. Did you want Todd Elliot to come into your home?"

"No."

"Did you *invite* him into your home? Maybe you wanted

to continue the—intimate relationship—that you had started several years earlier?"

"No!"

"And maybe when your boyfriend showed up you *panicked*?"

"*No*! That's not how it was! Ryan wasn't—"

"You had to give him a story. A story why you and Todd were going at it in the atrium."

"He *attacked* me! In my *home*! How can you say that?"

This was not good. For Catharine or the trial. She had lost control.

"What is your relationship with Detective Ryan Doherty?"

Ryan held his breath.

Catharine leaned back in the chair. "Excuse me?"

"You heard me. Are you intimately involved with Detective Ryan Doherty of the Chicago Police Department?"

"Objection. Relevance."

Ryan blew out the breath he had been holding. Jane was on her toes, at least. He knew he could trust her.

Brant explained to the judge, "This goes to show that she may have altered her story for the detective's benefit."

"I'll allow it," Judge Geithner's voice said from a distance.

Catharine looked to another spot to the right of the camera and shook her head. She must be looking at Jane, he thought.

"Detective Doherty and I are seeing each other. Now."

"You are seeing each other *romantically*?"

"Yes."

"Ms. Lulling, did Todd Elliot attack you or is that the story you told the detective because you didn't want to tell him the truth? That you and Todd were having an affair?"

"We weren't having an affair. He attacked me. That was the truth. That *is* the truth."

"Okay, so you say."

Ryan hated Brant. Almost as much as he hated Elliot. He

was glad he had decided to finish watching the testimony. He was going to give the man hell in court tomorrow.

"Ms. Lulling, what was the exact extent of your injuries? When your head hit that rock, did you bleed?"

"No, I just had a bump."

"You said that Mr. Elliot pulled your hair. You have beautiful hair, by the way."

Ryan's fist clenched, his jaw tightened. That sonofa-bitch—

"Did he pull any of it out?"

"No, not that I remember."

"No, what?"

"No, he didn't pull out any of my hair."

"And what were the extent of Todd's injuries? Do you remember?"

"My dogs bit him on the neck and on the shoulder. He got stitches, I believe."

"Do you recall that Todd got a total of one hundred and twenty stitches from the dogs tearing at his flesh?"

"I didn't know that, but okay," she said. Catharine appeared to have regained her composure again.

"So *you* had a bump on the head and *Mr. Elliot* was shocked with a deadly weapon *and* had his neck torn apart by vicious dogs. Who, exactly, is the victim here, Ms. Lulling?"

"Objection!"

Good girl, Jane.

"Withdrawn," Brant said. "No more questions. Thank you, Ms. Lulling."

"Ms. Steffen, any redirect?" Judge Geithner's voice asked.

"No redirect, your honor."

"This concludes the testimony…"

The video faded to black and then reset on Catharine's image with the big play button superimposed on it. Ryan stared at the computer screen for several minutes, almost looking through it. Coming out of his daze, he picked up the bottle of water and chucked it against the wall, as hard as he could. The plastic bottle cracked as the carbonated water hissed like a snake down the wall.

Catharine. Jane. He couldn't even think anymore. He felt like a shell with no soul. Closing his eyes, he decided to retire for the night, hoping to sleep off this day from hell.

# CHAPTER 23

The squad room erupted in whistles and catcalls when Ryan walked in on Thursday morning wearing khaki pants, a navy-blue blazer, a crisp new dress shirt, and his one tie. He held his hand up, nodded, acknowledging the attention, and fell into his desk chair.

"Who died?" Jaworski called from the far side of the room.

"Your dick. At least that's what your wife told me," Ryan answered, in true squad room fashion.

"Ohhhhhh!" echoed the sentiment from the mass of detectives.

"Lookin' pretty spiffy there," Di Santo complimented.

"Thanks, D."

"You watch the video of Cat's testimony?"

"Yeah. It wasn't as bad as I expected. Jane and I went over what I should say on the stand and I think I'm ready. Leave in fifteen minutes?"

"Sure. Hey, check out Finfamous.com—Amy-Jo got a hold of your sister and they got a story up!" Ryan brought up his sister's blog on the screen.

"TERRICO AND MANDY!" the home page shouted with a badly cropped photo of the two artists promoting their tour. She was kissing him on the cheek and he looked physically dragged down by a mammoth gold necklace in the form of his own logo. Ryan scanned the story, which was all speculation, but exactly what they wanted.

"Reputable sources—didja read that? That's *me*! I'm a reputable source," Di Santo said with a grin.

Ryan read, "Reputable sources—ha!—have confirmed that Terrico James and Mandy Ross had been on-again/off-again for the past two years, up until his death. Friends of the couple say they met at Mandy's sixteenth birthday party at Sunset Studios. Blah, blah, blah, crucifixion."

Di Santo interrupted, "Oh, Fisk got the warrant for Reggie's car. It's now been impounded and the techs are going over it today. I put a copy on your desk. He pointed to one of the three piles of folders and papers on Ryan's desk. Someday he'd become paperless. Just not now. "But I got some bigger news for you!"

"What."

"The fingerprints came back on the equipment case. Our friend from Atlanta. Warren—L—Smith! Sarge is trying to coordinate an arrest warrant with Atlanta PD for desecration of a corpse. He'll need to be brought back to Illinois. Second set of prints, unidentified, but I'd bet my ass it was one of his creepy-ass followers."

"That is good news. How long will it take to get anything from Reggie's car? I'd like a little more evidence against the man than his half-assed confession. It still doesn't make sense to me. Why would you kill someone—your brother, for god's sake—right after he tells you he's going to make you rich? Part of the story is missing."

"Maybe he didn't want to go into rehab. Or maybe he needed a fix right then and there and Terrico wouldn't give him money. You know the fall from meth is dangerous. He could've been in quick withdrawal."

"Time to book him, I guess." Ryan felt uneasy about wrapping up the case with Reggie as the perp.

It was too simple, too quick, with too many open questions. He always went by the "Occam's Razor" rule: the simplest solution is usually the correct one. "*Scientists must use the simplest means of arriving at their results and ex-clude everything not perceived by the senses."*

But since he'd met Catharine, Ryan had come to rely more on his senses and intuition. The brain fired more neurons and kept more memories than people realized. But whether it was physical or metaphysical, conscious or unconscious, Ryan believed that when your gut told you something was wrong, you listened. In the department they called it "cop instinct." He decided to shelve it for now and concentrate on the trial and his testimony, which was going to start in exactly forty-two minutes.

Catharine checked the clock on her computer screen. She knew the trial was commencing in a couple of minutes and that Ryan was slated to give his testimony first. Since their fight she had tried calling him, but he wouldn't pick up. The situation made her despondent, tearful. She didn't know if their relationship would ever be the same or if he'd ever come back. If this hadn't had happened—if she had just told him about Todd prior to the testimony—everything would have been fine. She would be calling him right now and wishing him luck, encouraging him, telling him he was the strongest man she had ever met. Telling him that she loved him.

In desperation, she picked up her cell phone and decided to call Matthew.

"Heeeey, Cat." he answered. "I'll be right in," he called to someone else. And then back to her, "What's up?"

"Hi, Matthew."

"Hi, howsit going?"

"Is he testifying today?"

"Yep, in about ten minutes. We're already here at the courthouse."

She took a breath. "He won't talk to me."

She heard some footsteps, then Di Santo spoke in a hushed tone. "Cat—"

"Hmm?"

"You're my friend. You know I adore you. But Ry, he's my partner. I gotta support *him*."

"I'm not asking you to choose sides, Matthew."

"I know. But if you were? I'm telling you now which one I'd be on. I can't get in the middle of this." His voice was tender but firm, as if lecturing to a child.

"I just wanted to tell him good luck."

"I'll pass that along. If he lets me."

"Okay, I understand," she said. "It was unfair of me to call. I apologize."

"It'll work out, Cat. Just give him some space. I know that he loves you very much. He's not going to throw it all away."

She nodded, as if he could see her. "Goodbye, Matthew."

Her heart was heavy as she ended the call.

When Ryan entered the courtroom he saw that Todd Elliot was already at the defense table with his attorney, both in suits straight out of GQ. Jane sat at the State's table, confabbing with someone from her office. When she saw Ryan, she waved him over to the right-side gallery, as the prosecution was always on the side closest to the jury.

"Hi, you ready?" Jane asked.

She was in pluperfect form, every hair in place, business suit fitting her like a high-priced attorney from a multi-named firm. At least it wasn't one of her usual over-sized beige numbers.

"Yes. I watched the rest of the video last night. That helped, thanks."

She looked squarely in his eyes. "Good. Let's get them."

They slapped hands and Ryan turned around to find his

partner entering the courtroom, closing a call on his cell. He waved Di Santo over to their seats and scanned the courtroom. There weren't as many spectators as there were the day before—the scheduled testimony was not quite as riveting as the actual victim's.

"'Zat the sarge?" Ryan asked, nodding his head toward Di Santo's phone.

His partner shook his head and keyed his phone to silent. Ryan took out his phone and did the same.

After the bailiff ordered everyone to rise, Judge Geithner made his entrance from the left of the podium and took his seat at the helm of the courtroom. He put on a pair of bottle-bottom eyeglasses and pulled some papers down in front of him. The jurors came in and took their seats in the jury box, and the court reporter adjusted her chair.

Victor Brant rocked forward and back in his chair as if he were preparing for a 40-yard sprint. The judge gave the jury admonition and then nodded to Jane, handing the trial to the state.

"The state calls Detective Ryan Doherty of the Chicago Police Department," she announced, standing from her chair.

She looked back at him and watched while he buttoned his jacket and approached the bailiff. Ryan took his oath on the Bible and settled into the leather chair on the witness stand. Jane had told him to have his badge showing, so he hung it from his breast pocket, which he had never done before in his life. Too ostentatious. He scanned the faces in the jury box, throwing his winning Irish grin at the group.

The beginning of the direct examination was pretty straightforward. Jane established who he was and how long he had been on the force and asked for a brief description of the morning in question. Ryan hadn't really witnessed much: Catharine's escape from her home and the two officers leading Todd Elliot from the premises.

But then Jane went down a new path. One that they had not discussed, but a brilliant strategy. With her smarts, they had a good chance of winning this thing.

"Detective, that morning—the morning of the attack—you had just learned that Mr. Elliot had been released from jail, correct?"

"Yes, that is correct."

"And did you fear that Mr. Elliot would be a threat to Catharine Lulling?"

"Objection," Brant said, half standing. "Leading."

The judge thought for a moment. "Sustained. Counselor, be careful with your questions, please."

Jane held up a hand in contrition. "I'll rephrase. Detective Doherty, when you heard Mr. Elliot was released from jail, what was your reaction?"

Ryan almost laughed. Jane was good. She had just instructed him how to answer with a faux faux-pas. "I felt Mr. Elliot was a clear danger to Ms. Lulling," he said, keeping a straight face.

Jane was satisfied with the answer. "And what was it that made you think that Mr. Elliot would be a threat to her?"

"A week prior to the attack, my partner and I were called to the county jail. We had been summoned by the defendant, who told us he had information on the murders of his employers, Carly and Scott Redding. We thought he might have been offering up a confession, so we went to County—to the Cook County Jail—to talk with him. Mr. Elliot."

Jane stopped right in front of the jury box. "And how did the defendant appear to you at that time?"

"He was disheveled and incoherent and was saying some pretty wacky stuff."

Jane turned back to him as if he'd said something unexpectedly interesting. "Wacky stuff? What wacky stuff?"

"He said that Catharine—Ms. Lulling—had come to his cell the previous night in the middle of the night and threatened him. He also said that she had murdered Scott and Carly Redding with her mind." He smirked and shook his head at the jury.

"With her mind?" Jane leaned back, feigning surprise.

"Yes."

Jane chuckled and several members of the jury laughed along with her.

"Wow. Okay, and *had* Catharine visited him in the jail?"

"No," Ryan said, smiling along with the jury. "We reviewed the sign-in logs at the jail, interviewed the guards, and verified it on their security video. She had not visited at any time during his incarceration."

He thought back to the real reason he had known Catharine wasn't there—she had been with him in bed that night. But luckily, he had covered himself by verifying with the county jail's logs.

"So his state of mind led you to believe that, when he was released, he might be violent and go after Catharine Lulling?"

The judge interrupted. "Ms. Steffen…"

"Sorry. So, judging from his erratic behavior in jail, you said you feared for Ms. Lulling's safety?"

"Yes, we both did. My partner, Detective Matt Di Santo, and I were both concerned for Cat—Ms. Lulling's welfare. We believed that Elliot could definitely commit a violent act."

"Objection, conjecture," Brant said, raising up a few inches from the chair and then down again.

"Sustained," the judge answered. "Detective, please only speak for yourself."

"I'm sorry. I was convinced, from the conversation with Mr. Elliot, that he would be a threat to Ms. Lulling."

Jane nodded. Her eyes lit up with excitement when she was performing in court. She was in top form. "So after speaking with Mr. Elliot in the jail, and hearing his statements about Catharine Lulling, how would you have characterized his mental state?"

"Objection," interrupted Brant again. "The detective is

not qualified as a mental professional to make that diagnosis."

"Sustained. Proceed with opinion only," Geithner ruled.

Jane prompted him, "In your *opinion*, Detective Doherty, from your sixteen years of experience on the police force, did Todd Elliot appear to you to be of sound mind?"

"No, he appeared to be out of it. Delusional." He looked Todd Elliot straight in the eyes. "In my *opinion*," he tagged on, with a smirk to the jury box.

Every one of the twelve jury members studied Todd Elliot.

"And what was your relationship with Catharine Lulling at the time of the alleged attack?" Jane asked bluntly. She was getting the issue out of the way, like she told him she would, the night before.

"We were friends."

"*Just* friends?"

"Yes."

"Catharine Lulling testified on her video that you and she are currently in a relationship."

"That is correct." In truth, he didn't really know where it stood, but for the sake of the trial he knew he hadn't perjured himself with that answer.

"But at the time of the attack, you were just friends?"

"Just friends."

Todd Elliot made some sound of disbelief, causing Brant to put a hand on his client's shoulder. Ryan almost flipped him the bird.

Jane went back to her notes. "Detective, you heard in the testimony of Catharine Lulling—you heard Mr. Brant put forth the theory that perhaps Ms. Lulling was having a relationship with Mr. Elliot at the time of the attack and had invited him into her home."

"Yes, I heard that." His fists clenched involuntarily, although his expression remained stoic.

"Do you believe that to be true?"

"No."

"Why not, Detective?" Perfect setup.

"Because we had run Ms. Lulling's telephone records. To eliminate her as a suspect for the homicide of her employers, Scott and Carly Redding, we ran her home phone and cell phone records six months back. We then cross-referenced her incoming and outgoing calls and texts to Town Red Media, and the home and cell phones of Scott Redding, Carly Redding, and—Todd Elliot."

Victor Brant's head whipped up. They'd grabbed his attention. Jane strode over to her table, picked up a stack of papers, and walked them to the witness stand.

"Is this the telephone record report you ran, Detective?"

Ryan looked through the pages and then leaned forward to the microphone. "Yes, this is it."

"I'd like to enter the police department's Line Usage Detail Report of Catharine Lulling's phone records into evidence as Exhibit D, your honor."

"Objection!" cried Brant. "These were not shared with the defense prior to testimony."

"They don't need to be, your honor," responded Jane. "It doesn't go toward culpability or sentencing. Just to disprove their defense theory."

"She's right. Overruled," the judge explained. "You brought up the theory, Mr. Brant, so they have the right to disprove it. The court accepts Exhibit D, report of Catharine Lulling's phone records, submitted by the prosecution."

Relieved that they'd gotten the records into evidence, Ryan inhaled deeply and relaxed back in the witness chair.

Jane continued her questioning. "And what was your conclusion from this report, Detective?"

"That there were not any incoming or outgoing calls or texts on Catharine Lulling's lines to or from Todd Elliot for the six months prior to the homicides on October eleventh."

"You stated previously that you and Catharine Lulling are now in a romantic relationship."

"Yes."

"And how many times a day would you say you call or text Ms. Lulling now?"

"Me?" He thought for several seconds. "Um, two, three times a day, maybe more."

Until yesterday.

"And how many times a day does she call or text you?"

"About the same: many more texts, maybe one or two calls a day."

"With that in mind, Detective, would it be possible for two people in a relationship to have *no* calls or text messages to each other whatsoever? In six months?"

"In my opinion, no. That would be impossible."

"Thank you, Detective. No more questions."

There was an audible group exhale in the courtroom as Jane sat down. After a moment, Victor Brant stood up and buttoned his suit jacket. Ryan glanced at Di Santo in the gallery who gave him a thumbs-up. He responded with a half-smile, sitting up straighter and slightly forward in his seat, preparing for the cross-examination.

# CHAPTER 24

"Good morning, Detective," began the defense attorney.

"Good morning, Mr. Brant," Ryan answered, maintaining direct eye contact.

"Thank you for taking time in your busy schedule to be here today."

"Thank you for having me," Ryan said and flashed another smile at Brant and at the jury. One older female jury member smiled back.

"Detective, you just stated that you and Catharine Lulling are in a relationship," he asked, more as a statement.

"Yes."

"A romantic relationship?"

"Yes."

"Are you *in love* with Catharine Lulling?"

The question caught him off guard, and he knew, immediately, that it was Brant's full intention to do so. He looked at Jane to see if she was going to object, but she was staring down at a yellow legal pad. He slowly leaned forward so his lips were millimeters away from the microphone.

Taking a short breath, he said, "I am."

*Ohhhhs* and *awwws* erupted in the courtroom. Di Santo grinned. Jane's eyes remained on her notes, her left hand rubbing her forehead, shading her eyes.

"So, Detective, this case is personal to you. It's about defending the honor of the woman—you—love."

"I'm here as an official law enforcement officer of the County of Cook. We are duly sworn to uphold the laws of the city, the county, and the State of Illinois."

"Yes, I'm sure you are. But this man," he said, pointing to the defendant, "is accused of the attempted rape of Catharine Lulling, the woman you love. Surely, there's a personal motivation for you to perhaps *stretch the truth* in order to get him convicted?"

"Objection!" Jane was on her feet before she finished the word.

"Sustained," said the judge. "Mr. Brant, the detective is an officer of the law and he is *not* on trial here. Change your line of questioning. *Now.*"

"Yes, your honor." Brant took some time and flipped through a small spiral notebook. He walked over to the jury box to ask his next question.

"Detective, is Catharine Lulling under psychiatric care?"

Ryan clenched his jaw and was about to object himself when Jane jumped up again.

"Sidebar, your honor," she requested.

The judge waved the two attorneys in and the court reporter rolled her stenograph machine over to the huddle. The judge turned off his microphone. Ryan dropped his head, pretending not to listen but straining his hardest to try to hear the conversation six feet to his left. He heard Jane's spitting words, and Brant's fluid confidence.

"...put it out there, let him answer, and that's it," Jane said, a little louder. She was instructing Ryan indirectly, and he caught it without looking at her.

"Okay," said the judge as the attorneys walked back to their respective tables. "The detective will answer the question, and then Mr. Brant must end the line of questioning. Mr. Brant, repeat the question."

"Thank you, Your Honor. I asked, Detective, if Ms. Lulling is under psychiatric care?"

Ryan looked at Jane while he answered. "No, she is not."

That was the truth. Catharine was not seeing a *psychiatrist* for her agoraphobia. Her therapist, Sandra Lampe, had a Ph.D. in holistic medicine. Since Brant was allowed only one question on the subject, it was closed. The defense attorney turned his back on the witness stand and looked at the jury as he asked the next question.

"Detective, what is Catharine Lulling's current occupation?"

Ryan leaned back in the witness chair, squinting, trying to determine how to put it without it sounding damning. "She's a consultant."

"A *consultant*," Brant said, spinning around to face him. "That's pretty vague. Can you elaborate, please?"

Ryan swallowed. "She consults privately, with people and organizations, such as the Police Department, to..."

"To what, Detective?"

Ryan held his chin up. "She's a psychic—"

"A *psychic*!" Brant exclaimed as if he'd heard it for the first time. He turned to the jury box with feigned surprise.

"Yes. A psychic empath. That means she helps people clear their pain—physical or emotional."

"So, a psychic *healer*?"

"I guess you could say that. And she can also find things."

"Find things? Like what?"

"Like lost pets, items, missing persons."

"Their checkbooks, their credit cards, their bank accounts," listed the attorney, matching Ryan's tone. Some snickers echoed in the gallery.

"Catharine doesn't charge for her services. She doesn't have to."

Brant suddenly froze, caught off guard. He must not have read the fine print on Catharine's website.

"So Ms. Lulling calls herself a '*psychic*,' a '*healer,*' and can find things," the attorney said, flailing his hand around in the air, "and you call *my* client delusional?"

"Objection!" Jane was on it.

"Withdrawn." Brant leaned against the jury box and chuckled, trying to get the jury to laugh along with him, but most of them sneered or looked away.

It appeared as if they had bonded with Catharine, approved of Ryan, and had started to hate Brant. Brant must have sensed it, too, because he stood back up and made a split-second decision.

"Thank you, Detective, no more questions."

Surprised, Ryan looked to Jane. *That's it?*

She rose from her chair. "The People dismiss Detective Ryan Doherty."

And at that, the judge ordered a ninety-minute lunch break.

As Ryan disembarked from the witness stand, most of the jury members smiled at him and he nodded back. When he got back to the front row of the gallery, Di Santo jumped up and shook his hand.

"Great job! You really had them!"

"You think?"

"I think every lady in that jury is gonna go out and buy a Detective Doherty pillowcase."

"You're an idiot." Ryan caught Jane's arm as she attempted to maneuver around the detectives. "Hey, Jane. Did we do good?"

"Yes, Ryan, I think we really have a chance now. Thanks for helping save it."

He noticed something in Jane's eyes—not defeat but a little wounded nonetheless.

"You sure? You think it's going to go our way?" he prompted her.

She wouldn't look at him. "No way to tell until the end," she said, stuffing her notebooks into her briefcase. "I think that's all we need. I'm going to go prepare for the afternoon. Matt, you're up next. You ready?"

"Sure, I'll be back in about an hour," Di Santo said, then to Ryan, "So are you gonna call Cat?"

Ryan didn't answer him. He watched Jane walk out the side door of the courtroom without so much as a farewell. Di Santo gave him a tap on the arm with the back of his hand.

"C'mon, you just told the entire world you were in love with her! Kiss and make up."

"It's more complicated than that." Ryan picked up his pace and walked up the aisle ahead of his partner, trying to avoid the subject.

They headed downstairs to the lunch van parked in front of courthouse, which fed the myriad of attorneys, jurors, and courthouse personnel. Di Santo ordered for both of them, as they always ordered the special from this particular truck.

"Pastrami. On rye," Di Santo said. "Two of them. Don't worry, this one's on me."

Ryan thanked him. They stood aside and waited for their order. Di Santo kept shifting on his feet and looking up at Ryan as if he had something to say.

"What?" Ryan finally said.

"Cat called me, you know, this morning." There it was. "She said you're avoiding her calls." The cook called their names. They retrieved the two lunches and headed to the courthouse cafeteria, choosing a table in the back corner. "So you're not cutting her a break?" Di Santo continued.

"Look, she shouldn't have called you. It's none of your business," Ryan said, giving him a straight look to back off.

"If you love her, like you said, you guys'll work it out, right?"

Ryan shook his head and put down his sandwich. "Sometimes, I don't even know what I was thinking. We're nothing alike. I think, is this it? Is this how it ends? 'Cause it's gonna end sometime. How's it gonna end?"

"What makes you keep thinking about the end? You guys are great together."

"Look, first of all, how would we ever live together? Due to the city's rules, all employees of the city of Chicago must live within city limits. So I can't move to Evanston even if I wanted to. So she's going to move out of her multi-million-dollar estate to live in my one-bedroom apartment in Rogers Park? That just shows how far apart our worlds are."

"You don't have to be a cop forever. Or you could always move to the Evanston force."

Ryan let out a bitter laugh. "I am Chicago. Born and raised. I can't work another force. And a suburban one? I'd die."

"You could retire. Get your pension, let her support you. The chick does have thirty million in the bank."

"It's more than that, now, with all of her investments," Ryan said. Di Santo whistled. "Cat has already hinted that she wants me to quit police work. Too dangerous, she says. She knew what and who I was when we started going out. She thinks I should teach criminology or some such shit. I'd be in *her* house, with *her* money, with *her* dictating what I do. That's not me, D."

"You're exaggerating. She's not a shrew, for god sake. What, do you want to be a struggling schmoe all your life? The chick's money is a plus, but that's not what Cat's about. You know that."

"The other day? She got a hundred-and-fifty-thousand dollar check. Some dividend from an investment. She says, 'I don't know what to do with this. I don't need it.' I say, 'Then donate it. Give it to one of your tree charities or something.' You know what she says?"

Di Santo looked up at him and quickly shook his head.

"She says, 'Do you want a new car or something?' I'm like, '*What?* A hundred-thousand-dollar car in my neighborhood? Parked on the street?' And can you see me roll into the eighteenth in something like that?"

"You'd have IAD all up in your face," Di Santo said, pointing his pastrami toward him.

They both laughed at the thought.

The emerald green Rolex popped into Ryan's head, but

he immediately dismissed it. "Yeah, well, that's not the point." Ryan stabbed at the three-lettuce-leaf salad that came with the sandwich, angry at the salad and at Cat's offer, all over again.

Di Santo swallowed. "I know, I know. It's emaska-lating, right? You want to be the breadwinner."

"Something like that."

"So what are you going to do?"

"I don't know. I just need time. Space. Think on things. I don't want to go over there right now. To that house. Fall into it again. It's too..."

"*Good?*" Di Santo said with a smirk.

"In a way, yeah. It's too good. It's not a real life."

With Ryan doing all the talking for a change, Di Santo finished his sandwich, held his hand over his mouth, and let out a big meaty belch. Losing his appetite, Ryan pitched the rest of his lunch into a nearby trashcan from his chair. He gulped down the root beer and checked his watch.

"Nineteen more minutes until you're on the stand," Ryan said.

"And what about Jane? You better not run over to her house like the last time you and Cat had a fight." Di Santo was rocking on his chair now, looking up from under his brow.

His partner knew him well, although Ryan would never admit it to him. So he rolled his eyes and replied, "I'm not an idiot. We're just friends."

"I've never known you to have a female friend," said Di Santo. "At least one you haven't bonked. You two are awfully close."

"She's like a sister to me. Nothing more."

"Does *she* know that? I think she's biding her time. Waiting, waiting, waiting!"

"She's dating some guy—guys. She told me last night. Seeing several people, she said. See? We talk to each other like girlfriends."

"Last *night?*"

"We had dinner."

"Mmm-hmmm. I'm just warning you…"

"This conversation is over." Ryan stood up, and Di Santo followed. "When you're up on the stand just cover everything I said." He stopped and turned to his partner. "And leave out the part where I was about to shoot Elliot in the head. That never happened."

"Never happened," Di Santo agreed. They made their way out of the cafeteria. "You know, I could use a new car. I really like that new red Cadillac. Can I be Catharine's charity case? I can limp."

Ryan slapped his partner on the back of the head.

# CHAPTER 25

I've come to view Jesus much the way I view Elvis—I love the guy, but a lot of his fan clubs really freak me out!

~ *John Fugelsang*

Di Santo's testimony was short and recapped most of what Ryan had said, with the addition of questions on police procedure and with the exception of questions on Catharine. When court was adjourned for the day, Ryan gave Di Santo his props and tried to catch Jane before she left, but he lost her in the crowd.

When he stepped out of the courthouse, a reporter shoved a microphone into his face.

"Detective Doherty, why isn't Catharine Lulling attending this trial?"

He put his hand in front of the television camera. "No comment."

"Come on, Detective, something? Was the attack related to the Town Red case? Do you think Todd Elliot still has something to do with the murders of Carly and Scott Redding?" The reporter's voice trailed off as Ryan jogged down the courthouse steps, Di Santo following.

When they got back to the 18th, the sarge called Ryan into his office.

"So, Doherty," Besko began. "You wanted extra hours and I got some for you. With a free vacation to boot! Well, not so much a vacation, but a working vacation."

Di Santo whined, "Extra hours? I don't want extra hours. Who wants extra hours?"

The sarge ignored him. "Atlanta PD wants you two on a plane today."

Ryan frowned. "Atlanta? Does this have to do with Smith?"

"That would be affirmative. I had a warrant sent to Georgia for his arrest and extradition. Apparently now he has barricaded himself in their offices, *with* his followers. And despite all efforts by Atlanta police, he will not surrender. Before Atlanta gets the Feds involved, they wanted you on the scene."

"Why us?"

"Well, the guy asked for you, Doherty, but I talked Atlanta into sending you *and* Di Santo. I told them you guys are a team and I wanted him there to back you up."

"But again, why me?" Ryan asked.

"Because Smith asked for you by name. Said he'd only surrender to you."

Ryan didn't mind the thought of getting on a plane to Atlanta. It would be another collar on his record and working non-stop always distracted him from everything else. "Okay, then."

"But be careful with these guys, D. We don't want another Waco over there. Di Santo—make sure he's safe."

"Gee thanks. Who am I, his bodyguard?"

"You guys have each other's backs, you know it. Now hustle and pack, you have two hours to takeoff. Here—here's the flight information. The chief's assistant already booked you. Here's his number."

Besko handed him a sheet from his notebook with the airline info scribbled on it while Ryan reviewed the situation in his head: Religious group, barricade. The remark about Waco troubled him. He hoped they didn't have a standoff on their hands.

"Do you know if they're armed?" he asked the sarge.

"I don't have any details. The Atlanta PD chief will give you a rundown on the sitch when you get there. Just hurry and get to O'Hare. Oh, and we don't have time to complete the paperwork for you guys to fly with your weapons, so leave them. Atlanta will issue you firearms when you get there."

Luckily, American Airlines offered Wi-Fi on the flight, so Ryan used the time to research the One Divine Life organization. He read through their website, to get a feel for their personnel and philosophies; reviewed the Wikipedia entry; and followed the links on the bottom to read the supporting articles. Most of them were favorable, from Christian periodicals to local Atlanta magazines. Di Santo donned his noise-canceling earphones, bobbed his head to a stream of music, and enjoyed a five-dollar martini.

The plane got to the gate at 7:22 p.m. Atlanta time and Ryan checked in with their contact on the Atlanta force, Chief Steven Burke. Burke told him they had a patrol car waiting for them outside of the luggage terminal, ready to escort them directly to the ODL offices. Ryan had hoped they would have time to check into the hotel first, but sometimes this was what policing was about: working it straight through.

They rode in the patrol car to the east side of town, eventually pulling into a non-descript business park lined with one-story concrete buildings fronted by charcoal tinted windows. As far as he could see, there was no press here yet, just a swarm of uniformed officers in body armor. When Ryan and Di Santo got out of the car, they were greeted by Chief Burke in person. Burke stood taller than Ryan, about six-foot-three, sporting a sturdy lean frame like an ex-basketball player. He appeared to be in his upper-upper forties or early fifties, dark skin, with a military haircut, slightly greying at the temples. He wore the standard police blues, four stripes and four stars indicating his rank on the cuffs and lapel, with a standard-issue vest over his jacket.

"Thank you, gentlemen, for coming out here on such short notice," Burke said, jumping right into it. "The attorney for this—organization—just showed up. He's said he's spoken with you before. A Mr. Harlan Copeland?"

"The third," confirmed Di Santo.

"We spoke to him on the phone briefly," Ryan explained.

"Let me introduce you, then." He led them over to a makeshift tent that swarmed with a tactical unit of the Atlanta SWAT. Burke introduced them to an older, plump white man in dress slacks and a vest. Copeland was seated in a plastic folding chair, fanning himself with a manila folder, his shirtsleeves rolled up to his elbows. He stood up to greet the detectives.

"Welcome to Atlanta, boys, where the days are hot and the nights are hotter. We appreciate you comin' in for the situation, here."

"Could you fill us in on what's going on in there?" Ryan asked, while they shook hands. "We don't know anything other than that Smith asked for me."

"Well, we received your warrant, here," he tapped a folder sitting on a folding table beside him. "Mr. Smith was none too pleased about it. I tried to get him to come in peacefully, but he was being quite belligerent. He has something to say and he only wants to say it to you. As you can see, Mr. Smith and his constituents have barricaded themselves inside their office, and despite our efforts in the last four hours, we cannot get them to come out."

Chief Burke took over the briefing. "Twelve hundred square feet, approximately thirteen persons, male and female, no kids," he said. "Their offices have two common walls with adjacent businesses in the building, one main door serving as both entrance and exit, here in front, directly into the reception area. The back door is covered with SWAT and two snipers. They've been in there for almost twenty-two hours now, since ten o'clock last night."

"Weapons?" Ryan asked.

Burke glanced at Harlan Copeland and said, "Undetermined."

"Copeland?" asked Ryan, raising his voice. "If you know something that you are not revealing, that is obstruction. Is there something you know that can save an officer's life in there?"

"I have no knowledge of any weapons inside the ODL." Copeland stated, as if he were being deposed.

The man dropped eye contact but Ryan stared at him until the attorney returned his gaze and shrugged. Ryan wanted to beat a new answer out of him.

Chief Burke continued, "We've procured vests and weapons for both of you. Everyone on the scene must wear a vest." He showed them to the tactical van where he handed each of them body armor and a standard issue firearm. A deputy held out a clipboard so each of them could sign a form acknowledging receipt of the guns. Ryan examined the make and model of the firearm and checked the cartridge. Full. He put the safety back on and placed it into its holster.

"We last spoke with Mr. Smith at 5:37 p.m., when he asked for food and drinks for the entire group. We wanted to wait to deliver them until you were here."

Ryan checked the time: exactly ten after eight.

"Three hours ago? You didn't worry that would make them really cranky by now?" asked Di Santo.

"It's a tactic. They'll be tired, hungry, and thirsty. Doherty, you go in with what they need and they'll trust you. See you as a friend."

"You're going in, D? Alone?" asked Di Santo.

"I've got my HNC cert. I'm fine going in," Ryan said, reassuring his partner while also informing the chief of his creds. "The last time we talked they seemed friendly enough. I'm hoping he'll trust me enough to talk about the equipment case and the cross." Then to the chief, "Smith's got several priors, I've seen his sheet. But anything major? Have I missed something?"

"No, nothing big. Minor harassment charges, trespassing on private property, abortion clinics," Burke said.

Ryan thought about the latter. "Did anything happen at the abortion clinics? Did they ever get violent?"

"No. But the group displayed some pretty gruesome signs to the women entering and exiting the clinic. Stuff like that."

Abortion clinics were a hot-button issue. Ryan wanted to make sure they didn't have any proclivity toward home-grown explosives. As he fastened the Velcro straps on his vest, he thought of Warren L. Smith and his calm demeanor during the luncheon. He replayed their conversation in his head. Tried to picture the faces of the group. Then some-thing caught his eye: a sky blue van with the words "One Divine Life" written in script on the side. He pulled out his cell phone and went to the voice recorder app. Tapped the date and time he'd interviewed Smith in the pizza parlor and played it for himself, with Di Santo and Burke listening in.

He dragged the slider to bypass the chit-chat and eventu-ally found what he was searching for: "*Well, Detectives, our plane arrived around five-thirty p.m., so after we got our luggage and picked up our rental van, we didn't get to the hotel until about seven.*"

"The ODL rented a van," he said, specifically to Di San-to. "While I'm in there, call all the rental companies in and around the airports and find that van. If it's white, call the sarge and let him in on this. He can get a warrant." Ryan turned to Burke and tapped the holster on his hip. "I can take this in with me, right?"

The chief nodded. "Abso-fuckin'-lutely. You're in the South, now, son. You don't go into a situation like this with-out a weapon. We're also going to wire you and listen to everything that goes on. You give the signal and SWAT will be in there in one-point-three seconds."

Ryan respected the man's accuracy. "What's the signal?"

"Two quick sniffs. So I hope you're not allergic to Christians."

The chief guffawed at his own joke. Several SWAT team members followed suit, and Ryan indulged them.

Di Santo wasn't laughing. He twitched with energy, bouncing on the balls of his feet. "I don't like this, D. You don't know what's in there."

"I'll be fine. Two sniffs and I've got General Custer's army in there with me."

"Custer fuckin' *lost*!" Di Santo said, throwing his hands up in the air.

Chief Burke puffed out his chest. "Not today, he won't. Let's give a call inside to Mr. Smith." He picked up a phone cradled in a large silver-sided briefcase, with a recording device attached. After he dialed, he pressed the speakerphone button and placed the handset down.

"One Divine Life. Are you having a blessed day?" a female voice answered on the line. Ryan recognized it as the same woman he spoke to the previous week when he called, although now she sounded shaky and distracted.

"This is Chief Burke. I have Detective Ryan Doherty here for Mr. Smith."

# CHAPTER 26

After being put on hold for several seconds, a familiar voice came on the line. "Detective Doherty!" Warren L. Smith said with his recognizable drawl. "You here in Atlanta?"

"Hello, Mr. Smith. Yes, I am right in front of your building. You said wanted to talk?"

"Please! Call me Warren. I believe I asked for some dinner for my friends. They're getting restless and tired. Any news on that first?"

"Well, Warren. You could let them go," Ryan said.

"I'm not holding them against their will, Detective. We're all in this together." Ryan flashed on Jonestown and Heaven's Gate, two previous incidents triggered by fundamental fanaticism. History he didn't want to repeat.

Chief Burke nodded to Ryan, then the office building. He got the message. "May I come in, Warren? I'll bring your dinner and drinks in with me. We can talk, share a meal, just like we did in Chicago." Burke nodded, approving of his technique. The line was silent. "Warren? You still there?"

"Yes, Detective."

"Hey, you asked to talk to me, so let's do it man to man. Face to face. What do you say?"

"I guess that would be acceptable. How soon can we have the food?"

The chief motioned to several boxes on a table in the tent.

"I've got your dinner right here, Warren," Ryan confirmed. "I'll be in real soon. 'Kay? Are we cool?"

"Yes, Detective, we are cool. See you soon."

A young uniformed Atlanta P.D. officer held up a wireless microphone to Ryan. She placed the box inside one of his vest pockets and lifted his shirt to thread the wire up inside it. He held his arms up for her to maneuver and studied the woman. Cute blonde, hair pulled back into a French braid at the back of her head. Most departments didn't allow the female officers to wear their hair loose, as it would make them too vulnerable during an attack.

"Pardon me for the personal touch," she said, positioning the microphone. "I hope my hands aren't cold."

"No, they're good," he said.

'*Don't even think about it,*' his former partner's voice echoed in his head.

She met the mic with her outside hand and clipped it to the inside of his collar. After she pulled the bottom of his polo shirt down from under the vest, she moved to tuck the ends back into his waistband.

"Uh, I can handle that," Ryan said, and tucked his own shirt into his belt.

She rounded behind him and placed another smaller box onto the inside back of the vest collar and pulled a coiled wire over his ear lobe, placing a tiny ear bud into his left ear. Ryan adjusted the bud to make sure it stayed in position while the officer came back around in front of him to assess her work. She ran her fingers through his hair to cover the earpiece. When their eyes met, he recognized the invitation he used to see in cop-bar women. Pre-Catharine. He hadn't seen that look for seven months now. Or maybe he just wasn't looking.

"We don't want it to be obvious you're wired," she explained.

He glanced at her full lips, but quickly rejected the

thoughts that entered his male brain. She turned him around and adjusted the volume knob on the box at the back of his neck, just slightly brushing his hairline. A chill went through him to the top of his head. When she was finished, the officer went back to the tent, about twenty yards away, and tested the earpiece.

"Can you hear me, Detective?" He could swear her voice sounded breathier through the headphone.

"Loud and clear."

"Too loud?"

"No, just right."

"Say your ABCs so we can get a level?"

"*A—B—C—D—E—F—*"

"That's fine. Thank you, Detective Doherty."

"Thanks." He tried to sound professional, official, not like he was picturing her without her vest. Or uniform. Why did his mind always turn to sex when he was under duress? A Doherty calming technique, no doubt.

The chief cut through his thoughts. "If they try to disarm you, tell them that's not in the rules," he said. "Tell them that you need your firearm to protect *them*. Maybe they'll buy it, maybe they won't. If we feel that you're hesitating in any way, we'll tell you what to say through the earpiece." He tapped his own ear. "I'll be at the other end."

"Aw, not *her*?" Ryan said, glancing back at the blonde. He threw her a wink. She smiled. Damned flirt mechanism.

One of the SWAT guys handed him the two food boxes, one stacked on top of the other, stamped with a TexMex Grill logo. They put a third, with the drinks, right next to the door. Chief Burke called the ODL office line again and informed them they needed to open the door for Detective Doherty to enter.

Ryan stood at the door, taking a moment to scan the parking lot and scrutinize the entire scene. He spotted at least six SWAT guys with rifles. The snipers weren't visible, but he knew they were out there. He gave a thumbs up and turned back to the ODL door when he heard the lock flip.

A plain, dark-haired woman opened the door with one arm, wide enough for Ryan to enter. She gasped when she saw the scene outside the building. Apparently she hadn't looked out the window lately.

"It's perfectly fine. No one will hurt you," Ryan assured her. "That's why I'm here."

He entered the building and immediately surveyed the interior of the office: wide open reception area, with large groups of desks on either side. Warren L. Smith greeted him with another guy he recognized from the lunch at Uno's, who took the boxes.

"There are drinks outside the door," he said to Smith, cocking his head.

"I think you should get them, Detective," Smith said. "Dave, you and Rachel bring the food to the conference room."

Ryan turned back to the front door and the same woman was there to assist him. She held the door open while he grabbed the drinks and walked them into the conference room where the rest of the ODL members were already helping themselves to tacos, nachos, and chicken quesadillas. A small container of hot sauce had opened and dripped on Ryan's fingers. He wiped it on his pants.

Smith stood next to him, eyeing the gun in his holster. "We're peace-loving citizens, here, Detective. There's no need for that." The grin on his face was a little disturbing.

"It's more for your protection than mine. Just want to make sure you all stay safe."

*"Good!"* Chief Burke barked in his earpiece.

"Fair enough," Smith replied. "Do you mind if I eat before we talk? Please, feel free to sit with us."

Ryan took a deep breath, celebrating the fact that he had passed the first hurdle. He remembered from hostage negotiation training that he should count the people inside. Thirteen, as they had expected, all taking seats at the oblong conference room table. He couldn't help make the association with Da Vinci's Last Supper, and hoped this story had a better ending.

"I hope we have enough food for all thirteen of you," Ryan said, sending the number back to the unit.

"It looks fine, Detective," Smith answered, before he took a delicate bite of a soft taco.

He ate the rest of his meal deliberately, stood up, and nodded to the next room. Ryan followed him into a private office on the far side of the office space.

A large sketch of a smiling Jesus hung on the wall behind Smith's desk chair. Christ knelt before two adoring children, a boy and a girl. A placid lamb stood to the side. On the wall to the right was a flag with a symbol on it. He'd seen that symbol before. Something Irish—then he remembered. It was the symbol on Fisk's tie clasp.

"I'm happy that you came," Smith said. He took a seat in his desk chair and held his hand out for Ryan to take the guest chair opposite him. "I wanted to explain the situation to you before we turned ourselves in. I'm hoping our story will get us some leniency."

"*Tell him you'll do what you can*," Burke said in his earpiece.

"I'll do what I can, Warren, I really want to help you."

"*He needs an attorney present if he's going to confess to anything!*" He heard the faint voice of Harland Copeland III argue with the chief in his ear. Burke's voice came in loud and clear, "*Attempt the Miranda, Doherty, you have to ask if he wants his attorney.*"

"Before you say anything, Warren, I have to let you know that you have a right to have an attorney present. Mr. Copeland is right outside. Would you like him to come in and join us?"

"No, I would not," answered Smith, waiving his right. Done deal.

"*Son of a bitch*—" Copeland shouted faintly in his earpiece, followed by silence.

Ryan sat back in his chair and folded his hands in his lap,

appearing to have a casual chat. "Okay then. Let's start at the beginning."

"The beginning. Well, it began the night before the concert. Friday night," Smith said. Ryan prompted him to continue with a nod. "Several of us were having a late dinner at the hotel restaurant. When we came out into the lobby we saw Mr. James exit the hotel with another man. He didn't have his bodyguards with him, so I thought it would be a good opportunity to talk, one on one. Try to get him to repent and renounce his blasphemy."

"So you followed them outside?"

"We did."

Ryan kicked himself for not viewing the security footage *after* Terrico James left the hotel. They would have recognized Smith—seen him exit the lobby—and might have been able to do something before this entire situation had blown out of control. He reached around behind him, checking his handcuffs. He was encouraged at the thought of having a suspect in custody within the hour.

"Can I have the names of the men who helped you?" he asked, trying to mask his anticipation.

Smith leaned forward, cupping his chin into his laced fingers. "Detective, I am perfectly willing to atone for my own acts, but please, don't ask me to bring harm to my associates. Let's just say they were helpers."

"Okay, so you—and your helpers—followed James outside. Then what?"

Smith inhaled and exhaled as if he were about to embark on a long story, or attempting to fabricate one. His shoulders hunched forward. "Liar's posture," they called it in the PD.

"Well, when I went outside, I couldn't find him. But I heard two people yelling from the alley next to the hotel. It sounded like a fight."

*Surprisingly consistent with Ben's story,* Ryan thought. *So far.* "Did you hear the fight? Was it a physical fight or just verbal?"

"Two men screaming at each other, obviously *black* by

their manner of speech. But I didn't catch the words, sorry."
Ryan nodded for him to continue. "After several minutes, it
died down. I was afraid to approach. Then one man came
out of the alley and walked away, down the street."

"And you want me to believe that that man is the murderer?"

"I assume it was, yes."

"Did you happen to see that man's face? Could you identify him?" Ryan expected a hasty negative.

"Yes, actually, it was Terrico James's brother, Reggie
Robinson. I recognized him when I saw him on television."

"And why didn't you tell us this when we first interviewed you? At the pizza place? You were a material witness to a homicide." Ryan hissed. It was time to antagonize.

"Well, like I said, I was frightened, Detective," Smith
said, leaning back in his chair. "That man was a homicidal
maniac and I feared he might come after me if I identified
him. Not to mention, I would have put myself at the scene
of the crime. Not a good situation at-all, at-all." Smith
sported a reptilian grin as he recounted his story, causing
Ryan to squirm in his seat.

"Keep him talking, this is great," said Chief Burke's
voice over the earphone.

"Okay, go on," Ryan prompted.

Smith leaned back in his chair, put his hands behind his
head and glanced at the ceiling. "So Reggie Robinson came
out of the alley and walked down the street. But Terrico did
not come out of the alley." He looked directly at Ryan. "I
was curious to see what he was doing. I had no idea a *homicide* had been committed. Goodness gracious. I had thoroughly expected Mr. James to round the corner and I was
preparing to speak to him. Man to man. I waited for a while
and when he didn't come out of that alley, we went in. Cau-
tiously. It was very dark and I could hardly see anything. No
one was there. Or so I thought. But then I saw someone *was*
there—Terrico James. But he was already lying dead, under
a blanket."

"Already dead," Ryan repeated. He didn't believe Smith's story for a minute, but he urged him to continue, grateful that APD was recording every word.

"Once my eyes adjusted to the dim light of the alley, I saw a lump under a blanket, about halfway down. I thought it may be a homeless person and shouted 'hello.' Some guy in the back of the alley shouted hello back, but it wasn't the bundle. I kicked it. Felt like a body. When I looked under the blanket, I found Mr. James dead. Bleeding."

"Which was it? Was he dead or bleeding?" Ryan asked. "When you're dead, your heart stops pumping. So was the blood pumping? Or just pooled?"

Smith gave him a chilling, blank stare. "Terrico James was already dead, Detective."

"That must have been very disturbing for you," Ryan said, baiting him. Smith's lack of expression had betrayed him to be either the perpetrator of this crime or a sociopath. Maybe both. Getting a confession was crucial. "And then what did you do?"

"Then we got the idea for the cross. I had seen photos of his concerts—the sacrilegious spectacle of him coming down on a cross. A cross! So I thought how fitting it would be for him to come down on it like Jesus. He wanted to be Jesus, we would make him Jesus. For his final act. His fans, his followers, these foolish people who swallowed his blasphemy, we would make them see what happens when you try to put yourself above the Lord. My—associates—helped me take the body from the alley and we transported it to the arena. Nobody was there."

"And you used the equipment case to transport the body?"

"Wasn't that lucky? It was just sitting there, waiting for us. As if God, himself, had provided the assistance."

Ryan did his best not to recoil from the comment. "And how many of you did it take to carry Terrico James's body up to the rafters?"

Smith paused before answering, reveling in the memory

of his handiwork. "Once we got him up there, I could feel Jesus, himself, smiling down on us. We nailed that man up like a work of art."

"You didn't answer my question. You said you did this with several of your associates. What *associates*?"

Smith's gaze flickered to a pamphlet on his desk. *The Knight's Brotherhood.* Even viewing it upside-down, its message was apparent. The cover photo flaunted five smiling white men with semi-automatic weapons, that cross emblazoned on their chests. The only things missing were the white hoods.

*My hood is black and his is white...* Ryan recalled Terrico's rap. He realized, then, that James hadn't been referring to neighborhoods.

"Was one of your associates Wyatt Fisk?" It had to have been Fisk. Smith and Fisk were both from Atlanta, and now he had evidence that they were both connected to this *brotherhood.* If Fisk was involved, it would be a PR nightmare for the Chicago Police Department. An embarrassment.

"That's all I'm going to say, Detective. I choose to not implicate any other individual. I believe the charge on the warrant is desecration of a human corpse? I'm willing to take it. But please, leave my flock out of this. They did nothing."

Ryan rubbed his face as he thought on the confession. He wanted more on this guy, but if he brought him in for the current charges, he was sure he could go at him to get the real story.

Smith got up from his desk and started to pace as he spoke. "The entire 'rap industry' is a sham. All these guys just make up words and they're instantly elevated to superstars among their community. And what have they done? They rhyme. They rhyme words. Does rhyming give you the right to say you're on the same terms as our Lord and savior Jesus Christ? Rhyming? Nothing they say is poetic.

It's anti-American, anti-white drivel." Spittle flew from his mouth along with the words of hate.

Ryan's left nostril started to burn. He rubbed it with his index finger, trying to alleviate the sensation. He then sniffed once, out of reflex. "What do you mean, anti-white? Are you saying Terrico James was racist?"

"Look, Detective, you're a red-blooded, God-fearing Christian man. Don't you hate the fact that these people have become so rich doing so little?"

"*These people*? What people?"

"The n—Negroes."

Ryan flinched at the antiquated term while the inside of his nostrils started to sting—burn—beyond belief. Must have been the hot sauce. He rubbed his nose again, but then suddenly stopped, realizing that the finger he was using to rub it must have been sauce-infected.

"Are you okay, Detective?"

"Yeah, I just—" The pain became unbearable as he sniffed again and then froze, realizing what he had just done.

# CHAPTER 27

N o, *no!*" Ryan shouted into his mic. "That wasn't—"
Within seconds the front door blew open and twenty fully-suited and armed SWAT members started
shouting, their commands muffled by their facemasks.

"*DOWN, DOWN! GET DOWN ON THE GROUND—
NOW!*"

Ryan jumped up and formed a barrier between the SWAT
team and Smith.

"No, you got it wrong—"

"*GET DOWN NOW!*" a SWAT guy roared at him. Ryan
turned to see Smith opening his desk drawer. Their eyes
locked.

"Warren, don't do it."

"*I SAID DOWN!*" the SWAT guy screamed behind him.

Smith put his hand into the drawer.

"*Warren!*" Ryan screamed at him. "You don't want it to
end this way!"

Ryan felt a hand at the back of his collar, fiercely yank-
ing him back, throwing him down on the floor, to the left of
Smith's desk. When he recouped from the fall, he looked
back at Smith, who had removed a revolver from his desk.

"*DROP IT!*" shouted the lead SWAT guy. Smith smiled
at each of them and cocked the gun.

"Warren—*don't!*" Ryan warned. The burning worsened and he rubbed his nose, again, with the wrong hand.

"*DROP THE WEAPON OR WE'RE SHOOTING IN ONE!*" the leader of the SWAT team shouted, although he was within a foot of the suspect.

"*Don't do it!*" Ryan yelled—a message to both Smith and the SWAT team. He scrambled to pull Smith down to the floor with him. But just as he grabbed the leg of Smith's pants, a deafening crack rang out. Smith's body thumped back against the wall and slid down in front of him. Blood oozed from the large crimson cavity left in his chest where Smith's heart used to be. His face stared back, already blank and soulless, with the faint smile remaining.

*Dead or bleeding?*

Ryan averted his gaze, back to the sketch of Jesus and the children, where Jesus was still smiling, the children were still adoring, and the lamb still placid. He rubbed his eyes and they, too, started to burn.

"*Shit!*" Ryan pounded his fists into the wall behind him. When dark gray SWAT boots surrounded him like a forest of burnt redwoods, he realized he was still on the floor. He lifted himself up with the hand of a SWAT member, who escorted him back out to the front parking lot. They trailed directly behind the remaining twelve ODL members who were panicked, weeping, and shouting Bible verses.

*Lucky thirteen* was all Ryan could think of at that moment, and the next image was Di Santo running up to him.

"D, you all right?" His partner studied his face. "What's with your eyes? Have you been crying? What happened in there?"

"Get me some water, please. *Now.*"

The female cop came up and handed him a water bottle, which he cracked open and splashed in his face. And then on his right hand. He swore to himself that the hot sauce debacle would remain his secret until the day he died, already guilt-ridden with the death of Warren L. Smith. The uniformed officer rushed to unhook the box from the back of his neck and pulled the earpiece from his ear, trying to rescue it from the sudden water bath.

"Oh, sorry," Ryan said to her.

"That's okay. I'm glad you're all right," she said and gave him a quick hug.

After she was out of earshot, Di Santo whispered, "You're treading on thin ice with that cop, D. Don't go there."

Ryan didn't reply.

"You did good, Detective," Chief Burke said, placing a hand on his shoulder. "Smith was obviously armed and you were in grave danger."

"No," Ryan said, hanging his head. "I wasn't in danger. He was going to surrender."

"You were, actually," Burke corrected him. "My team just radioed. They found a case of HK-416 assault rifles in the back room. Twenty in all. Plus a big pile of grenades. They were definitely stockpiling." Ryan couldn't hide his surprise at that news. "We're also finding a stash of white supremacist propaganda, especially in the back room. These guys had been trying to hide it behind their religion. They were dangerous. You did a good thing. Seriously."

Ryan nodded. "I saw some of it in his office. He talked about being part of a 'brotherhood.' Do you think that was—"

"Klan? Could be. Smith grew up in a rural area down south that had a very substantial KKK presence. We'll look into it."

The cross. Ryan pulled out his phone and opened the browser. He searched for "Celtic cross KKK" and found it. That particular cross was a symbol of white supremacy. And Fisk had worn it in plain sight. As a police officer. The thought made Ryan nauseous. He had to talk to the sarge before confronting Fisk as there was protocol in accusing a fellow officer of any kind of wrongdoing. And Ryan needed hard evidence to support Fisk's involvement with the cruci-fixion.

Di Santo patted him on the back. "See? The chief said you did good. So why so glum, my chum? You're alive!"

For some reason, the commendation still didn't absolve his mistake. As putrid as the man was, Ryan wished at this moment that Warren L. Smith had his day in court. "Just tired, I guess."

They hung around the scene for another hour while they turned in their body armor and firearms and assisted with the breakdown of the operation. Ryan accepted congratulations from the SWAT team and various uniformed officers. He returned the compliments for a job well done while the takedown plagued him in his head.

The last of the patrol cars were pulling out when Burke shook both their hands. "Doherty, you had true balls in there. We'll call your sergeant and let him know what went down. Appreciate all the help you boys gave us. That patrol over there will get you back to the hotel. Let's debrief in the morning. I want to go over Smith's statement. Go back and rest now." They agreed. "We'll meet you at Atlanta headquarters at…" He looked at his watch. "Oh-nine-hundred. That gives you gentlemen a little time to sleep in. It's been a long day. We'll send a car to pick you up at 8:45. We good?"

"Yeah, we're good," Ryan answered. He felt like his eyes were about to close right then and there.

By the time they checked into the hotel it was 11:23 p.m.

"Mr. Doherty and Mr. Di Santo, we have the reservations right here," said the front desk woman. The Southern drawls were jarring to Ryan's ear, making everyone sound way too congenial. "You have already been checked in by Atlanta PD so all I have to do now is give you your keycards."

Ryan thanked his One Divine Lord that Atlanta had booked them two separate rooms. Aside from wanting to be alone and decompress, Di Santo snored like a warthog. He thanked the woman and they headed to the elevator lobby.

"Pretty swank for public service," Di Santo commented on the upscale accommodations.

"I just want a bed."

They rode the elevator up alone, and silence hung in the air as he watched the numbers light up in ascending order. It stopped at the three and Di Santo stepped out, catching the elevator doors with one hand.

"Don't beat yourself up over this, D," he said. "They had enough firepower in there to take us all out."

Ryan nodded and put his hand up as a goodnight. He ran his fingers through his hair and pressed the already lit button for the eighth floor.

When he turned out of the elevator, he checked a wall plaque to find room number 810. He followed the left arrow to the long carpeted left wing. He scanned the numbers on each door as he approached the end of the carpeted hallway. The next sign indicated his room was to the left, again, down another corridor. When he turned to proceed down that hallway, there was no question which door was his: the one with the blonde uniformed officer leaning against it. As he approached, he noticed that her hair now fell loosely onto the epaulets of her uniform, making her look even younger than she did at the ODL scene. Straight out of the academy, he figured, with a hard body to prove it.

"Officer..." He angled the silver rectangular nameplate up from her chest with one finger. "Hill?"

"Doherty."

"What can I do for you?"

Her chin lifted slightly as she gazed up at him, a faint smile forming on her lips. "I'm here for protection."

"Protection," he repeated. "From what?"

"Nightmares."

He let out a fatigued chuckle.

Officer Hill tossed a strand of hair out of her face. "Seriously, it was rough out there. Thought you might need some company."

His eyes met hers and then roamed her tight, uniformed torso. She had shed her vest and utility belt, revealing a perfect curve at the hip. His thoughts went to Catharine then the image of Catharine and Todd together. Entwined. In that conference room.

He inserted his keycard into the lock. When the little green light came on, he turned the knob and held the door open for her.

# CHAPTER 28

The room phone rang at exactly eight a.m. It was one of those old-fashioned phone bells, clanging Ryan out of a deep dark sleep. He reached for it, eyes still shut in half-slumber.

"Yeah, Doherty," he answered, not remembering exactly where he was.

He heard light music on the other end of the line and then a recording: "Your wake-up call is now complete."

He sat up and put his feet on the floor, rubbing his eyes while the memory of the previous night's activities rushed back into his head. He checked the other side of the bed. Empty.

He scanned the room for any sign of Officer Hill, but there was nothing out of place. No leftover bra or panties. No holster. What was her first name? Did he ever ask?

He headed over to the small bathroom, emptied his bladder, and washed up, splashing cold water on his face. While drying his hands on the thick white hotel towel, he spotted a small piece of white paper peeking underneath the hotel room door. He bent over, picked it up, and unfolded it.

*Woke up early, going to HQ. Meet you there.*

At first, he thought it might have been from Officer Hill, but the idea quickly vanished when he recognized the writing. Plus, it was signed "D."

He dropped the note back on the floor and stepped back into the bathroom to shower and shave.

At exactly 8:45 a.m. he met the patrol car in front of the hotel, arriving at the Atlanta Police headquarters eleven minutes later. The guys at the 18th would get a good laugh out of the fact that this city's police headquarters was located on *Peachtree* Avenue. That wouldn't fly in the macho home of Da Bears.

Ryan entered the headquarters and noted how vastly different this building was to the 18th district station—even from their own main headquarters, downtown. The Chicago buildings were old, or as the sarge liked to say, "historical-like." The construction on the Atlanta building appeared to be fairly new—built within the last ten to fifteen years—of polished marble and glass.

Inside, the sun from the windows combined with the fluorescent light from above bounced off every surface, making the reception area look more like a modern upscale hotel than a police headquarters. The desk sergeant directed Ryan to the office of the chief, which was located at the end of a hallway on the ground floor of the building. Like Besko's office, it was situated in the back of a large space, but instead of it being in a detective unit, it appeared to be more of a common area for all of the officers in the building. A large-screen television hung on one wall, currently dark, and a full lunchroom (behind glass) bordered the right side of the room. Several uniformed and plainclothes officers gathered in the lunchroom getting their morning coffee, either ending their graveyard shift or beginning their day shift. Two restrooms were located behind the lunchroom, and next to them a doorway led to an annex with a maze of desks and cubicles.

Above the various voices in the room, he heard the familiar squawk of his partner's voice.

"Hey, D! Over here." Di Santo called out to him from a round table surrounded by several Atlanta officers.

Ryan slapped hands with the cops, whom he recognized

from the previous day, while scanning the room for someone else he might recognize. She probably wasn't on the
morning shift. He tolerated more kudos from the cops on
the newly dubbed "Cult Raid" and thanked them with genuine modesty.

At exactly nine o'clock Chief Burke entered and motioned the detectives toward the back of the room, to his
office. His large, mahogany desk was on the left side of his
space with two chairs facing it. It was basically the same
setup as Besko's office, if the sarge's office was fifty square
feet larger and held expensive mahogany furniture.

"Cute kids," Di Santo commented, referring to a picture
on the chief's desk.

"Grandkids, thanks. They're a handful! You guys have
kids?"

Di Santo shook his head and then glanced in Ryan's direction.

"Nope," Ryan responded and rubbed his nose.

Di Santo stared at him as if he had just lied on the stand,
but Ryan ignored it. It very well could be completely over
with Cat, and he had to prepare himself emotionally to separate from her and her boys.

Chief Burke had Ryan write out his statement on the
previous evening on a standard Atlanta PD statement form
and sign the bottom of it when he had finished. They then
listened to the audio recording of his ill-fated visit to ODL,
which now sat as a digital file on Burke's computer. Ryan
was embarrassed by how loud his personal movements
sounded on the audio track, but it made sense since the mic
was sitting directly on his chest. Every headshake, shift,
cough, and utterance was about three decibels louder than
the other sounds on the recording. His voice boomed over
the other dialogue that was directed at him, but at least
Smith's voice was audible. And then came the sniffs. He
looked down at the floor as soon as he heard the first one,
and his eyes remained there when he heard SWAT shouting
and then eventually the boom of the assault weapon that

took the life of Warren L. Smith. Ryan lifted his head again when the recording stopped.

"We'll send you a copy along with the transcript, for your files," Burke said. "We've got the other members in custody, but that attorney's not letting them make any statements at this time. With them all lawyering up, I don't think we're gonna get any info that we don't already have. You boys don't have to stick around if you don't want to, but you're welcome to stay if you need anything else from us."

Ryan didn't hear the chief's last couple of words because his eyes had locked onto Officer Hill through the glass wall. She crossed the open space quickly, heading to the lunch-room. "Excuse me, I'm going to get some coffee, if that's okay," Ryan announced.

He got up from his chair without waiting for approval and made his way across the space to the lunchroom. Acute-ly aware that Burke and Di Santo could see them from the Chief's office, he purposely turned his back to the men.

Officer Hill was dressed in crisp new police blues, her hair back up on her head, tightly braided, giving off a slight smell of baby shampoo.

"Hill," Ryan greeted her. He racked his brain for her giv-en name but none surfaced.

"Doherty. Want some coffee?" she held up the coffee pot with a grim expression on her face.

"Sure. Black, thanks."

She opened a cabinet and took out two mismatched mugs. Even though there was nobody else within earshot, Ryan lowered his voice.

"I want to apologize again for last night. It's not you."

She chuckled. "Seriously? You're going to do the whole *it's-not-you-it's-me* thing?"

"Yeah, well…"

She filled his mug with black muddy liquid, and then her own. "I can't say I've ever been kicked out of a guy's room before. *Before* sex, that is. But we're good, no worries."

"I shouldn't have let you in in the first place. I was—it was a long night."

"It would've been fun," Hill said, raising her mug to take a sip. "But I guess it was for the best. Since you're *involved*…" She lifted her chin as she said it, almost in challenge. "Had a talk with your partner this morning. He was here early."

Ryan's head whipped around and he glared at Di Santo through the two walls of glass. Di Santo caught his gaze with a curious expression.

"Yeah, well, sometimes he doesn't get all the facts straight."

Hill locked onto his eyes and took another shallow sip of the steaming coffee. "And what about you, Doherty? Do *you* have the all facts straight? Do you have a girlfriend or not?"

When he didn't answer, Hill shook her head, left the lunchroom, and turned into the annex. Ryan's jaw clenched. He placed his mug down on the lunchroom counter and strode back to the Burke's office.

"Sorry, Chief. Can I have a word with my partner?" He hoped he gave Di Santo a look like he was drilling into his skull. "Outside."

Di Santo followed Ryan out of the squad room and down the hall, practically jogging to catch up to him. "What's up, D?"

"Shut up." Ryan exited the building and took the front stairs two at a time. When he reached the lawn in front of the headquarters, he turned back to Di Santo. "What'd I tell you about staying out of my business?" he said, poking Di Santo's shoulder.

"You were making a big mistake with Blondie in there! I was trying to help you!"

"Maybe I don't want your help right now." Ryan shoved his partner.

"Think about Cat, D. Don't throw away a good thing!"

"Who are you, my mother? My priest?" He kept poking

Di Santo's shoulder hoping to irritate him, start a fight. When Di Santo finally dodged his hand, Ryan slapped him on the opposite side of his head.

"What the hell are you doing?" Di Santo said, his voice rising in pitch. "We're partners, we're buds!" The little guy's eyes darted around for witnesses.

"You're *not* my friend. You're my partner. That's all." That seemed to hit Di Santo harder than his hand. "You think that gives you the right to take over my life? We're co-workers. *Capisce*?" With the last word, he pushed Di Santo back with both hands.

"You're gonna wanna stop touching me, D," Di Santo warned. He cracked his neck and made two fists.

"Fuck you. Make me." Ryan kept pushing him.

"I'm serious."

"Do it!"

Di Santo then threw a quick right jab, which landed sharply on Ryan's left cheek. Ryan felt a sting and a dribble of blood.

"Oh, sorry, my class ring," Di Santo said.

After a quick breath, Ryan tackled Di Santo and they fell to the ground. He got a few sharp punches into Di Santo's ribcage and was about to smash his jaw when he felt some-one grab him and pull him up by his shirt and shoulders. Glancing behind him, he saw it was a couple of uniformed cops, who let him go as soon as they righted him and he could stand on his own. If it hadn't been for the badge on his belt, they would have been hauling his ass into lockup. A third officer helped Di Santo up, and the uniforms stood looking at the two of them, probably trying to ascertain the state of the conflict.

Ryan waved, dismissing his partner's existence. "Just stay the hell away from me today," he shouted at Di Santo, then turned and sprinted up the marble steps and back into the building. Back in the brightly lit squad room, he headed directly to the restroom in back.

He had to clean up before he returned to Burke's office. This was not how he wanted the Chicago PD to be repped in another city.

The men's room was a single-seater: just a toilet, a urinal and sink. He had started the tap on the sink when he heard a soft knock at the door.

"What." It had better not be Di Santo or he was in for another beating.

"It's me," Officer Hill's voice came in through the door. "I've got first aid."

# CHAPTER 29

Ryan unlocked the restroom door and opened it a crack to make sure Hill didn't have anyone else in tow. She stood close to the jamb, holding up a small plastic box bearing the obligatory red cross. He let her in and locked the door behind her.

"I saw the blood on your face when you came in," she said, wiping his cheek with her thumb.

He winced. She walked over to the sink, pulled two brown paper towels from the dispenser, and ran them under the cold water. When she returned, Ryan leaned against the wall and let her dab his face with the towel. The cool water felt good. He realized he was overheated from fighting, not to mention the heavy, wet Georgia air.

"Scoot down," she said, and he bent his legs slightly so he was at her level. She angled her head, assessing the cut on his cheek. "It's not bad, just a lot of blood. But it's slowing down now." She pulled out a square package containing an alcohol wipe and ripped it open with one hand and her teeth.

"Thanks."

"It's Heather, by the way."

Busted. "Heather Hill. Nice name," he said.

She flashed him a smile and dabbed the wound with the alcohol wipe. He drew in a breath when the delayed sting hit him. Hill put a hand on his chest for comfort. "I hope this wasn't over me."

"No," he lied.

Hill met his gaze with suspicious cop eyes. His Irish smile softened her expression.

"When are you going back?" she asked. "Tonight? Tomorrow?"

"Not sure," Ryan answered. It was the truth.

The next question remained unasked. He studied her face and deep green eyes, which reminded him of Kelly's. With the exception of the blonde hair, she looked a lot like his ex-girlfriend. About ten years ago.

"How old are you, anyway?" he asked her.

She stopped dabbing for a split second and then threw the alcohol pad into the trash.

"Twenty-two. Why?"

The number hit him harder than Di Santo's right hook. Only three years older than Hank and Duke. He blinked his eyes rapidly as that processed.

When his conscience kicked in, he said, "You don't want a one-nighter."

She unpeeled the wrapper from a medium-sized Band-Aid, pulled off the two backing strips, and placed the bandage on an angle across his cheek.

"How do you know what I want?" she asked him, tossing the wrapper.

"You deserve better than that."

She leaned in closely to him and he could feel her breath on his mouth.

"I deserve better than that, huh?"

He glanced at her full lips and she took it as an invitation, touching them to his—hesitantly, at first. Then she leaned in, pressing him against the wall, and kissed him deeper. Her tongue parted his lips and playfully teased his. Just as he felt himself kissing her back, he broke it off.

"Um, Hill—Heather. I can't."

"You can't or you won't?" she asked.

"Both."

She studied him. Patted his chest. "You kicking me out, again?"

"Sorta, yeah," he said, rubbing her kiss off of his mouth. "Matt was right. I am involved with someone. She—well—it's complicated."

"Fair enough." She turned away from him, closed the first aid kit and headed to the door. Before she left she looked back and said, "Keep that face clean."

The door clicked shut, echoing behind her, and Ryan blew out the air that had gathered in his lungs. Although he hadn't responded to the kiss, he immediately felt like shit. He hadn't kissed another woman since he had met Catharine. He thought about their first night together. They slept—just slept—side-by-side. Nothing else. It had almost killed him. He'd wanted so much to know what it felt like to kiss her and had even told her so. In the morning, she'd blessed him with their first kiss. '*That's what it feels like,*' she whispered into his ear. It changed his life. She changed his life.

The rush of that moment washed through him and the desire to be with Catharine was overpowering. He wanted to lie beside the woman in her big, white bed and run his fingers through her hair from her temples to her waist.

Remembering where he was, Ryan shook off the image and went to the sink, running his hands under the cold water and then through his own hair. He lightly touched the bandage with his index finger while he chastised himself over the close call with Hill, Heather.

When he left the men's room, he scanned the squad, but Officer Hill was nowhere to be seen. Neither was Di Santo, and he was grateful for both. When he stuck his head in to Chief Burke's office, it too was empty.

"Detective Doherty?" A young uniformed officer addressed him.

"Yes."

"Chief Burke had to leave for a meeting, but he told me

to tell you that you were done for the day and if you'd like to head back to Chicago, I can get y'all on a 3:55 flight. You'd be home by dinnertime. Would you like me to book that for you?"

"Yes, please," Ryan answered.

The young officer pounded the keys on his computer for a few minutes until a paper confirmation came out of the printer beside him.

Ryan jotted down a phone number on a yellow pad beside the officer.

"Please call my partner and tell him to meet me at the airport," he instructed.

Ryan toted his duffel and laptop bag into the waiting area of the airline terminal at the Hartsfield-Jackson International airport. When he got to the gate, he spotted Di Santo in a row of black vinyl seats near the window. Their plane had already arrived, with the previous flight's passengers debarking through walkway door. Ryan calculated that they had about fifteen or twenty minutes before their flight began boarding.

He mazed his way through the rows of chairs and took an empty seat next to his partner, placing his bags on the floor.

"Hey," Di Santo said, pulling off his headphones.

"Hey."

They reconciled in silence.

After a minute, Di Santo studied Ryan's cheek. "Sorry 'bout that," he said, pointing to the bandage.

"Just a little scrape."

"It was the ring. Didn't really want to hurt you or nothing."

"I know." Ryan glanced at his watch, then around at the various travelers, seeing if there were any babies that could potentially make their two-hour flight a miserable one. He tapped his fingers on the black armrest.

"Nothing happened," Ryan finally said. "With the cop."

"Yeah, I figured," Di Santo answered.

He knew that wasn't the end of it. He had one more thing to say. "And I'm sorry about that friend thing. You are my partner—and my bud. You've been a good one. And you were just watching out."

"I always will."

They bumped fists and the subject was closed.

# CHAPTER 30

Distracted from her gardening, Catharine alighted the stairs to her bedroom. She needed to decompress and attempted to take a short nap. After almost a half hour of gazing up through her skylight at the afternoon clouds, she figured sleep was not going to happen and decided to meditate, instead.

She inhaled deeply as she focused her mind, as she envisioned a swirling, light pink energy radiating from her body. It picked up speed, curved around her room, and created a funnel above her, climbing higher and higher until it reached the skylight and traveled through it into the trees, above. It then slowed its climb, circling back and descending, falling, until it came back, trickling down through her ceiling and back into her.

Catharine's thoughts turned to Ryan. Ryan in the past and the present. It had been days since they had spoken and she wanted to get a feeling or an impression on where he was at that very moment. To feel him and hear his voice. She pictured the 18th district police station and his desk. An empty chair. Her thoughts went to his apartment—although she had never actually been there, she tried to picture it in her mind's eye. The bed wasn't slept in. She tried to feel his energy perhaps running along the lakeshore, but that didn't feel right, either.

Catharine's head rolled slowly to the left, and her body followed. She pulled her knees up to her chest and curled into a fetal position. She concentrated on the heart chakra and its associated color: green. She imagined herself covered in a warm, pine-green blanket. She closed her eyes and another set of eyes appeared in her consciousness. Green eyes. Female. Smiling eyes. She bristled. Ryan wouldn't be with another woman. Not possible.

She then felt his presence. Ryan was with her, next to her—in bed. She could smell him. She could feel his thumb lightly brush her lips, the other four fingers lingering at her temple then slowly making a journey down through her hair. It gave her chills down her spine and out through her toes.

Then he vanished.

Catharine opened her eyes but remained still, trying to take in the space around her. The afternoon sun shone yellow against her all-white walls. Outside, the birds performed delicate mating cantatas, sweetly calling for love. The room, itself, was silent except for her own heavy breathing and pounding heart.

*He'll be back.* She was sure of it. Or was she?

She sat up, opened her nightstand drawer, and removed a red silk pouch. In it were her crystals. The special crystals that she believed could enhance her innate abilities.

Catharine placed one quartz bar in each hand and shut her eyes. The instant images were as clear as a video screen, but flashing in and out so quickly, she couldn't catch any of them for more than a second. *The rapper on the cross, grenades, Mandy and Hank, concertgoers, a dark alley, blood. Lots of blood.* Her palms pulsed with a small ache. *Money, children. A fence with flowers. A memorial. A buzzing fly.* The pain sharpened, as if needles were piercing her palms. *Rapper on the cross. A knife in the chest.* The pain grew unbearable to the point where she dropped the crystals and opened her eyes. Blinking, unfocussed, she thought she saw blood oozing from two puncture wounds, one in each palm.

Before it could drip on her white bed sheets, she pressed

her hands together, leaped out of bed, and ran to her bathroom.

She turned on the cold faucet and wrung her hands under the faucet in true Lady Macbeth form, expecting the water to run pink, but only clear water fell and circled down the drain. Another study of the front and back of her hands revealed no blood, no puncture wounds. The pain had subsided. An abstract phenomenon. A vision of stigmata, not reality.

She was startled from her thoughts by an unexpected rap on the bedroom door.

"Yes?" Catharine called out, rushing to dry her hands on the white towel. She double-checked to make sure there were no bloodstains before exiting the bathroom.

"Ma, it's us," she heard Hank say through the closed door.

"Hi, babies, come on in."

She sat back down on the bed and picked up a book, pretending she had been reading all along. Hank and Duke bounded down into the bedroom in their stocking feet and sat on either side of the bed. Duke leaned over and kissed his mother on the cheek. She accepted it with a smile.

"What's up?" she asked.

"How *are* you?" Hank said.

"I'm fine," she answered and gave him a sideways glance. "Why, what do you want?"

"Nothing," answered Hank.

The boys locked eyes, conversing silently in that way twins communicated.

"*Guys?*"

"Ma, Hank and I were talking," Duke said.

He glanced at his brother to continue.

Hank took his cue. "We noticed that you've been kind of down," he said. "You don't usually nap in the middle of the day."

They paused and she knew they wanted her to say something, but she didn't know what to say. How could you explain the complications of your love life to your children? In the fifteen years since she had divorced Eric, there had been maybe two or three short-term relationships, none long enough for Catharine to bring the man into her household. Not one long enough for the man to create a bond with the boys.

Hank continued the inquiry. "Yeah, and we noticed that Ryan hasn't been around for a day or two. And, well, we heard you crying earlier."

Catharine took a deep breath and considered how she was going to explain the situation to them.

"We want to know if something happened," added Duke.

Even though they were large-framed, nineteen-year-old linebackers, when they hung their heads and looked up at her like this with their big, saucer-like eyes, they were still her little boys—the same boys that used to grab at her skirt and chase each other around her legs. She flashed on another time they had those same faces, looking at her for answers.

"Remember that day, when you were four? I sat you down and I tried to explain to you that your father wasn't going to live with us anymore?"

Duke punched the bed, jumping to conclusions. She took his fist, uncurled it, and held it in her hand.

"I don't think you boys understood, really, what was going on. Duke, you looked at me and said, 'Okay, can we go bowling now?'"

Duke pouted, staring down at his lap.

Hank's jaw tightened. "I did," he said. "I knew what was happening. I could tell it in your face. Like now."

"Me too, I knew," Duke added. "I just didn't want to say it out loud. It would've made it real and I still wanted you and Dad—"

"I know," Catharine said. She was still holding Duke's hand and she reached out and took Hank's as well, looking back and forth between them.

"Is it another woman?" Hank asked. "'Cause if it's another woman, I'll kill him!"

Catharine flashed on the green eyes, but just couldn't grasp hold of the concept. There was nobody else.

"No, no, it's not another woman," she answered. "But honestly, what it is, is between me and Ryan. It's *our* issue, and it's up to the two of us to work it out. If we can work it out." She focused on Hank. "Did I interfere with you and Mandy?" He shook his head. "No, I didn't. Because I trusted you to make the best decision for *you*. Even if I thought it was a mistake. Right?" She lifted his chin with two fingers. He nodded. "If it doesn't work out with Ryan, then it wasn't meant to be. I have enough love in this house to last me ten lifetimes, and I am so grateful for that."

A tear rolled down Duke's cheek. She leaned over, wiped the tear, and kissed his cheek. She'd always known him to be the more sensitive of the two. He took adversity a lot harder than his twin.

"What about Saturday?" Hank asked. "It's Ryan's birthday, right? Are we still going to have a birthday dinner?"

Catharine shrugged. "I don't know, sweetie. He won't answer my calls."

"Is he coming back?" Duke asked.

"I hope so."

"Me too," Duke said. "He's a good guy."

'*Cat, I need to talk to you,*' a male voice called out from behind the boys.

Catharine leaned to look past her sons—straining to see if there was anyone else in the room. Standing in the doorway was a figure of a person, ensconced in light.

The twins followed her gaze behind them to see what had caught her attention. "Ma? What is it?" Hank asked. "Are you seeing something?"

"Don't you?" she asked them.

The haze entered the bedroom and circled the perimeter of the round space as she felt a vibration in the air. Heavy, but pounding.

"I—I don't see anything," Duke answered, glancing at his brother.

Hank shook his head. "Me neither. Maybe you need to rest."

Her initial instinct was to get the boys out and see what this specter—if it was a specter—wanted. "Oh, it must have been just a flash of light from the sun," she told them, appeasing their concern. "You boys are right. I could use a short nap. I'll be down in a half hour."

When Hank and Duke left the room and Catharine stood up, ready to confront the entity in her bedroom.

"Hello? Who are you?"

Like a Polaroid, a blurred image of a man developed before her. She recognized him from the photos on Ryan's phone.

"Jonathan," she said, with almost a sigh of relief.

She knew Jonathan Lange from Ryan's anecdotes and memories of his former partner. He seemed to be a good person and, from what she'd heard, an exemplary police officer. She hoped that translated into the afterlife as a good spirit. She took a deep breath and willed herself to relax, the vibrations still swirled in the room, ebbing and flowing like ocean waves.

"So good to finally meet you," she greeted him. "I thought this day might come."

'*Cat,*' he said, as if already familiar with her. '*I wish I could hug you, but it just won't work.*' His white grin almost glistened against his chocolate complexion.

Catharine giggled, half out of nerves, half at his joke.

Jon was a tall, broad black man with closely cropped hair and a thick neck. The crinkles next to his eyes revealed his age at the date of death: early forties. He wore faded blue jeans and a Chicago PD tee shirt, identical to the outfit that Ryan wore to work regularly.

"Why are you here?" she said, taking a tiny step towards the vision. "Is Ryan in danger?"

'*No, Cat. He's okay. He'll be back.*' The assurance

warmed her heart. '*It's time for me to leave, now. I have to leave him...*' The man's form began to fade.

"What?" Catharine moved closer to the mist he had become. "Jonathan! What are you saying?"

His outline sharpened just a bit. '*He has you, Cat. I need to leave. Tell him...he was like a brother to me.*'

"I know he was," she said. She tried to reach for him, instinctively, but her hand cut through the cold mist. "Will you be okay?"

'*The brother...hood. It was the brother...*'

Like a distant radio station, his voice was peppered with white noise, becoming less and less audible.

"Jonathan?"

Jon Lange's spirit had faded into nothingness, leaving Catharine's heart pounding with residual adrenaline. She called his name several more times, hoping for him to rematerialize. But his energy had left the room. The vibrating had ceased.

Catharine went over the man's message in her head, but she couldn't piece it together. Should she even relay it to Ryan? She wondered if the "brother" had to do with Terrico James. They had arrested Terrico's brother for the murder, so maybe Jon was merely confirming that they had the right person in custody.

She picked up her cell from the nightstand and dialed Ryan. Straight to voice mail. "Ryan, it's me. Please listen...I know you don't want to talk right now, but it's very important you call me. It's about Jonathan Lange. I love you. Take care."

# CHAPTER 31

Ryan clicked "Ignore" on his cell when a call came in from Catharine. He just couldn't deal with the relationship before the flight. He'd see how he felt when he got home.

"I'm guessing that was Cat?" Di Santo asked.

Ryan glared at him until Di Santo mimed locking his mouth and throwing away the key. Yeah, that would last for a minute and a half.

A tabloid headline caught his eye from across the aisle of airport chairs. *TERRICO AND MANDY'S LOVE CHILD!* The face of the reader was hidden behind the paper, but a blue church hat peeked out over the tabloid pages while two chubby brown hands held it on either side. Ryan elbowed his partner and pointed to the photo underneath the headline, which showed Terrico James holding a small freckle-faced baby.

Di Santo leaned into the aisle. "Hey, ma'am, can we see that magazine for a minute?" The magazine lowered and a big, black woman squinted her eyes at him. Di Santo pulled out his badge and added "Police business."

Ryan chuckled silently.

"Mm-hmmm," she said with a smirk and then handed him the mag. "I'm gonna want it back!"

Di Santo agreed, took the paper with a smile, and

thumbed through the pages while Ryan looked over his shoulder. On page three, they found the article: *MANDY ROSS, TEEN MOTHER.*

"What does it say?" asked Ryan.

"Hold on…"

"It could be a bunch of crap, this isn't exactly the *New York Times*," Ryan said.

"Yeah, but I wanna know 'cause I've got an inquiring mind!"

"Hunh!" grunted the woman across the aisle.

"Okay, it says that—Wow! According to the popular celebrity crime blog *Finfamous.com*, when Mandy was sixteen, she supposedly went into 'rehab' for four months. But they suspect she was really in a private spa in the Caribbean having Terrico's baby!" Di Santo hit the page with the back of his hand.

Ryan couldn't help but be a bit proud of his sister. She had edged her blog into being a legitimate source. Even for this trashy paper. "And?"

"'Kay, hold on…yadda, yadda…Terrico wanted to keep it, but Mandy gave it up for adoption."

Ryan took the tabloid. "Wait a second, let me see that." He reviewed several photos on the inner page with Terrico and his alleged love child. "I've seen this baby. This is Chris's baby girl."

"Who's Chris?" asked the woman across the aisle. The detectives ignored her.

"Some photographer may have just gotten pictures of Terrico holding his niece and they made a story out of it," Ryan said.

"Or…" Di Santo said.

"Or what?" asked the woman, eager to insert herself into the conversation.

Di Santo lowered his voice and leaned in to Ryan. "Or that *could* be Mandy's baby. She does kinda look a little…mocha." Di Santo handed the magazine back to the woman.

"Mmm-hmm," she answered. "This baby ain't dark chocolate! And Terrico is dark chocolate! Well he *was,* God rest his soul." She crossed herself.

Ryan stared back at the cover, squinting his eyes. "What are you thinking, D?" Di Santo asked.

"Maybe this whole thing centers around that baby." Ryan took out his cell phone. He noticed that their conversation about Terrico's love child was starting to attract attention, so he got up and headed to a secluded corner of the terminal.

"Hey, Jane, this is Ryan. I need a favor," he told her voice mail. "See if there are any cases—family court, custody in particular—in either Illinois or California that involve Terrico James. It may be under his real name, Terrence James Robinson. And if not, check his brother's name, Christopher Robinson. I know it's a common name, but you can use the same address on Reggie Robinson's arrest warrant to isolate it. They all live in the same house. Thanks and let me know."

The flight attendant announced that boarding was about to begin when Ryan returned to their seats. Di Santo and the tabloid owner were in deep conversation.

"I left a message for Jane at the SA's office. We should also talk to Chris."

"Oh, Detective, your partner was telling me all about the Terrico case, that you were *there* when it happened! Did he really—"

"Sorry, ma'am, but we can't talk about an ongoing investigation." It was more a reprimand for Di Santo than an apology to the woman.

Ryan got home to his apartment by 8:17 p.m. thanks to the residual rush hour on the Eisenhower. He threw his duffel bag on his bed and took a quick rinse in the shower. Airplanes always made him feel dirty, no matter how short the flight. He towel-dried his hair, and pulled the James file from his laptop bag. He had planned to go through it detail by detail but had fallen asleep on the flight back, with lingering exhaustion from yesterday's raid.

He checked his texts and emails, and then played Cat's voice mail message.

"Ryan, it's me. Please listen…I know you don't want to talk right now, but it's very important you call me. It's about Jonathan Lange. I love you. Take care."

He almost pressed "Dial" but he couldn't bring himself to talk to her tonight. Jon had been gone for two years, nine months, and twenty-nine days now. It couldn't be that pressing.

He got a beer from the fridge and plopped down into his recliner. He could feel her presence. In a way, he could sense when she was thinking about him. They had a strong connection—maybe psychic, maybe just emotional.

Ryan missed her from his life already, and it had been only two days. Catharine had become his other half, his best friend. It was really tough losing your best friend, the person you shared everything with. And it had already become a habit to want to share everything with her, instinctively. That funny cat video, the new HBO show, the current case. Without her, there was no one to share with. A lonely-ass feeling. Shit, she didn't even know he had been out of town.

He shook off the desolation and dialed into his work voice mail at the 18th. The automated voice told him he had three new messages.

"Hey, Ryan, this is Zach. I heard you were in some kind of a shootout or something! Call me when you get back. You, me, and Matt should grab a drink at the McGinty's. I wanna hear all about it!"

News traveled fast in the department. He wasn't sure if or when he wanted to rehash the ODL debacle.

Delete.

"Chief Burke, Atlanta PD. I didn't get the opportunity to say goodbye to you and Detective Di Santo. I just wanted to thank you again for your extreme bravery yesterday. Commendations have been sent to your superior officer and the superintendent of police over there in Chicago. I'll be talking with the Illinois State's Attorney's office to see if they want to still press charges on the corpse desecration thing and if they want to reopen the murder investigation in light of the ODL's involvement. In the meantime, I hope you get a coupl'a days off. You deserve 'em! Take care, Detective."

Save.

"Hey, it's Jane. Just wanted you to know that we wrapped up closing arguments in the Elliot trial today and the jury's probably going into deliberations on Monday. I'll let you know when we have a verdict. And I wondered if you were on shift tomorrow. Bye."

That last sentence was in a weird sing-songy tone, very un-Jane. He hoped it didn't have anything to do with his birthday.

Delete.

"You have no more new messages."

He disconnected and thought about calling Jane back, but was reminded of Di Santo's warning. He couldn't run to her every time he and Cat had a fight.

When he opened the browser on his phone, the Celtic cross was still there from his search:

He scanned the variants of the symbol, the scariest being the one surrounded by the words, *White Pride, World Wide*. His heart ached as he reflected on the continued hatred in the world. As a white man, he would never truly understand the pain of discrimination, but he'd heard Jon's stories on many occasions.

The injustice, the frustration. Being stopped by other cops when he was off duty and out of uniform. How Jon loved to pull out his badge and shove it in their faces. But it was disgusting that he had to even qualify himself with the badge. What about all the law-abiding citizens who didn't have a badge to flash and had to tolerate the abuse? He knew the department still had its throwbacks, and Fisk was one of them. Luckily, it was a top priority of Superintendent Grady to clean up that shit.

He shot off an email to Sergeant Besko, relaying his suspicions about Fisk. And at that, Detective Ryan Doherty was done for the night. He shut down the laptop as he shut down his brain, popped the top on the Goose Island brew, and decided to take the whole weekend off. No Terrico, no trial. No Catharine, no Jane. No ODL, no Fisk. No phone.

Offline.

Tomorrow he'd celebrate his thirty-ninth alone. Celebrate himself *by* himself. He'd hit the gym, take a long run along the lakefront, and maybe even spend all day Sunday at North Avenue beach. Hadn't done that for years, and he missed the combined smell of the fishy lake, the sweaty sunscreen, and the greasy food trucks.

It was a plan. He'd earned a weekend off.

# CHAPTER 32

The four-on, two-off schedule had been all but demolished with the Terrico James case, and although he was not technically on duty, Di Santo came into the 18th on Saturday for a very special reason: to oversee the birthday decorations. He and Officer Paige Riley did a number on Ryan's desk, from streamers to floating Mylar balloons tethered to his chair and phone. He couldn't wait to see his partner's face on Monday.

As they were putting the final touches on it, Jane entered the squad. She grinned at the sight of Ryan's desk. "He's going to hate it."

"Woah, look at you!" Di Santo said, taking in the sight of the prosecutor in casual attire. "You actually own a pair of jeans! Who knew?"

"You should talk, Di Santo. I think this is the first time I've known you that I haven't seen you all suited up."

"The pair of us, right? Nothing wrong with dressing the part. Dress for success, and all that. So why are you here?"

"Oh, I just wanted to drop something off for him," she said, nodding to Ryan's desk. "Is he coming in today too?"

"Nah, Sarge gave us the weekend off. Just getting this all fixed up for Monday. So whatcha got?"

Jane pulled a manila envelope from her sizable designer bag. "I have a report he asked me to run." She handed him the manila envelope and then dove back into her purse and pulled out a small blue one. "Just a little birthday card," she tossed off as she propped it up against the keyboard on Ryan's desk. It didn't look out of place amidst Riley's decorations.

Di Santo studied the card and the blush that saturated Jane's face and made a critical split-second decision.

"Jane, come with me." He put a hand on her back and turned her around, while he picked up the card in the blue envelope.

"Come with you *where?* Where are we going?"

He escorted her back through the double doors. "Across the street. I'm buying you breakfast."

"But I don't want—"

"Jane, I'm buying you breakfast," he said, as a command. "It's Saturday morning. What else are you going to do? We've never talked, just you and me, and I want to get to know you. You have time?"

"No." She looked at her phone. "Yes. Okay."

Looking confused, she allowed herself to be gently pushed down the marble stairway and out the stationhouse door. He was surprised, too, because the woman had about three inches and probably ten pounds on him. Not that she was hefty. Jane Steffen was athletic. She worked out.

Keeping his hand on Jane's back, Di Santo guided her across the street and held the door open to the diner. The Stripes Café was one of the oldest eateries in the neighborhood, specifically constructed in the late 1940s to feed the cops in the 18th district station. It had gone through several bouts of ownership since, but was now owned by a husband and wife, Charlie and Viv Pulaski. They kept it clean and honest and somehow managed to employ the best short order cooks in town.

Bells jingled as the door opened and closed behind them. Di Santo motioned to the regular waitress that they were taking a table. She nodded.

Jane scooted into the green vinyl booth, placing her

purse next to her. Di Santo took a seat across from her and placed the birthday card on the seat beside him.

The waitress came right up to the table before he could begin the conversation.

"Hey, Detective, what can I get for you?"

Grace wasn't as old as she pretended to be, probably early thirties, but he could see she savored the role of diner waitress and played it to the hilt with her ruby red lips and her hair elevated into a baby beehive.

"Hi, Gracie. Just coffee for me. Jane? You want pancakes or something?"

Jane glared at him as if he were an alien from Mars. "Actually, I don't eat breakfast. I'll take coffee, too. Black, thanks." Jane flashed a smile at the waitress and a scowl at Di Santo.

"You got it, sweetie." Grace tucked an order pad back in her apron and turned away from the table.

Jane slapped the table. "So?"

"So." Di Santo echoed, glancing around at everything but Jane, trying to figure out a way to say what he had to say.

"This a date, Di Santo? Or do you have an agenda?" she said. Impatient with no answer, she took out her phone and checked something.

Grace returned with two white mugs, which she flipped and filled in front of them. Di Santo waited until she left the table before he began.

"Jane, I'm telling this to you as a friend. And as Ryan's partner. I think you need to back off."

Jane pulled back as if he had struck her. She furrowed her brows, and her hazel eyes squinted until they were just slits. She took in a deep breath, probably to protest, when he continued.

"I don't know what's going on, and frankly, I really don't wanna know, but I know Ryan loves Cat. And that's where he belongs. And you? You just confuse the guy. And that's no good. For him or for you."

She shook her head and chuffed as if she couldn't be bothered by his accusation. "We're *friends*, Matt. That's it." Jane picked up her coffee, blew off the steam, and took a tentative drink.

"You really believe that?"

"Of course, I believe it. I know it. Nothing more has ever happened between us."

"You think I'm an idiot, Jane?" She looked up at him. "There's a reason I made detective at a young age," he continued. "I've got a keen sense of observation. And I know people. I know how they work, how they tick. I'm like a psychologist, without the degree."

She rolled her eyes. "A psychologist. Okay, Matt. And what, exactly, do you think is going on?"

"I think you're fooling him into believing you're friends."

"Who the *fuck* are you to—"

"Shut up and let me talk!" he hissed, staring straight into her eyes. "I think you're fooling Ryan *and yourself* into believing you're friends. You're no dummy, Miss Ivy League. You know what you're doing and I know what you're doing, and I don't know if our friend is too stupid to know what you're doing or just thinking with his dick, but I'm nipping it in the bud, right here." He tapped the Formica table with his index finger.

"You are *so* out of line," she said, shaking her head.

"I'm out of line, eh? This is what I think: I think you're taking advantage of Catharine's situation. You give him what she can't: companionship outside of the house, dinners out, police work. Everything but sex. It's like an opposite affair. Usually it's the sex that gets guys to step out, but you, you're doing it backward. You're giving him the social stuff he can't get from Catharine, and you're just biding your time until he gives you the rest."

She sobered and looked down at her coffee mug, mulling over his words in that super-smart brain of hers.

"Today is Ryan's thirty-ninth birthday," Di Santo said, a

little more quietly. Jane's eyes lifted to his. "Yeah, you know that, because you came in to bring him this."

He slapped the card onto the table, keeping his hand on top of it. Her eyes went to the blue envelope, and he noted a hint of shame in them. Jane's breathing became erratic and he could see her shoulders twitch, slightly. But he had more to say.

"What if I opened this card? What if I read it to the squad? In the card, I'm sure you wrote a 'just friends,' 'just coworkers' sentiment, right?"

"Don't you dare!"

"Well, can I read it?"

"No." She reached for the card but he pulled it back. "Ryan and I—we have—"

"You have diddly-squat, my friend. Nothing. Ryan Doherty should be with Catharine Lulling. And I am going to do my best to see that it happens. They belong together. And she's going to get better and get out of the house so they can have a normal life together. I am going to make damn sure they make up and that no one gets in the way, because for the past two years he was a mess. His partner died. Then his girlfriend left, and he was just a shell. I found out I really didn't *know* him until he met Cat. Because then he came out of it. She brought him back to the land of the living. It's like he became a whole person. He's happy. He's not drinking. He's going to make up with her. And you are going to stop your little friendship game and leave—him— alone."

Her expression remained stoic, but as she gazed at the blue envelope her eyes brimmed with tears.

"There she is," Di Santo said. "*That's* the woman I'm trying to reach. The one underneath the hardcore I'm-a- tough-lawyer shell." He gave her a few moments. "I know it hurts, but better now than before everything gets all fucked up. And it would, Jane, it would get fucked up if you and Ryan continued this so-called 'friendship.' You know it. Deep down, you're probably already fucked up."

She looked up at him, questioning the statement.

He elaborated: "Wanting him and not having him. Must be hard. Like leading a thirsty horse to water, but not letting it drink."

It was a standard investigation technique. Empathize, sympathize with the suspect. Let her feel that you understand. It was working. Although Jane remained as still as a statue, the tears began to slide down her cheeks.

"I know him better than anyone outside of his family, Jane," Di Santo continued. "And what I know is that his life changed the day he met Catharine. *He* changed. Profoundly. For the better. And as his partner, I have to protect him. I'm not going to let anything get in the way of that."

"Everything okay?" the waitress said, checking in on them.

"Yeah, thanks, Gracie. We're okay," Di Santo said quietly. He handed her a ten. "Keep the change."

The waitress nodded and left them. He turned his attention back to Jane, who was trying to clear the tears with the backs of her thumbs. He leaned his elbows on the table and tried to put his hand on hers, but she quickly snapped it away.

"So. What you're going to do is let him go," Di Santo said softly. "Stop the dates, the jokes, the texts, the emails. You're not his friend. You're not going to *be* his friend. You're going to let go. For him and for yourself." He took the first drink of coffee since he started his speech and watched Jane study the table.

He didn't know what was going through her mind, but he figured she was hearing him, since she hadn't screamed and stormed out of the diner. Yet.

After a minute of letting his words sink in, she started to nod, slowly, wordlessly. She had agreed.

Di Santo got up out of the booth and ripped the blue envelope in half, drawing her attention. He tucked the two halves of the card into a pocket of her briefcase as he looked straight into her eyes.

"Let him go," he reiterated and then left the diner.

He jogged back across the street, but before he alighted the front steps to the station, he turned to look at Jane through the diner window.

Grace had taken the seat opposite her, where Di Santo had been, and had her hand on Jane's. Satisfied he had gotten through to her, he went back to work.

# CHAPTER 33

Ryan ran into Di Santo in the lobby as he entered the 18th District station bright and early Monday morning.

"Happy belated birthday, partner!" Di Santo shouted, as they climbed in tandem up the stairway to the second floor. "You didn't answer any of my texts on Saturday. Didja have a good one? Didja see Cat?"

"Yes, and no." Subject closed. "You just getting in?"

"No, I've been here a while…"

As soon as they entered the squad room, the rest of the detectives broke out in a chorus of "Happy Birthday."

Ryan smiled and waited for the cacophony to end while he stared in the direction of his desk. It was transformed into a monstrosity of balloons and streamers. This was going to be a long day.

"Hey, D," one of the other guys shouted from a cubicle. "This the big four-oh?"

"One more year, guys. Don't put me in the grave yet."

Di Santo went to the snack room while Ryan put down his laptop case and went to a manila envelope that had been left on his party desk. Inside, was a report with a note clipped to it: *You owe me!* ☺ *Jane*

He took the note off, paperclip flying off somewhere to the left of his desk. It was an Illinois court filing: *Robinson v. Robinson*, in Illinois family court for the custody of a female child named Tyree Amanda Robinson.

"Holy shit, the baby *is* Mandy's."

Di Santo came out of the snack room with a coffee in one hand and once-bitten donut in the other. "I told you! *Mocha!*" he said, spitting powdered sugar. "How do you know?"

"The baby's name is Tyree *Amanda* Robinson—after Mandy." Ryan read the papers aloud. "The filing lists the father *and* mother's name...yep! Amanda Louise Ross. She had relinquished all parental rights when Tyree was born. According to this, Terrico had given the baby to Chris when she was born, but she was never legally adopted. He had since changed his mind and was suing for custody. Wanted the baby with him, back in L.A. Asked for these records to be sealed."

"Wow, I wonder how Jane got them?"

"She's got connections."

"So you think this custody battle has something to do with Reggie killing Terrico?"

"I don't know. I want to go through the case file again." Ryan studied the papers one by one and then stopped and said, "Where's the money?"

"What money?" Di Santo asked, putting down his coffee and donut and dusting the powdered sugar from his hands.

Balloons kept drifting in front of Ryan's face, and he batted them away. "The will, the inheritance, any life insurance. Where's the money?"

"I think Kim Brant said he didn't have a will. It was a big issue. All his guys were fighting over it."

"And if someone doesn't have a will, then money automatically goes to..."

Di Santo punched his fist into the opposite palm. "Terrico's heir!"

Ryan nodded like a teacher approving the right answer. He looked back at the file and flipped through it. "Okay, here's one life insurance policy, taken out by the production company."

"Yeah, that's been pretty standard since the whole Michael Jackson thing. Jackson's production company paid off all his debts and he was going to make it up from the proceeds of his tour."

Ryan thought for a moment as a red balloon drifted between them. He batted it away. "So in that respect, Terrico was more valuable to them alive."

"Definitely so."

"Okay, then. Back to the Robinson family." The red balloon drifted back into his sightline. Ryan grabbed a scissors out of his pen cup and popped it. Then, as long as he had it in his hand, popped the remaining balloons that surrounded him, despite Di Santo's disappointed frown. One of the younger cops in the squad reacted to the noise by reaching for his weapon until he realized what had happened.

When the howls and teasing died down, they went back to case. "There could be family contention regarding the baby. Custody and money. That's a lot of motive."

"Motive for Chris, not Reggie, though." Di Santo took another sip of coffee, making enough of a slurp that the desk sergeant on the floor below could've heard it.

Ryan went to the brown case folder and re-read the ME's report, reviewing every word and phrase.

"There was a bruise in the form of a hand print on Terrico's right shoulder, and the knife wound angled up, from left to right, Zach said." Ryan made the gesture with his right hand, slicing the air with an invisible knife. "So the attacker would have had to be left handed." He went back to the file and flipped through the pages.

"So what does that mean?" Di Santo asked.

"I think it means Reggie didn't do it. I saw Reggie fill out and sign his statement. With his *right* hand. I think he's taking the fall for someone." He searched his memory for every left-handed subject. Usually he noticed those kinds of details. "The publicist," Ryan recalled, flipping through his notes. "Here she is, Kim Barnett." I remember handing her my business card. She took it with her left hand."

"The whole Terrico crew flew back to L.A.," Di Santo said. "They were going to come back for the funeral once Barone released the body."

"Call your girlfriend."

"Who?" said Di Santo, plopping down in his chair and twirling around in a circle.

"Amy-Jo. Tell her to call Kim Barnett, the publicist, and tell her we're going to do a press conference about Terrico and we need her here for it. If we tell Kim we want to question her, she may not come all the way back to Chicago. But for her job, she might."

"How did you know?"

"How did I know what?"

"Me and Amy-Jo."

"No shit, really? I was just—*really*?"

"Maybe," Di Santo threw him a wide grin.

Ryan rolled his eyes, picked up the tennis ball from his desk, and threw it at his partner's head. Di Santo caught it before it could connect.

"Just call her."

Amy-Jo Slater called back several minutes later and told Di Santo that Kim was due to fly in Thursday.

"Okay, then. Let's go talk to Chris," Ryan said. "But before we do that, I have to go tell the sarge we're about to reopen a homicide that he told the supe was closed."

"Don't worry. Right now he thinks you're golden because the Atlanta chief called him. I think he's in there now, ordering you a birthday cake."

Ryan strode over to his boss's office and held up a hand before Besko could wish him anything.

"Sarge, I have a couple things before you go celebrating my awesomeness today. One, I don't think Reggie killed Terrico James. We found some new evidence that is not consistent with his confession." Before Besko could curse him into next week, he added, "Oh, and I sent you an email.

You're going to want to look into Wyatt Fisk. I think he aided and abetted in stringing the body up on that cross at Payton Arena. I have reason to believe he has ties to the Klan. Call his previous department before notifying IAD and see if you can eke out some info. Thanks."

The sarge stared at him in disbelief. "You trying to kill me, D? A heart attack at fifty-seven, is that what you want?"

Ryan flashed him the famous Irish grin and slapped the doorjamb. "Thanks, Sarge."

"Fuck you very much, Doherty."

Back at his desk, Ryan picked up the keys to the Impala, and tossed them to his partner. "Let's go see what Chris has to say."

"Are we calling for backup this time?" Di Santo asked as they drove back to the lower south of the city.

Ryan was brimming with energy, wishing that Di Santo would at least break the speed limit. "We don't need backup."

"That's what you said last time."

"We can handle it."

When they pulled up in front of Mae Robinson's house, Ryan noticed the shrine to Terrico James had started to decay. In just a week, the pictures had faded and the flowers withered. A Jesus candle sat off to the side, gray and burnt down to the bottom of the glass holder. Someone had stuck the Love Child photo from the tabloid through a hole in the fence.

They walked up the steps to the now-familiar white iron door. Di Santo stood behind Ryan with his hand hovering over his weapon. He kept turning his head left and right and behind him to look at the street.

"A little jumpy there, Tonto?" Ryan asked.

"It's just a little too quiet, D."

Ryan knocked. They waited about ten seconds and then exchanged a glance. Di Santo went down the steps and looked up at the second floor while Ryan knocked again.

"Ms. Mae? Chris?" he called into the door.

After a minute, he heard the inner door open. He could only see a shadow.

"What do *you* want?" Tracey's voice didn't sound as accommodating as the previous two times they had met.

"Hey, Tracey. Can we come in? We'd like to talk to you."

"What about?" She remained behind the iron door without unlocking it. She was definitely not granting them access. He thought maybe she didn't see them through the door. "It's Detective Doherty and Di Santo. From your brother-in-law's case?"

"I know who you are. Tell me, what is this about?"

"Is Chris home?"

"He's at work. Downtown."

"Can we talk to you?"

"I think we're done talking to the police. Our family has been pulled apart by this whole thing. One brother is dead and the other's in jail. I think it's time you leave us all alone."

She almost had the door shut until Ryan palmed it.

"Tracey, if Chris had anything to do with Terrico's murder—"

"*What?*" She pulled the door open wide again. "You think my husband killed his brother? Reggie *confessed*. Why do you want to involve Chris, now? Is this because we're black? Is that it? Well, let me tell you something. My husband is a college-educated, fully employed family man. How dare you come to my house with this bullshit!" Tracey slammed the door before he could refute her accusation, and the two detectives retreated back to the Impala.

Ryan turned the engine and blasted the air conditioning while they idled.

"I think I know where Chris works downtown," he said. "Hold on."

He took out his wallet and fingered through several business cards until he found the one for the general manager at the security firm, then dialed the number on his cell.

"Celestial Security, may I help you?"

"Yes, may I speak to Chris Robinson?" Ryan said in a friendly tone.

"Sure, who may I ask is calling?"

He rushed to concoct a false identity. "Clancy Ray."

"Clancy Ray?" the woman said, as if she didn't believe him. Shit, maybe she knew Ray. Ryan sounded nothing like him. "Please hold."

He waited while a vintage low-rider pulled up next to them. The bass booming out of the rear sub-woofers rattled their sedan's windows. The vehicle was quite a sight: custom paint job, bright gumball blue on the bottom, school bus yellow on the top. Three men peered out from the windows—driver, passenger, and rear passenger, all extremely interested in the Impala and its occupants. The three men held eye contact as the car rolled by, with the driver flashing them a white and gold-toothed grin.

"Yo, they five-oh!" shouted the backseat passenger. The car kicked into gear and they screeched away.

"Gee, I think we've been made," Di Santo quipped.

A man answered the line. "This is Chris Robinson."

Ryan hung up. "He's there. Let's go."

# CHAPTER 34

Di Santo complained about the downtown parking rates as they pulled into the garage descending into base of the skyscraper. "Highway robbery!" he shouted to the attendant, who appeared to be biding his time until his next cigarette break.

They rode the elevator to the fifteenth floor and entered the reception area for Celestial Security. Ryan held out his badge to the receptionist, a young black woman with doe eyes and short-cropped, natural hair.

"Hello. We're here to see Chris Robinson?" he asked, flashing his shield. "Detectives Doherty and Di Santo. It's about his brother."

"Oh, you sure you're not *Clancy Ray?*" she said with a head wag. Ryan shrugged and the receptionist rolled her eyes. "I assume you're with the other guy?"

"What other guy?" Di Santo asked.

"That other detective," she said, as she glanced at her notepad. "Fisk. He just went back to talk to Chris. You're with him, right?"

Ryan locked eyes with Di Santo as he answered. "Yeah. He's with us. Can we go back?"

"Well, just hold on, hold on. I have to announce you." She picked up her headset and punched some buttons on the phone console.

Di Santo paced around reception while Ryan picked up one of the company's brochures: *Commercial Security, Residential Security, Personal Security, Crowd Control, Bodyguards.* The faces on the brochure were all black, from businessmen to recognizable celebrities. He hadn't noticed the previous time he was here that they had a specific target market. Smart.

"He's not answering," the receptionist informed them after hanging up the phone. "Wait here, and I'll go get him for you. Have a seat." The woman sashayed out from behind the desk and disappeared down the corporate carpeted hallway.

Ryan grew restless as the minutes passed. He glanced at the time on his phone. "What's going on down there?" he asked Di Santo. His partner shrugged. "I'm not getting a good feeling about this. Let's move in."

Ryan didn't pull his weapon, but unlocked the strap on its holster. They rounded the corner to the hall and Ryan spotted the receptionist about two-thirds of the way down, talking through an open door into an office.

"Everything okay?" he called down the hall to her.

The receptionist glanced in their direction and shook her head, slightly. Her expression said it all.

"Draw your weapon," Ryan said to his partner.

"We're engaging? We don't have our vests!"

"Keep your piece down. No pointing. Not yet. We have to see what's going on in that office."

Ryan and Di Santo treaded lightly down the hall, in the direction of the open office. The receptionist's attention was still drawn to something inside, her fear tangible—even from a distance.

"Stand back," Ryan shouted at her.

He motioned for Di Santo to stand against the wall, while he made his way behind the woman. Inside the office, Fisk had his service weapon up to the side of Chris Robinson's temple.

"Fisk, what are you doing?" Ryan said as he pulled his

Glock and raised it in less than two seconds. "Put down your weapon."

"This boy, here, needs to learn some respect for the law," Fisk answered. He appeared fully delighted at the situation. "He's got some crazy theories that his brother didn't kill Terrico James and I wanted to drive home the point that he can't mess with us."

On the word *mess*, he shoved Chris's head with the barrel of the gun.

Chris winced, shutting his eyes as if he truly believed a bullet was coming next. "I went through TJ's file," he said, eyes still shut. "I found several threats from a group calling itself the Knight's Brotherhood. I—I did some research on it. It's Klan. I called you guys and—and—*he* showed up."

"Crockashit," Fisk said. "Trying to blame this on the white man."

"Fisk. Drop—your—weapon," Ryan repeated. "We can handle this."

Detective Fisk took a moment to inhale deeply and lowered his arm. But before they could blink, he lifted it and took a shot at the doorway. Ryan jumped back and pulled the receptionist with him.

She screamed.

He spun her around and pushed her in the direction of reception. "Call 9-1-1!" he shouted.

The woman took off, stumbling once when a high heel caught on the carpet.

Di Santo was still hanging back, pressed against the wall on the opposite side of the doorway. Ryan had to process the fact that a fellow police officer had just shot at them. That made Fisk: 1.) an immediate threat and 2.) a suspect with a hostage. In response to both points, there was only one tack he could take: shoot to kill.

Before he could round his Glock into the room, Fisk came bursting out of it with Chris Robinson in tow, the gun now pressed against Chris's ribcage. He turned to Ryan, "Doherty, I really don't want to do this, but you've left me no choice. You should'a left me in charge of this investigation, and now you done mucked it up."

The man didn't realize Di Santo was behind him until the little guy pounced on his back. A brave move, but risky.

Caught by surprise, Fisk let off a shot and Chris fell to the floor. Ryan ducked down to aid Chris as Di Santo gripped the back of Fisk's shirt, riding his bucking form like a rodeo cowboy.

Chris held his foot, blood from the gunshot wound already seeping through his shoe. Ryan helped him up, and shoved him in the direction of the lobby. The receptionist caught him at the end and helped Chris hobble around the corner, into safety.

When Ryan turned back to the melee, Fisk had Di Santo in a chokehold, dragging him away down the hall.

Shit. "C'mon, Wyatt, it doesn't have to be like this."

"Like I said, Doherty, you should'a just let sleeping dogs lie. Or should I say confessing dogs confess. We had this in the bag with Reggie. It was closed."

It dawned on Ryan why Fisk was so agitated when they took Reggie's statement. Why he kept clearing his throat. He'd been intimidating the witness, signaling Reggie to cooperate and confess. It was all his doing.

Fisk's head spun left and right, searching for an escape. His gaze locked on a door with an exit sign over it.

"Don't do it," Ryan said, eyeing the door. "They just called for backup. You're not getting out of this."

Drops of sweat appeared just below Di Santo's hairline, as he attempted to signal something to Ryan. He kept making eye contact then dropping his gaze to Fisk's weapon. In his left hand. Not completely damning evidence that Fisk killed Terrico, but considering the current situation a feasible conclusion. Ryan nodded, letting Di Santo know that he got the message—and that he'd do everything in his power to get him out of this safely.

Fisk backed up to the exit door, gripped Di Santo's neck a little tighter as he reached around behind him with his gun hand, and opened the door. Both men's shoes scuffled on the gray metal stairwell. Ryan reached the exit door just as it was about to close and spotted them a half-floor down on the landing.

He followed them into the stairwell, the door shutting behind him. Knowing these corporate stairwells, it was most likely that it had locked behind him. Unless you had a keycard, the only way out was ground level, fifteen floors down. He didn't want his partner dragged fifteen floors.

Ryan sat on the top step and held up both hands, his Glock in the right. "Fisk! Stop! Let's deescalate this. Look, I'm putting down my weapon." He slowly placed it beside him and raised his hand again.

Fisk looked up at him, stumbling back against the gray cinderblock wall. Fear flushed across Di Santo's face.

"We can resolve this, calmly," Ryan said. "I trust you, Fisk. You were just trying to keep the case closed. Protect our work. I get it, now. No need to cross the blue line. We're in this together."

Fisk wiped the sweat on his brow with his suit jacket sleeve and flashed a glance down the stairwell.

"It's fifteen flights down, Fisk. Fifteen. I'd rather not chase you down those fifteen floors." Fisk probably knew three or four flights would wind him. Ryan was counting on it. "Tell me what you want."

Di Santo made a fist. They had trained for this. His partner was going to count down, out of Fisk's sightline, and then they would make the move together. Ryan prepared while he kept direct eye contact with Fisk.

"I want the case to remain closed. Forget Chris Robinson and his conspiracy theories. The Brotherhood, w—they had nothing to do with it. He's just trying to get his thug brother out of the can. Reggie killed Terrico James."

Di Santo flashed one finger.

Ryan nodded. "That Klan stuff—totally off the wall," he lied to Fisk. "You're right. We all know it's Reggie."

Di Santo flashed two fingers.

Ryan didn't even make one micro movement toward his Glock or Fisk would've caught it. Di Santo flashed three fingers then dug his heel into Fisk's instep. Ryan went for his weapon. Fisk screamed and loosened the chokehold. Di Santo ducked away from his captor giving Ryan a clear shot. He fired a bullet into Fisk's torso.

Fisk went down to his knees and Di Santo jumped on top of him. Ryan took the half-flight two stairs at a time, and when he got to the landing, kicked Fisk's service weapon down to the fourteenth floor.

"Get off him," he said to Di Santo, pulling him off the man. "Not worth it."

Di Santo pulled himself up off the man with one last kick to the ribs. "White-supremacist shithead. It's fuckheads like you who set the world back fifty years!"

"Chicago PD! Identify yourselves!" came a shout from below, along with a thunder of footsteps up the metal stairs. The lovely, but late, Tac Team.

Ryan called back down with his creds. "Officer down, bleeding. GSR to left shoulder," he added. He turned to his partner. "You okay?"

"Phew! Yeah, I'm fine. Thanks, D. You saved my life."

"Lucky for you, I'm a good shot. I was *not* going to lose another partner."

Di Santo bud-slapped him on the shoulder as the Tac Team's footsteps thundered up the stairwell. When they finally made it to fourteen and a half, Ryan clasped hands with the team lead and explained the incident. "After treatment Detective Fisk is to be taken into custody."

# CHAPTER 35

The first order of business when they got back to the 18th was to release Reggie Robinson. Ryan had to find out why he was willing to take the fall for Terrico's murder. Since Cook County Jail was frothing over with criminals, Reggie was still being held downstairs, in their local cellblock. Di Santo announced that his birthday gift to Ryan was to complete the rest of the paperwork for the case—there was always a shitload of paperwork—so he alighted the steps to the second floor while Ryan went down to Holding.

"Yo, what's going on?" Reggie said, as Ryan instructed the guard to open the cell door.

"You're free to leave, Reggie. We know you didn't kill your brother."

Reggie picked at his head, confused. "Yeah, I did. That detective tol' me so."

"No, Reggie, you didn't. And we're dropping the firearm charge. As long as you turn in your gun."

"Wait, I didn't kill TJ?" The man seemed genuinely confused.

"You know you didn't." Ryan sat down quietly next to him on the cot. "So why did you confess to a murder you didn't commit?"

"I thought I did it. That other detective—the big one—he

kept coming in and talking to me. Convincing me that in that alley—I dunno. I'm just nothing. A nobody. The black sheep of the family an' all that. Sounds like something I would do, and there are times I don't remember things." Reggie shook his head as his eyes dampened.

Ryan put a hand on the man's slumped shoulder. "Reggie, you're not a nothing. Terrence believed in you, didn't he? He believed you could clean up. Hundred grand or no, do his memory a service and get some help. The State can get you into a rehab center. I'll make sure of it." Reggie sat up a bit straighter and looked at him with the curiosity of a five-year-old child. "Look, what you *were* doesn't dictate what you can be. Believe me. Two years ago, I lost my best friend *and* my girlfriend. All within a week. I was a mess. It wasn't until recently that I got my shit together. Took two years, but I did it. There's always time to turn around."

"Yeah, man. I guess I could try. For TJ…"

"For TJ. And Ms. Mae, and Chris, and Tracey, Simone and Tyree. They need you."

"I love them, man. They all I've got."

"I know you do." Ryan clasped Reggie's hand and brought him in for short man-hug. He then handed him a card for Victim Services.

"'Kay, man. I'll do it! And you know what? I was thinking of maybe throwing down some rhymes myself. While I was sitting here in jail I came up with one—a kind of an answer to that happy dude's song. Wanna hear it?"

Ryan nodded. "I sure do."

Reggie stopped to think for a moment then held his hand out in front of him, keeping the beat.

> "You say you're happy, but yo' hair's still nappy,
> Just like your seventy-seven-year-old Grandpap-py!
> So shut up yo' mouth and stop being so sappy.
> 'Cause some of us still got lives that are crappy!"

He ended his concoction with a swoosh of the hand and a

grin. Ryan grinned back, if only to give a small spark of encouragement.

"It's got potential."

"I know, right?" Reggie said, glowing with pride.

"What I do know, is that you have a good chance getting heard with Terrico's name behind you."

"Thanks, man. I 'preciate it, I really do." Reggie came in for another handclasp and hug.

Ryan obliged then instructed the guard to process him out.

Back in the squad, Ryan caught the sarge on his way to the break room and briefed him on the Celestial Security incident. Besko scheduled a meeting with his captain so they could give their official statements, a mandatory follow-up for all officer-involved shootings.

As Ryan gathered his stuff to leave for the day, Amy-Jo Slater burst into the squad room like a whirling dervish. This time she had a grin on her face. It almost made her look human.

"You guys! Check this out," she said, gesturing to his computer. Ryan rounded the desk pod to look. Amy-Jo clicked some keys and brought up Finn's blog. Ryan groaned.

A photo of Mandy Ross took up the entire width of the home page, with the pop star attempting to fend off the photographer. She wore a faux incognito outfit complete with yes-I'm-a-celebrity sunglasses. The headline above the photo read, *Mandy's a Mother, Not a Killer*.

"She's heading overseas to start a new European tour," Amy-Jo explained. "Still denies the child is hers."

Di Santo scrolled down and underneath the photo of the couple was an image of Tyree's birth certificate. "Ha! Guess she can't deny anything, now."

Midway down the page, there was sidebar about the ODL, with a small photo of Smith and his band of brothers, linking to a "related" article. Di Santo clicked through—most likely searching for his own name.

Ryan scanned through the ODL article. Nothing about Fisk. Good. His sister had promised him she'd keep the PD out of it, but he couldn't be sure when it came to his sister. She was a journalist, after all.

As he read through Finn's accounting of the murder and crucifixion—almost in the exact words he had fed her—he recalled questioning Smith the night of the concert. Not yet twenty-four hours after the man had executed the homicide and several hours before they even knew a homicide had been committed, Ryan was drawn to him in the parking lot of Payton Arena. His instinct had been right on—it was a textbook example of Occam's Razor: look to the simplest solution. Or maybe some of Catharine's sixth sense was rubbing off on him. Either way, he promised himself he'd pay more attention to his own instincts.

"Glad it's over," Ryan announced, dismissing himself from the workday.

When he lifted his eyes from the screen, he noticed Amy-Jo's hand on Di Santo's shoulder. Too intimate. It looked like his partner was getting a little something-something after all. He smiled, privately, packed up his laptop, and headed out for the day.

By the time he got back to his Rogers Park apartment it was after nine. Premature fireworks rang out in the distance. He had almost forgotten that tomorrow was the Fourth of July.

Falling down onto his bed, he tried to remember if anyone had invited him to a celebration, cookout, or Cubs game, and resolved that he would be spending the holiday alone.

He eventually nodded off and was dead to the world until the bright rays of the sun woke him the next day at 9:48 a.m. He hadn't slept in that late for months.

Ryan padded into his small bathroom, splashed water on his face, and leaned both hands on the sink so he could study his face in the mirror.

"Thirty-nine," he said to his image, trying on the number. "T-minus-one."

He rubbed the stubble on his chin and took out his shaving gear. After his face was made smooth by the triple-edged blade, he ambled into his bedroom. It was dark, dreary.

He had forgotten why he'd even walked there, so he went back out into the living room and took a good look around.

The apartment appeared depressingly empty. Instead of the sofa, he saw an empty couch. Instead of a television, he saw a dark void. He couldn't imagine watching his shows without Cat snuggling up beside him, laughing when he laughed, or burying her face in his chest during the scary scenes.

He turned to the breakfast bar where two stools stood against the counter, glaringly unoccupied. In the kitchen no one was preparing a meal. He couldn't remember the last time he used the oven. Or stovetop. Maybe he had boiled water last week for mac and cheese.

The refrigerator doors were devoid of magnets. No shopping list, no family photos. No reminders to take out the trash or the dog to the vet. Because he didn't have a dog. Or a vet.

Or a family.

His apartment had become a crypt. A crypt with a big brass plaque that stated: "Detective Ryan Doherty, First Grade, slept here...and slept here...and slept here."

He realized that the space in which he was standing was not his home anymore. He grabbed his phone and his keys and left the apartment.

He had to go home.

# CHAPTER 36

She knelt among the purple and white anemones in her atrium, pruning back the blooms that had taken over the roots of her indoor oak tree. Catharine felt the need for solitude. She'd therefore texted Sara and Lisa and told them to take the day off. The boys were out with friends.

Ryan's birthday had come and gone without a word, which saddened her since it was his first since they had started dating. She had waited—hoped—all day Saturday that he would call. That he would want to share it with her. She had been so tired and frustrated from checking her phone, that by eight o'clock at night she threw it across her bedroom, took a bath, and relinquished herself to bed. No sleep had come to her until after midnight that night, but at least she wasn't pacing the mansion.

Beethoven's *Moonlight Sonata* played from the atrium's sound system and the birds outside seemed to sing along. Catharine had assembled a playlist of melancholy songs to match her mood. She hummed along, herself, to the instrumental lament.

When she heard the dogs bark, she stopped clipping and turned to look toward the front of the gardens. Keys rattled in the front door, it opened, and then the dogs were silent again. Assuming the boys had returned home early, she turned her attention back to the garden and continued to hum along to Beethoven.

"Cat." Her name rang out in his voice.

Wondering if it was clairaudience or if he was really there, she turned and looked over her shoulder. Ryan stood at the head of the atrium's path, keys in hand. Bully and Buddy circled his legs, tails wagging, panting and smiling as only dogs can smile. It drew a smile from her as well.

Ryan made his way toward the spot where she was working. She stood up and he pulled her into his arms. He held her so close—so tightly—that she almost stopped breathing. After several moments, he softened the embrace and moved his lips close to her ear.

"I love—the way you sing to your flowers," he whispered. "I love—the little sound you make when I'm about kiss you." His breath in her ear made her own breathing rhythm slow and synchronize to his. "I love—watching you watch the stars before you fall asleep." He paused in between each phrase, letting her take it in, rocking her a little, front to back. "I love—that you're not perfect. That would make life so boring."

At that, her eyes closed, taking in the miracle of the moment.

"I can't remember my life before I met you," he said, and then pulled back to look into her eyes. "And I don't want to."

She shook her head, tears stinging her eyes. "I'm so sorry."

"Shhh. I know you are." He used his thumb to wipe a tear from her cheek. "I'm sorry, too. I overreacted. I know you were ashamed. And I can't be angry about something that happened six years ago. It was the fact that you didn't tell me. I thought we—our relationship—was stronger than that."

"It is. It is stronger," she replied.

"You have to promise to be honest with me, Cat. No secrets."

"No secrets, I promise." She placed a palm on his cheek, over a bandage. "What happened there? How did you get hurt?"

"Di Santo. He's got a mean right hook."

She didn't understand, but she didn't need to. Not now. The moment was about the two of them. She looked into his deep brown eyes, eyes that were painfully pleading for her honesty, her commitment.

Catharine brushed the bangs from his brow line, pulled him down until she could kiss him. Ryan leaned in and returned her kiss once, and again, and a third time.

She pulled back to take in his face, so elated he was actually there. "Happy belated birthday," she whispered, and buried herself in his arms for another hug.

They swayed to the music, gently rocking to the sounds of the sonata, the birds caroling, sun shadowing, and the trees exhaling.

He ran his hand through her hair and gathered it all over her right shoulder. He let his lips travel from just under her left ear to the curve of her clavicle.

"No one's here today because of the holiday," she said, glancing up at him in expectation.

"Annie's Song" started playing on the sound system as Ryan lowered her to the grassy patch next to the anemones.

Several hours later, Catharine woke up in the middle of a patch of ferns, with Ryan still asleep by her side. She took a deep breath and thanked God, Goddess, Whomever that he had come back to her.

A couple of minutes later, he opened his eyes, propped himself up on his elbow, and faced her. "Do you remember when we first did it here, in the atrium?"

"Mmm-hmmm," she said, stretching.

He ran his fingers through her hair. "When I was recu-

perating from the Town Red case. Remember we kept waiting because the doctor said we couldn't do it?"

"Oh, my gosh, I wanted you."

"Well, then you had me."

"It was great."

He smiled. "It *is* great."

"Mmmm-hmmm." Catharine repeated, recalling the feeling of new love. Her attention was drawn now to the bandage on his cheek. She touched it lightly with her index finger. "So, what happened with Matthew?" she asked.

"We got into a fist fight in Atlanta."

Catharine bristled. *"Atlanta*? When were you in Atlanta?"

"Last week. I don't really want to talk about it. Anyway,
I kicked his ass."

"Poor Matt." Catharine then realized why she hadn't
been able to place Ryan anywhere in her mind's eye. He
wasn't in town. "What was the fight about?" *The mystery
woman*?

"You." He kissed her on the nose. "He told me not to f—
mess this up, because you are the best thing that ever happened to me. And he was right, too, but don't tell him that."
Ryan moved in closer. "Want to go for round three?"

Catharine gazed up through the skylight trying to gauge
the time of day. "How long have we been out?" she asked.

Ryan reached over her to his cell phone, which was lying
next to his badge and wallet. "A couple hours. It's 2:15," he
said, tossing the phone back on the ground.

"Oh my gosh! I have to prepare for the cookout. The
boys are coming home."

An Aerosmith song rang out from somewhere in the
flowers. Ryan searched for his phone and found it among
the flowers. "It's Matt."

"You can answer."

He did. As he listened, his face transformed from serene
to troubled. "Yeah, thanks. See you tomorrow." He hung up
and exhaled.

"What? Bad news?"

"Verdict came in late yesterday. I guess Jane was trying to get a hold of you."

"Oh my gosh, I turned my phone off." By the look on his face, it wasn't good news. "Oh no, don't tell me—Todd's not *free*?"

Ryan took her hand in his. "No, no. That scum is going to jail. It's just that we didn't get what we wanted. He was found guilty of aggravated battery *with* a deadly weapon. Apparently Brant made a mistake and called the Taser a deadly weapon on your testimony video. That was good. He was also found guilty of two counts of animal abuse—for Tasering the dogs."

"Good!" Catharine responded.

"But—"

"What? But what?"

"He was found *not* guilty of breaking and entering and *not* guilty of attempted rape. I'm sorry, Cat."

She brooded for a moment, shaking her head. "How long?"

"Five years, eligible for parole in three. Minus the six months he's already served. This is fucked up. I'm calling Jane."

Before he could dial, Catharine gently took the phone from his hand and put it back down on the grass. "It's over, Ryan. He's gone. Let's not perpetuate the negativity in our lives anymore." She gave him a kiss to reinforce the message. "Are you hungry?"

"I am kind of hungry. We've been here all morning and part of the afternoon," he said, hovering his mouth near hers.

She softened, letting the trial—and Todd Elliot—float out of her head, out of the house, and into oblivion.

He planted another soft wet kiss on her lips and she fought her desire to go that extra round.

"Ryan…"

"Hmmm?"

She pushed him gently off of her and confessed, "I didn't get you a birthday present. I wasn't sure—"

"Cat, don't worry about it. You are my present. It's more than I could ask for. I was just telling Matt the other day—"

"Oh, I forgot," she said, hearing Matthew's name. "I had a vision. Of Jon, your old partner. He came to me the other day."

Ryan sat up. "Yeah, I didn't understand that message."

"He said he had to leave you. I believe he has to move on. And I think he said something about your case. Something about a brother—it was the brother who killed Terrico James, right?"

"Strangely enough, we thought it was his *brother*, but it was actually members of the Klan. They call themselves the '*brotherhood.*'"

"That's it! He did say brother-*hood*! Oh my gosh." Catharine shook her head in disbelief. "That's horrible. In this day and age. I just don't understand that kind of hatred."

"Me, neither. But it's out there. Unfortunately." Ryan leaned against her, taking a moment of silence while she stroked his hair. "So Jon's leaving? For good?"

"I'm sorry, but yes, I believe so. It's his time.'"

Ryan nodded, staring out into the anemones, and she let him process the message in silence until Bully and Buddy's toenails started clicking against the travertine floor, followed by their protective barking.

The deadbolt clicked in the front door and then the familiar call: "Maaaaaa! We're home!"

"Oh no, the boys!" Catharine gasped.

"*Shit*," Ryan said and moved quickly, grabbing the clothes he had shed in passion.

Catharine scanned the atrium floor for her blouse and skirt and rushed to pull them on.

Ryan was hopping on one leg, struggling to get his boxers on in the middle of a vine patch.

"The tree! Go behind the tree!" she instructed, and he scrambled over to hide behind a large oak.

"Maaaaa!" Hank called from the entryway.

Catharine didn't answer, hoping to give herself a little more time to arrange her clothes and hair. It didn't work.

"Hey, Ma," Hank said, coming down the atrium path. Duke followed behind, texting.

"Hey, babies, how are you?" Catharine said breathlessly. She greeted her boys with a big smile. "How was your day?"

"What's up with your hair?" Hank asked.

"What?" Catharine reached up and patted the top of her head.

"You've got like flower petals and stuff all up in it."

He pointed to his own head, indicating where the debris was located. Catharine felt around and picked a twig out from above her left ear. She then saw Hank's eyes go to a spot on the ground and she followed his gaze. Ryan's wallet, badge, and cell phone. Hank stopped short and put his arm out to stop his brother.

"What?" Duke said, lifting his face from the phone.

"Ryyyy?" Hank called out to the atrium.

A voice behind the oak tree answered, "Hey, guys."

Catharine blushed and squeezed her eyes shut. When she opened them, she saw her sons retreating away from her, backing up toward the door.

"I just forgot we—" said Hank.

"Yeah, we gotta go—" Duke added, pointing his thumb behind him.

"Bank."

"ATM."

The twins alternated excuses, finishing each other's sentences.

"We need money," Hank said.

"We'll stop—"

"At the store, too."

"What time are we eating?" Duke asked.

Catharine giggled at their embarrassment, determined not to be thrown. "Around three-thirty," she called to them.

"We'll be back," Hank said.

"Bye, Ryan! Happy birthday!" Duke called.

"Thanks," the oak tree answered. "See you guys later."

Just when Catharine thought she'd have to put the twins in therapy, she saw them slap hands on the way out.

# EPILOGUE

Log No. 76-61533
Excerpt of Transcript of Interview with Wyatt Earl Fisk, Chicago PD, District 18, transcribed by Elise Haywood
7 July – 1:35 p.m.

In attendance: Cptn. Roy Chen, Assigned Investigator, Internal Affairs Division; Sgt. Robert Besko, Dist. 18; Det. 1G Ryan Doherty, Dist. 18; Det. 3G Matthew Di Santo, Dist. 18; Det. 1G Wyatt Fisk, Dist. 18; Fred Roscoe, Attorney for the Defense.

CHEN: Wyatt Earl Fisk, you have been accused of murder in the first degree, brandishing a firearm, desecration of human remains, aiding and abetting the commission of a felony, and aiding and abetting in the commission of a hate crime, assault of a police officer. Your complainant is Detective First Grade Ryan Doherty of District 18. He has provided a sworn affidavit, in compliance with Illinois law 50 ILCS 725/3.8. Do you understand the charges as they have been brought against you?

FISK: Yes, sir.

CHEN: For the record, the State's Attorney has agreed to leniency in sentencing in exchange for your statement here today.

FISK: Yes, that is correct.

CHEN: Detective Fisk, would you please start by stating your full name, Chicago PD rank and badge number.

FISK: Wyatt Earl Fisk, Detective First Grade, Chicago Police, 18th District, 945303.

CHEN: Relative to the death of Terrence James Robinson, AKA Terrico James, please describe to us what transpired on the night of Friday, June twenty-third.

FISK: I was dining with a friend of mine, Warren Smith—rest his soul—and a couple of other gentlemen. We were having dinner at his hotel, the Westley.

CHEN: How did you know Mr. Warren Smith?

FISK: We knew each other from Atlanta. We belonged to the same fraternal organization.

CHEN: And the name of the organization?

FISK: The Knight's Brotherhood.

CHEN: The Knight's Brotherhood. Is that an alternate name for the Ku Klux Klan?

FISK: The name of the organization is the Knight's Brotherhood.

CHEN: Okay. Back to the evening of the twenty-third. What happened after dinner?

FISK: We saw Terrico James in the lobby. He then left the hotel and we followed him.

CHEN: What was your intent in following him?

ROSCOE: We are not going to discuss intent. Detective, you can just state the facts.

FISK: Mr. Smith and I and two of his associates—Greg and Joseph, I do not know their last names—the three of us exited the hotel and did not see Mr. James. Then we heard an argument to the left, coming from the alley. Mr. Smith motioned for us to stay put, looked into the alley next to the hotel. When he came back to our group, he told one of his associates—Greg, I think it was—to go get their van.

CHEN: Did you know why, at the time, he had asked Greg to get the van?

FISK: Yes.

CHEN: How did you know?

FISK: You see, James had been a target of ours for a while.

ROSCOE: Fisk, you don't have to go into detail. I'd advise—

FISK: What the hell, Fred. I've already got my deal. I want to tell it like it is.

CHEN: We appreciate that, Detective Fisk, thank you.

FISK: You're welcome. So yes, we planned confronting Terrico James, but not hurting him. That crap James spewed—it was disgusting. He thought he was the second coming. The way he opened his concert, on a cross? We needed to teach that boy a lesson.

DOHERTY: He was a man, not a boy.

FISK: So when he announced that his tour was coming through Chicago, it was the perfect opportunity. I went to Payton a couple months in advance and offered my services in security. They bit. We were in. Then it was just a matter of getting James alone. That's what we were talking about at dinner. But then when we saw him in the lobby without his usual security, well, then the perfect opportunity presented itself. Straight from God. We saw the sign and we acted on it.

DI SANTO: God had nothing to do with it, you sick—

CHEN: Detective Di Santo, please. Unless you have a question...

DI SANTO: Sorry.

CHEN: Continue, Detective Fisk. The man named Greg went to get the van...

FISK: Yes, it was in the parking garage. Took about five minutes. The rest of us were standing at the far end of the hotel, close to the alley, waiting for whatever was going on there to end. We weren't going to let James get out. The fellow he was speaking to walked away just as Greg drove up with the van. Warren motioned for him to pull in and block the alley exit.

CHEN: What was the plan, exactly?

FISK: Well, initially it was going to be to rough James up a bit and then put him up on that cross. He wanted to be Jesus, we'd make him Jesus. Beat his ass. See how he liked it. But he fought back. He shouldn't have fought back.

DOHERTY: May I? You said I could participate in questioning the witness.

CHEN: Go ahead, Detective Doherty. Without prejudice.

DOHERTY: Detective Fisk, did you kill Terrence James Robinson?

FISK: I did not.

DOHERTY: You are saying, on record, that you did not kill Terrico James AKA Terrence Robinson?

FISK: No, I did not kill Terrence Robinson.

DOHERTY: Then who, may I ask, stabbed him?

FISK: I don't know. It all went really fast. Greg had handed me the keys to the van. I was the designated driver because I knew the way to Payton Arena. But they went at him and I hung back. Smith pulled out a knife—I tried to intervene—and then it got out of hand. When I saw James go down, I knew we were in deep shit. So I told them to quick, load him in the van so we could get out of there.

DOHERTY: Well, it's very convenient to blame the crime on a dead man. You know Atlanta is conducting interviews with all of the ODL members. Will their stories back this up?

FISK: I have no idea what they will say. We shall see.

DOHERTY: Okay, so back to the alley. You witnessed a murder, Detective Fisk, and instead of calling for police assistance or any kind of medical help, you decided to let James die.

ROSCOE: I'm sorry, you are assuming intent in my client's statement.

CHEN: Detective Fisk. You loaded James into the van and then drove to Payton Arena? What was his physical condition at that time?

FISK: Well, I knew it was bad 'cause there wasn't a peep out of him during the ride.

DOHERTY: You could have driven him to a hospital.

CHEN: Doherty, let the man speak, please.

FISK: Continue? Okay. We were driving to the arena. One of Smith's guys was panicking. He kept saying, "Is he dead? Is he dead?" and Smith kept yelling at him to shut up. I was seriously concerned—Doherty—so I did inquire on the man's health. I remember shouting to the back, "Well, is he dead?" Because that wasn't what I signed up for. Seriously, it wasn't. It was not my intent to kill that man. Just teach him a lesson.

DOHERTY: So, you're saying it wasn't a lynching?

FISK: Lynching? Lord, no! What is this, 1952?

DOHERTY: Could've fooled me.

CHEN: Let's get back to the facts, gentlemen. What time did you arrive at Payton Arena?

FISK: About twenty minutes later.

CHEN: And what did you observe at that time regarding the condition of Terrico James?

FISK: When we unloaded, he was most definitely dead. Stab wound in the chest. Bled out.

CHEN: And at that time, you had decided to still go through with the crucifixion?

DI SANTO: Lynching.

CHEN: Detective Di Santo, do you have a question?

DI SANTO: No, sir.

CHEN: Okay. Detective Fisk, you said that you had observed James was dead, yet you were going to go one step further and hang up the body?

FISK: Well, we had come that far, so yes. There was no talking Warren out of it.

CHEN: Can you explain the mechanics of how you did that?

FISK: Sure. So when we got there, I drove around back to the loading dock. I've got all the keys, since I worked security. I unlocked one of the stage doors, disengaged the alarm and let them in. Smith was paranoid about security cameras. I told them there wasn't one on this particular door, but he didn't want to take a chance. He was trying to figure out a way for his guys to hold up a blanket while he and I transported the body. But again, I said I wasn't going to touch it. I found an empty equipment box just inside the hall and brought it out to them. They loaded the body in the box and wheeled it into the arena. I wasn't going to touch the box, either. I showed them a freight elevator that went up to the catwalk.

DI SANTO: Freight elevator? No wonder. I thought they had to get him up the spiral stairs.

FISK: No. The elevator goes from the loading dock, not the stage. Easy to miss. They use it to bring up lighting equipment and FX. Anyway, they got him up there and did their thing, while I stayed on the main floor as kind of a lookout.

CHEN: Where did they get the hardware? The hammer and nails?

FISK: There are tools all over. A guy asked me for a toolbox, and I unlocked a maintenance closet, nearby. I swear to you, I didn't think they were going to actually going to nail him to the thing. I thought once they got him up there, they'd just strap him in. But Smith—there was no stopping that guy. He's a true inspiration. Innovation and brilliance is what made him the Grande Master of the Knights, statewide. He thought way, way outside the box.

DI SANTO: Brilliance? Innovation? That's psychopathy, my friend. And I'm not so sure you don't fall into the category, too!

CHEN: Sergeant Besko, if you can't control your men, they'll have to leave the interview.

BESKO: Double-D. Last warning!

DI SANTO: Sorry, Sarge.

CHEN: What time was that? When they…crucified the body?

FISK: About twelve-thirty, one in the morning.

CHEN: And you left at what time?

FISK: When I got home it was 'round about two-fifteen.

DOHERTY: So, the next night, at the concert—who triggered the cross mechanism?

FISK: That would be me. I had the remote.

CHEN: We are going to talk about motive now. Is that okay with you, Mr. Roscoe?

FISK: I'm okay with it.

ROSCOE: Proceed.

CHEN: You said you were friends with Warren Smith. Can you tell us again, how you two met?

FISK: We both belong to an organization back in Georgia.

DI SANTO: Organization.

CHEN: Detective Di Santo?

DI SANTO: Nothing. Go on.

CHEN: And that was the Knight's Brotherhood?

FISK: That is correct.

DOHERTY: Let me say for the record that I've done some research and the Knight's Brotherhood is a pseudonym for the same organization referred to as the Ku Klux Klan.

CHEN: Thank you, Detective. Detective Fisk, what is the philosophy of the organization?

ROSCOE: Detective Fisk is not required nor is he qualified to go into the philosophy of the organization. You can research that, too.

CHEN: Did you and Warren Smith share the same views on African-Americans?

FISK: Warren Smith and I share the truth that the white race is superior in this great nation of ours, and we work to support that truth.

DOHERTY: And that was your motive for breaking the law, violating police policies, and aiding and abetting the commission of these crimes?

FISK: I am not going to justify my actions. I'm fine with what I did and if I have to do time for my beliefs, then so be it. I have no regrets.

DOHERTY: Do you understand why this is deemed a hate crime?

FISK: I consider it a love crime. An act of love for the white people. The man was an abomination. We had to show these people what happens when you put yourself above the Lord. He was a false prophet. An anti-Christ. A negative role model for the deranged society we live in. We had to set an example.

DI SANTO: You set an example, all right. An example of the lowest form of scum on earth: you.

BESKO: Di Santo, step out of the room.

DI SANTO: Sarge!

CHEN: We're almost finished, Sergeant. He can stay. Detective Fisk, is it your intention, then, to plead not guilty to the murder of Terrico James?

FISK: I had nothing to do with the death of that man.

CHEN: Okay, is there anything further you would like to add to your statement?

FISK: Only that I'm tired of this god-damned circus we call a police force now, with the affirmative action hiring, the mandatory acceptance of faggots and—

ROSCOE: I think we're done here, Captain.

CHEN: This concludes our interview. Your arraignment will be scheduled by the end of the week.

DOHERTY: You are a stain on the Department, you [STRICKEN FROM RECORD]

BESKO: Turn off the recorder.

# ACKNOWLEDGEMENTS

As always, I am grateful for the advice, knowledge and never ending generosity of the police officers of the 18th District Chicago P.D., especially Karen Wojcikowski and Casey O'Neill. I couldn't do the above without the expert editing and critique of Idria Barone Knecht, Jovana Grbic, Kate Glinsmann and my dudes in the L.A. Writers' Workshop (I listed you in the last book). I appreciate your honesty and true faith in my characters! Thanks to Chuck Reaume for creating yet another awesome book cover and his lovely wife, Jennifer Sykes, for the referral. Last, but never least, a big thank you to Lauri Wellington and the wonderful folks of Black Opal Books.

# About the Author

Jennifer Moss was born and raised in Evanston, Illinois and is a graduate of Northwestern University. In 1996, Moss launched one of the first parenting websites, BabyNames.com. She began her writing career as a freelance author for articles about the Internet industry. In 2008, she published her first book, *The One-in-a-Million Baby Name Book* (Perigee Press) as a companion to her website. Moss has appeared on national TV media, including CNN Headline News, MSNBC, FoxNews, CBS This Morning, as well as a multitude of international radio programs speaking about names and naming trends.

Moss is an active board member of the Northwestern University Club of Los Angeles, Los Angeles Female Business Owners (LAFBO), The Crescendo Young Musicians' Guild, and The Bully Police Squad, an organization founded by police officers to help schools define and enforce their bully prevention strategies.

Moss divides her time between Los Angeles and her home in the mountains near Yosemite National Park.

Made in the USA
Lexington, KY
25 January 2016